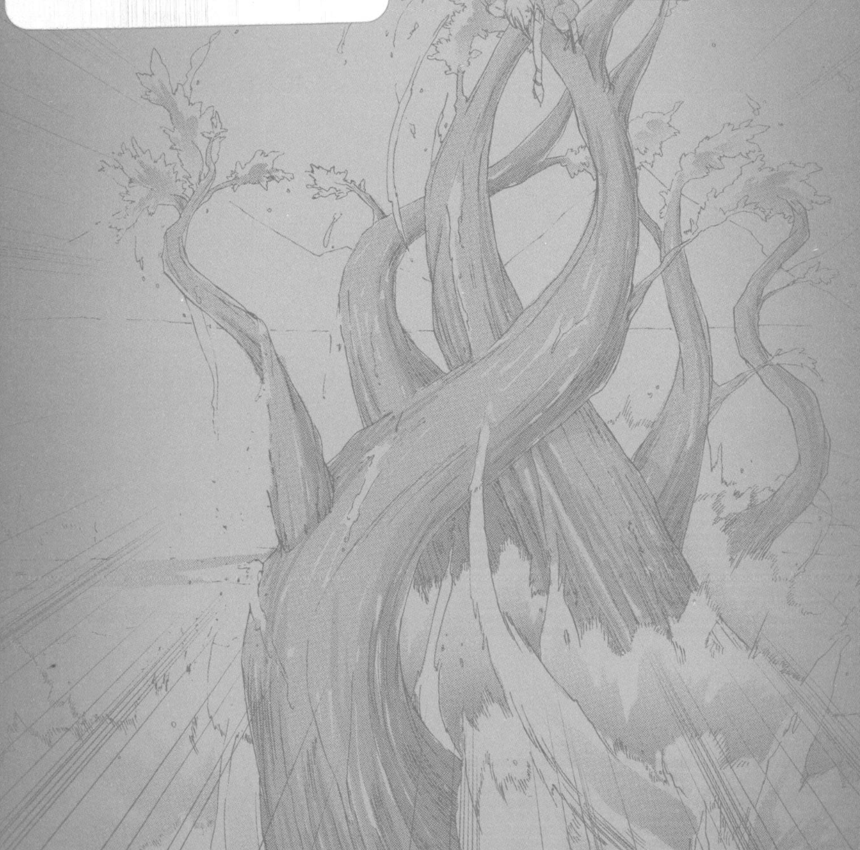

白

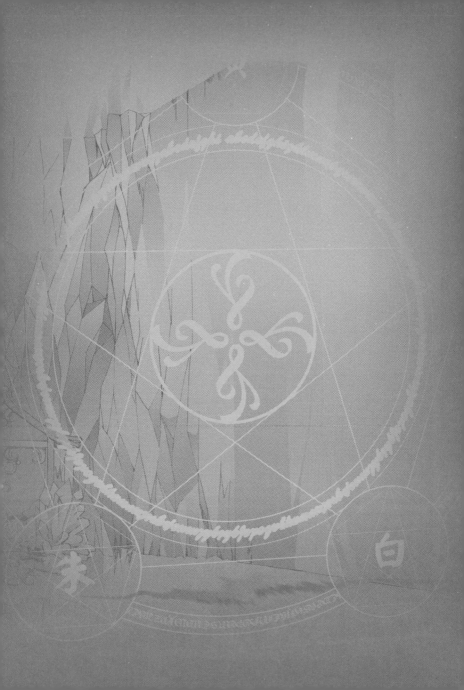

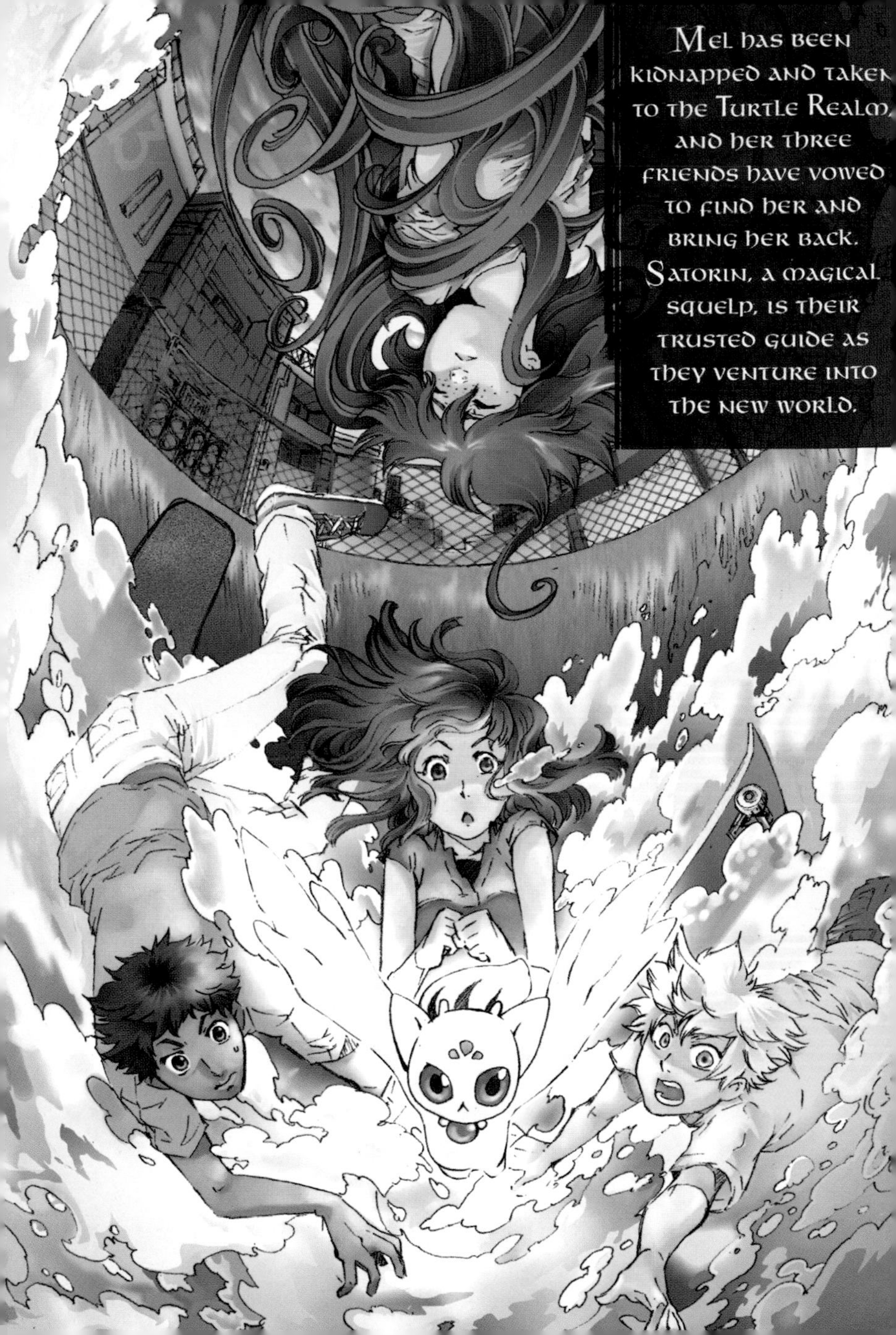
Mel has been kidnapped and taken to the Turtle Realm, and her three friends have vowed to find her and bring her back. Satorin, a magical squelp, is their trusted guide as they venture into the new world.

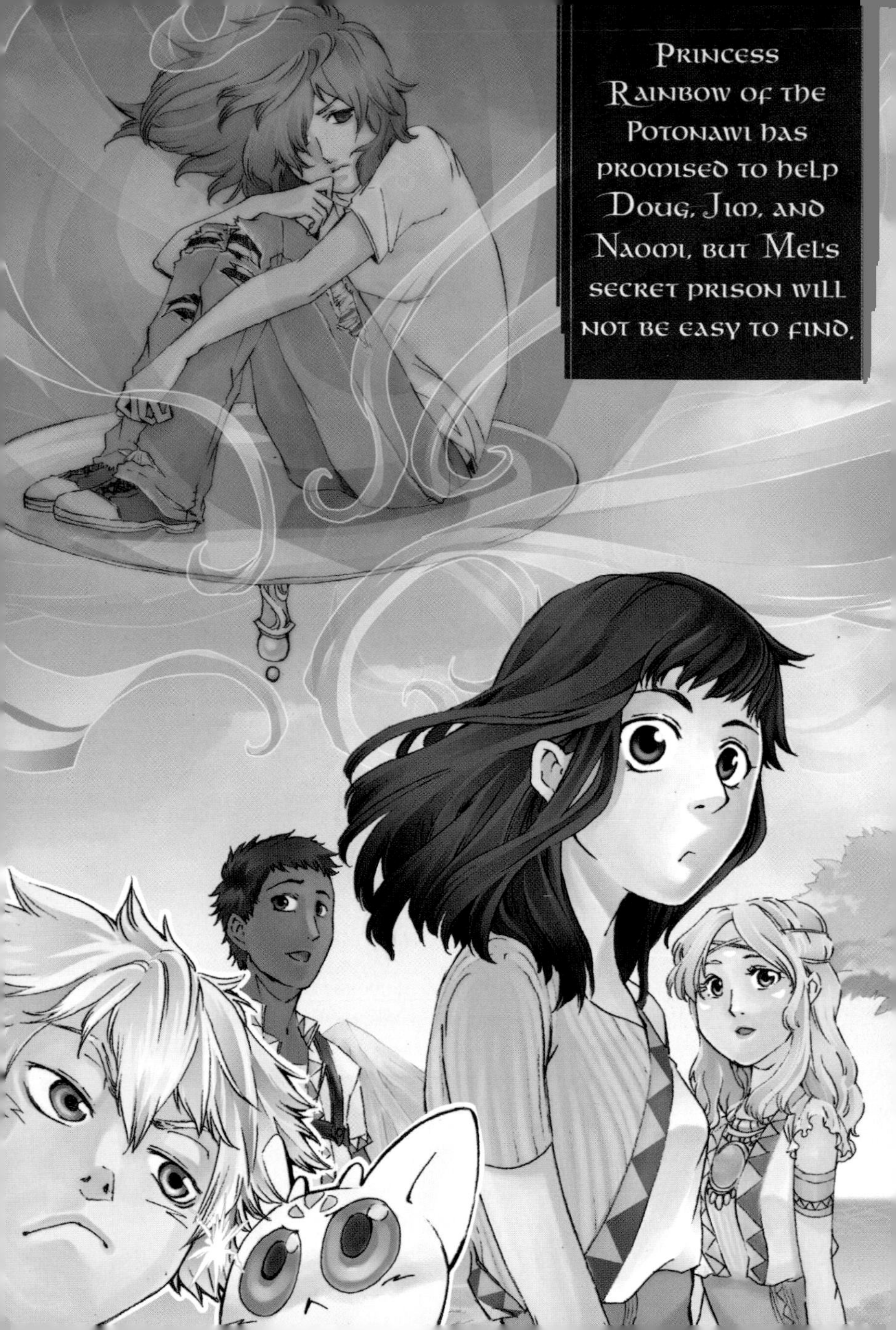
Princess Rainbow of the Potonawi has promised to help Doug, Jim, and Naomi, but Mel's secret prison will not be easy to find.

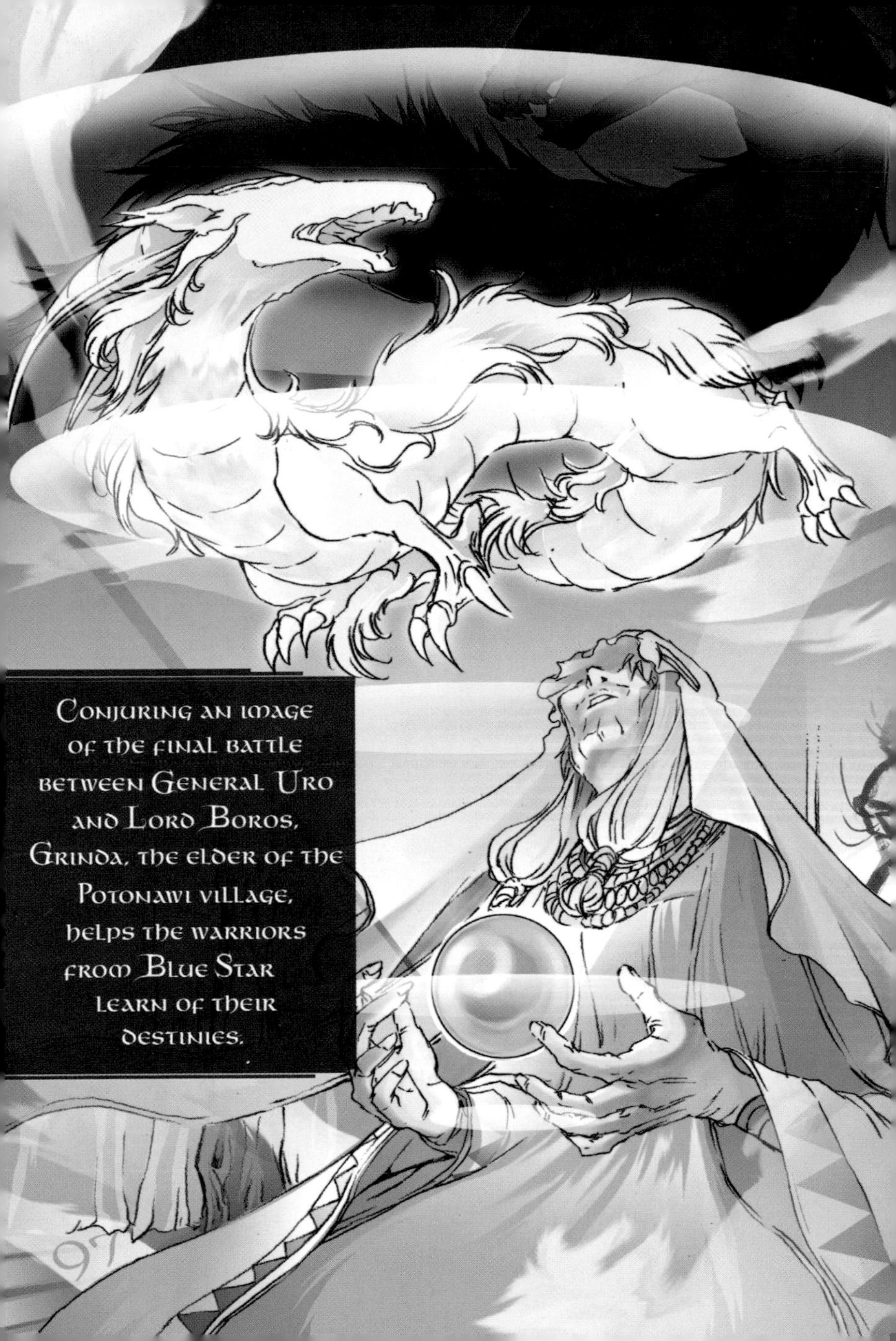
Conjuring an image of the final battle between General Uro and Lord Boros, Grinda, the elder of the Potonawi village, helps the warriors from Blue Star learn of their destinies.

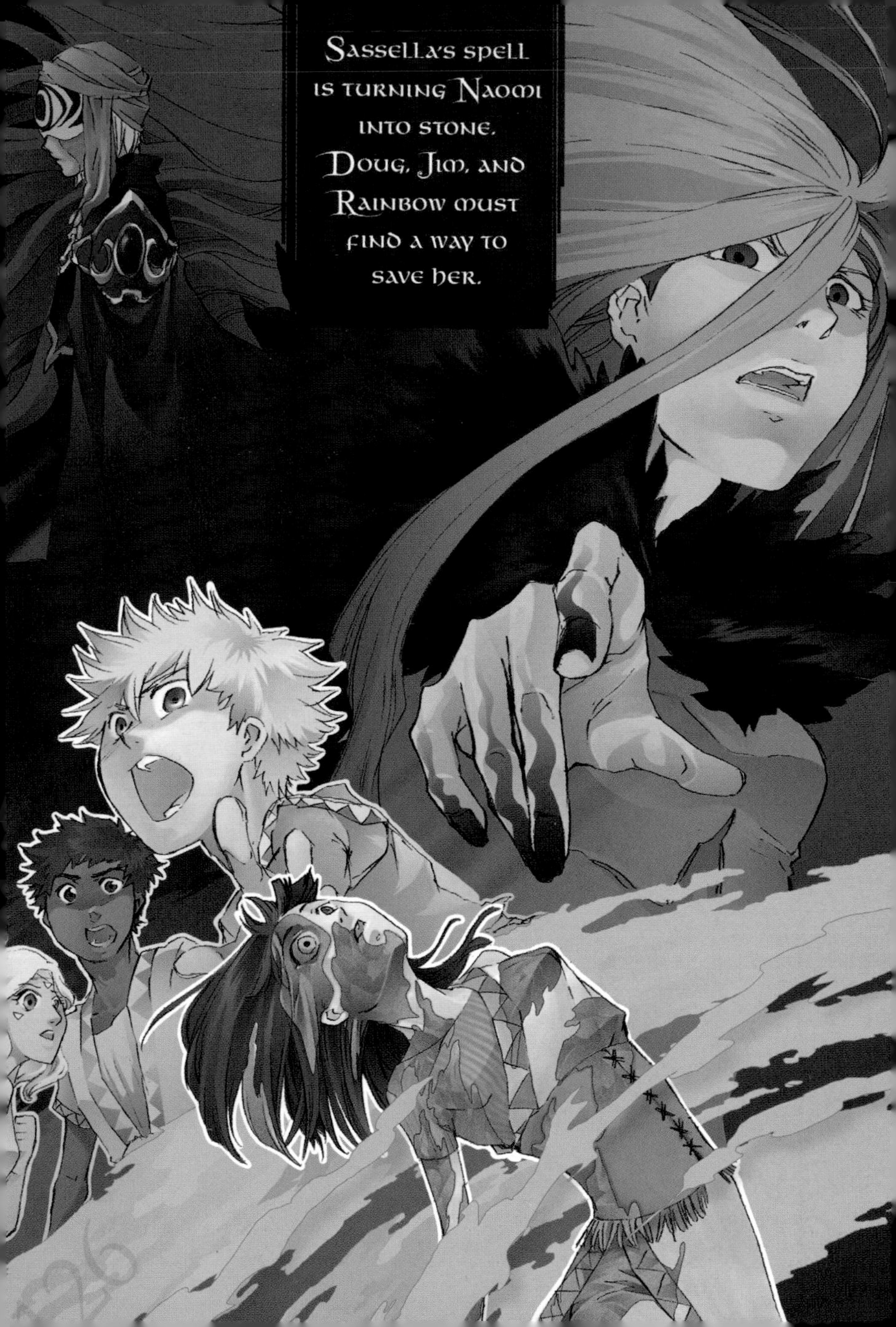
Sassella's spell
is turning Naomi
into stone.
Doug, Jim, and
Rainbow must
find a way to
save her.

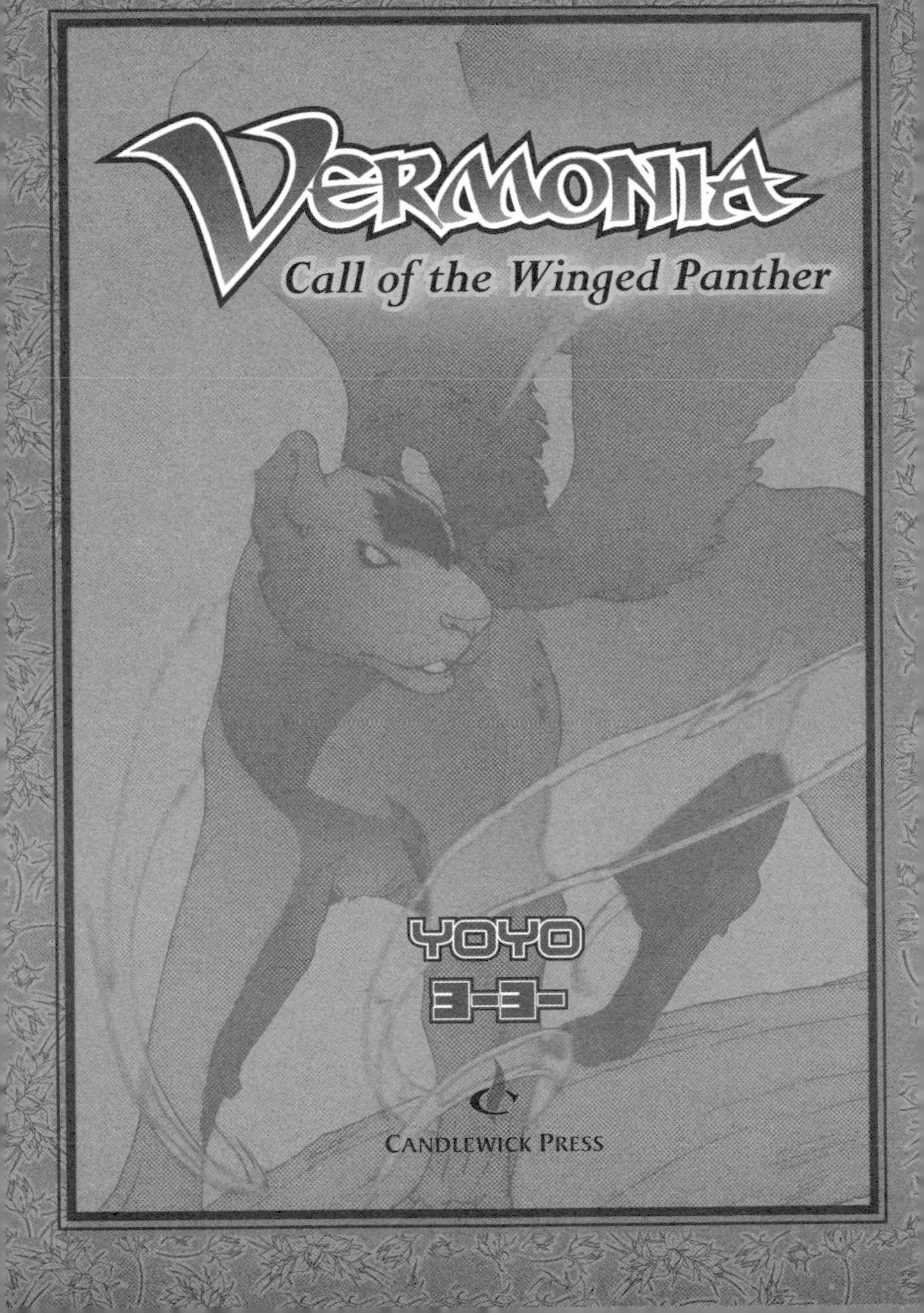

VERMONIA

Call of the Winged Panther

YOYO

ヨーヨー

CANDLEWICK PRESS

FIRST U.S. EDITION 2010

LIBRARY OF CONGRESS CATALOGING-IN-PUBLICATION DATA

09 10 11 12 13 14 SCP 10 9 8 7 6 5 4 3 2 1

PRINTED IN HUMEN, DONGGUAN, CHINA

THIS BOOK WAS TYPESET IN CCLADRONN ITALIC.

CANDLEWICK PRESS
99 DOVER STREET
SOMERVILLE, MASSACHUSETTS 02144

VISIT US AT WWW.CANDLEWICK.COM

WWW.VERMONIA.COM

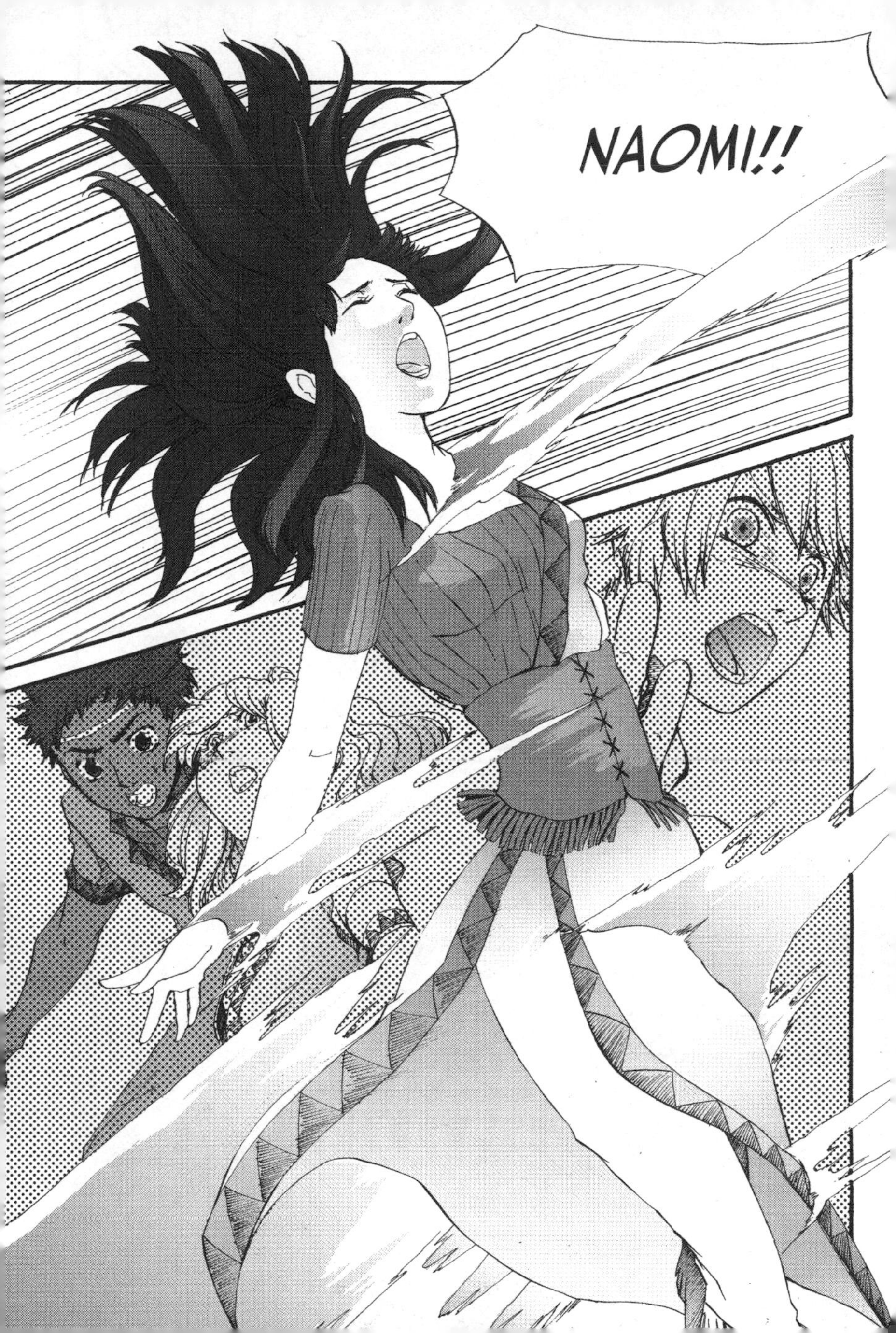
NAOMI!!

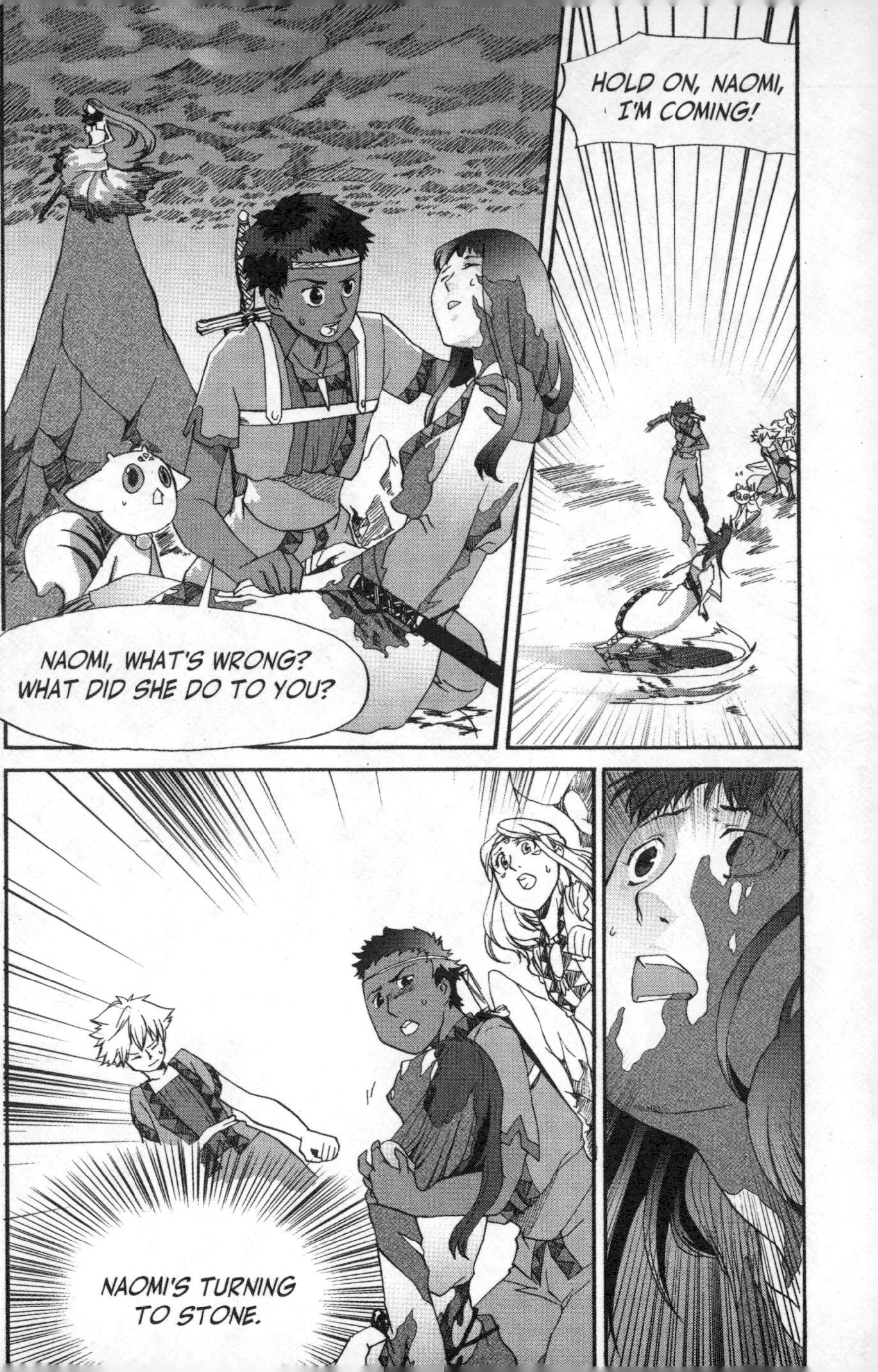
HOLD ON, NAOMI, I'M COMING!
NAOMI, WHAT'S WRONG? WHAT DID SHE DO TO YOU?
NAOMI'S TURNING TO STONE.

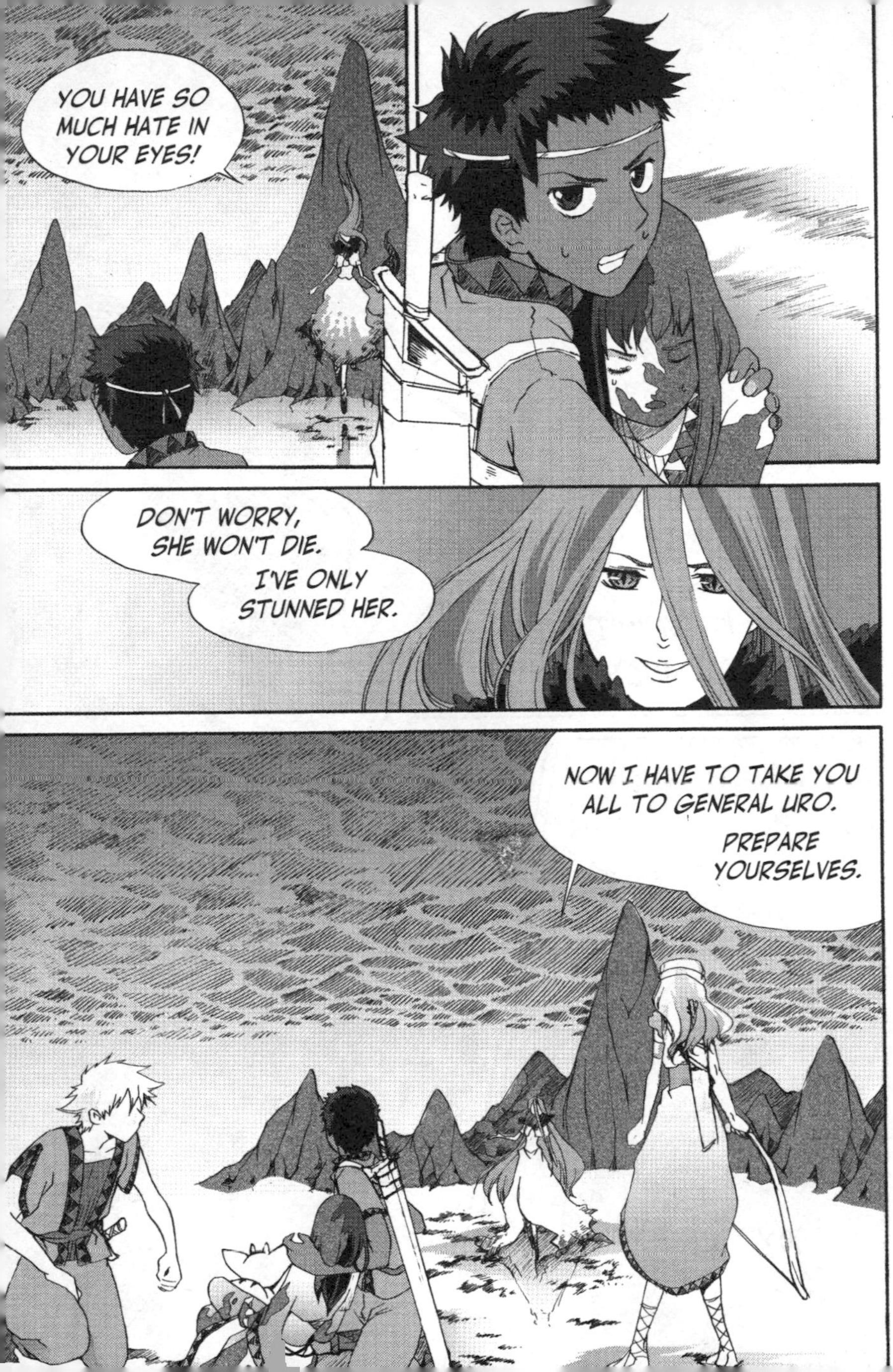
YOU HAVE SO MUCH HATE IN YOUR EYES!
DON'T WORRY, SHE WON'T DIE.
I'VE ONLY STUNNED HER.
NOW I HAVE TO TAKE YOU ALL TO GENERAL URO.
PREPARE YOURSELVES.

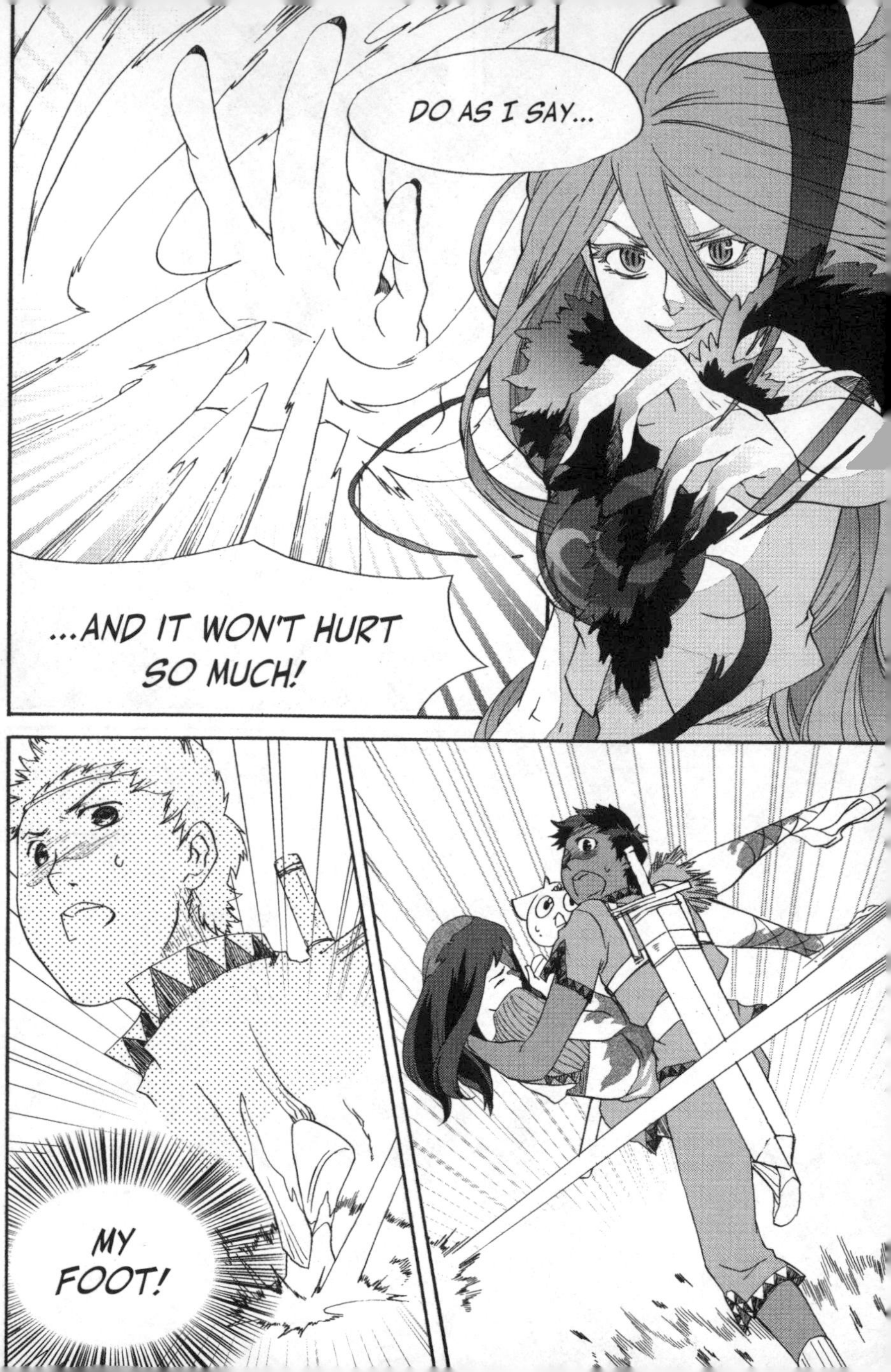
DO AS I SAY...
...AND IT WON'T HURT SO MUCH!
MY FOOT!

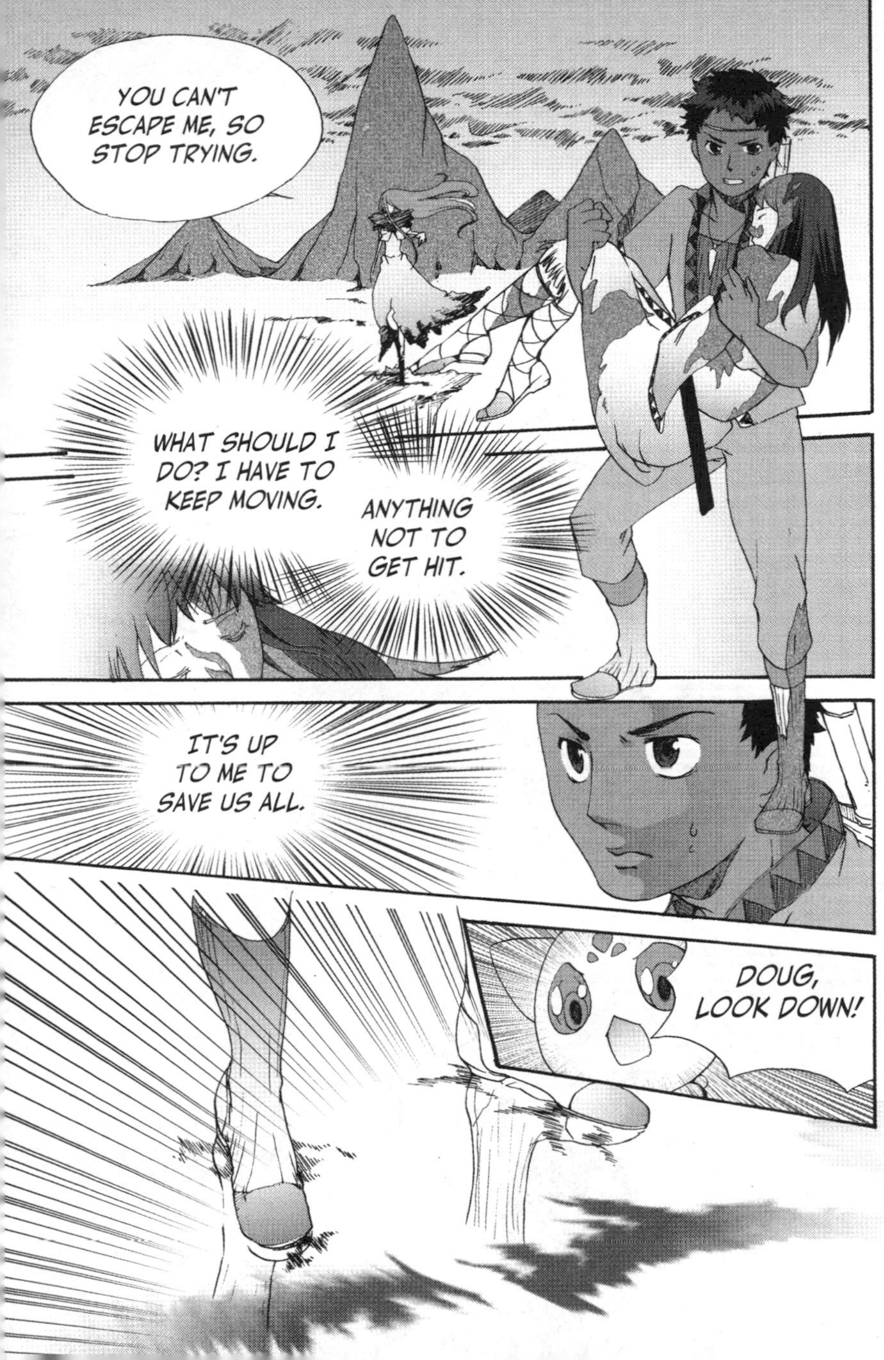
YOU CAN'T ESCAPE ME, SO STOP TRYING.
WHAT SHOULD I DO? I HAVE TO KEEP MOVING.
ANYTHING NOT TO GET HIT.
IT'S UP TO ME TO SAVE US ALL.
DOUG, LOOK DOWN!

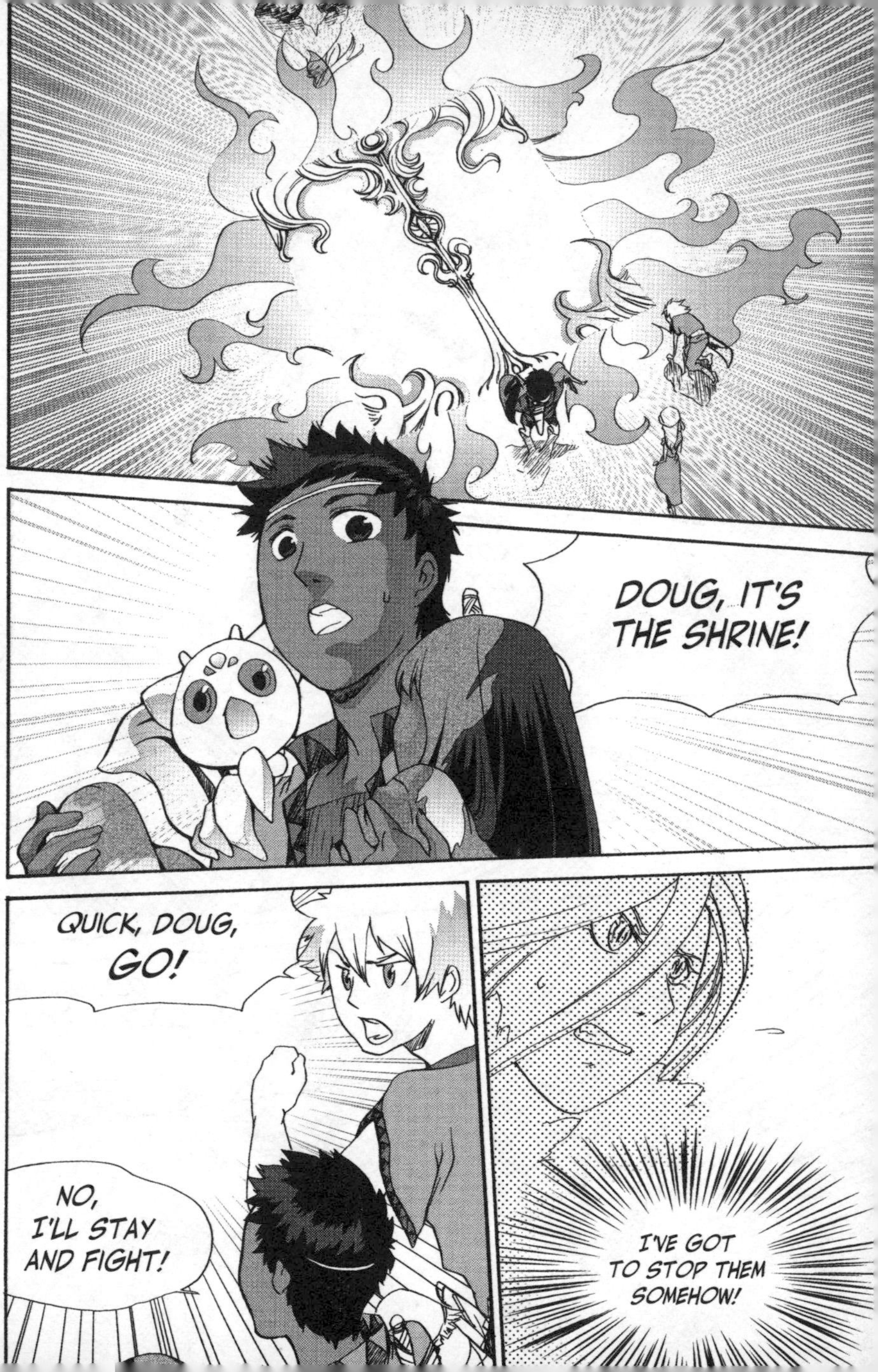
DOUG, IT'S THE SHRINE!
I'VE GOT TO STOP THEM SOMEHOW!
QUICK, DOUG, GO!
NO, I'LL STAY AND FIGHT!

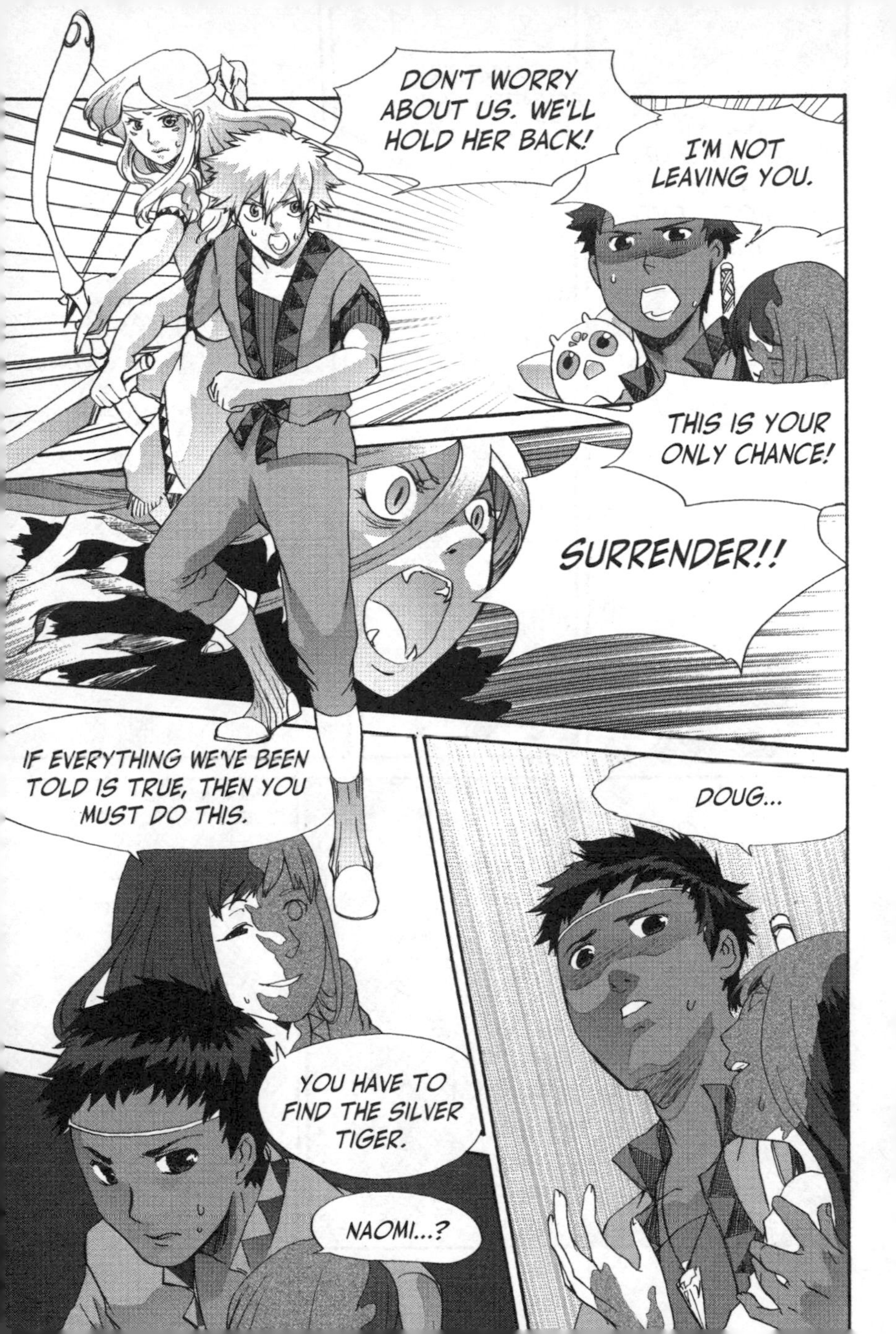
I'M NOT LEAVING YOU.
DON'T WORRY ABOUT US. WE'LL HOLD HER BACK!
THIS IS YOUR ONLY CHANCE!
SURRENDER!!
DOUG...
IF EVERYTHING WE'VE BEEN TOLD IS TRUE, THEN YOU MUST DO THIS.
YOU HAVE TO FIND THE SILVER TIGER.
NAOMI...?

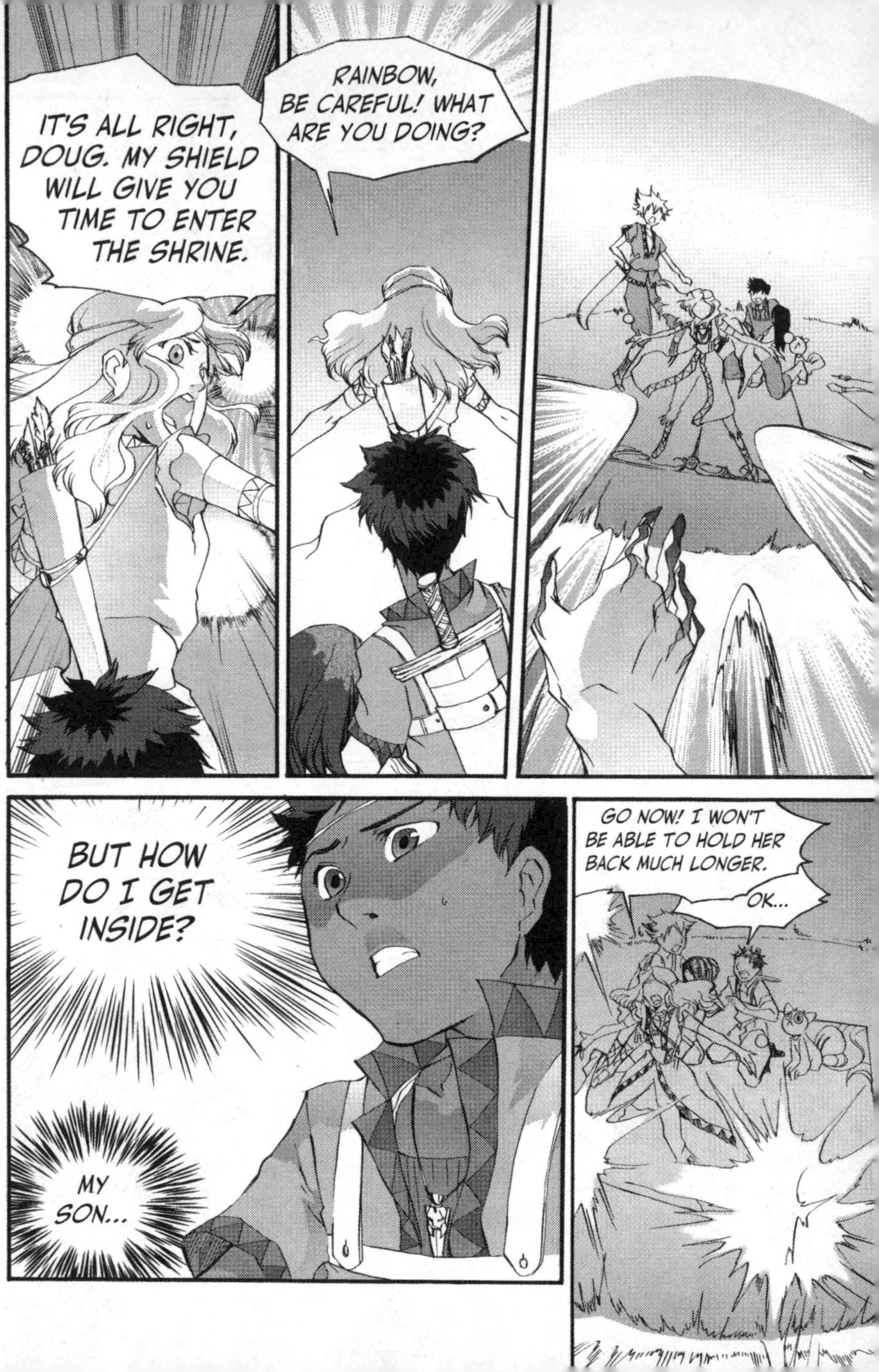
RAINBOW, BE CAREFUL! WHAT ARE YOU DOING?
IT'S ALL RIGHT, DOUG. MY SHIELD WILL GIVE YOU TIME TO ENTER THE SHRINE.
GO NOW! I WON'T BE ABLE TO HOLD HER BACK MUCH LONGER.
OK...
BUT HOW DO I GET INSIDE?
MY SON...

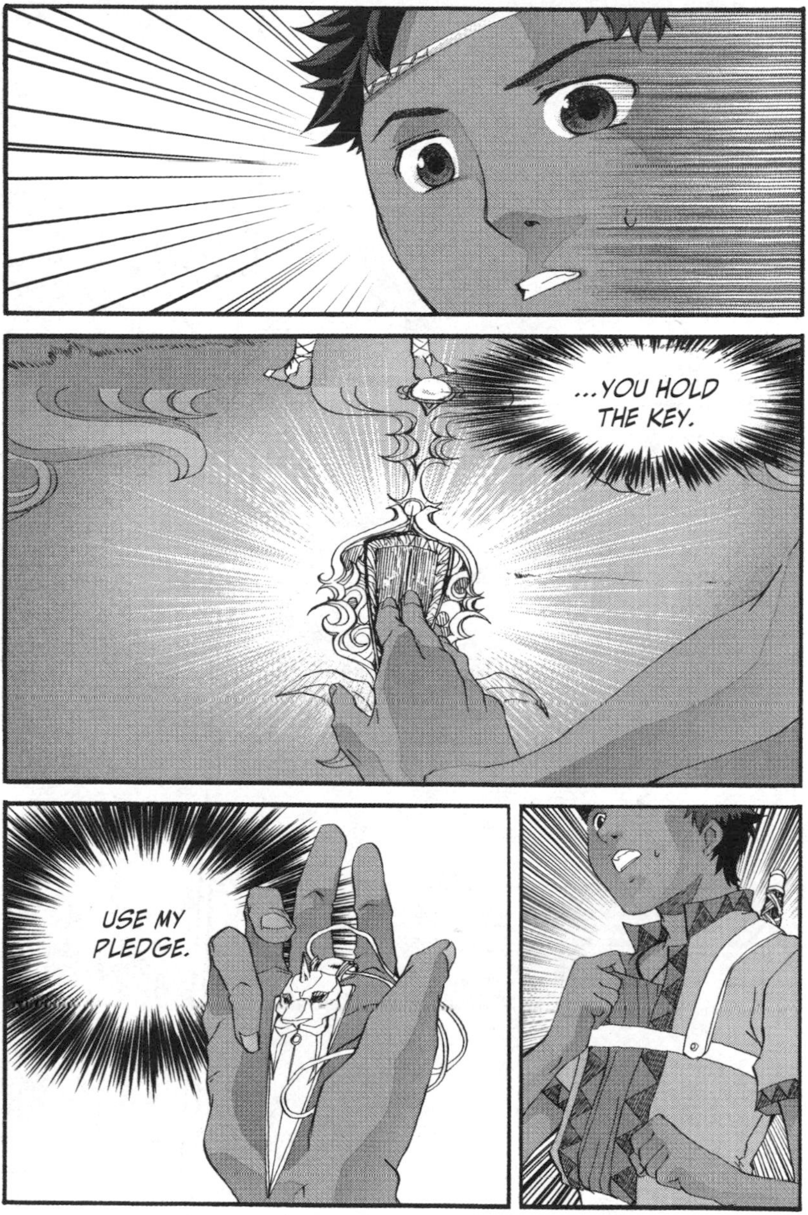
...YOU HOLD THE KEY.
USE MY PLEDGE.

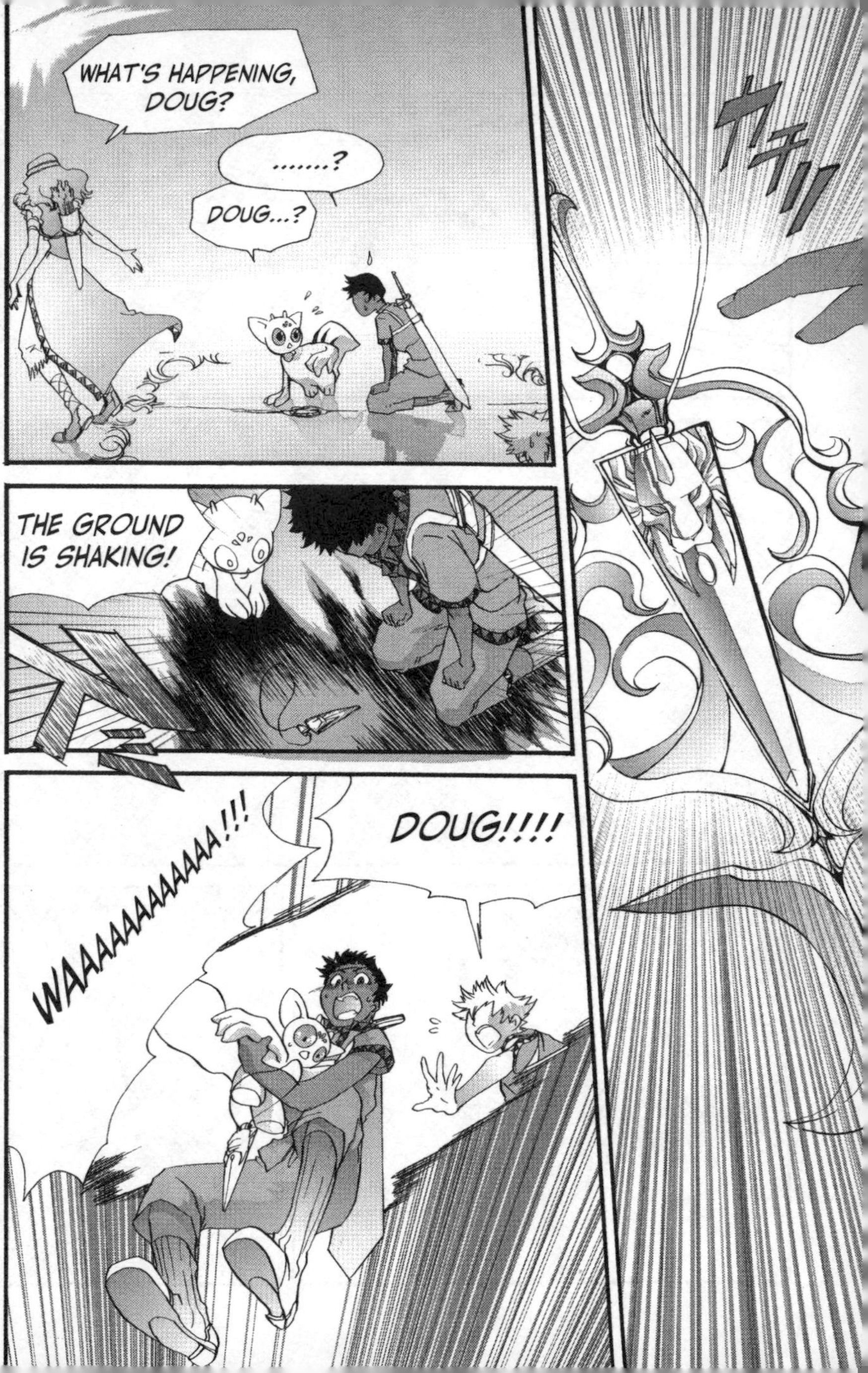
WHAT'S HAPPENING, DOUG?
.......?
DOUG...?
THE GROUND IS SHAKING!
DOUG!!!!
WAAAAAAAAAAA!!!

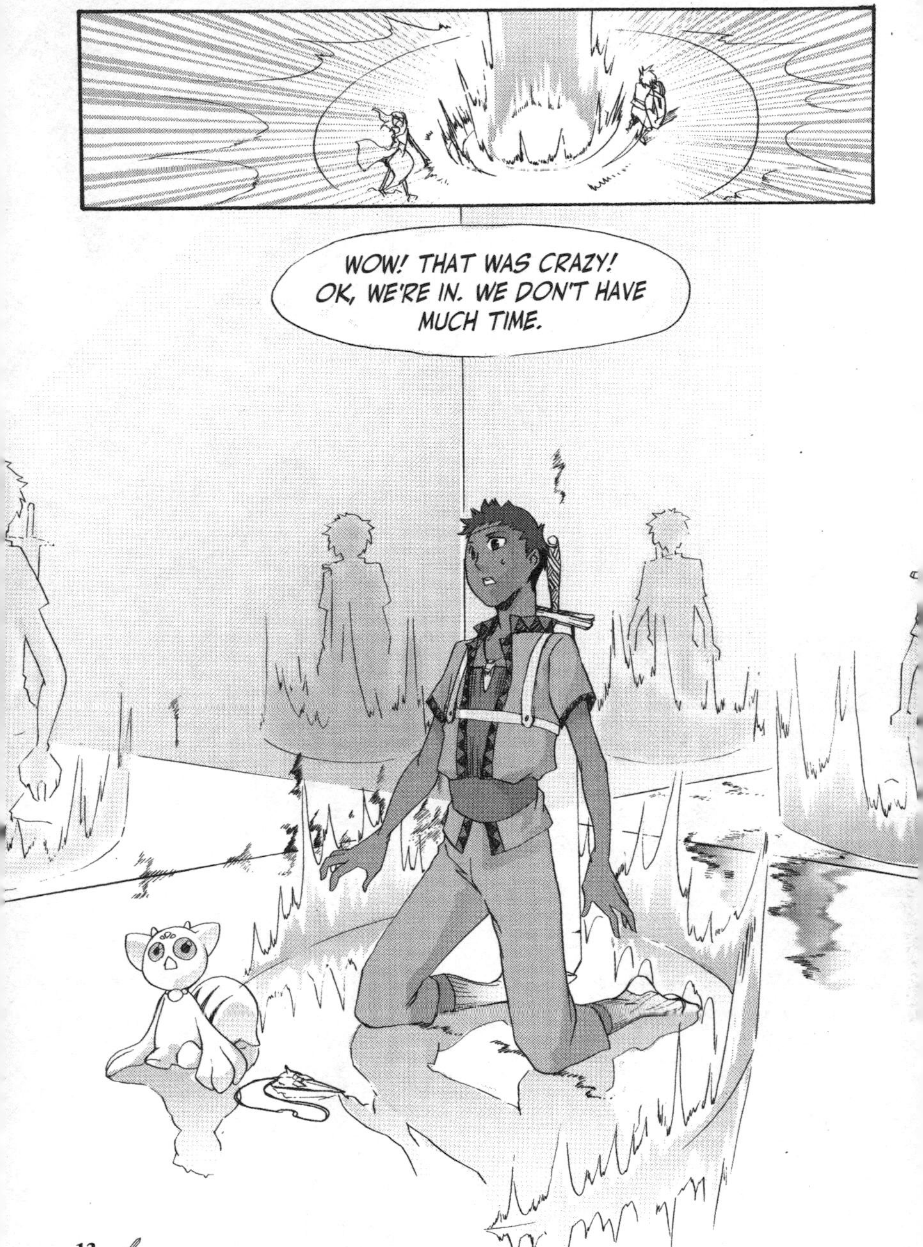
WOW! THAT WAS CRAZY! OK, WE'RE IN. WE DON'T HAVE MUCH TIME.

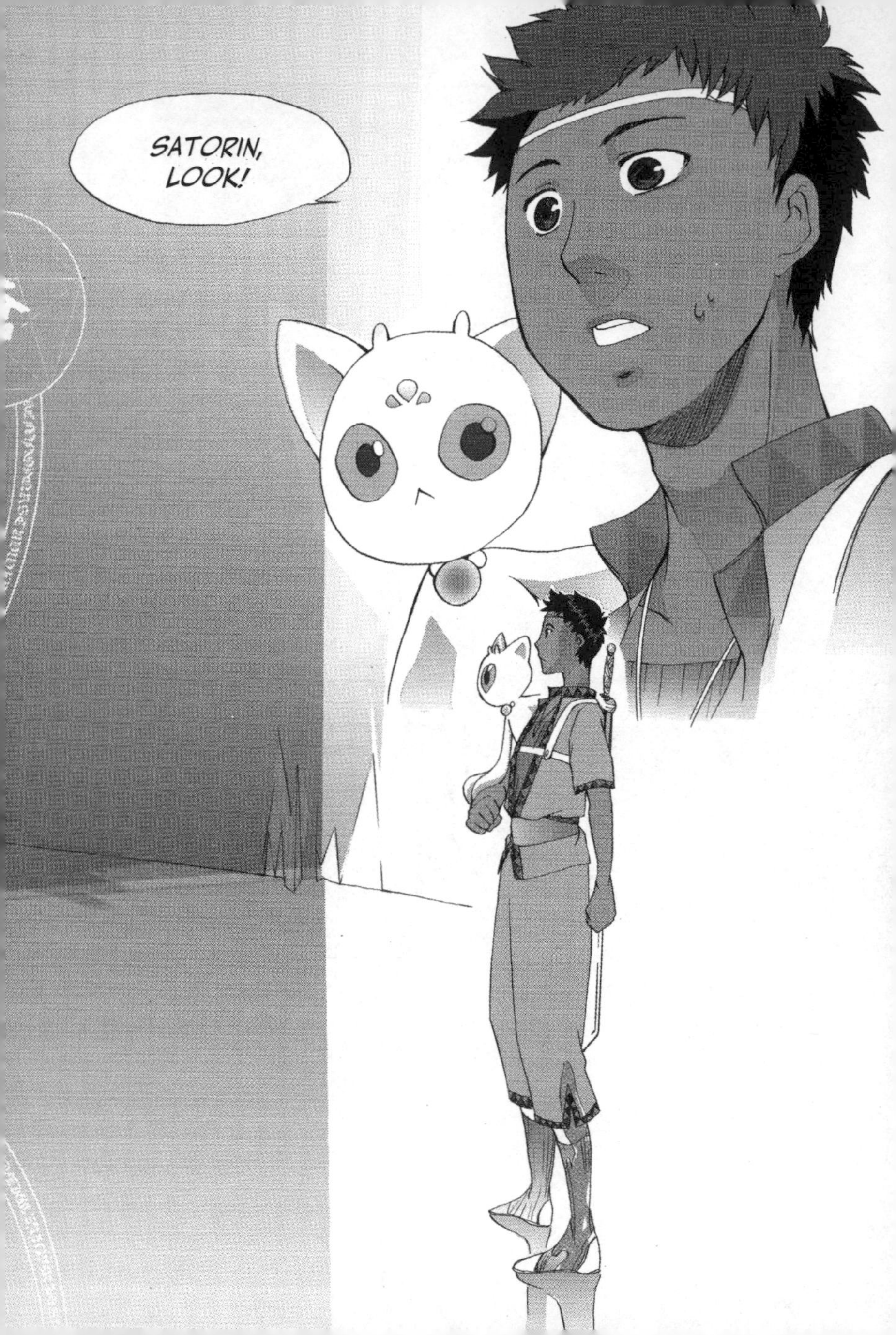
SATORIN, LOOK!

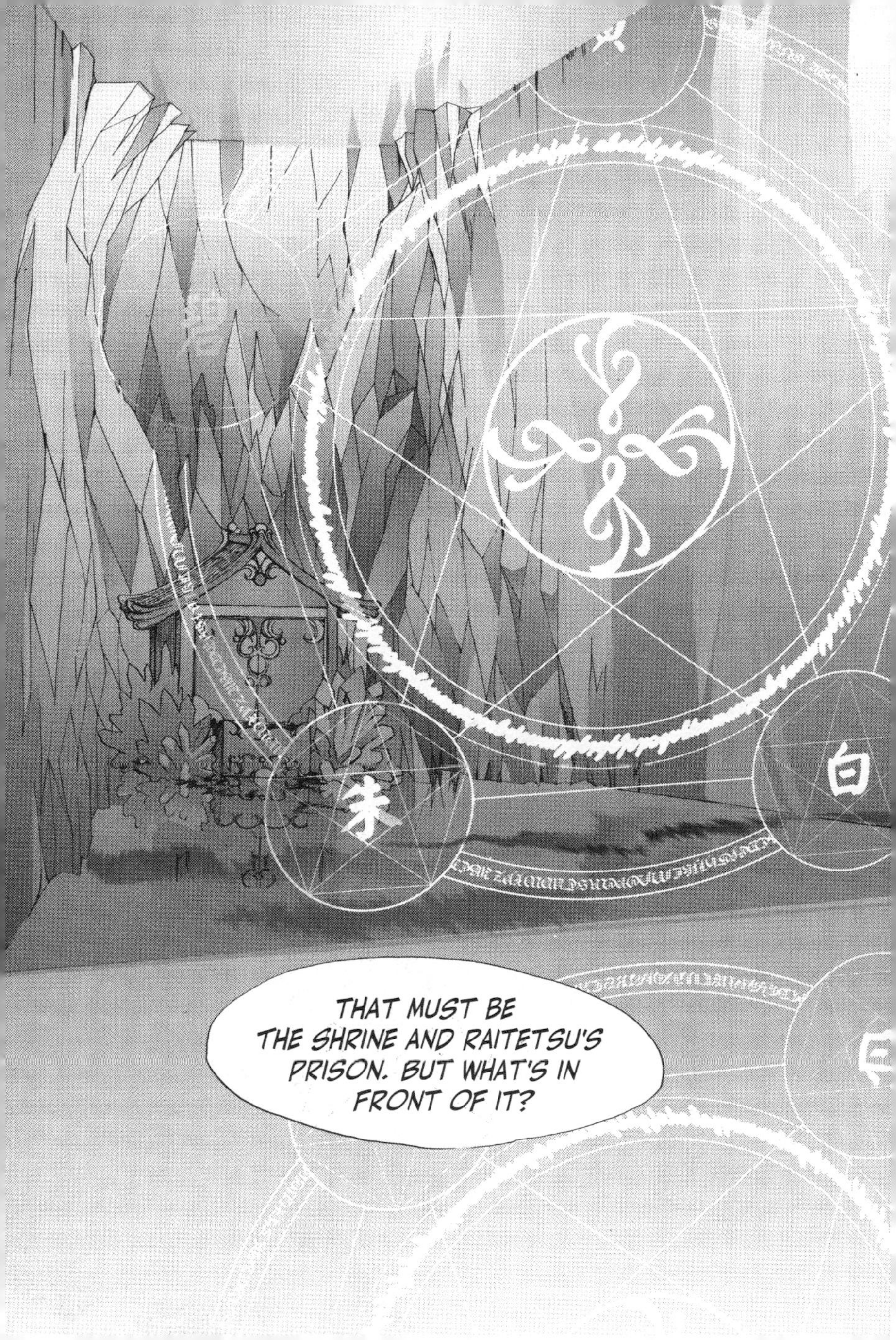
THAT MUST BE THE SHRINE AND RAITETSU'S PRISON. BUT WHAT'S IN FRONT OF IT?

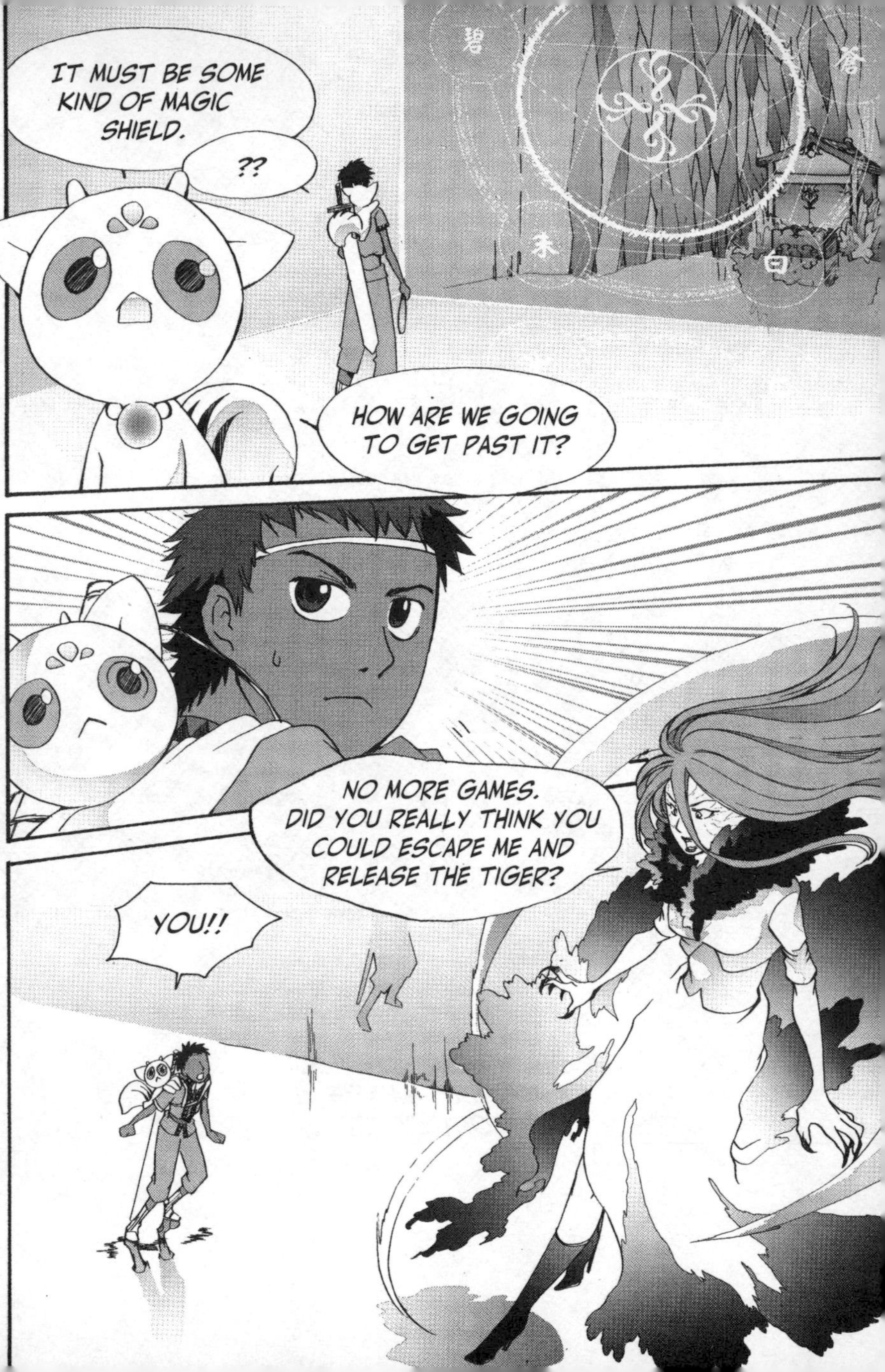
IT MUST BE SOME KIND OF MAGIC SHIELD.
??
HOW ARE WE GOING TO GET PAST IT?
NO MORE GAMES. DID YOU REALLY THINK YOU COULD ESCAPE ME AND RELEASE THE TIGER?
YOU!!

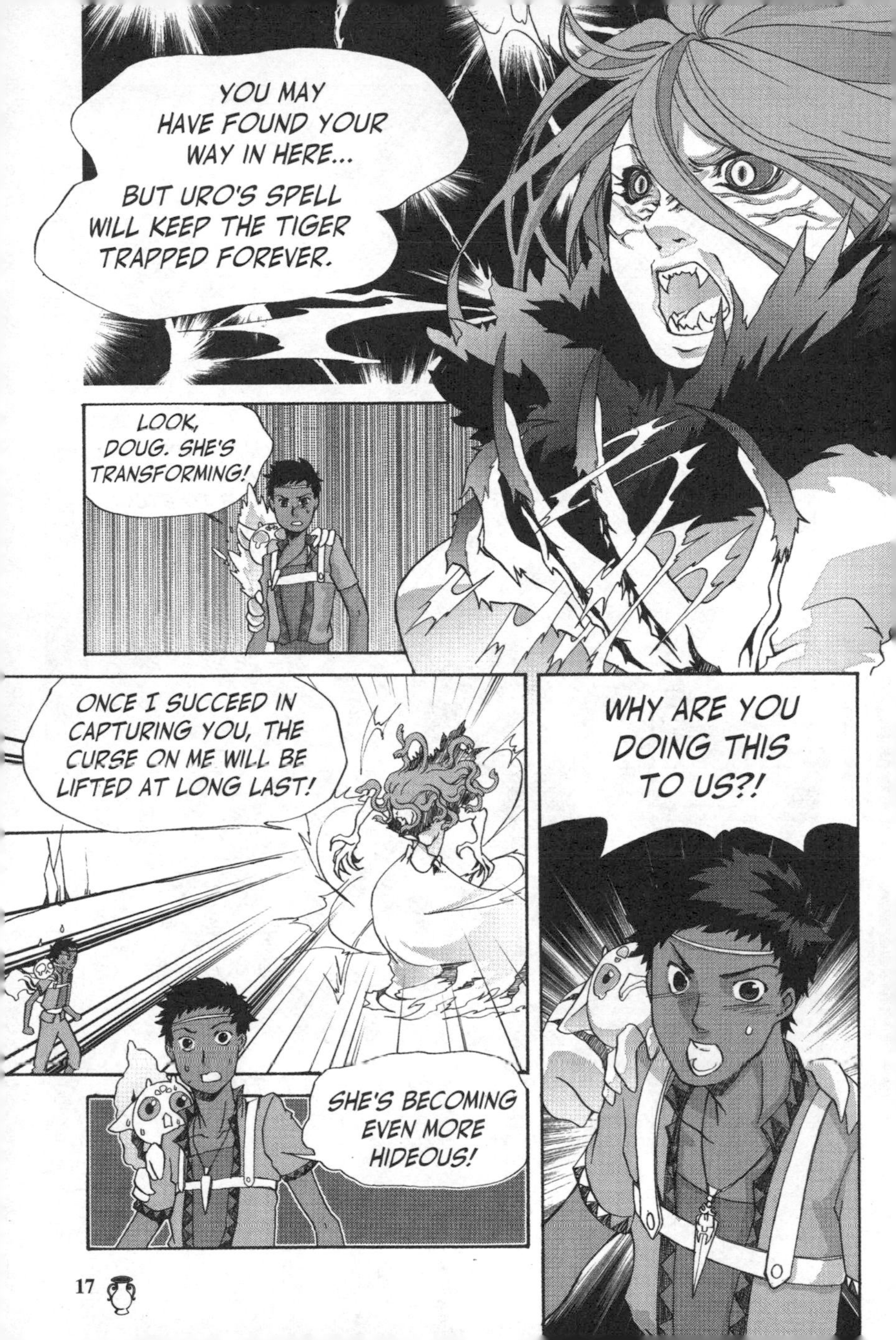
YOU MAY HAVE FOUND YOUR WAY IN HERE...
BUT URO'S SPELL WILL KEEP THE TIGER TRAPPED FOREVER.
LOOK, DOUG. SHE'S TRANSFORMING!
WHY ARE YOU DOING THIS TO US?!
ONCE I SUCCEED IN CAPTURING YOU, THE CURSE ON ME WILL BE LIFTED AT LONG LAST!
SHE'S BECOMING EVEN MORE HIDEOUS!

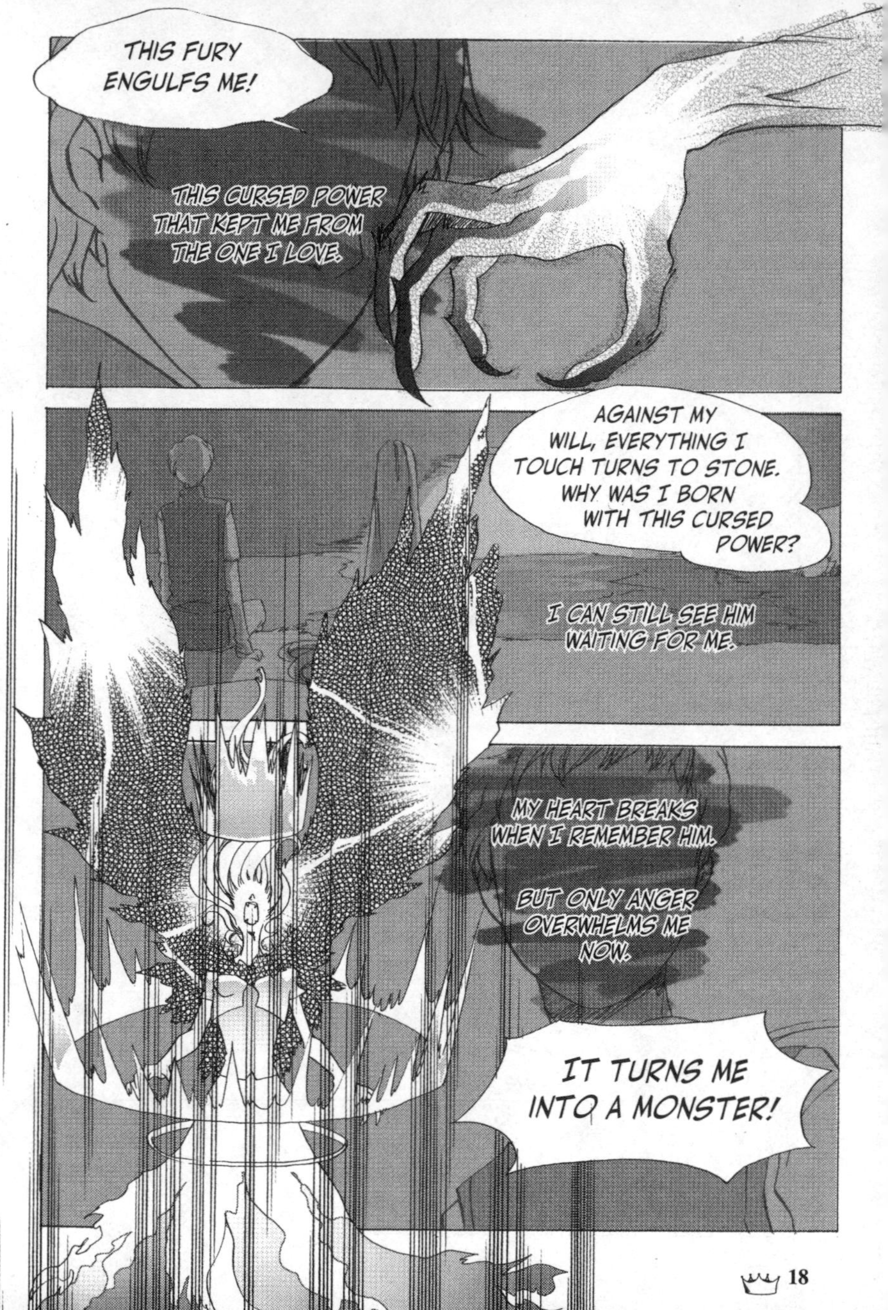
THIS FURY ENGULFS ME!
THIS CURSED POWER THAT KEPT ME FROM THE ONE I LOVE.
AGAINST MY WILL, EVERYTHING I TOUCH TURNS TO STONE. WHY WAS I BORN WITH THIS CURSED POWER?
I CAN STILL SEE HIM WAITING FOR ME.
MY HEART BREAKS WHEN I REMEMBER HIM.
BUT ONLY ANGER OVERWHELMS ME NOW.
IT TURNS ME INTO A MONSTER!

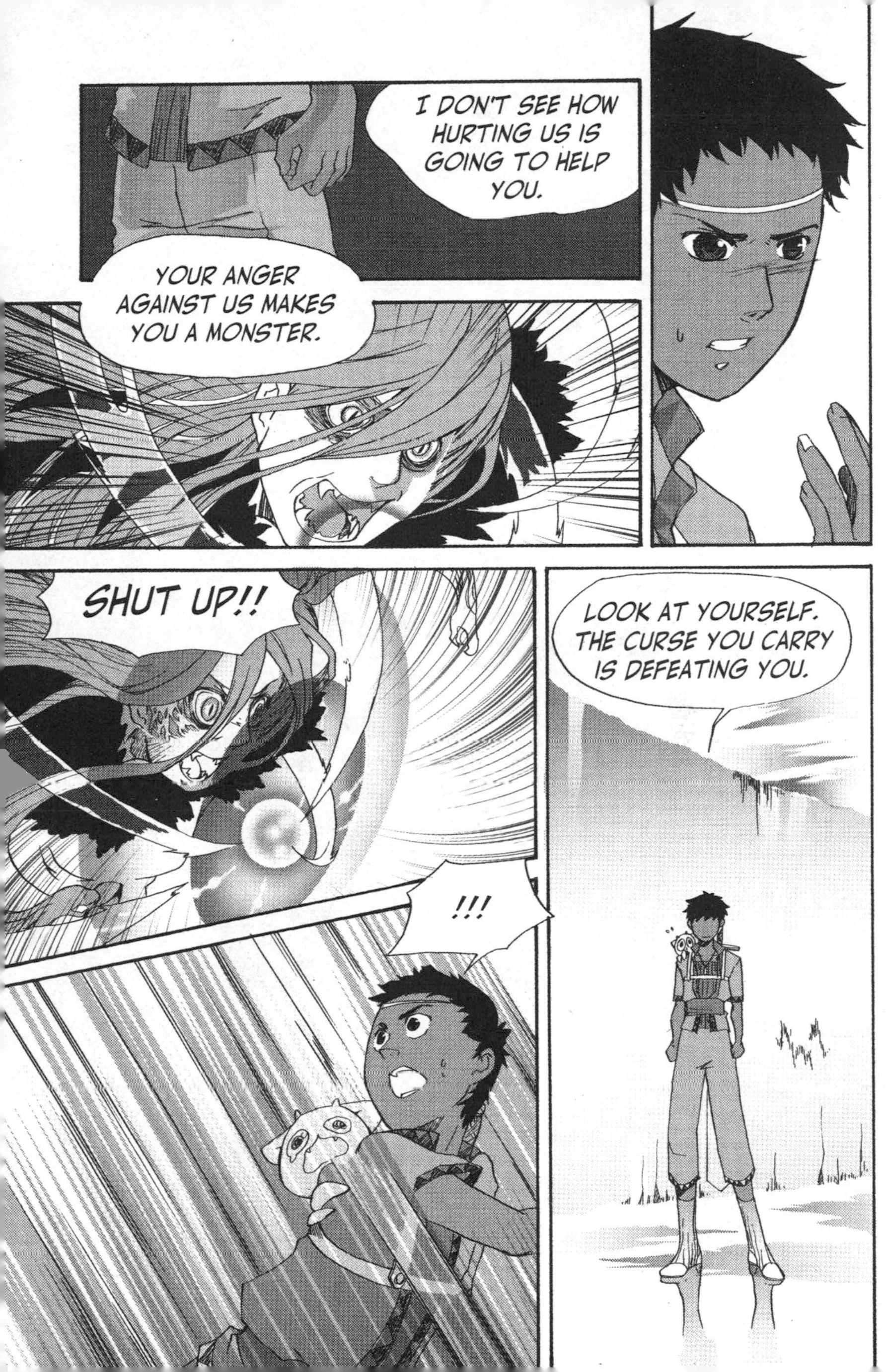
I DON'T SEE HOW HURTING US IS GOING TO HELP YOU.
YOUR ANGER AGAINST US MAKES YOU A MONSTER.
LOOK AT YOURSELF. THE CURSE YOU CARRY IS DEFEATING YOU.
SHUT UP!!
!!!

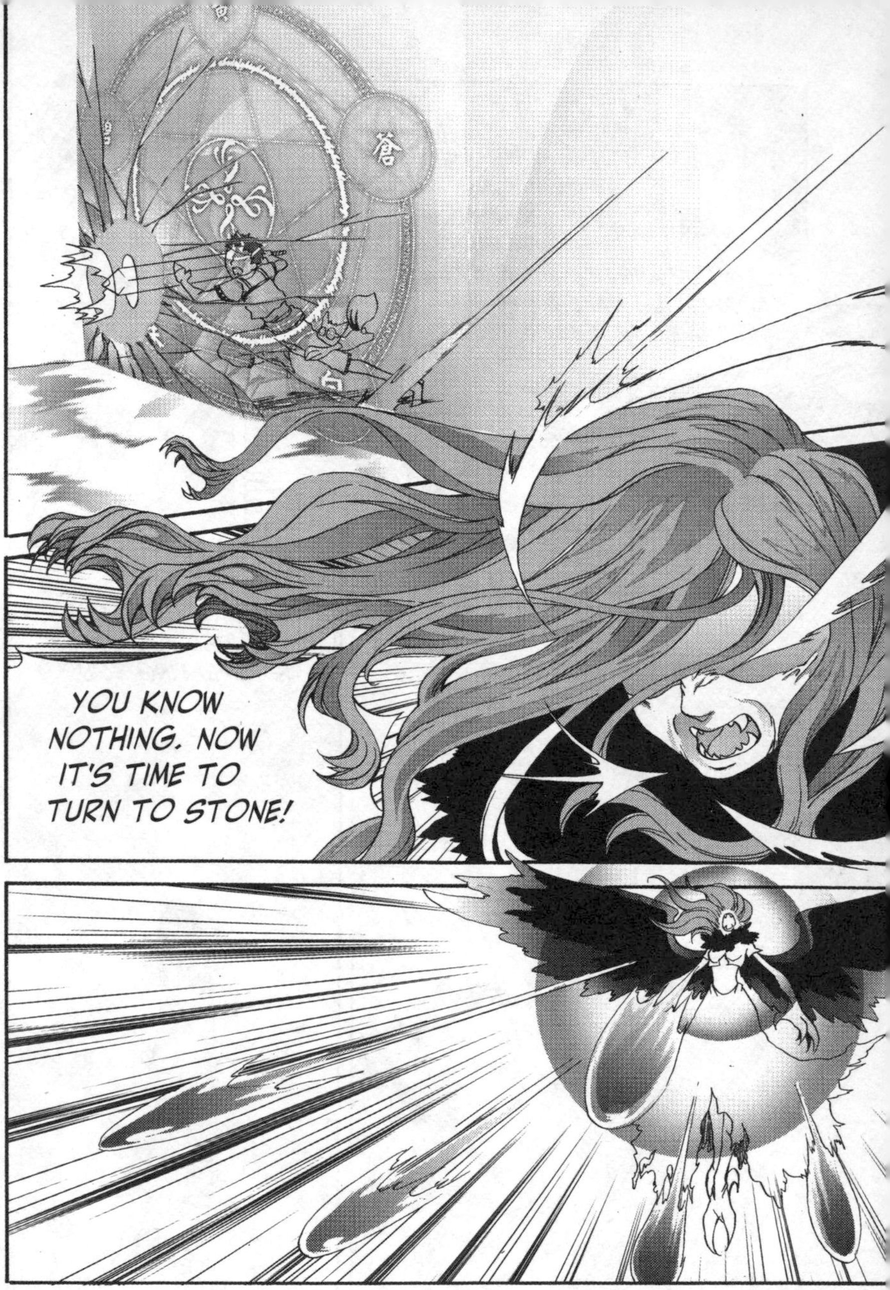
YOU KNOW NOTHING. NOW IT'S TIME TO TURN TO STONE!

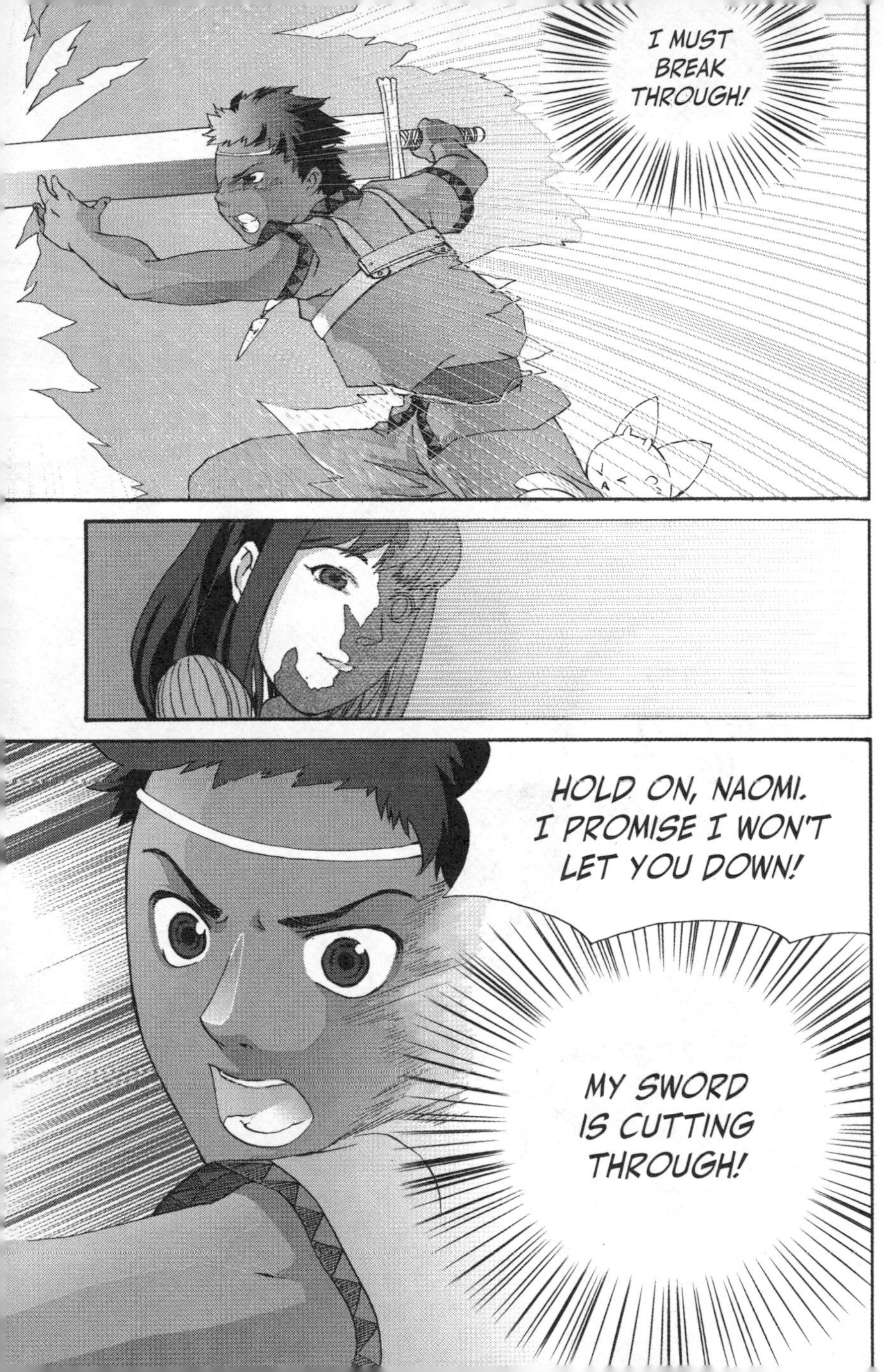
I MUST BREAK THROUGH!
HOLD ON, NAOMI. I PROMISE I WON'T LET YOU DOWN!
MY SWORD IS CUTTING THROUGH!

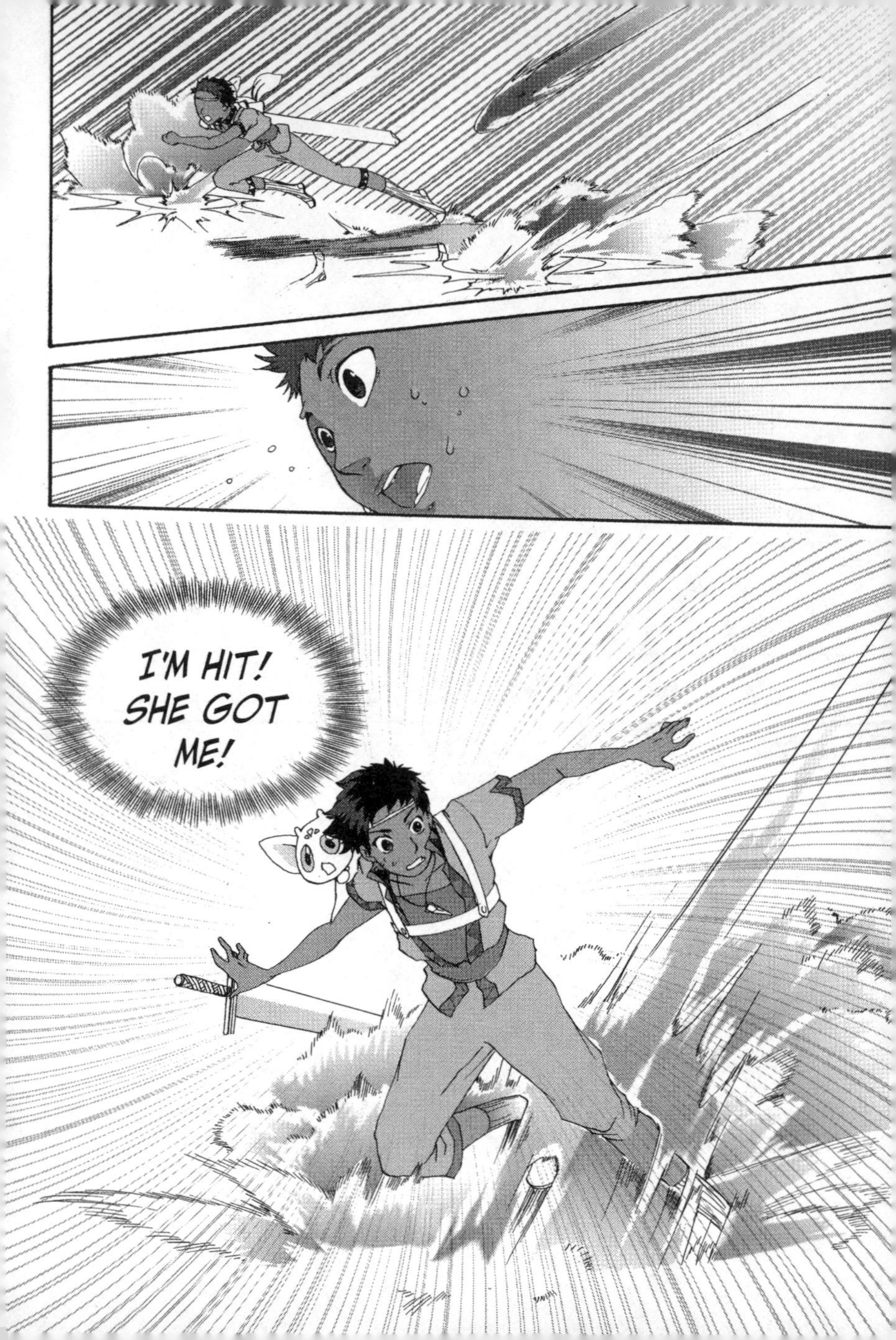
I'M HIT! SHE GOT ME!

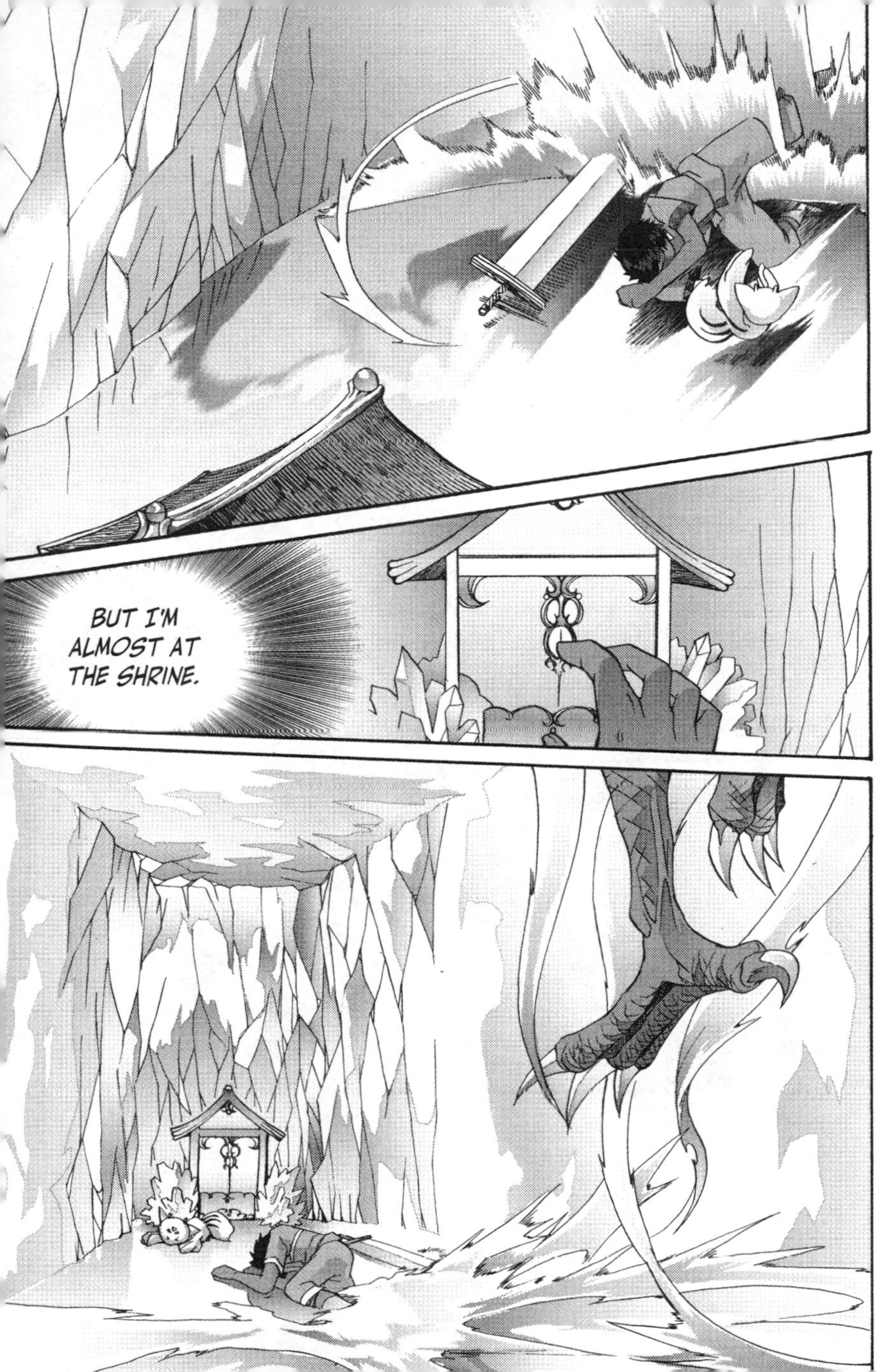
BUT I'M
ALMOST AT
THE SHRINE.

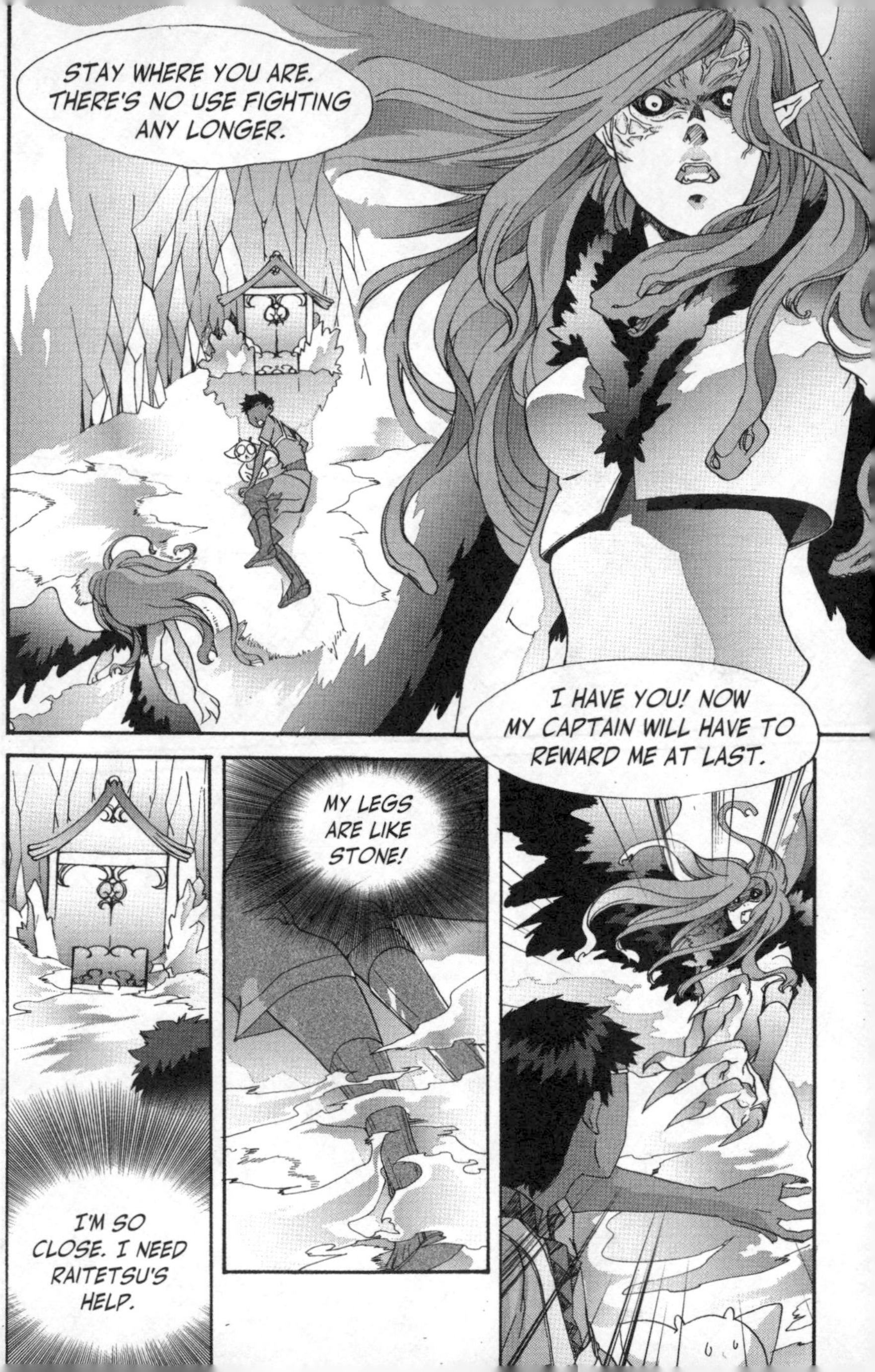
STAY WHERE YOU ARE. THERE'S NO USE FIGHTING ANY LONGER.
I HAVE YOU! NOW MY CAPTAIN WILL HAVE TO REWARD ME AT LAST.
MY LEGS ARE LIKE STONE!
I'M SO CLOSE. I NEED RAITETSU'S HELP.

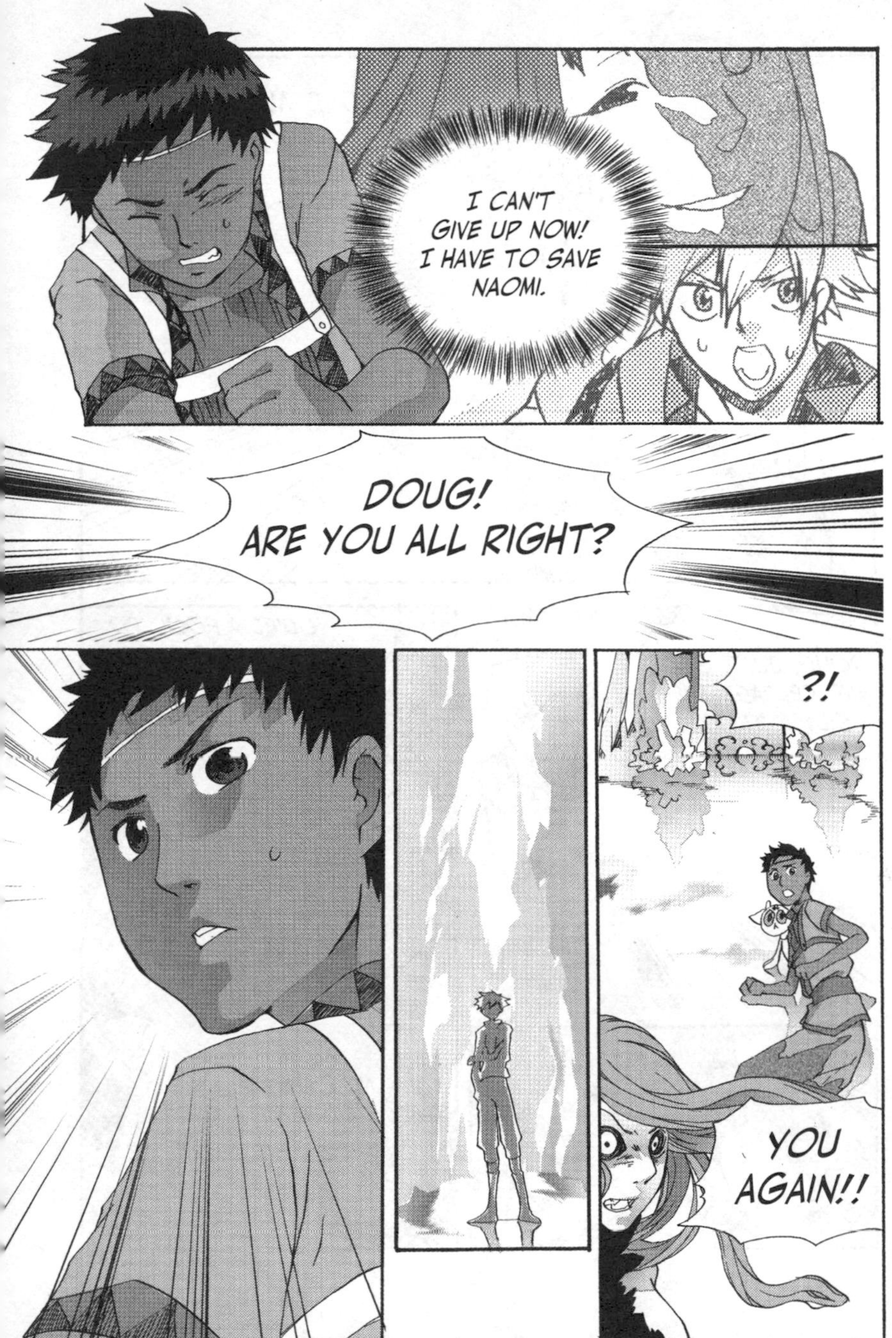
I CAN'T GIVE UP NOW! I HAVE TO SAVE NAOMI.
DOUG! ARE YOU ALL RIGHT?
?!
YOU AGAIN!!

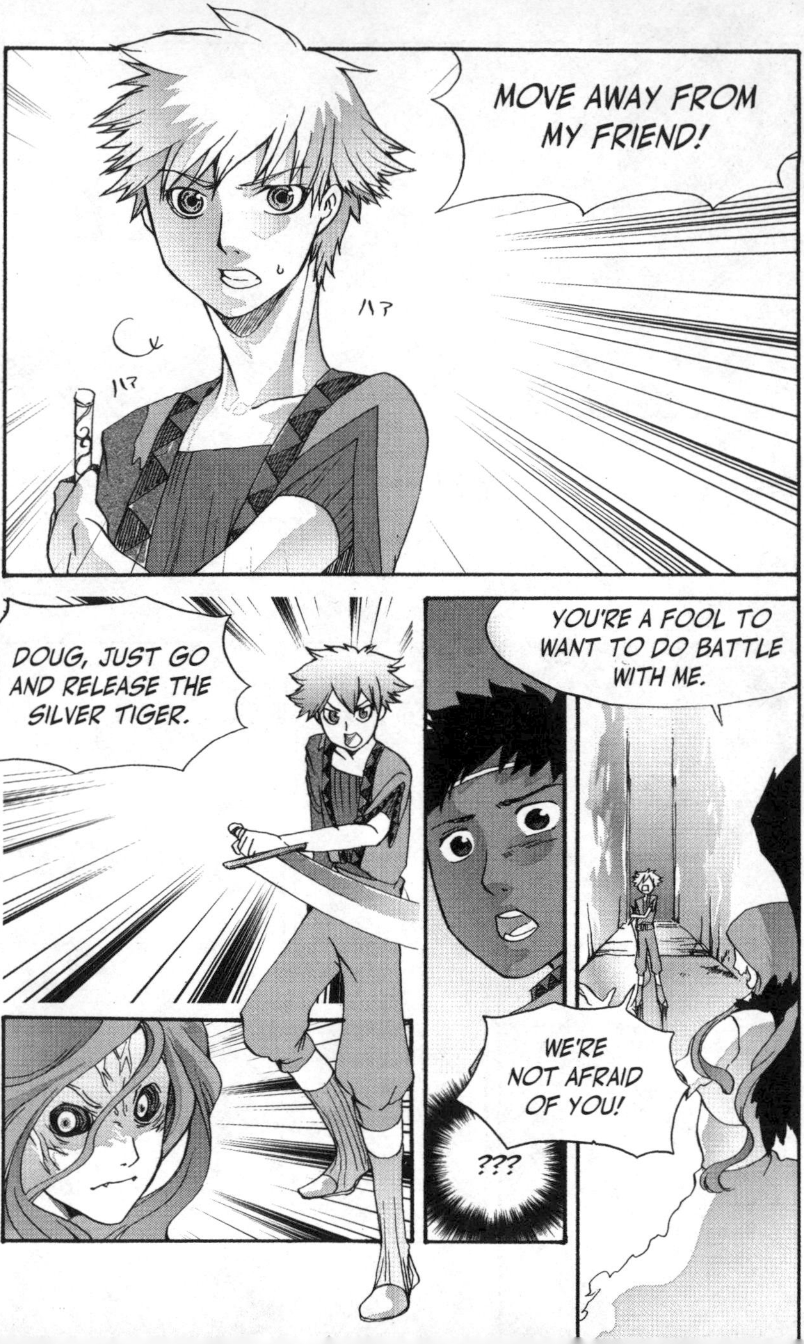
MOVE AWAY FROM MY FRIEND!
ハア
ハア
YOU'RE A FOOL TO WANT TO DO BATTLE WITH ME.
WE'RE NOT AFRAID OF YOU!
???
DOUG, JUST GO AND RELEASE THE SILVER TIGER.

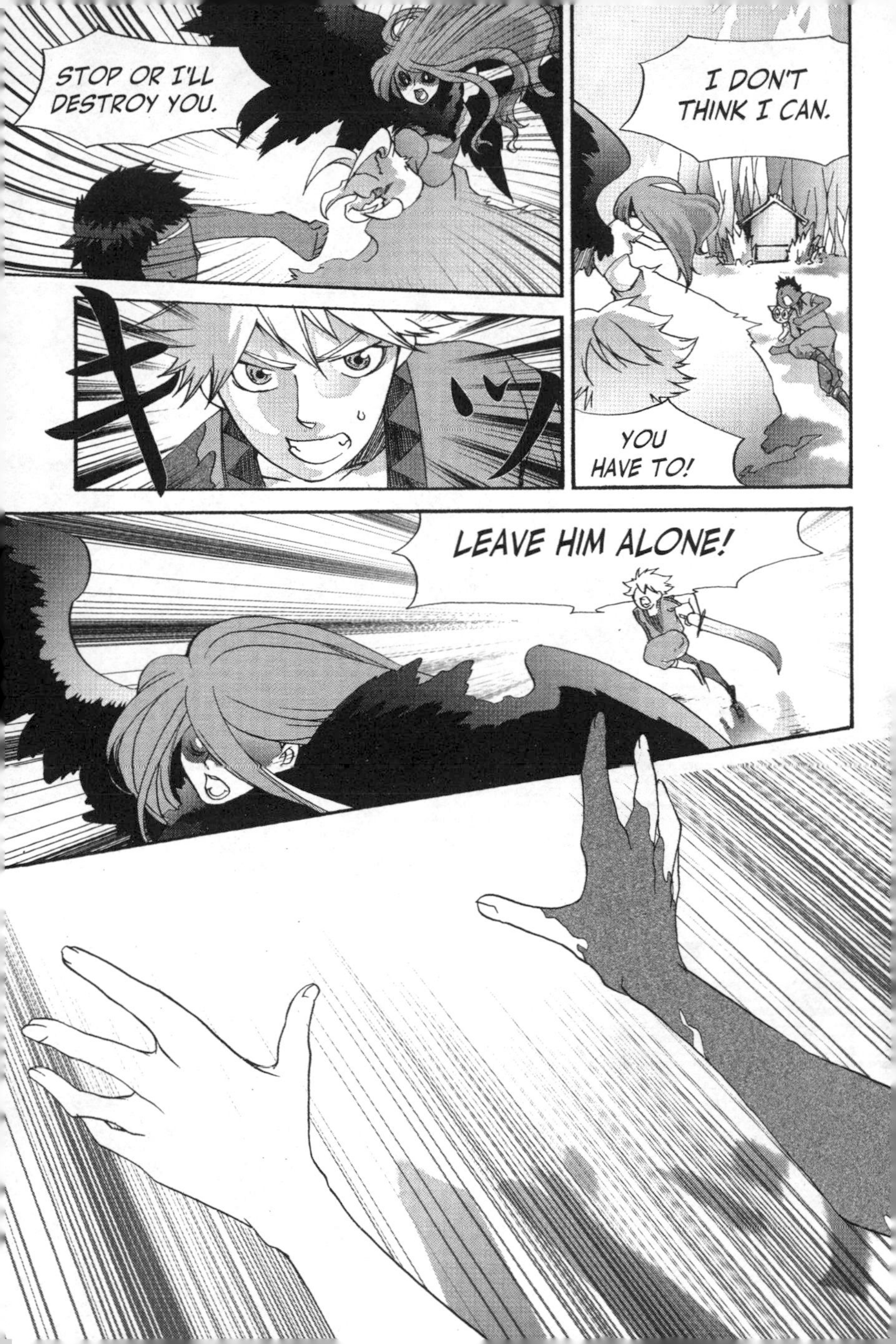
I DON'T THINK I CAN.
YOU HAVE TO!
STOP OR I'LL DESTROY YOU.
キッ
LEAVE HIM ALONE!

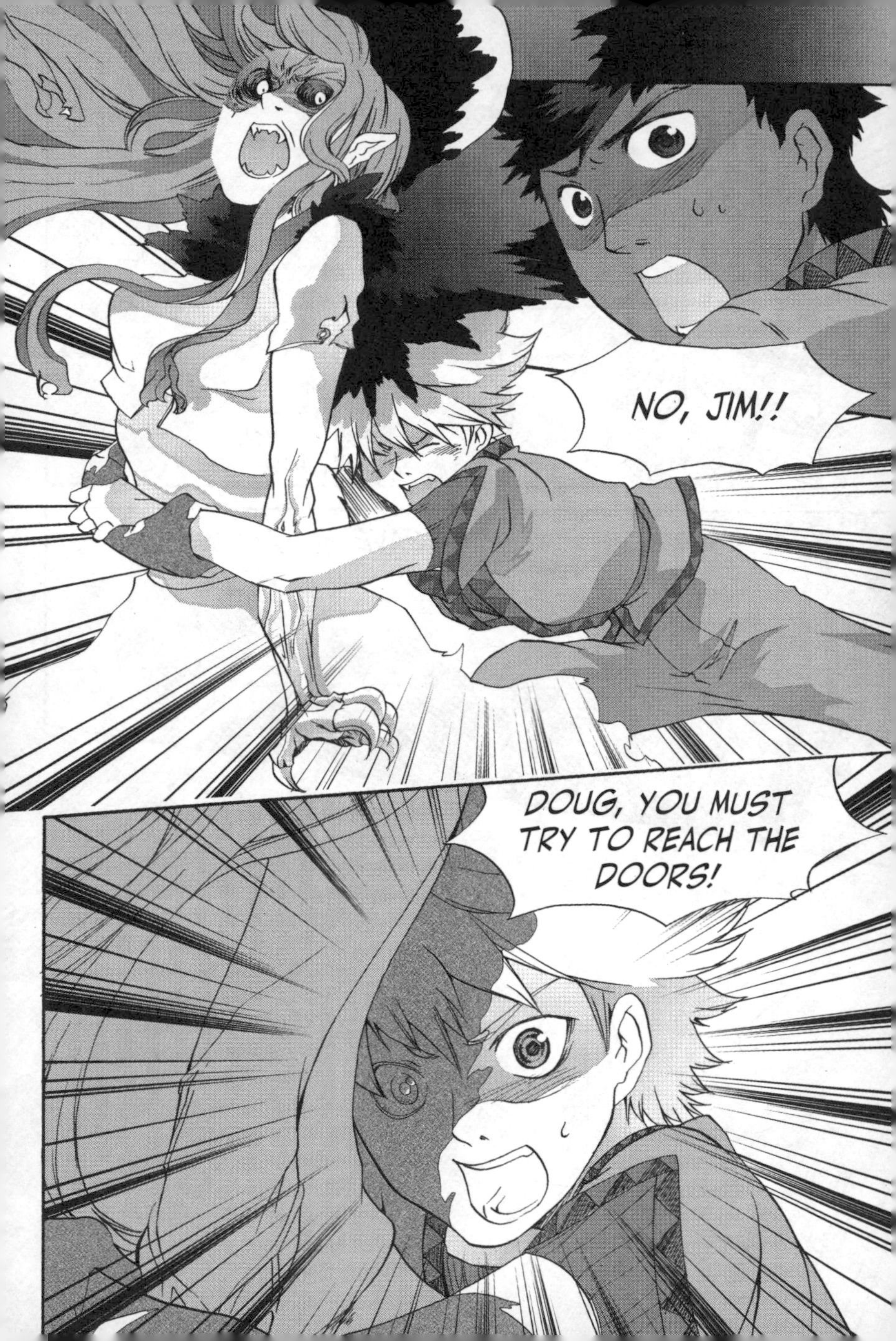
NO, JIM!!
DOUG, YOU MUST TRY TO REACH THE DOORS!

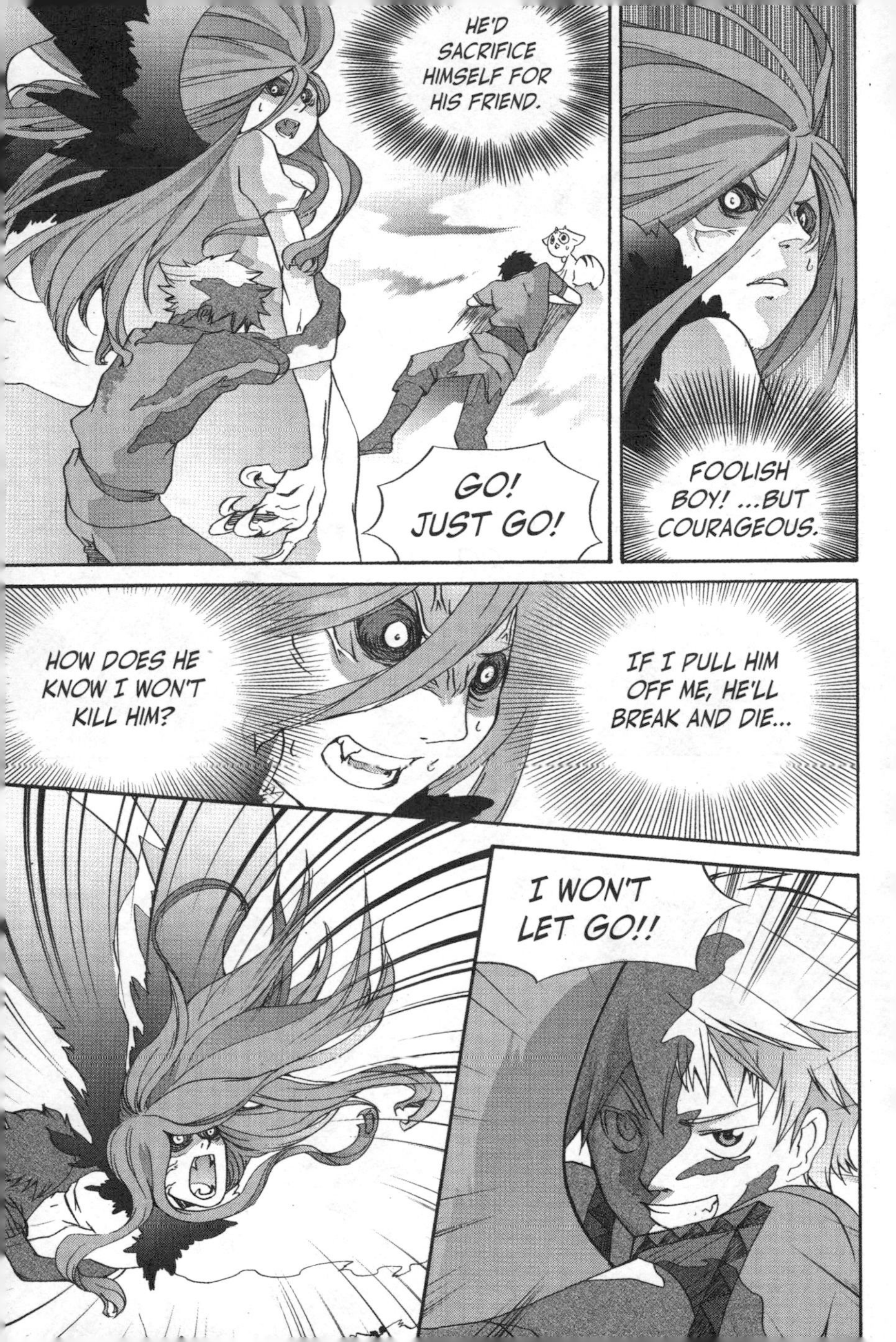
FOOLISH BOY! ...BUT COURAGEOUS.
HE'D SACRIFICE HIMSELF FOR HIS FRIEND.
GO! JUST GO!
IF I PULL HIM OFF ME, HE'LL BREAK AND DIE...
HOW DOES HE KNOW I WON'T KILL HIM?
I WON'T LET GO!!

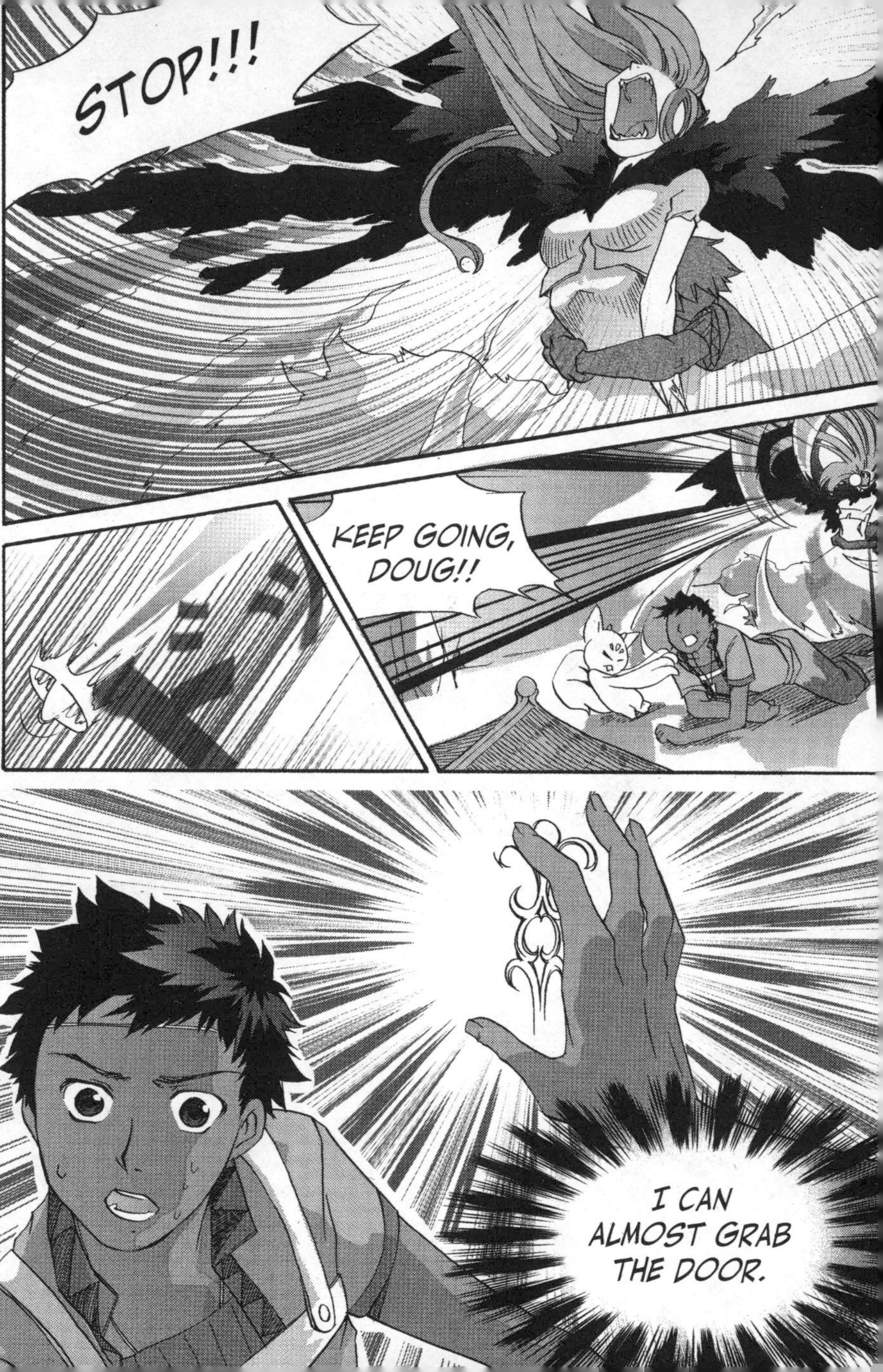
STOP!!!
KEEP GOING, DOUG!!
I CAN ALMOST GRAB THE DOOR.

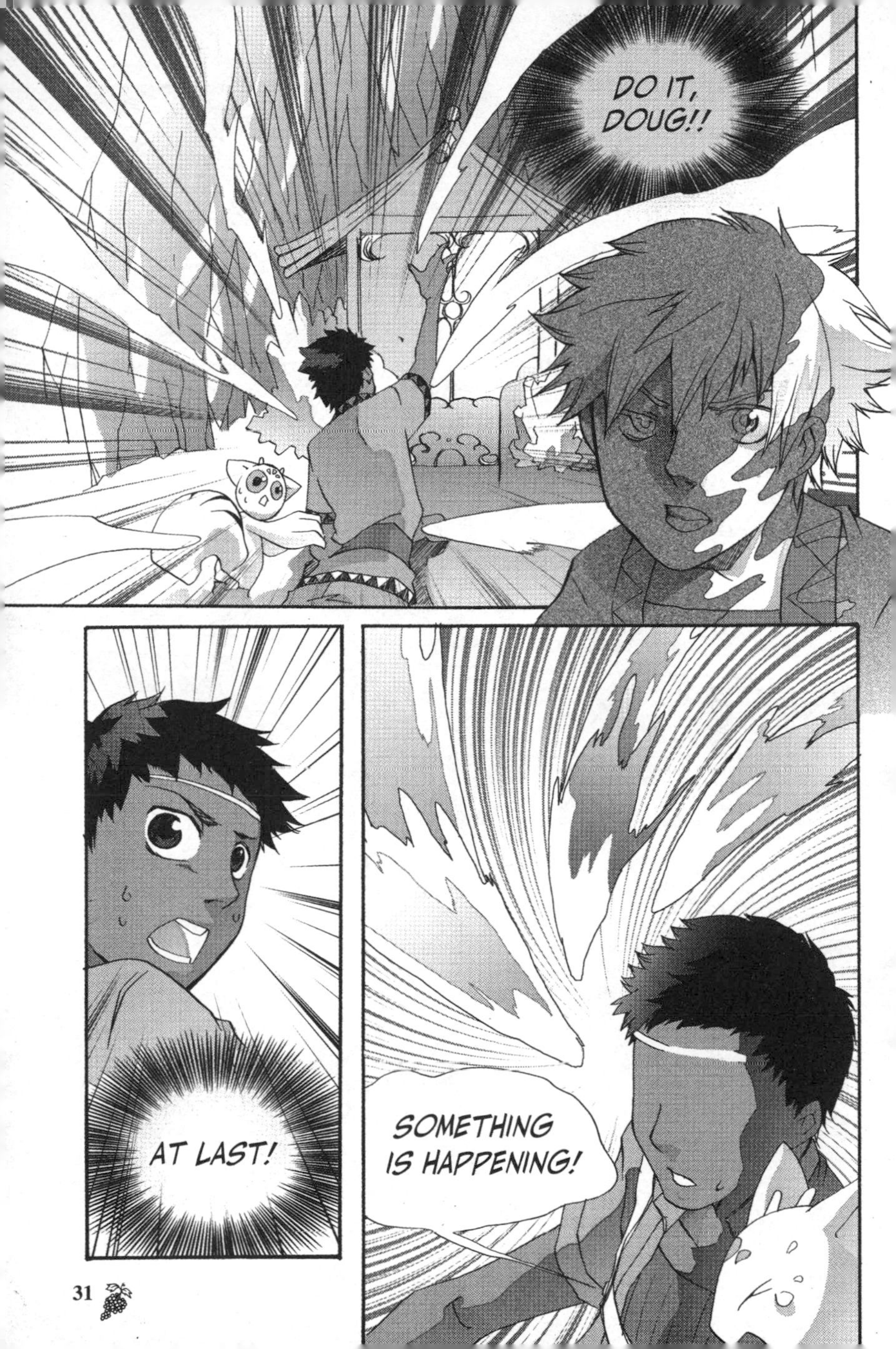
DO IT, DOUG!!
SOMETHING IS HAPPENING!
AT LAST!

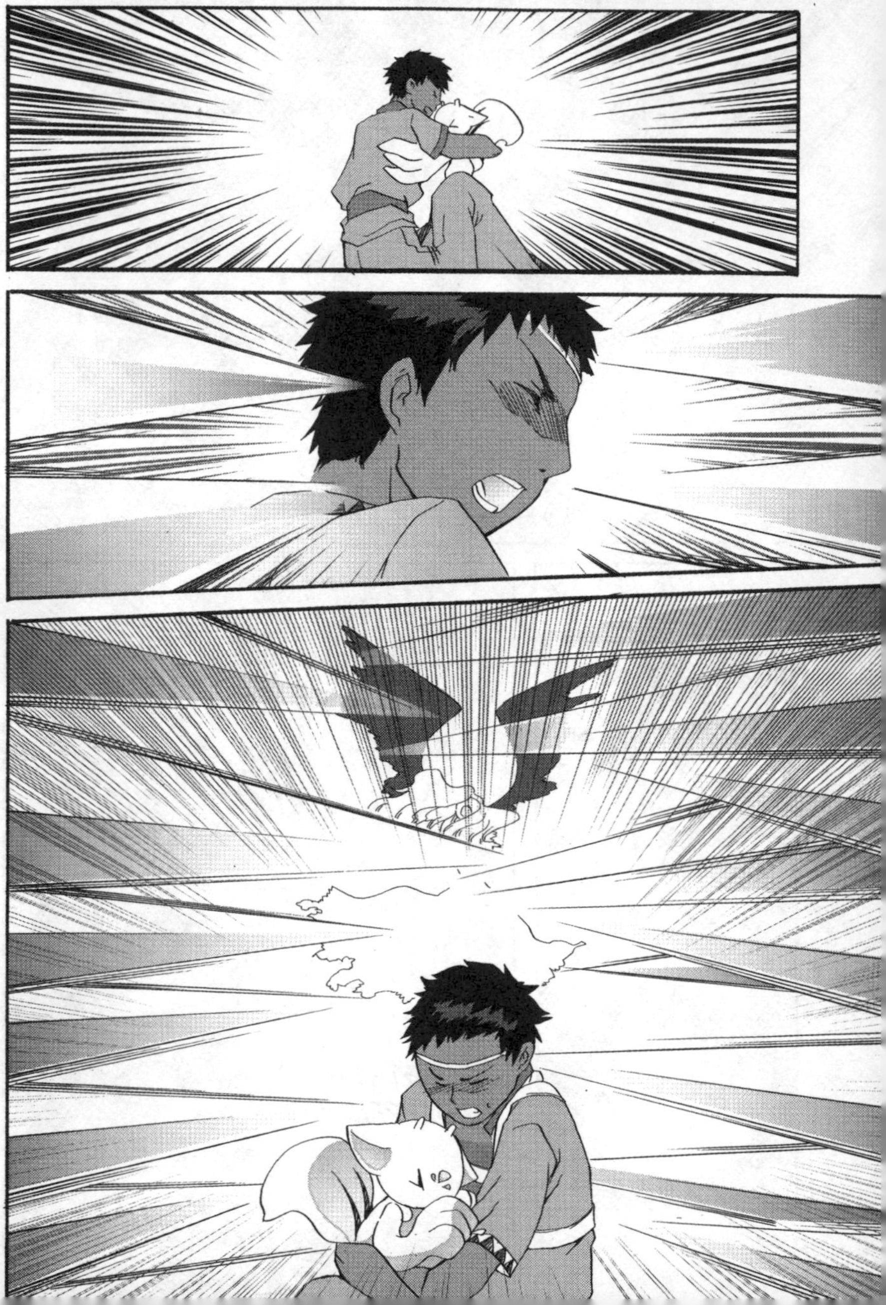

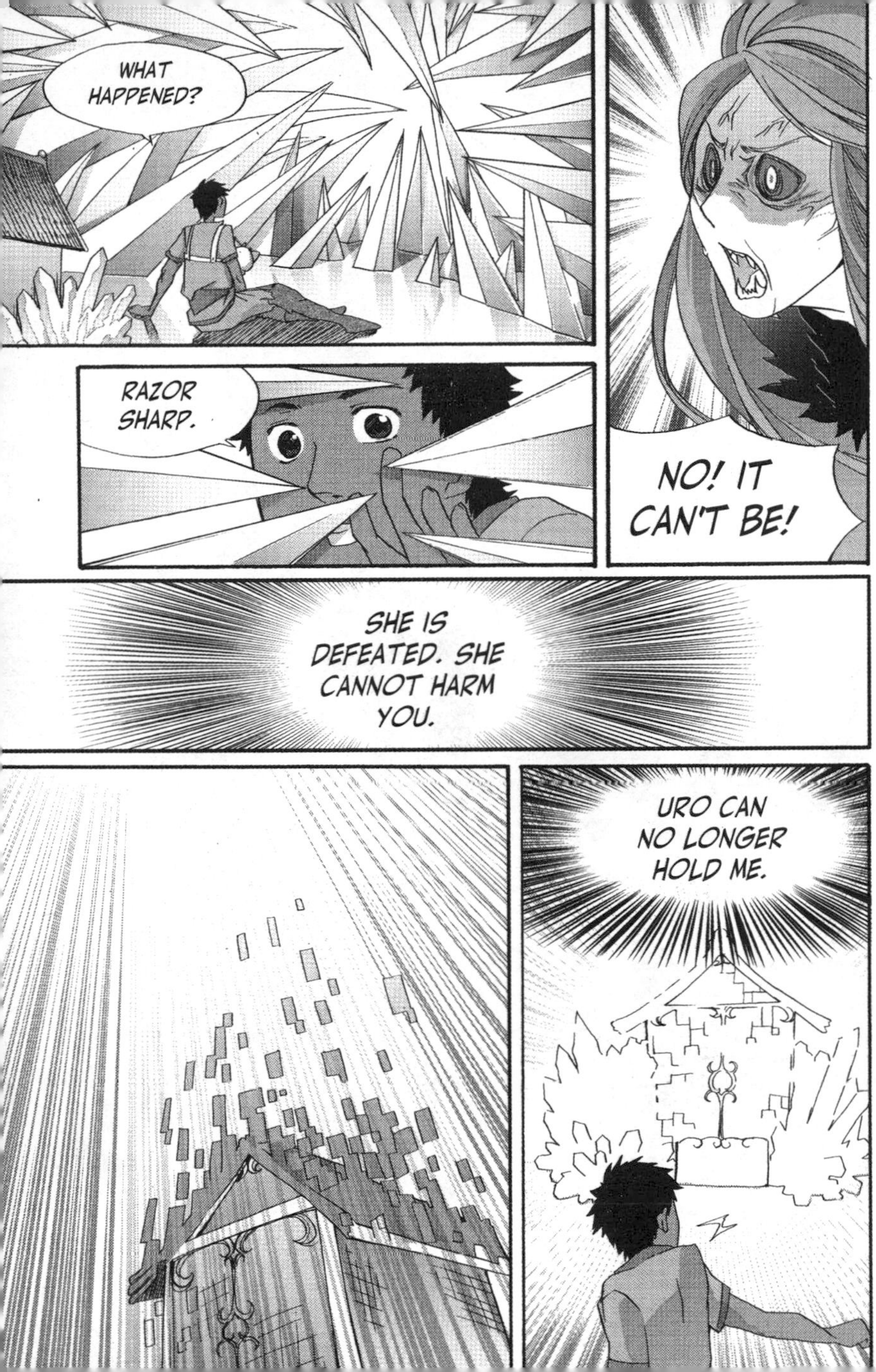
NO! IT CAN'T BE!
WHAT HAPPENED?
RAZOR SHARP.
SHE IS DEFEATED. SHE CANNOT HARM YOU.
URO CAN NO LONGER HOLD ME.

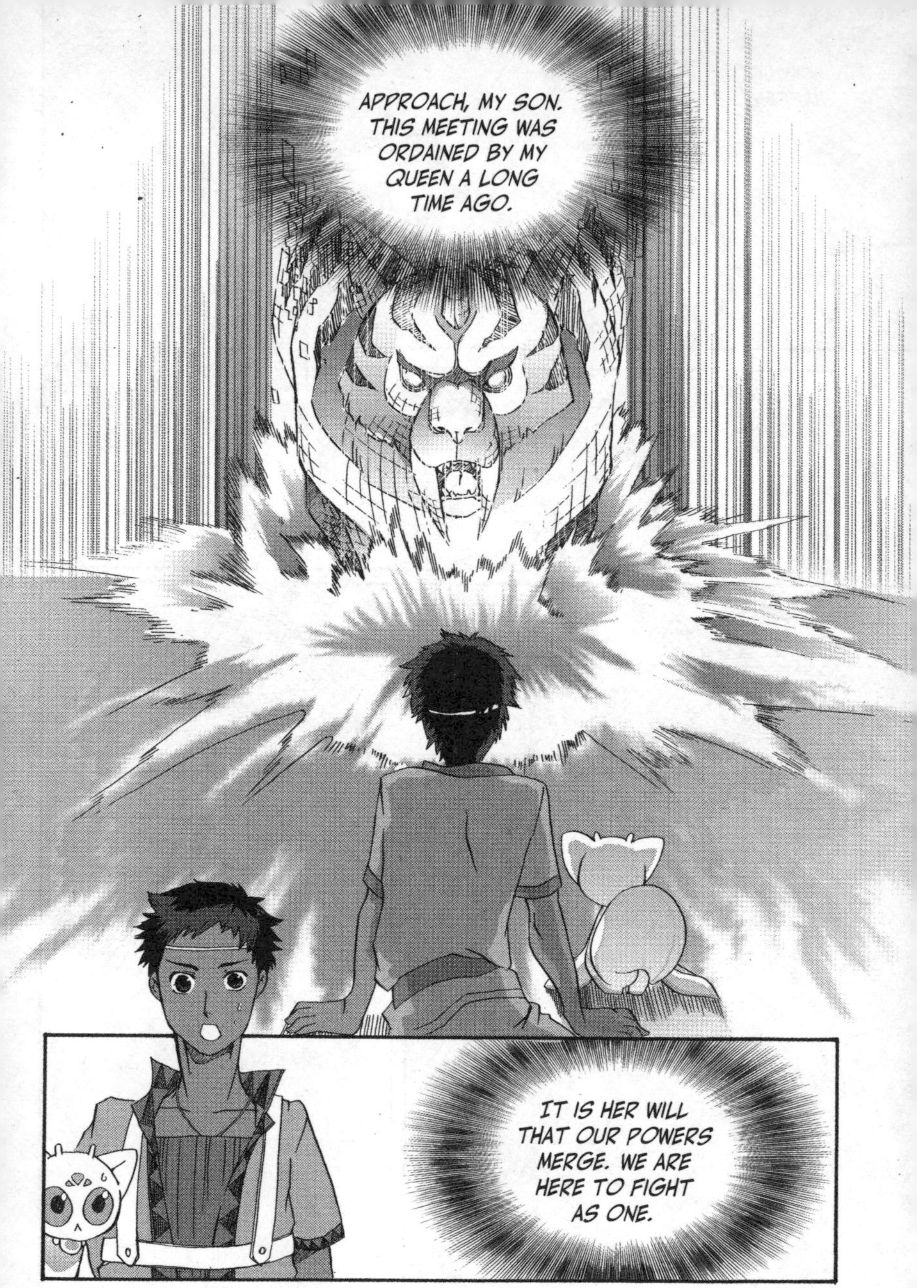
APPROACH, MY SON. THIS MEETING WAS ORDAINED BY MY QUEEN A LONG TIME AGO.
IT IS HER WILL THAT OUR POWERS MERGE. WE ARE HERE TO FIGHT AS ONE.

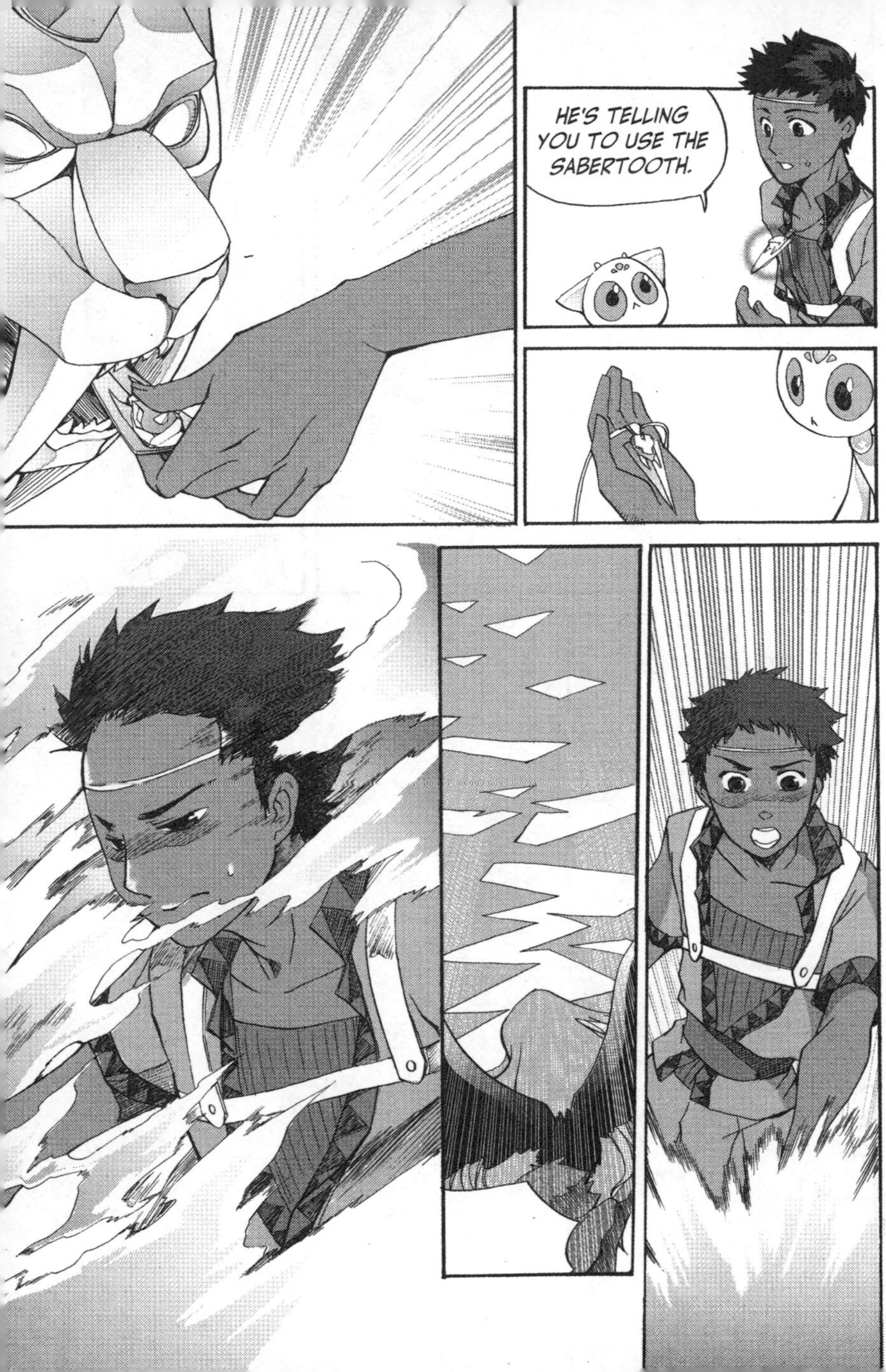
HE'S TELLING YOU TO USE THE SABERTOOTH.

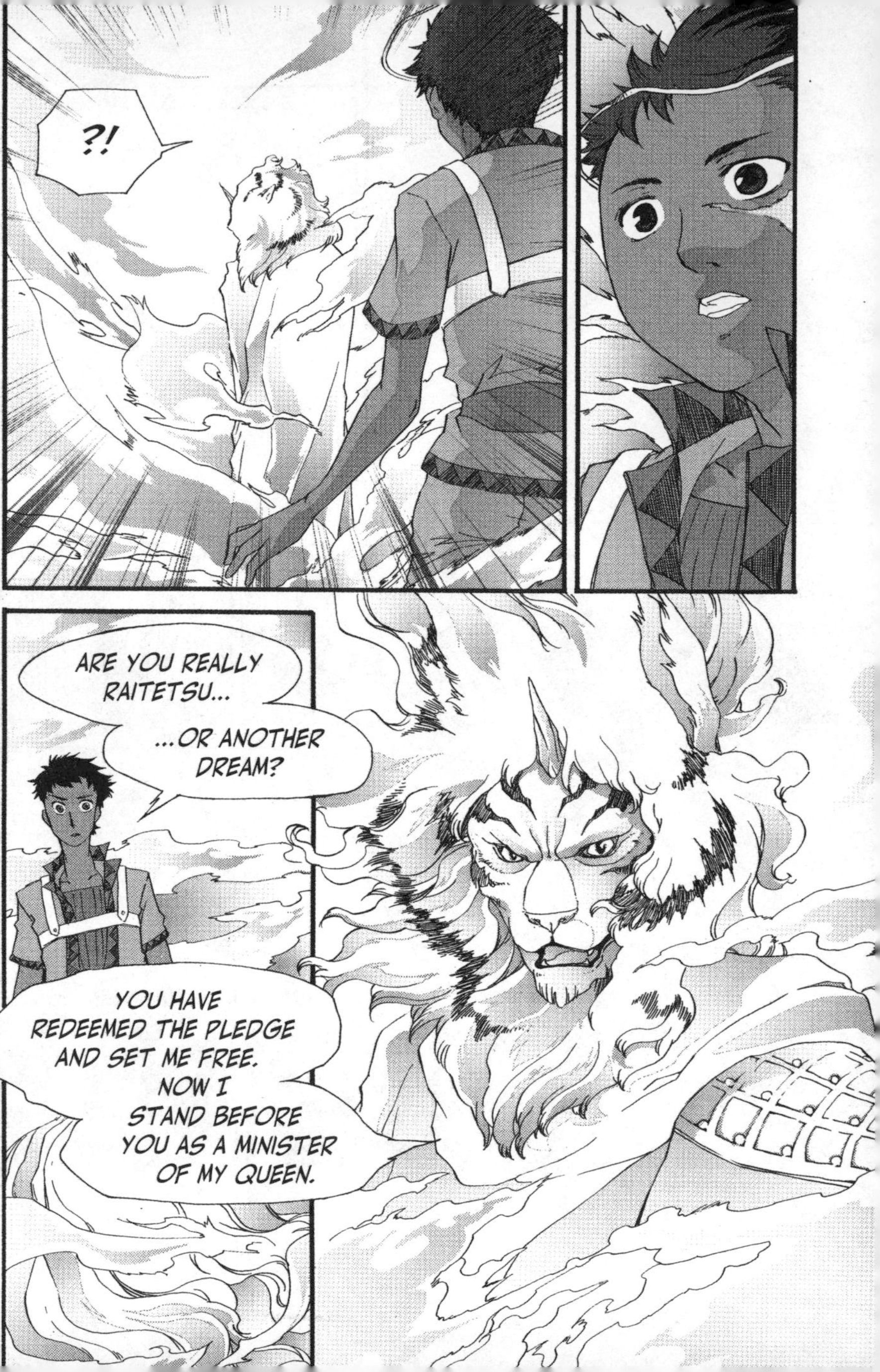
?!
ARE YOU REALLY RAITETSU...
...OR ANOTHER DREAM?
YOU HAVE REDEEMED THE PLEDGE AND SET ME FREE.
NOW I STAND BEFORE YOU AS A MINISTER OF MY QUEEN.

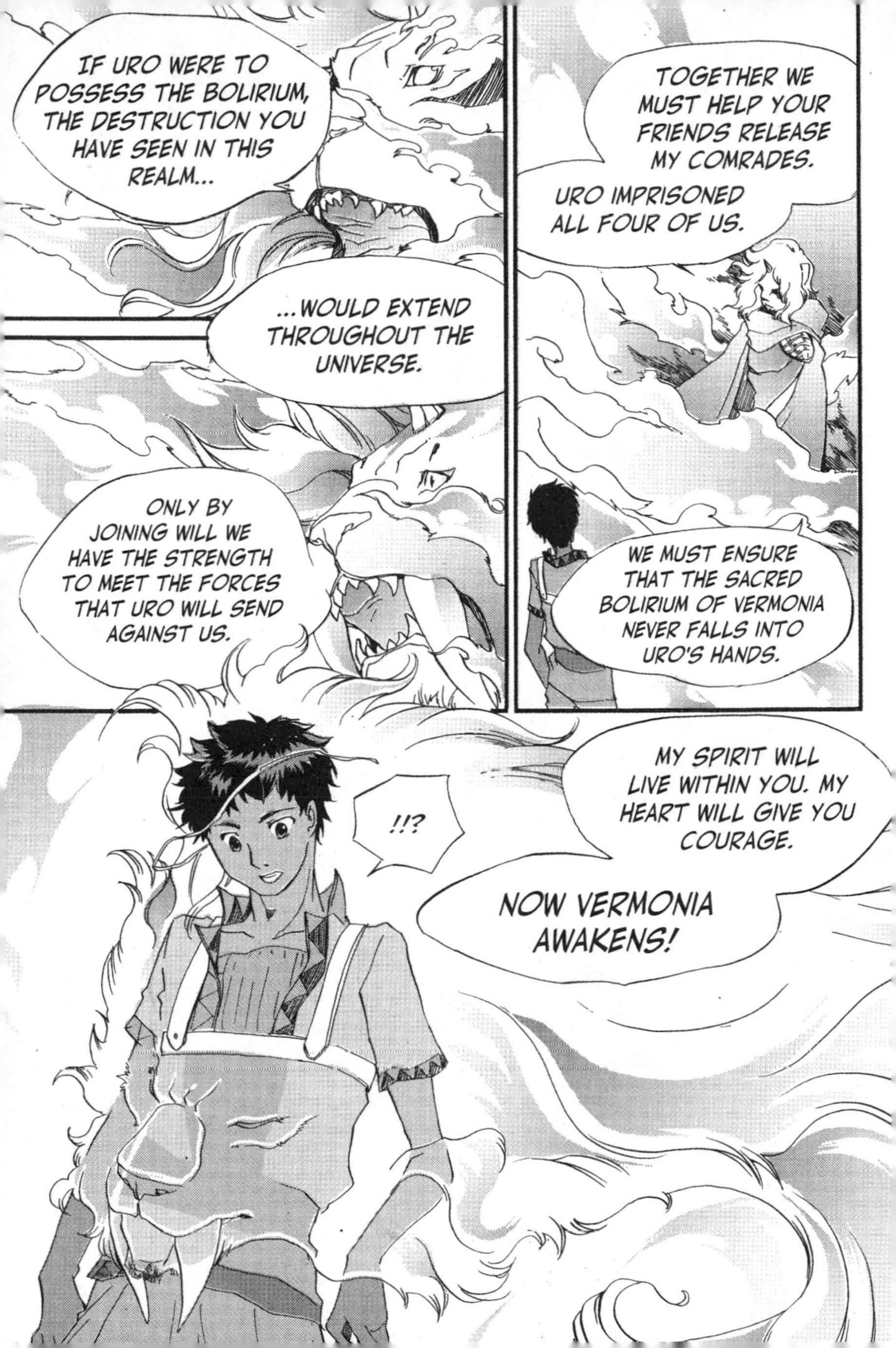
TOGETHER WE MUST HELP YOUR FRIENDS RELEASE MY COMRADES.
URO IMPRISONED ALL FOUR OF US.
WE MUST ENSURE THAT THE SACRED BOLIRIUM OF VERMONIA NEVER FALLS INTO URO'S HANDS.
IF URO WERE TO POSSESS THE BOLIRIUM, THE DESTRUCTION YOU HAVE SEEN IN THIS REALM...
...WOULD EXTEND THROUGHOUT THE UNIVERSE.
ONLY BY JOINING WILL WE HAVE THE STRENGTH TO MEET THE FORCES THAT URO WILL SEND AGAINST US.
MY SPIRIT WILL LIVE WITHIN YOU. MY HEART WILL GIVE YOU COURAGE.
!!?
NOW VERMONIA AWAKENS!

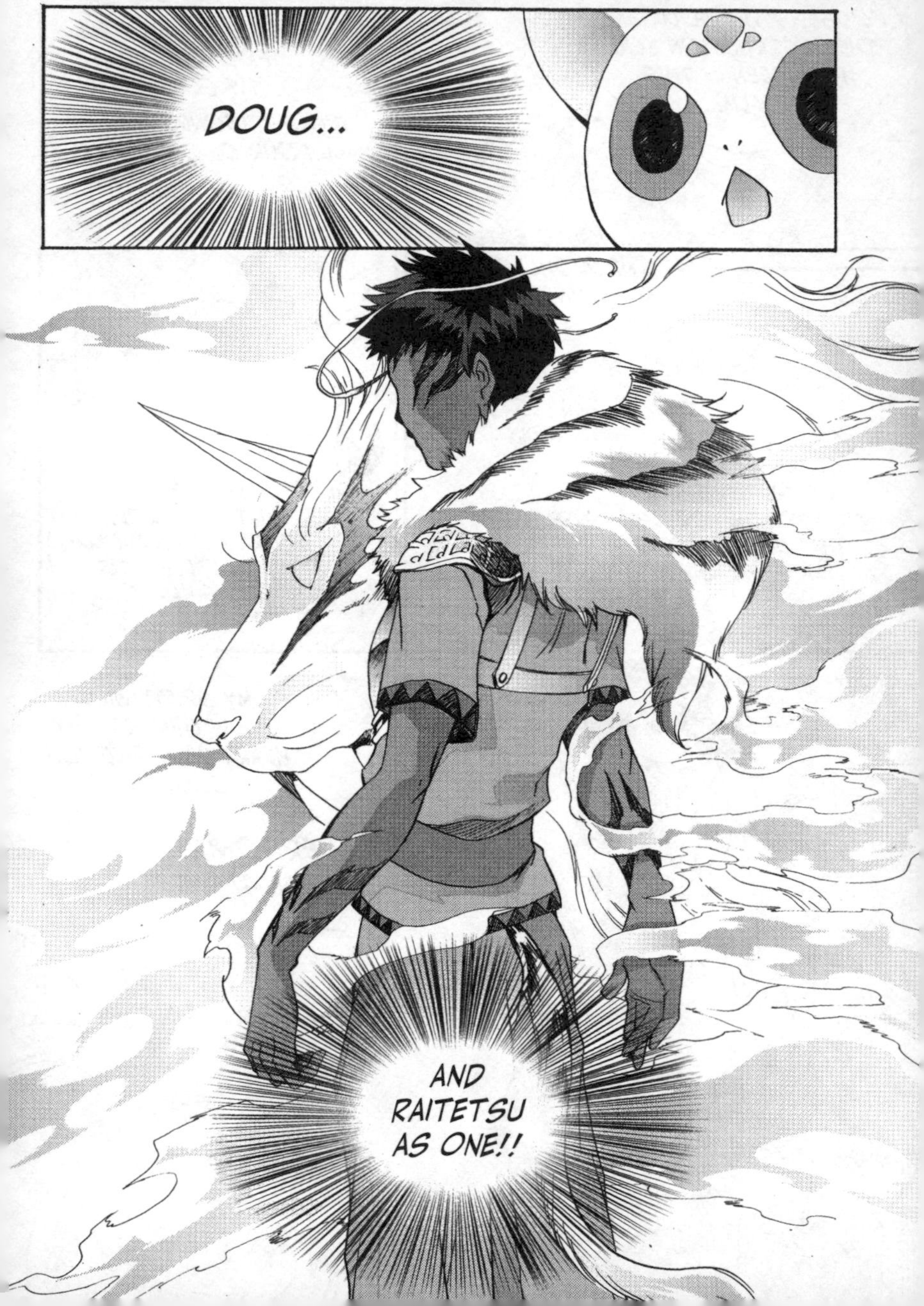
DOUG...
AND RAITETSU AS ONE!!

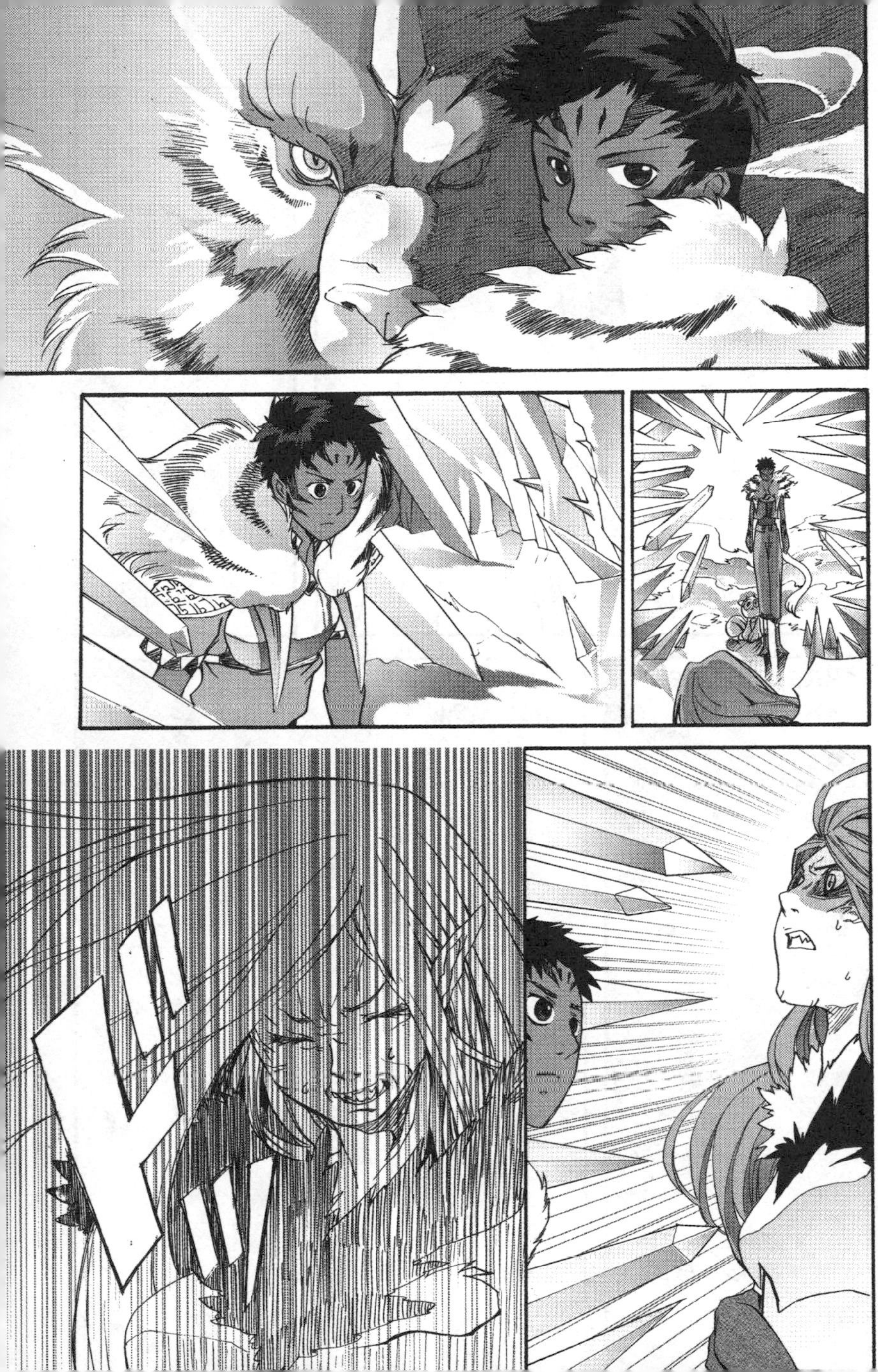

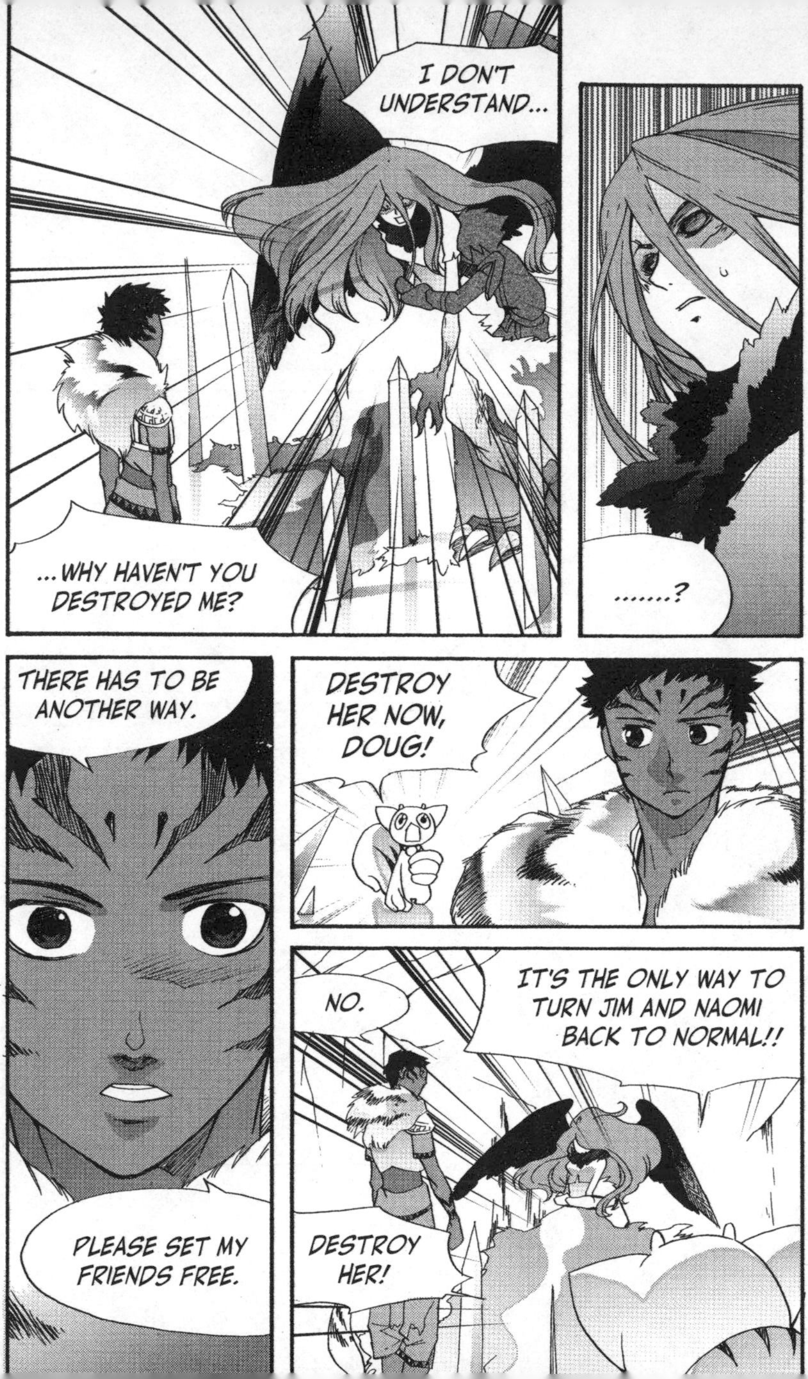
.......?
I DON'T UNDERSTAND...
...WHY HAVEN'T YOU DESTROYED ME?
DESTROY HER NOW, DOUG!
IT'S THE ONLY WAY TO TURN JIM AND NAOMI BACK TO NORMAL!!
NO.
DESTROY HER!
THERE HAS TO BE ANOTHER WAY.
PLEASE SET MY FRIENDS FREE.

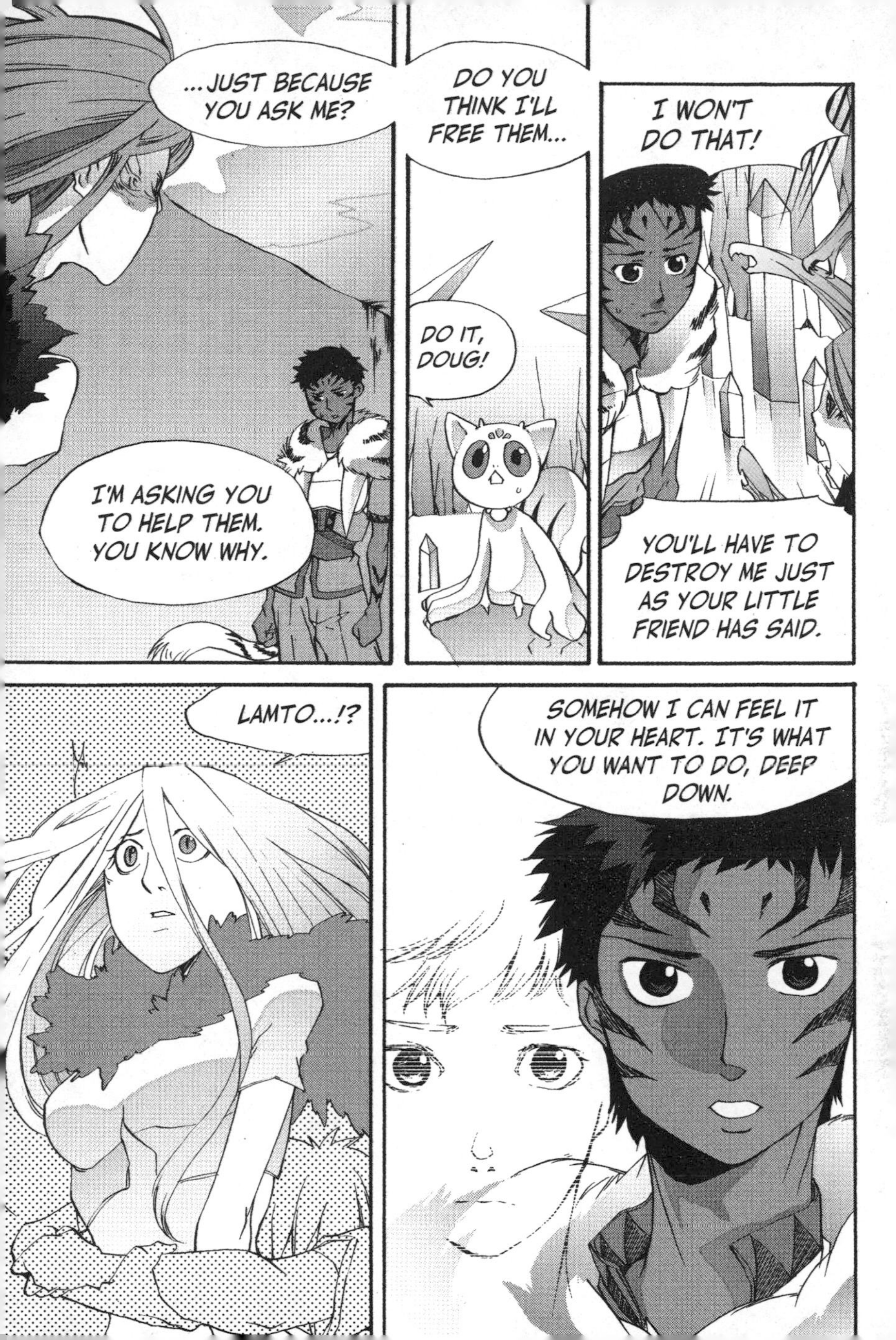
I'M ASKING YOU TO HELP THEM. YOU KNOW WHY.
DO YOU THINK I'LL FREE THEM...
...JUST BECAUSE YOU ASK ME?
DO IT, DOUG!
I WON'T DO THAT!
YOU'LL HAVE TO DESTROY ME JUST AS YOUR LITTLE FRIEND HAS SAID.
LAMTO...!?
SOMEHOW I CAN FEEL IT IN YOUR HEART. IT'S WHAT YOU WANT TO DO, DEEP DOWN.

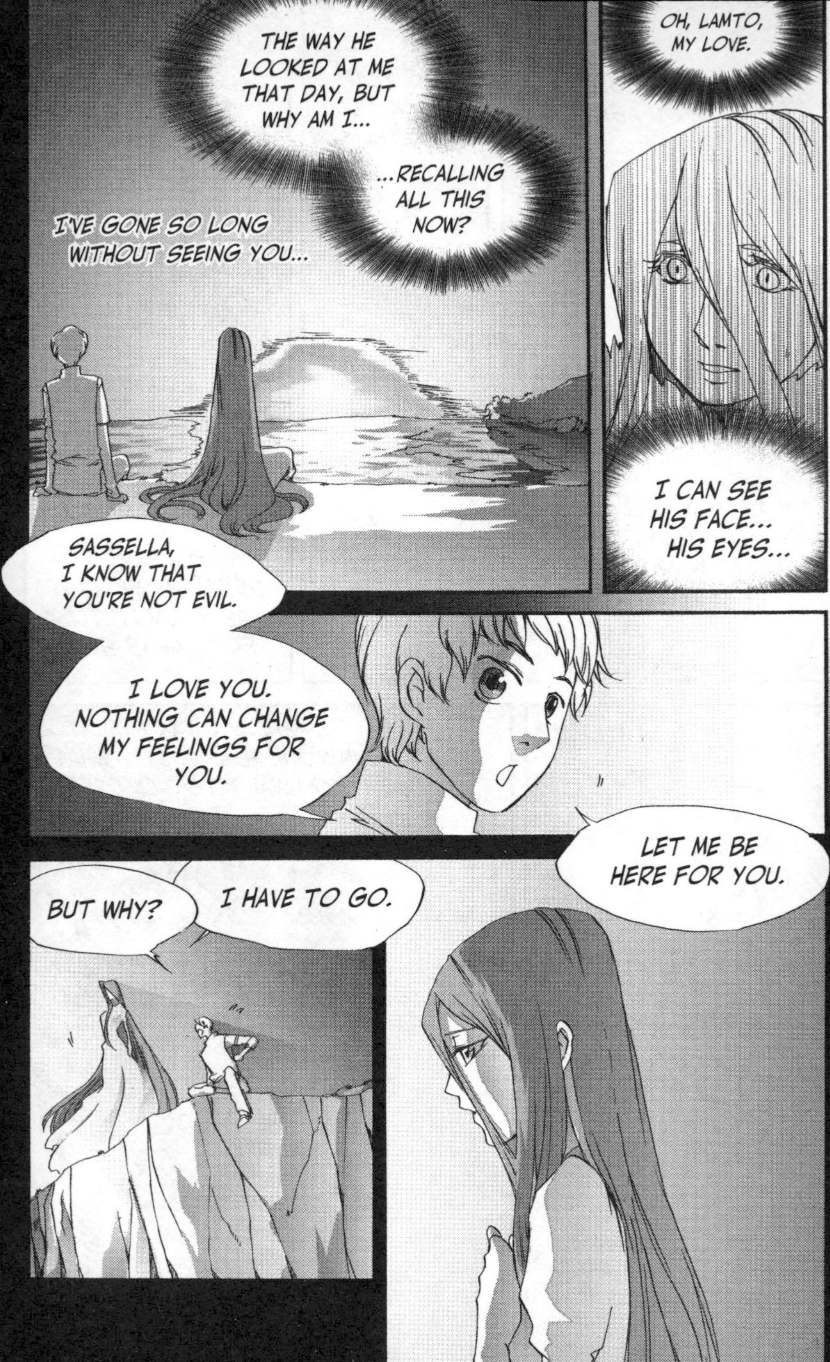
OH, LAMTO, MY LOVE.
I CAN SEE HIS FACE... HIS EYES...
THE WAY HE LOOKED AT ME THAT DAY, BUT WHY AM I...
...RECALLING ALL THIS NOW?
I'VE GONE SO LONG WITHOUT SEEING YOU...
SASSELLA, I KNOW THAT YOU'RE NOT EVIL.
I LOVE YOU. NOTHING CAN CHANGE MY FEELINGS FOR YOU.
LET ME BE HERE FOR YOU.
I HAVE TO GO.
BUT WHY?

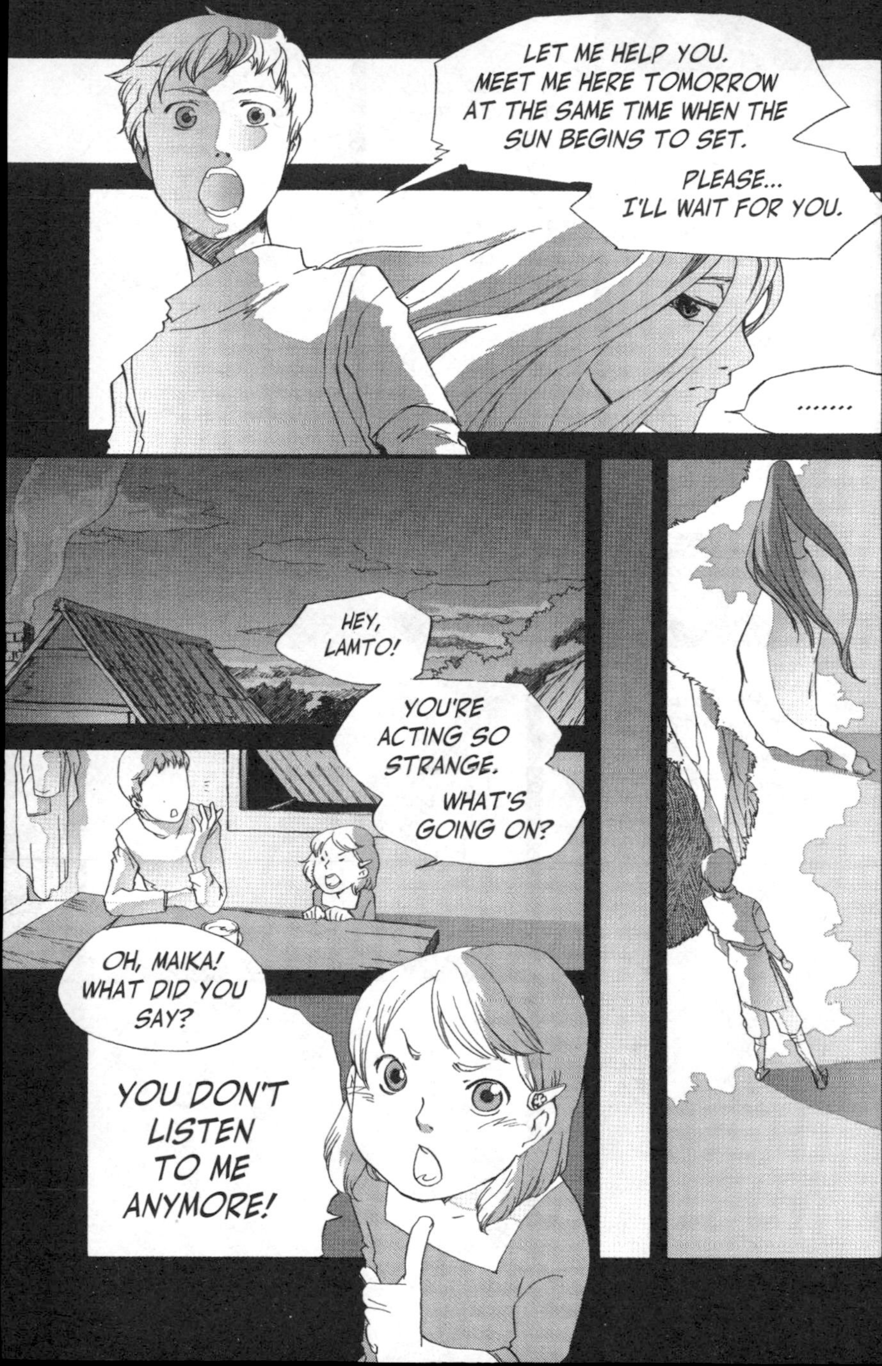
LET ME HELP YOU. MEET ME HERE TOMORROW AT THE SAME TIME WHEN THE SUN BEGINS TO SET.
PLEASE... I'LL WAIT FOR YOU.
....
HEY, LAMTO!
YOU'RE ACTING SO STRANGE.
WHAT'S GOING ON?
OH, MAIKA! WHAT DID YOU SAY?
YOU DON'T LISTEN TO ME ANYMORE!

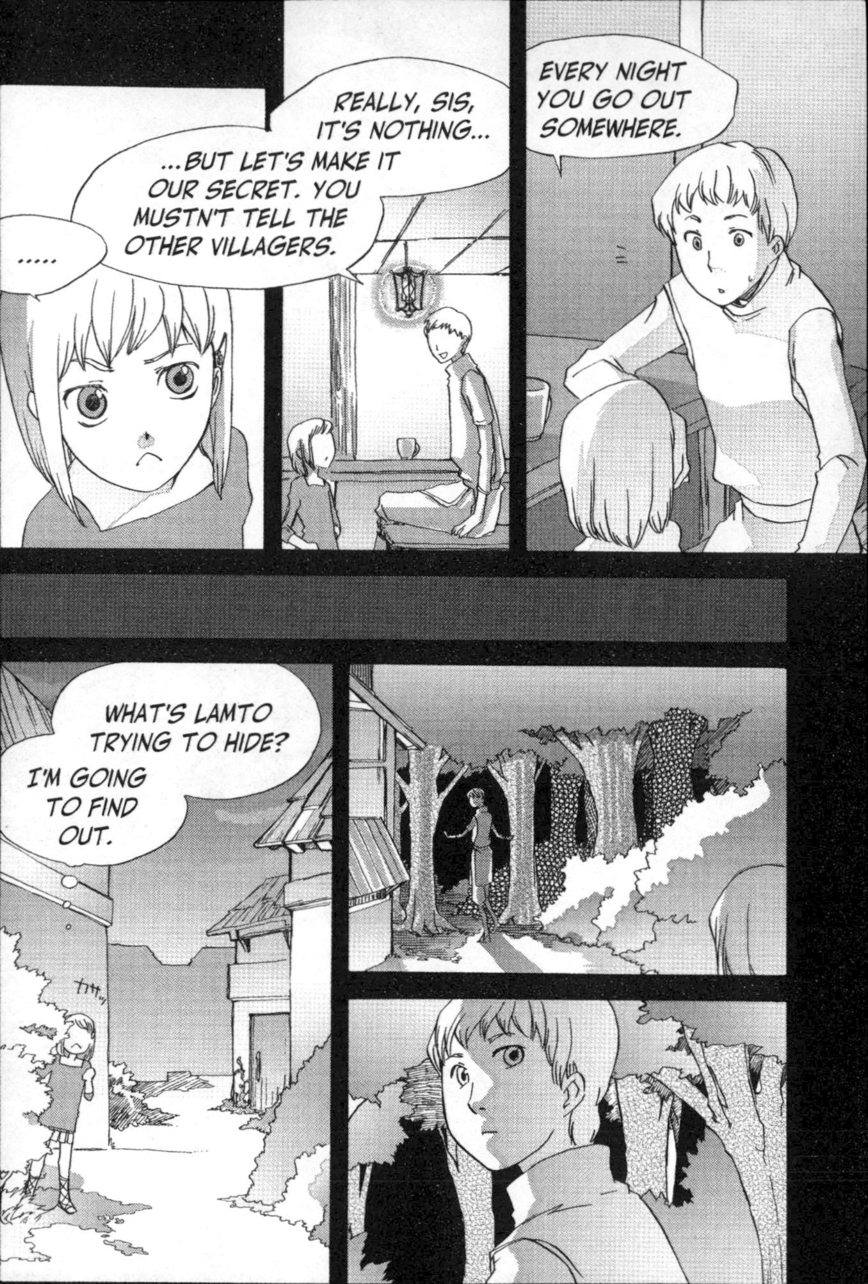
EVERY NIGHT YOU GO OUT SOMEWHERE.
REALLY, SIS, IT'S NOTHING...
...BUT LET'S MAKE IT OUR SECRET. YOU MUSTN'T TELL THE OTHER VILLAGERS.
.....
WHAT'S LAMTO TRYING TO HIDE?
I'M GOING TO FIND OUT.

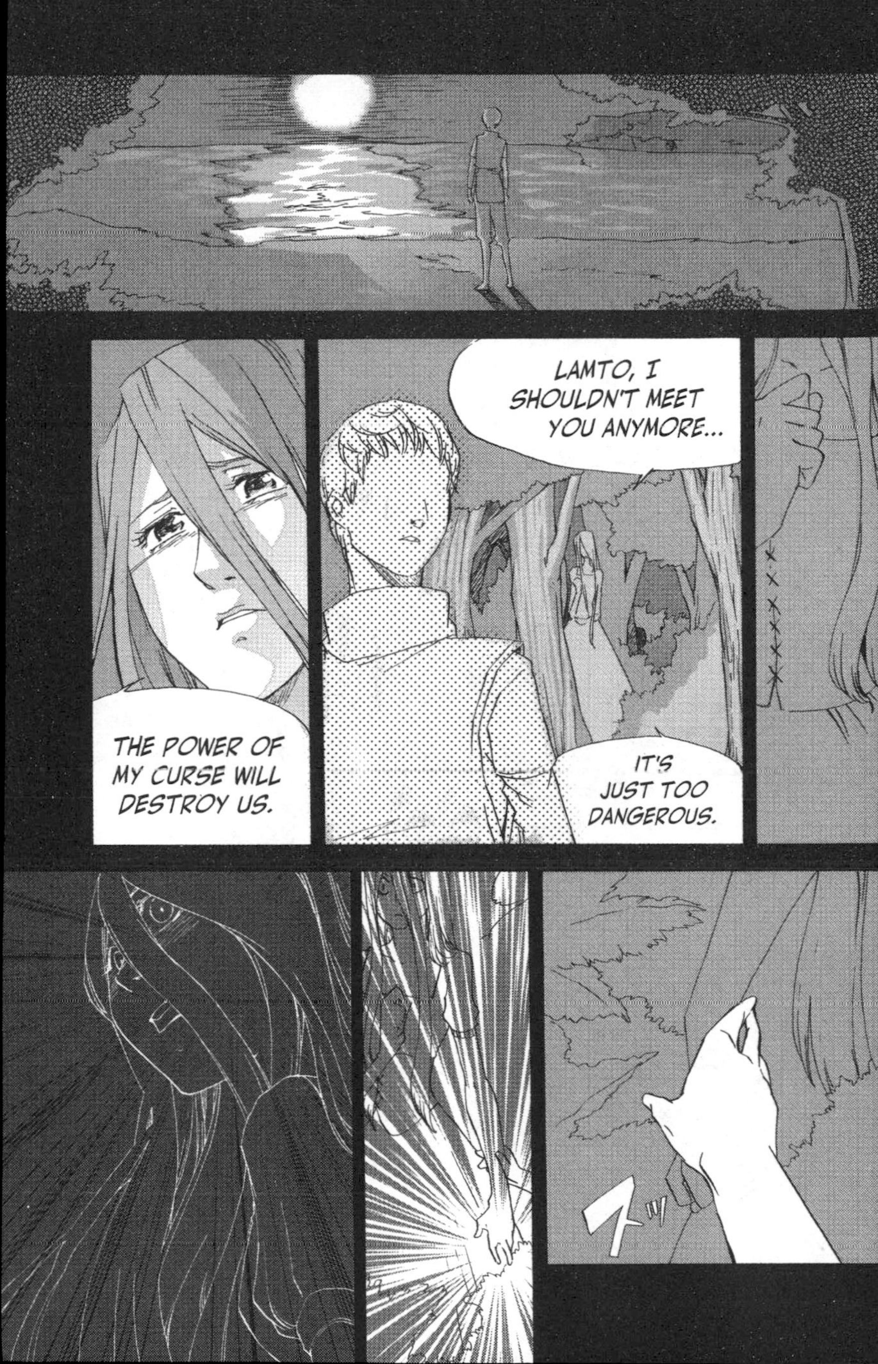
LAMTO, I SHOULDN'T MEET YOU ANYMORE...
IT'S JUST TOO DANGEROUS.
THE POWER OF MY CURSE WILL DESTROY US.
スッ

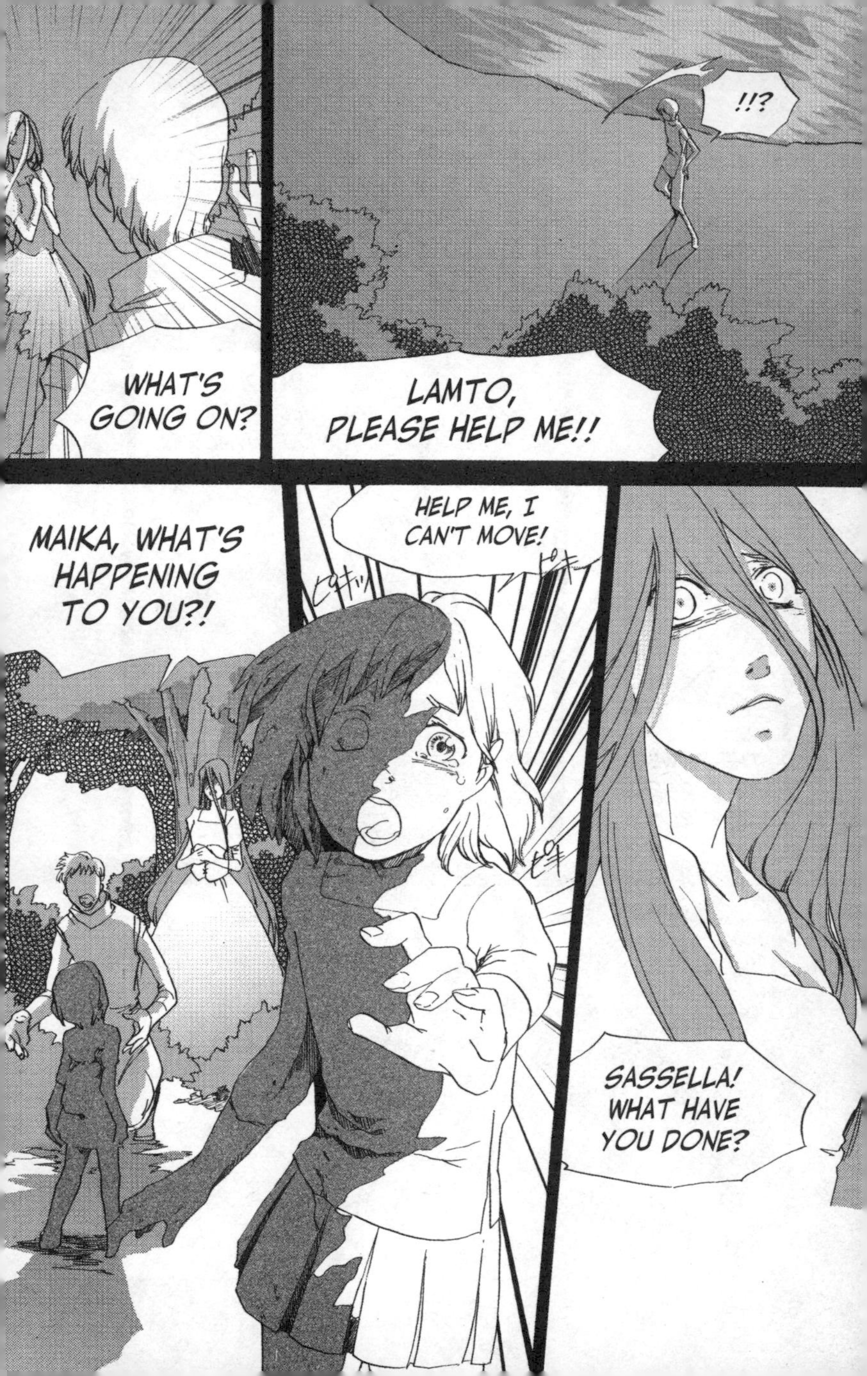
!!?
LAMTO, PLEASE HELP ME!!
WHAT'S GOING ON?
SASSELLA! WHAT HAVE YOU DONE?
HELP ME, I CAN'T MOVE!
MAIKA, WHAT'S HAPPENING TO YOU?!

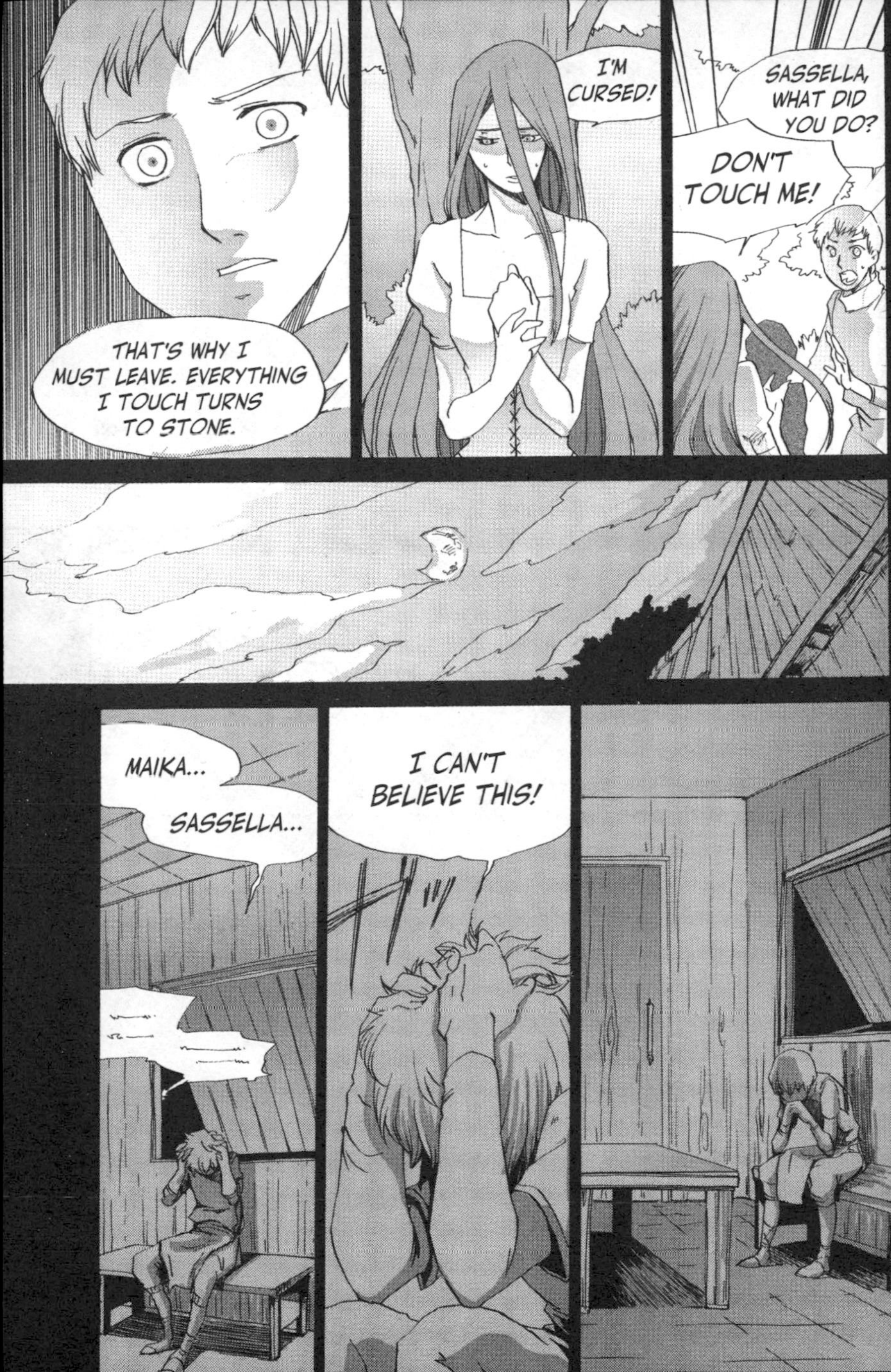
SASSELLA, WHAT DID YOU DO?
DON'T TOUCH ME!
I'M CURSED!
THAT'S WHY I MUST LEAVE. EVERYTHING I TOUCH TURNS TO STONE.
I CAN'T BELIEVE THIS!
MAIKA...
SASSELLA...

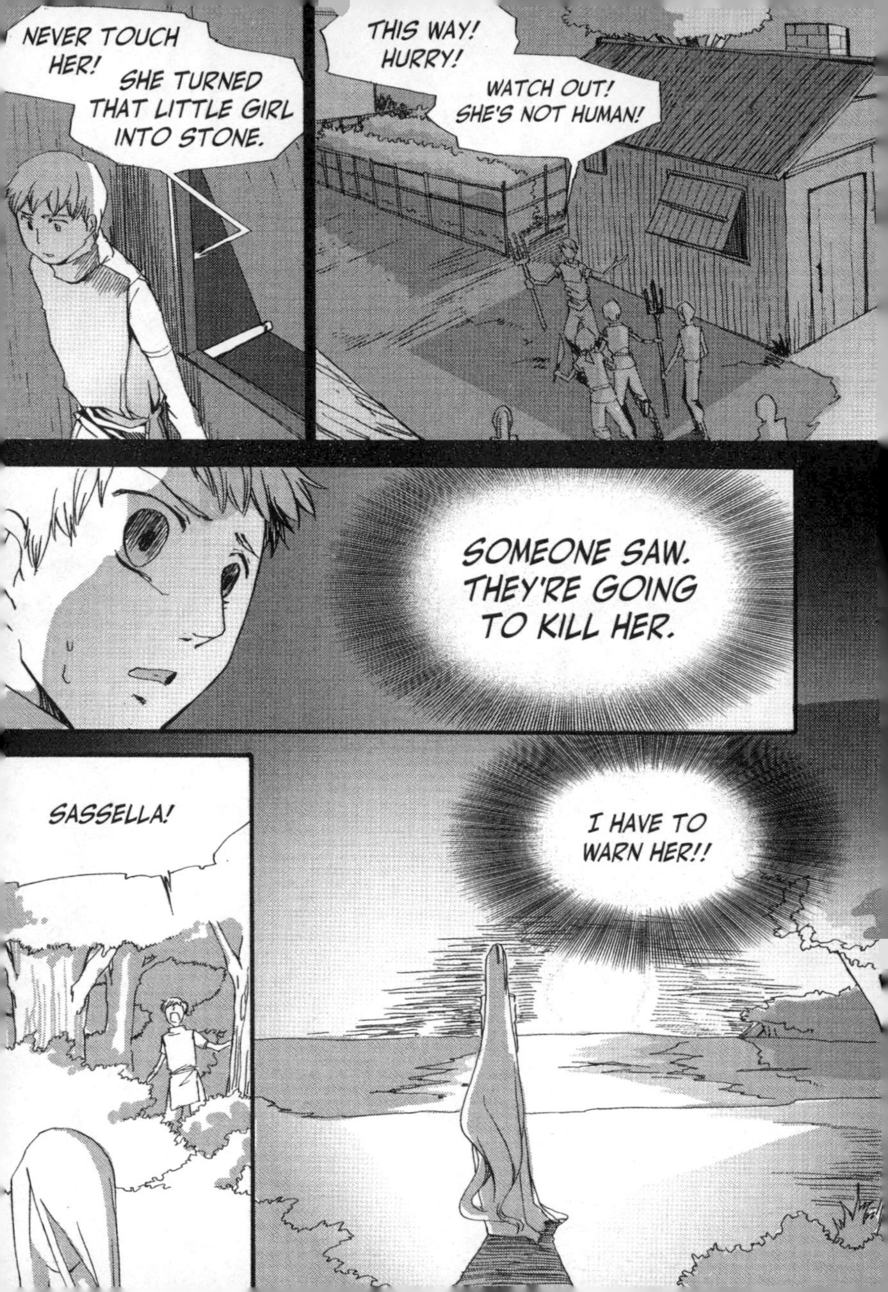
THIS WAY! HURRY!
WATCH OUT! SHE'S NOT HUMAN!
NEVER TOUCH HER!
SHE TURNED THAT LITTLE GIRL INTO STONE.
SOMEONE SAW. THEY'RE GOING TO KILL HER.
I HAVE TO WARN HER!!
SASSELLA!

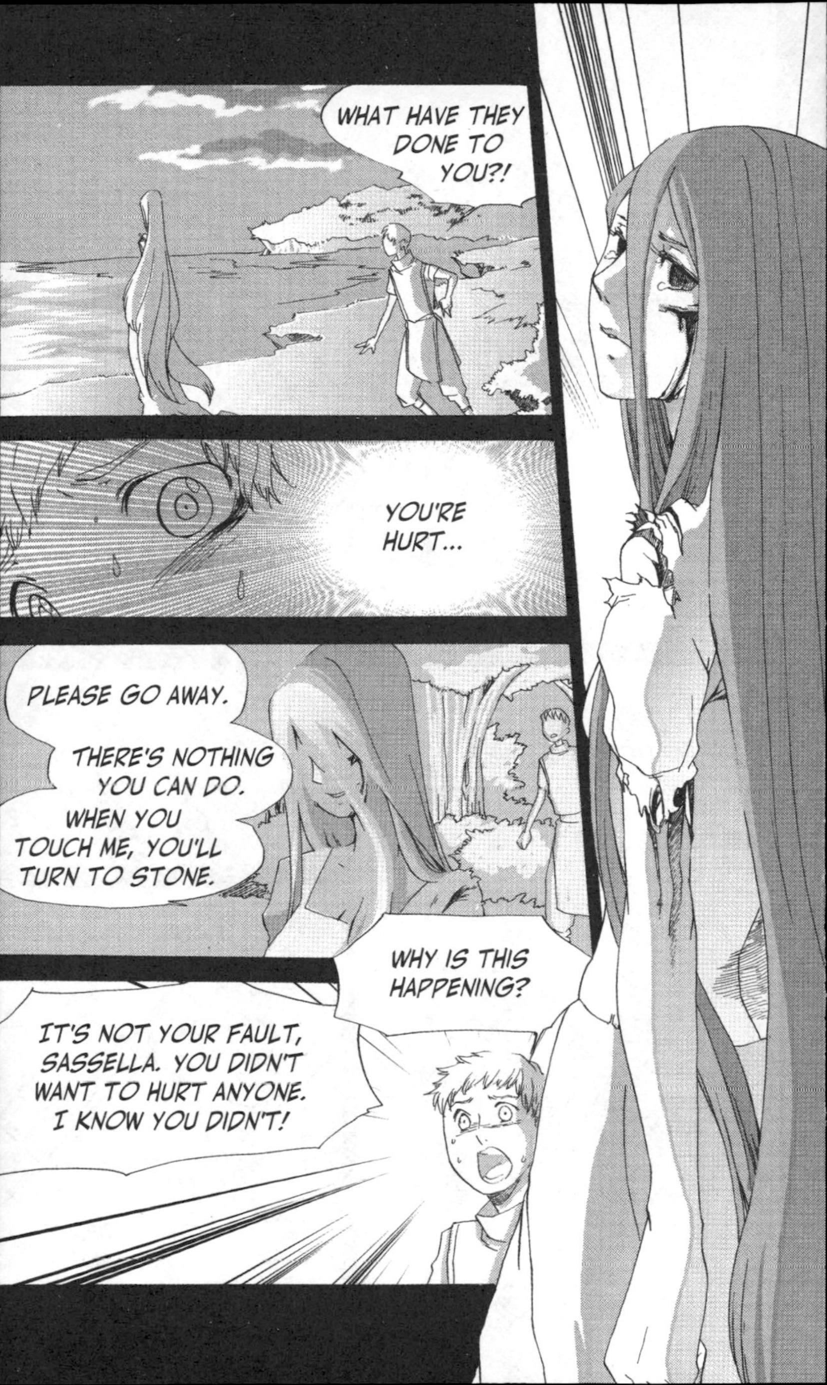

WHAT HAVE THEY DONE TO YOU?!
YOU'RE HURT...
PLEASE GO AWAY.
THERE'S NOTHING YOU CAN DO. WHEN YOU TOUCH ME, YOU'LL TURN TO STONE.
WHY IS THIS HAPPENING?
IT'S NOT YOUR FAULT, SASSELLA. YOU DIDN'T WANT TO HURT ANYONE. I KNOW YOU DIDN'T!

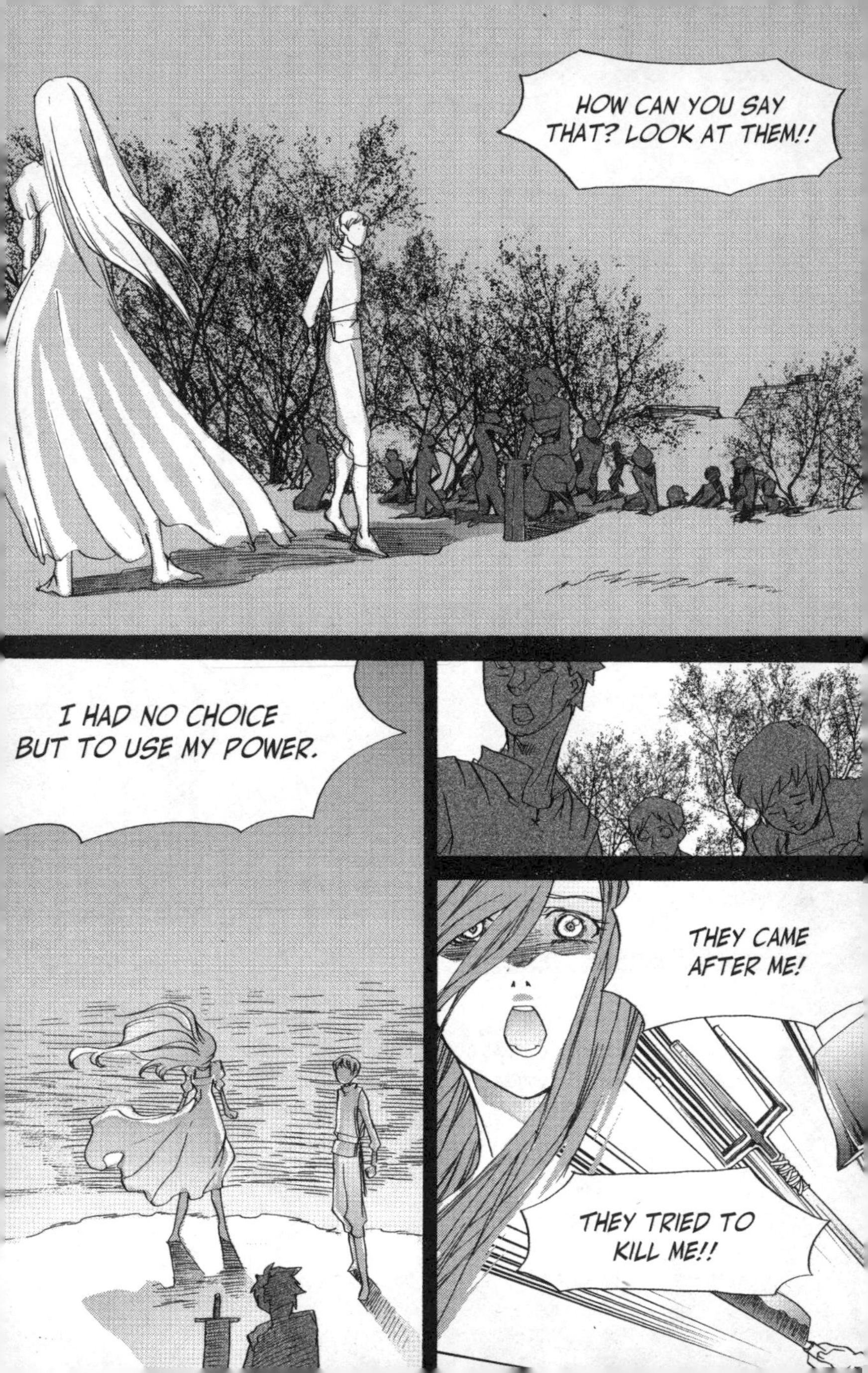
HOW CAN YOU SAY THAT? LOOK AT THEM!!
THEY CAME AFTER ME!
THEY TRIED TO KILL ME!!
I HAD NO CHOICE BUT TO USE MY POWER.

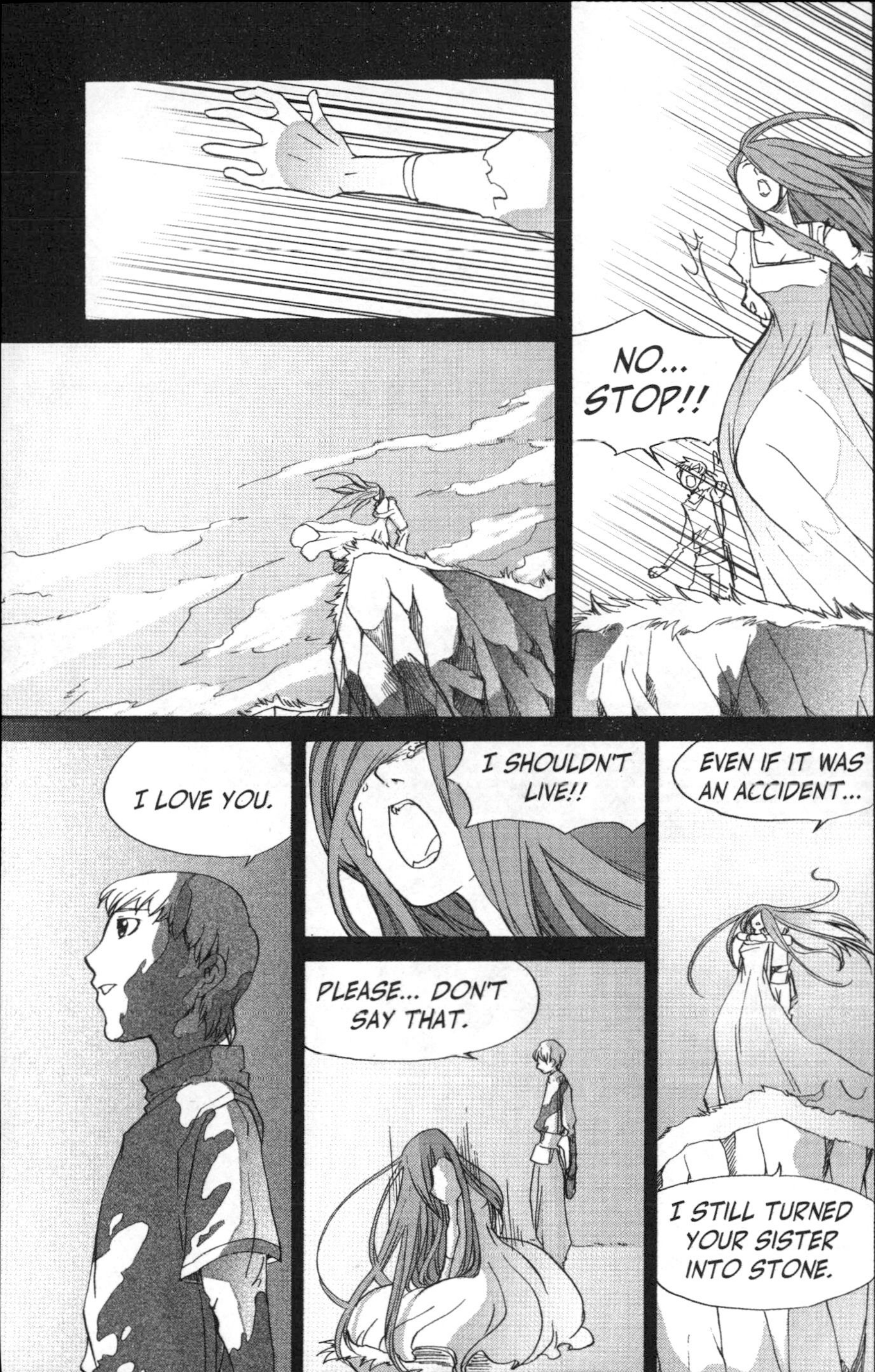
NO... STOP!!
EVEN IF IT WAS AN ACCIDENT...
I STILL TURNED YOUR SISTER INTO STONE.
I SHOULDN'T LIVE!!
PLEASE... DON'T SAY THAT.
I LOVE YOU.

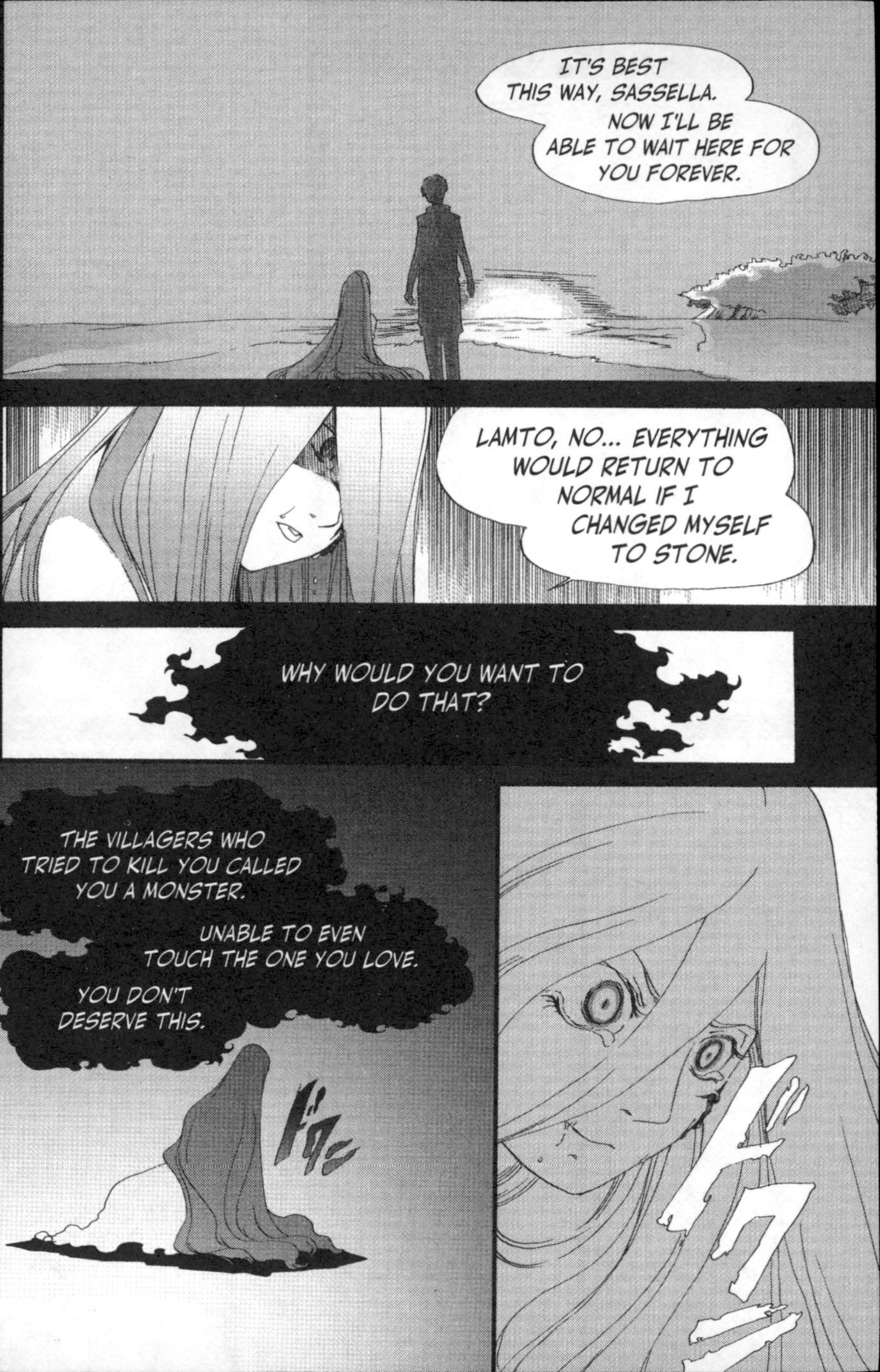
IT'S BEST THIS WAY, SASSELLA. NOW I'LL BE ABLE TO WAIT HERE FOR YOU FOREVER.
LAMTO, NO... EVERYTHING WOULD RETURN TO NORMAL IF I CHANGED MYSELF TO STONE.
WHY WOULD YOU WANT TO DO THAT?
THE VILLAGERS WHO TRIED TO KILL YOU CALLED YOU A MONSTER.
UNABLE TO EVEN TOUCH THE ONE YOU LOVE.
YOU DON'T DESERVE THIS.

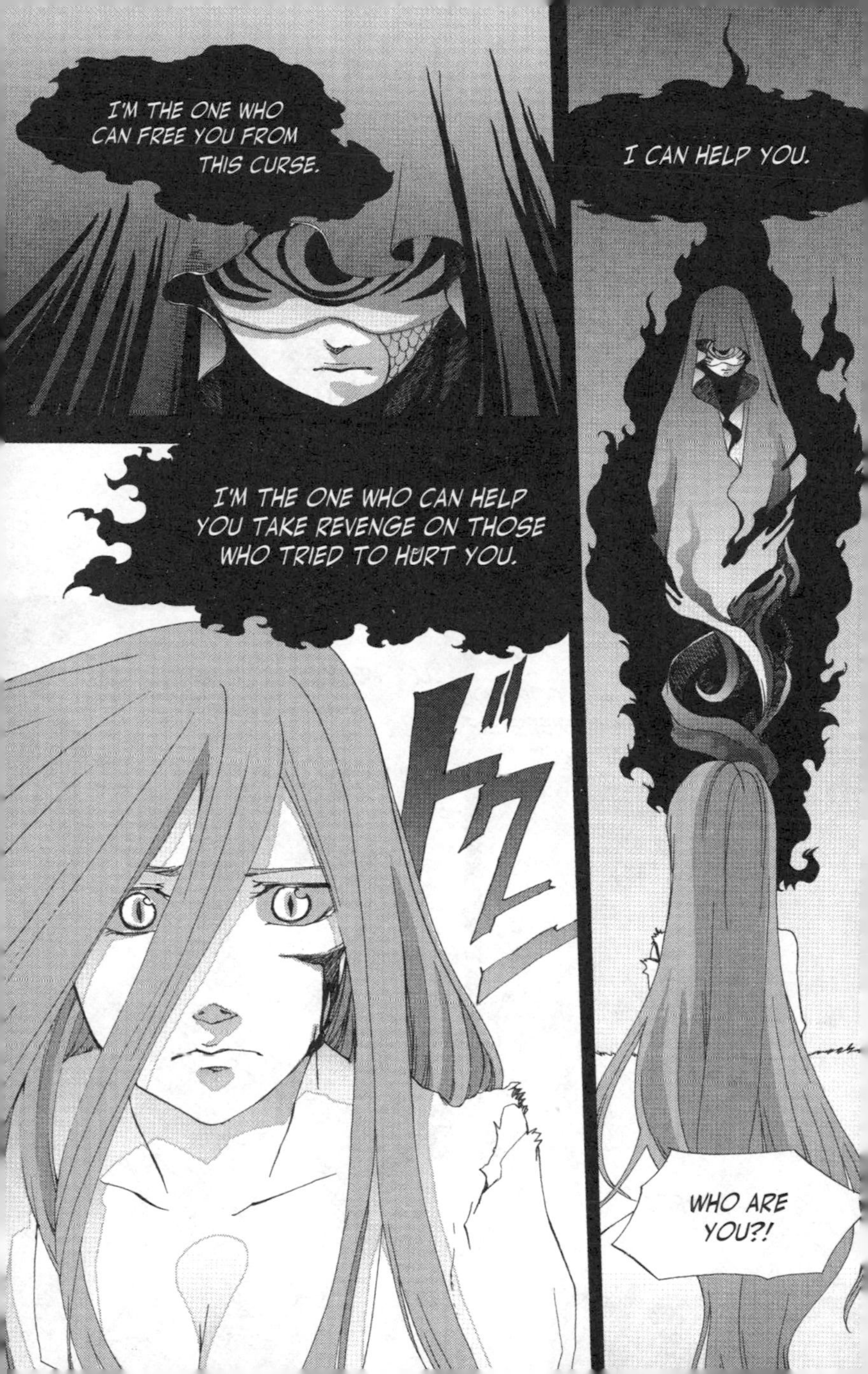
I CAN HELP YOU.
WHO ARE YOU?!
I'M THE ONE WHO CAN FREE YOU FROM THIS CURSE.
I'M THE ONE WHO CAN HELP YOU TAKE REVENGE ON THOSE WHO TRIED TO HURT YOU.

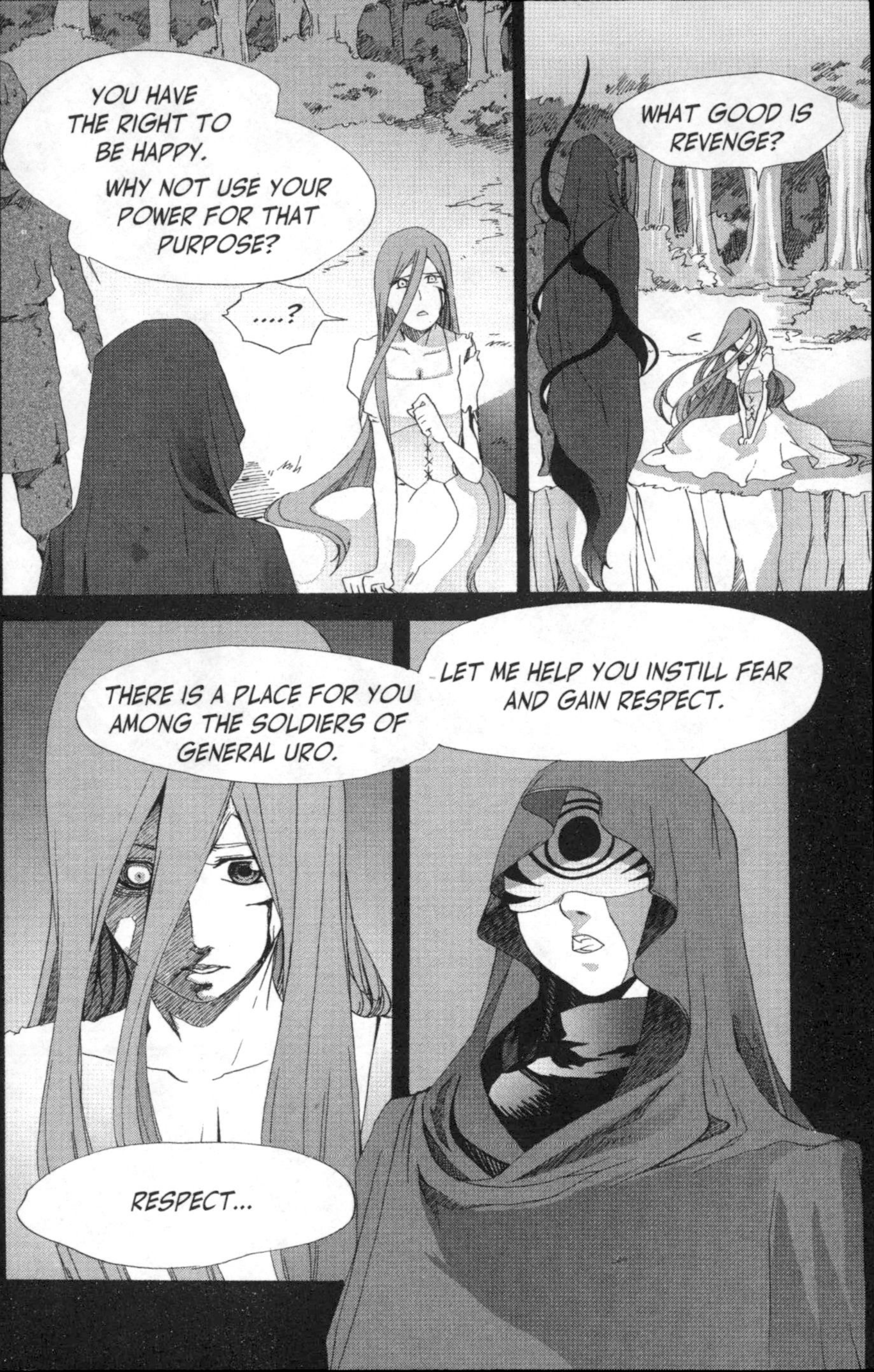
WHAT GOOD IS REVENGE?
YOU HAVE THE RIGHT TO BE HAPPY.
WHY NOT USE YOUR POWER FOR THAT PURPOSE?
....?
LET ME HELP YOU INSTILL FEAR AND GAIN RESPECT.
THERE IS A PLACE FOR YOU AMONG THE SOLDIERS OF GENERAL URO.
RESPECT...

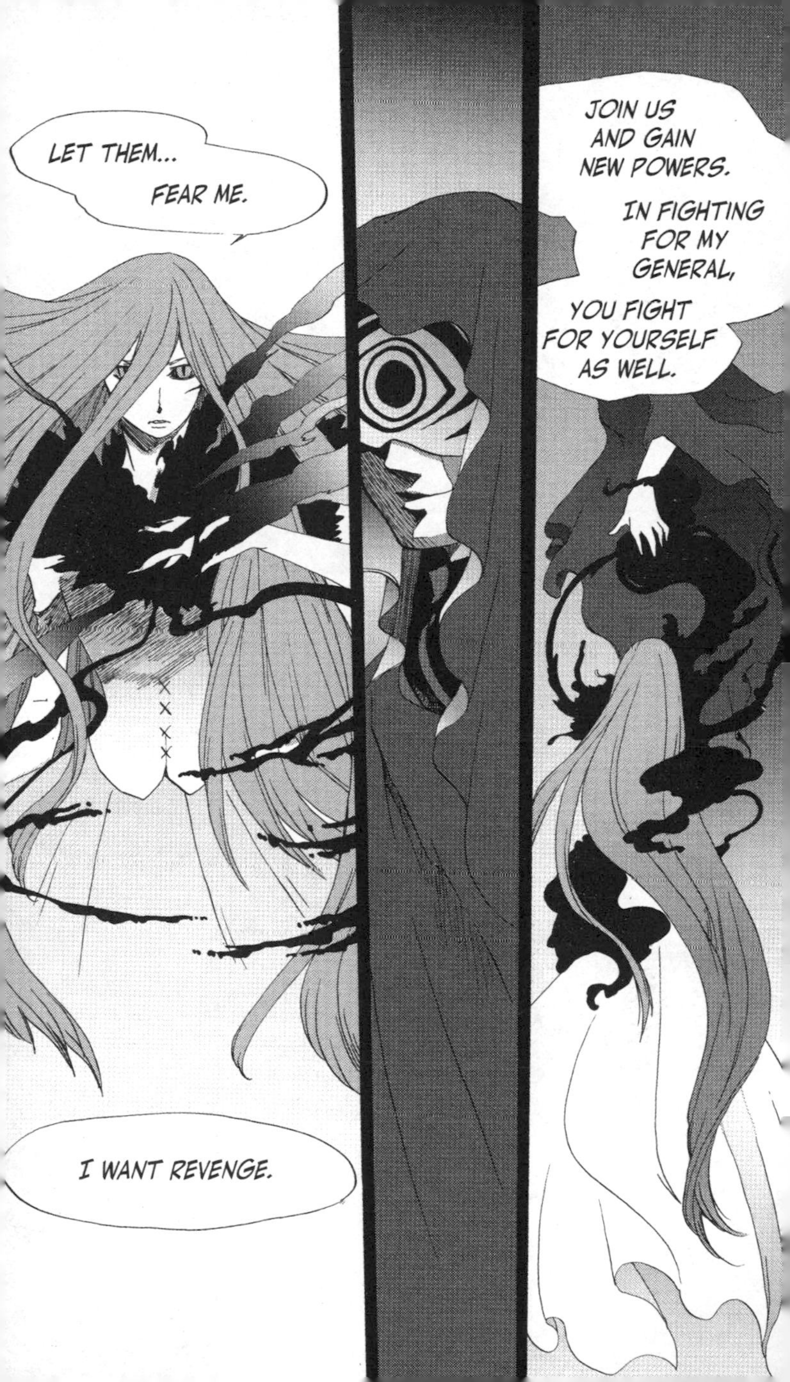
JOIN US AND GAIN NEW POWERS.
IN FIGHTING FOR MY GENERAL,
YOU FIGHT FOR YOURSELF AS WELL.
LET THEM... FEAR ME.
I WANT REVENGE.

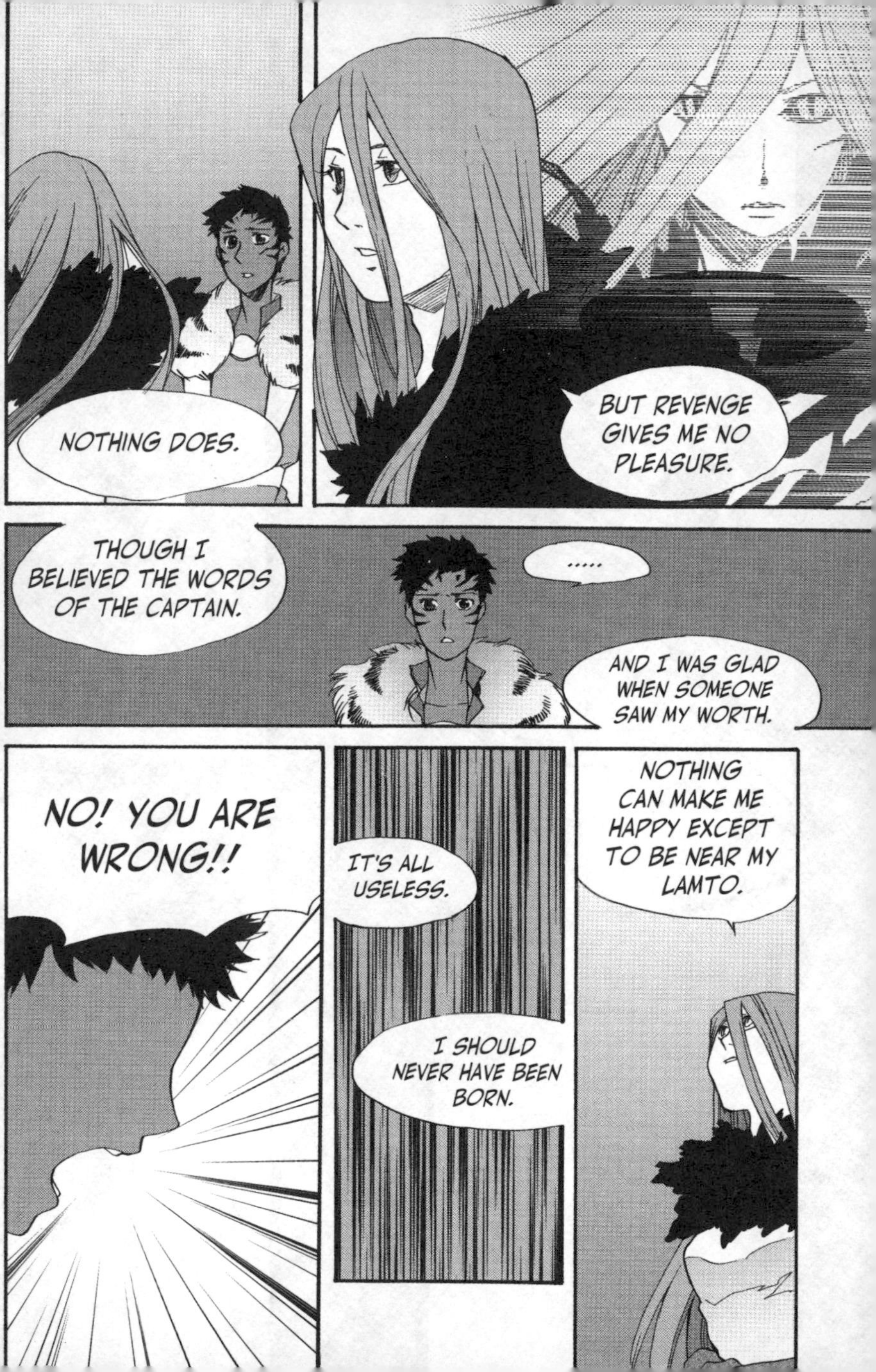
BUT REVENGE GIVES ME NO PLEASURE.
NOTHING DOES.
THOUGH I BELIEVED THE WORDS OF THE CAPTAIN.
.....
AND I WAS GLAD WHEN SOMEONE SAW MY WORTH.
NOTHING CAN MAKE ME HAPPY EXCEPT TO BE NEAR MY LAMTO.
IT'S ALL USELESS.
I SHOULD NEVER HAVE BEEN BORN.
NO! YOU ARE WRONG!!

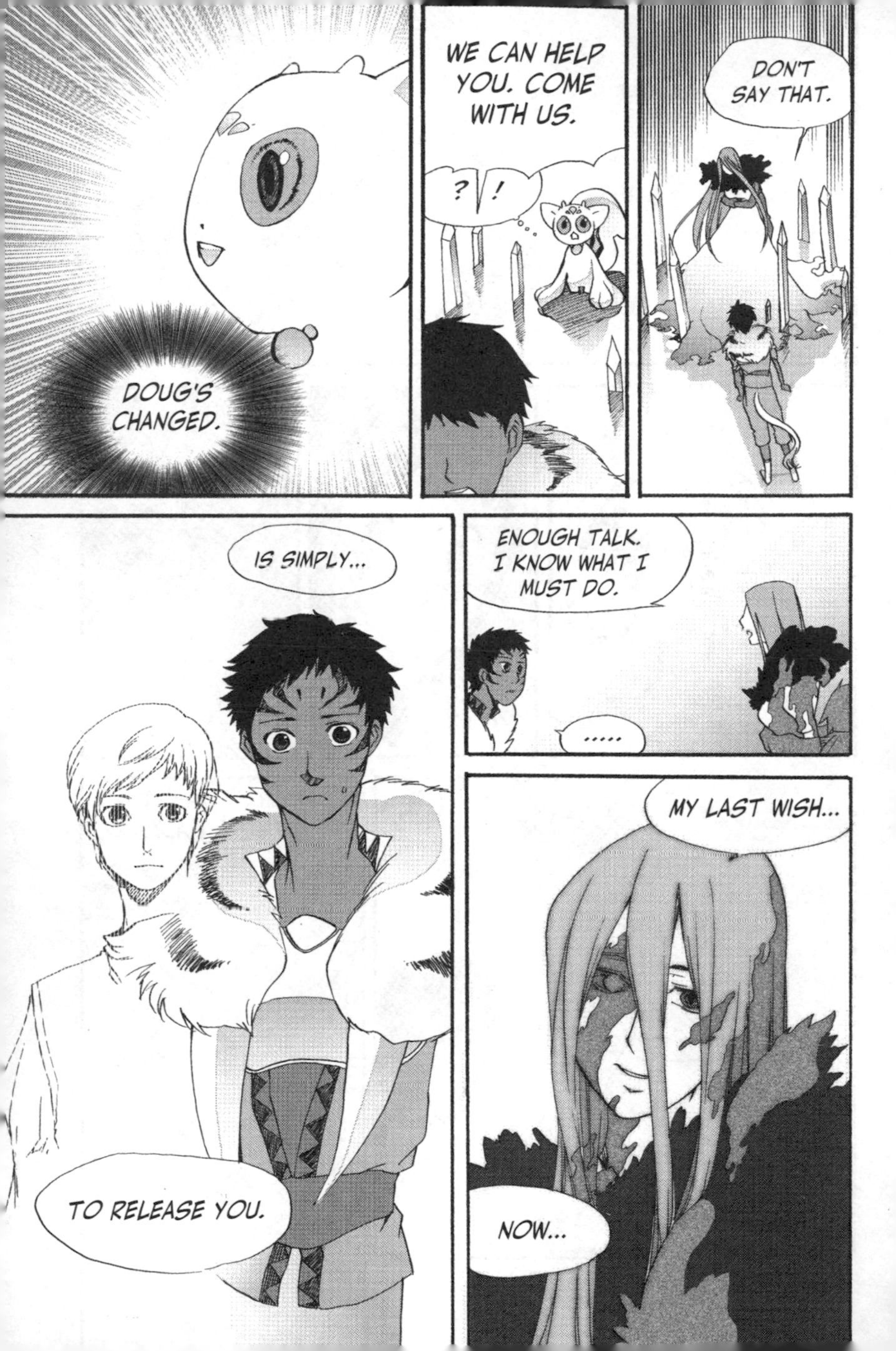
DON'T SAY THAT.
WE CAN HELP YOU. COME WITH US.
? / !
DOUG'S CHANGED.
ENOUGH TALK. I KNOW WHAT I MUST DO.
......
MY LAST WISH...
NOW...
IS SIMPLY...
TO RELEASE YOU.

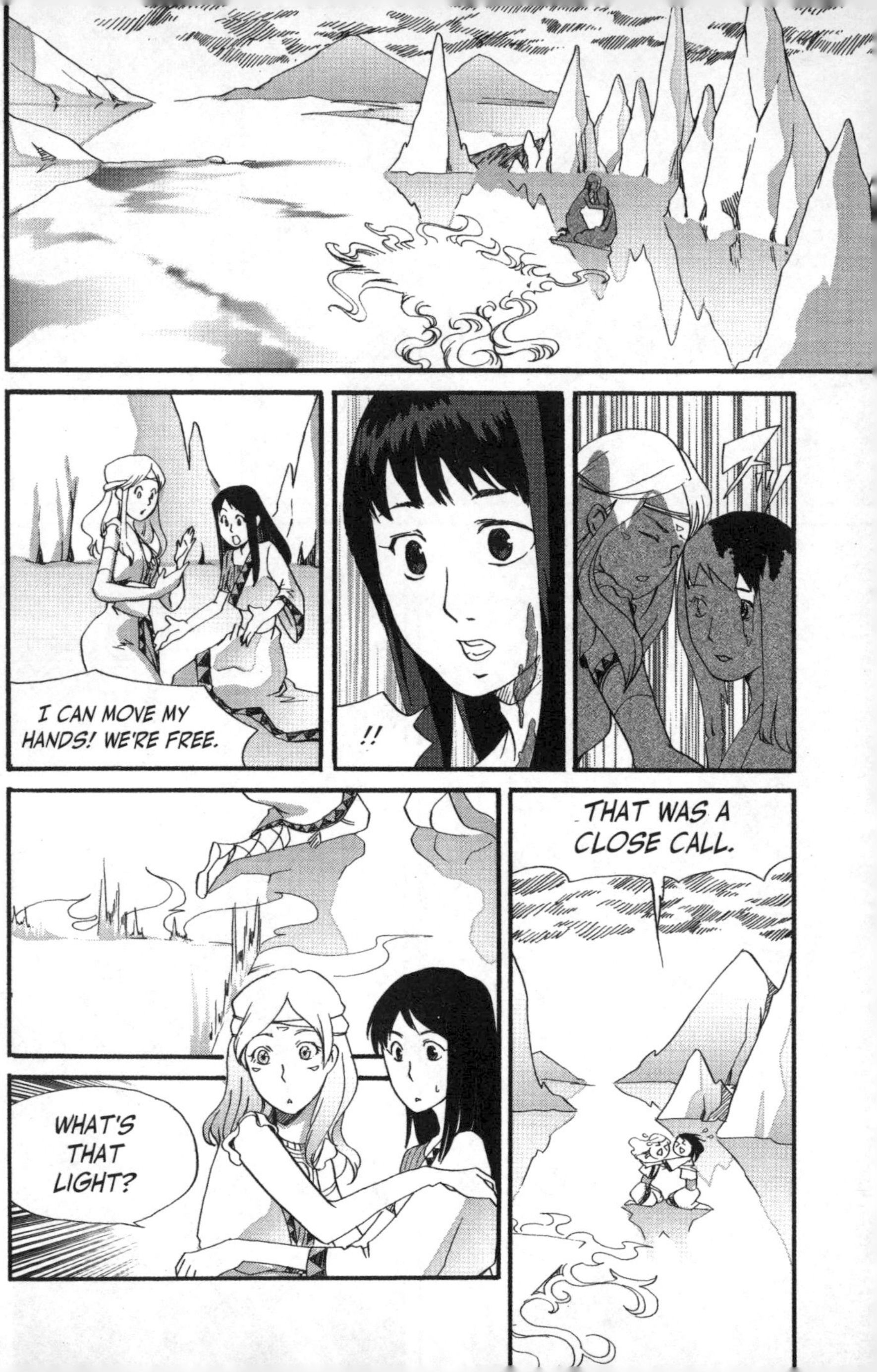
!!
I CAN MOVE MY HANDS! WE'RE FREE.
THAT WAS A CLOSE CALL.
WHAT'S THAT LIGHT?

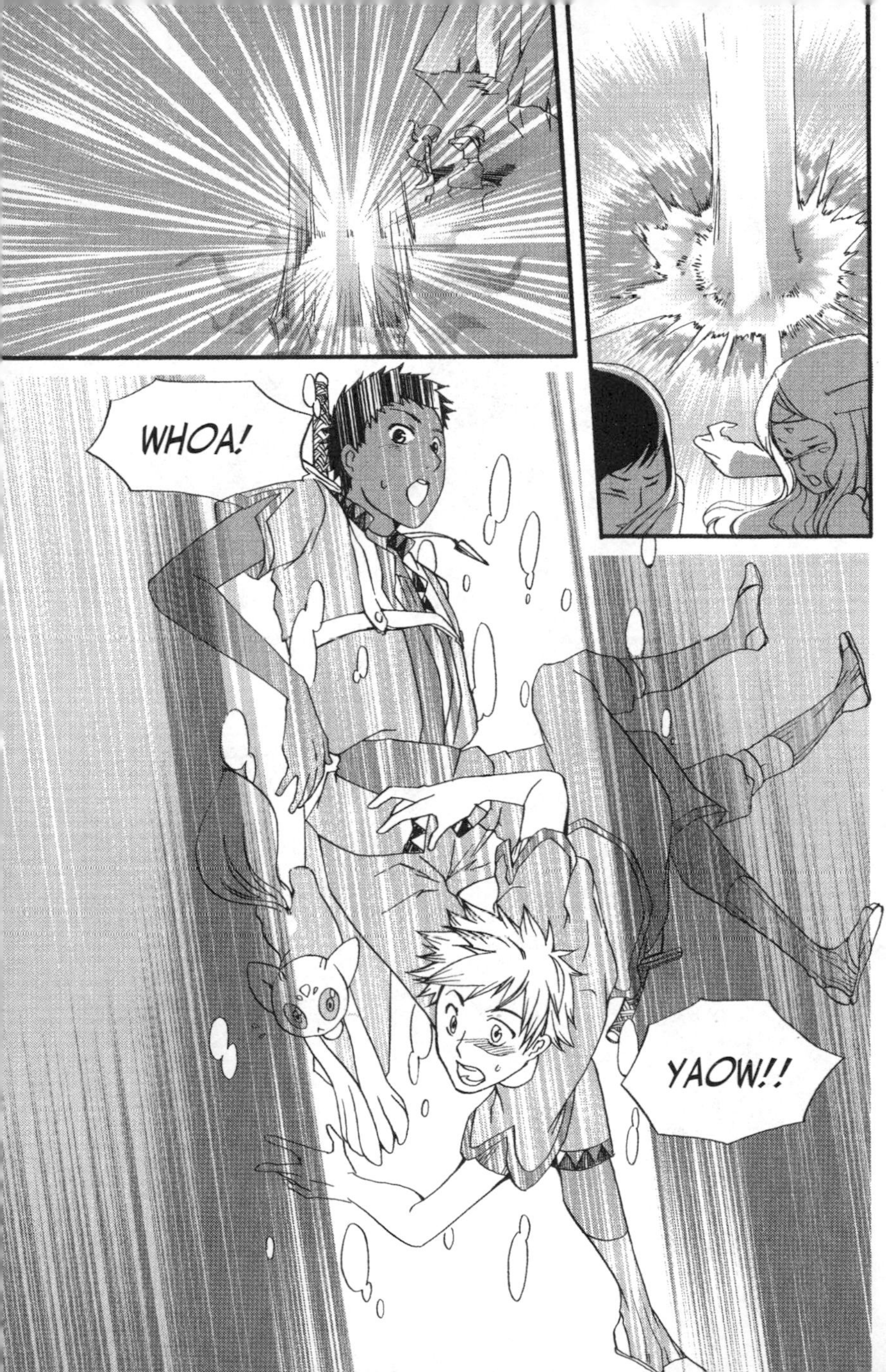
WHOA!
YAOW!!

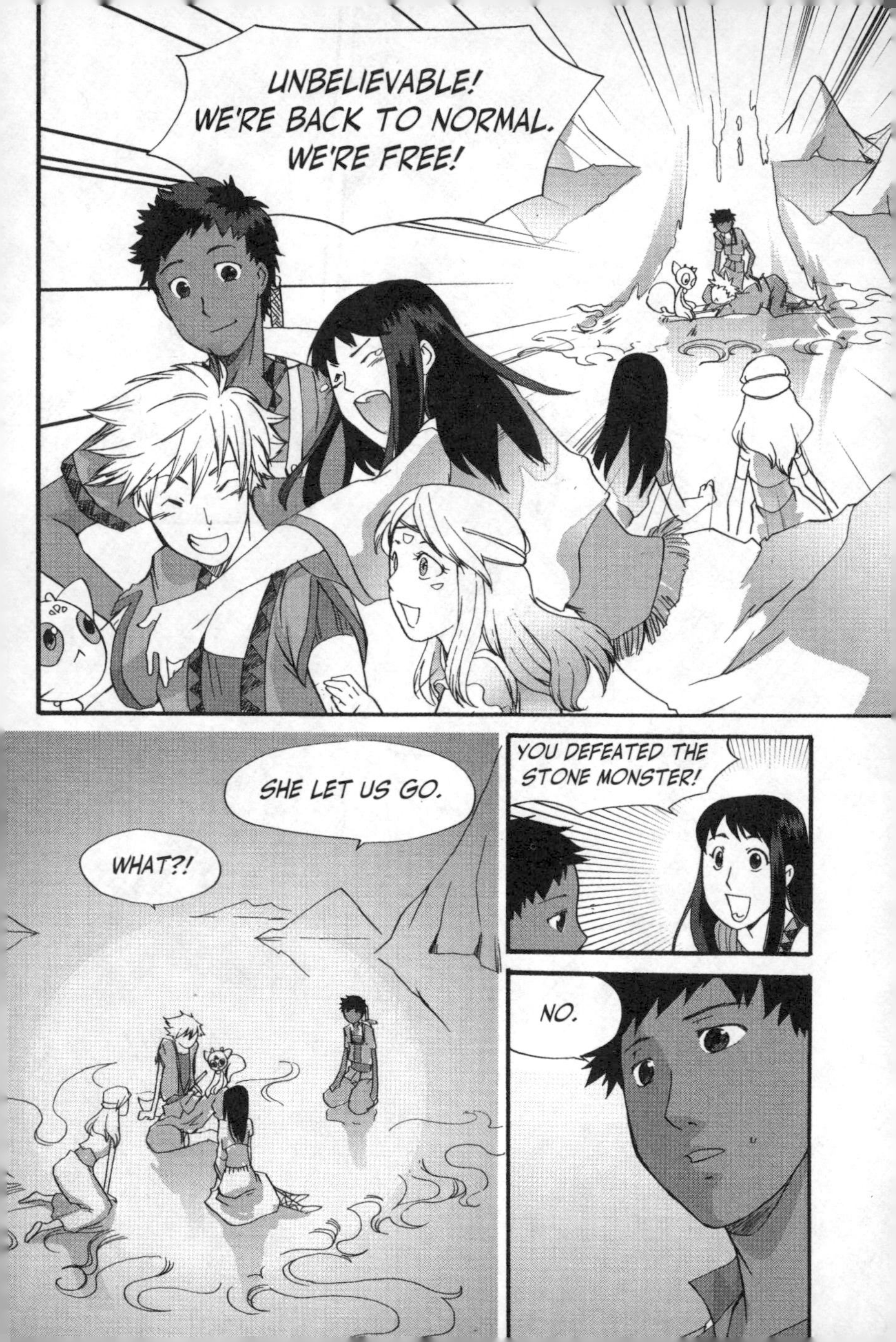
UNBELIEVABLE! WE'RE BACK TO NORMAL. WE'RE FREE!
YOU DEFEATED THE STONE MONSTER!
NO.
SHE LET US GO.
WHAT?!

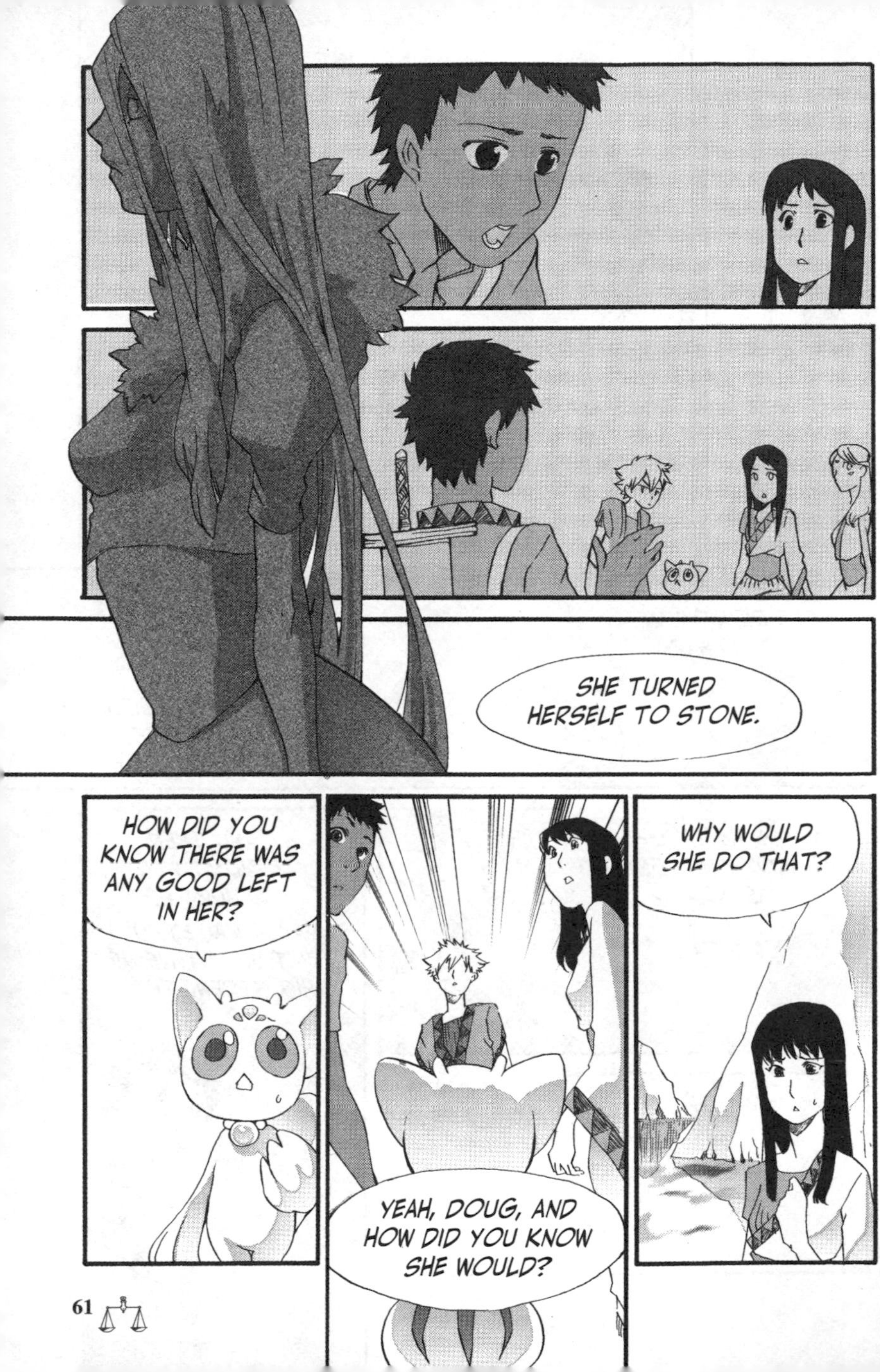
SHE TURNED HERSELF TO STONE.
WHY WOULD SHE DO THAT?
YEAH, DOUG, AND HOW DID YOU KNOW SHE WOULD?
HOW DID YOU KNOW THERE WAS ANY GOOD LEFT IN HER?

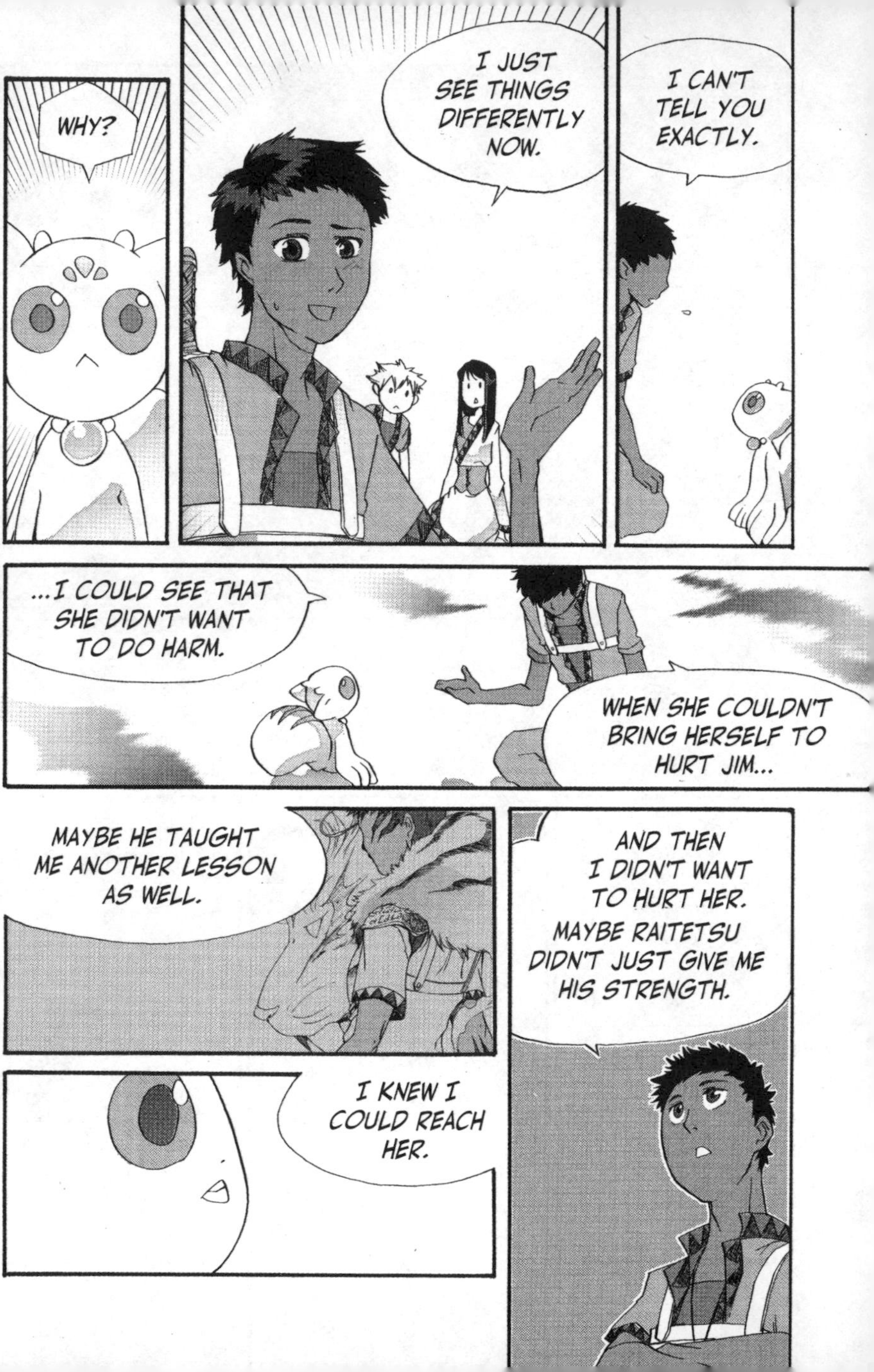
I CAN'T TELL YOU EXACTLY.
I JUST SEE THINGS DIFFERENTLY NOW.
WHY?
WHEN SHE COULDN'T BRING HERSELF TO HURT JIM...
...I COULD SEE THAT SHE DIDN'T WANT TO DO HARM.
AND THEN I DIDN'T WANT TO HURT HER.
MAYBE RAITETSU DIDN'T JUST GIVE ME HIS STRENGTH.
MAYBE HE TAUGHT ME ANOTHER LESSON AS WELL.
I KNEW I COULD REACH HER.

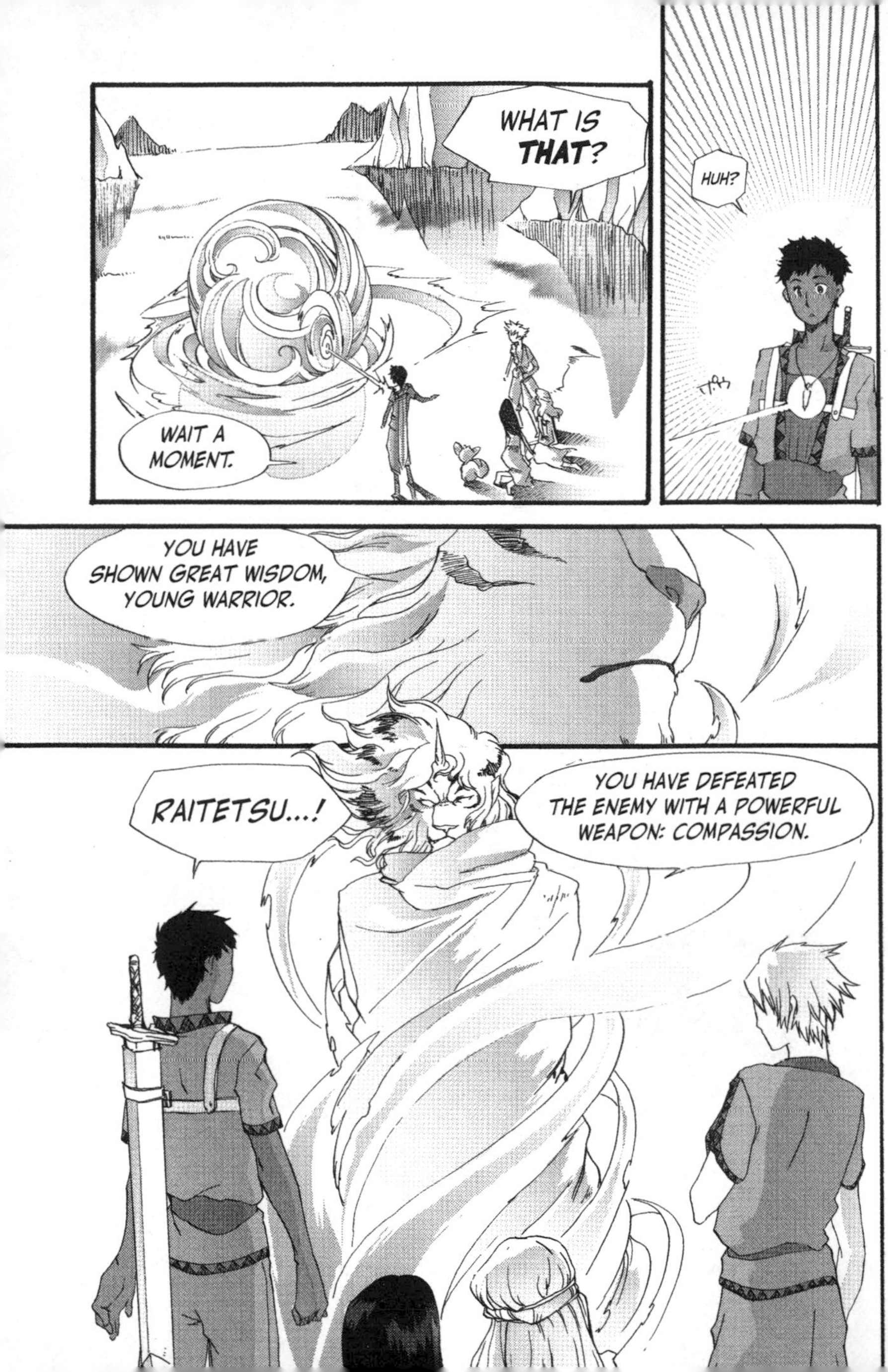
HUH?
WHAT IS THAT?
WAIT A MOMENT.
YOU HAVE SHOWN GREAT WISDOM, YOUNG WARRIOR.
YOU HAVE DEFEATED THE ENEMY WITH A POWERFUL WEAPON: COMPASSION.
RAITETSU...!

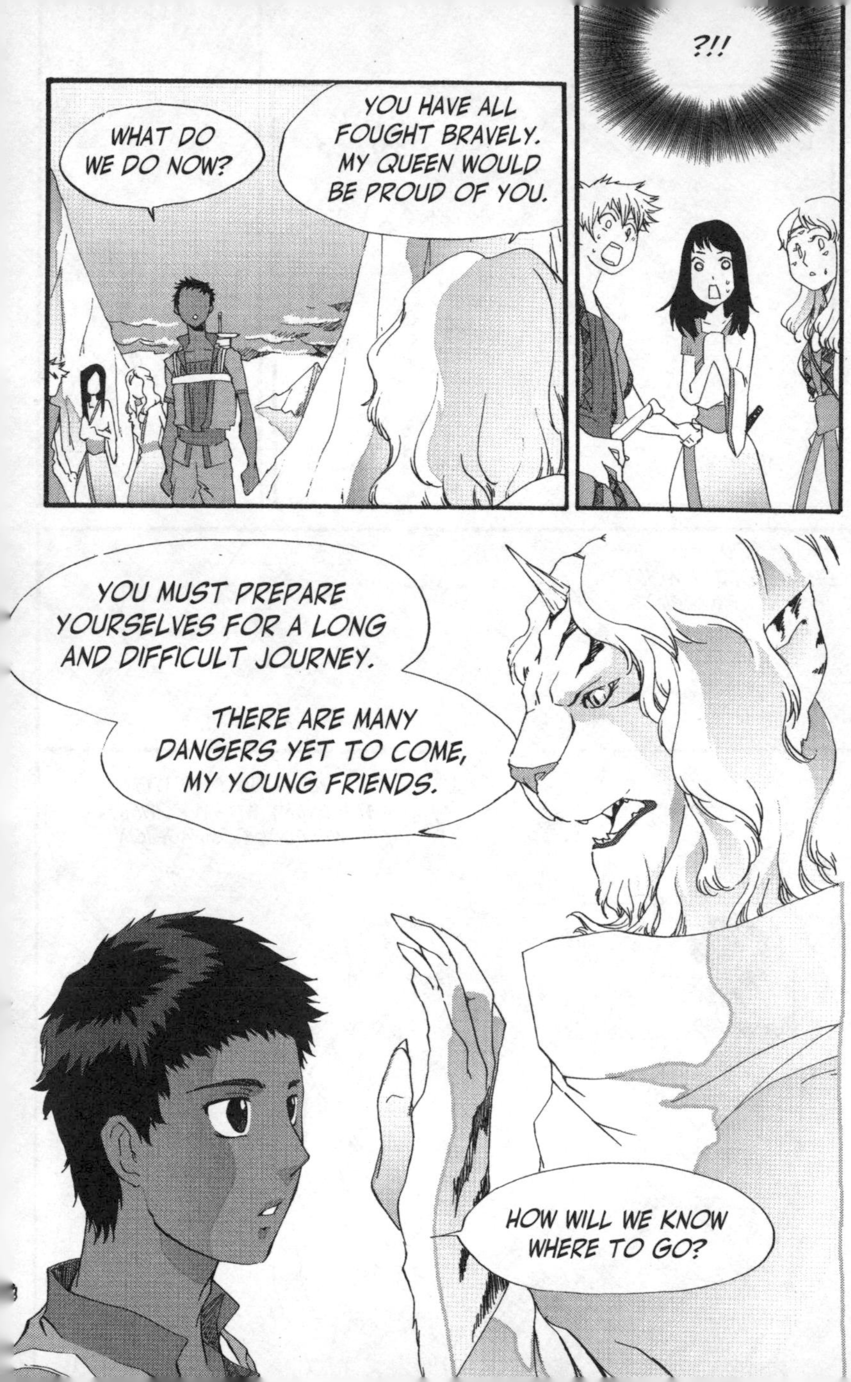
?!!
YOU HAVE ALL FOUGHT BRAVELY. MY QUEEN WOULD BE PROUD OF YOU.
WHAT DO WE DO NOW?
YOU MUST PREPARE YOURSELVES FOR A LONG AND DIFFICULT JOURNEY.
THERE ARE MANY DANGERS YET TO COME, MY YOUNG FRIENDS.
HOW WILL WE KNOW WHERE TO GO?

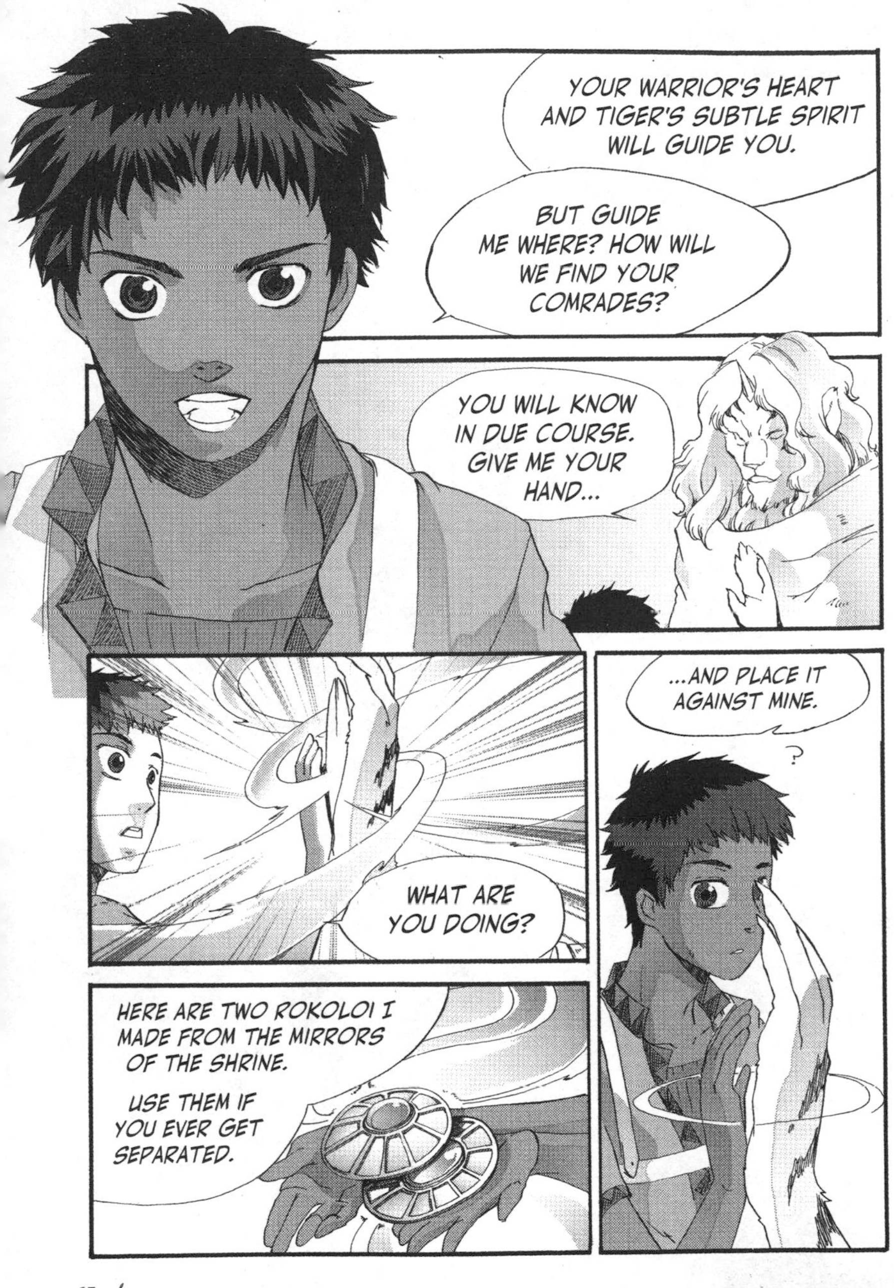
YOUR WARRIOR'S HEART AND TIGER'S SUBTLE SPIRIT WILL GUIDE YOU.
BUT GUIDE ME WHERE? HOW WILL WE FIND YOUR COMRADES?
YOU WILL KNOW IN DUE COURSE. GIVE ME YOUR HAND...
...AND PLACE IT AGAINST MINE.
?
WHAT ARE YOU DOING?
HERE ARE TWO ROKOLOI I MADE FROM THE MIRRORS OF THE SHRINE.
USE THEM IF YOU EVER GET SEPARATED.

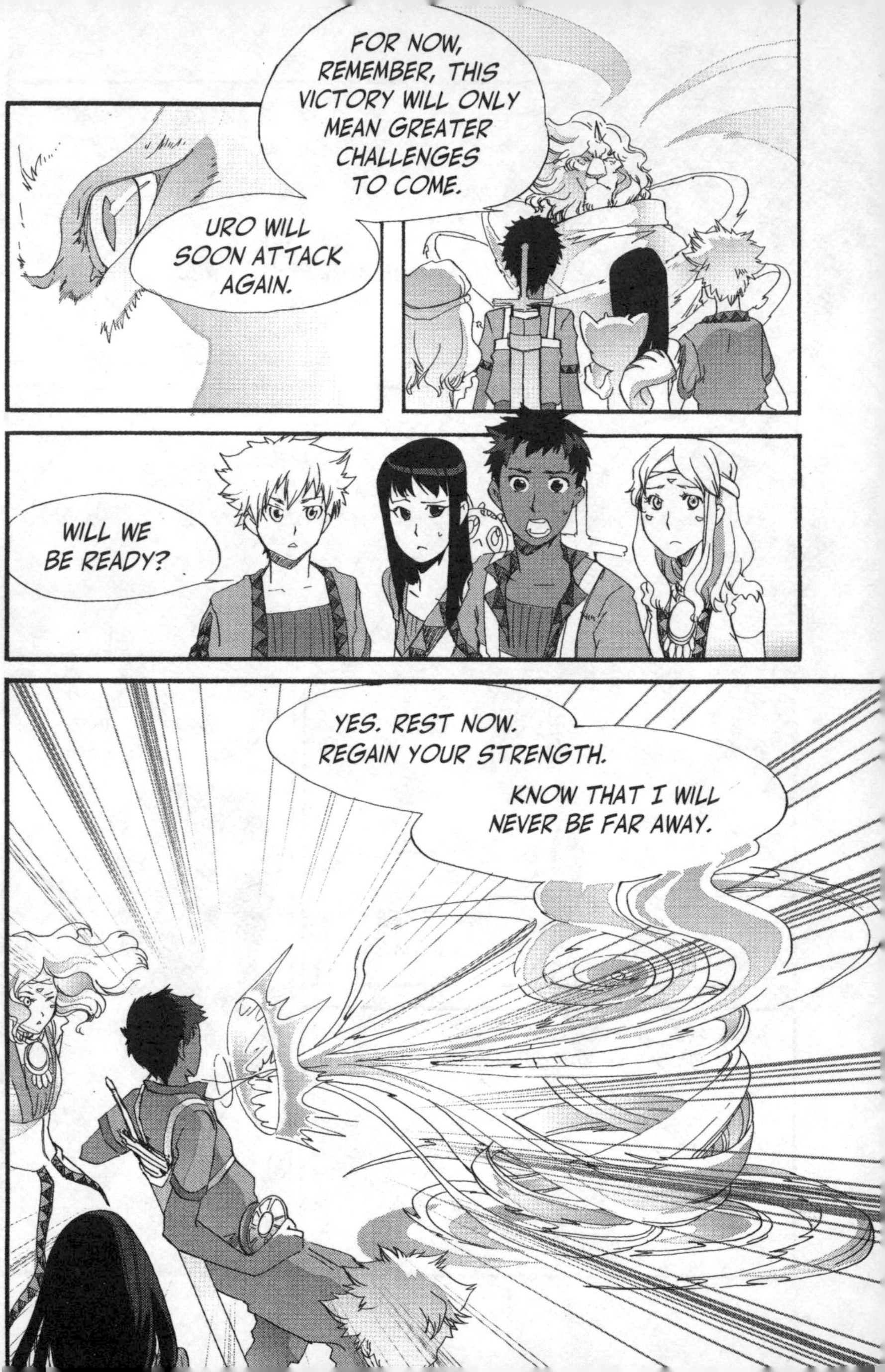
FOR NOW, REMEMBER, THIS VICTORY WILL ONLY MEAN GREATER CHALLENGES TO COME.
URO WILL SOON ATTACK AGAIN.
WILL WE BE READY?
YES. REST NOW. REGAIN YOUR STRENGTH.
KNOW THAT I WILL NEVER BE FAR AWAY.

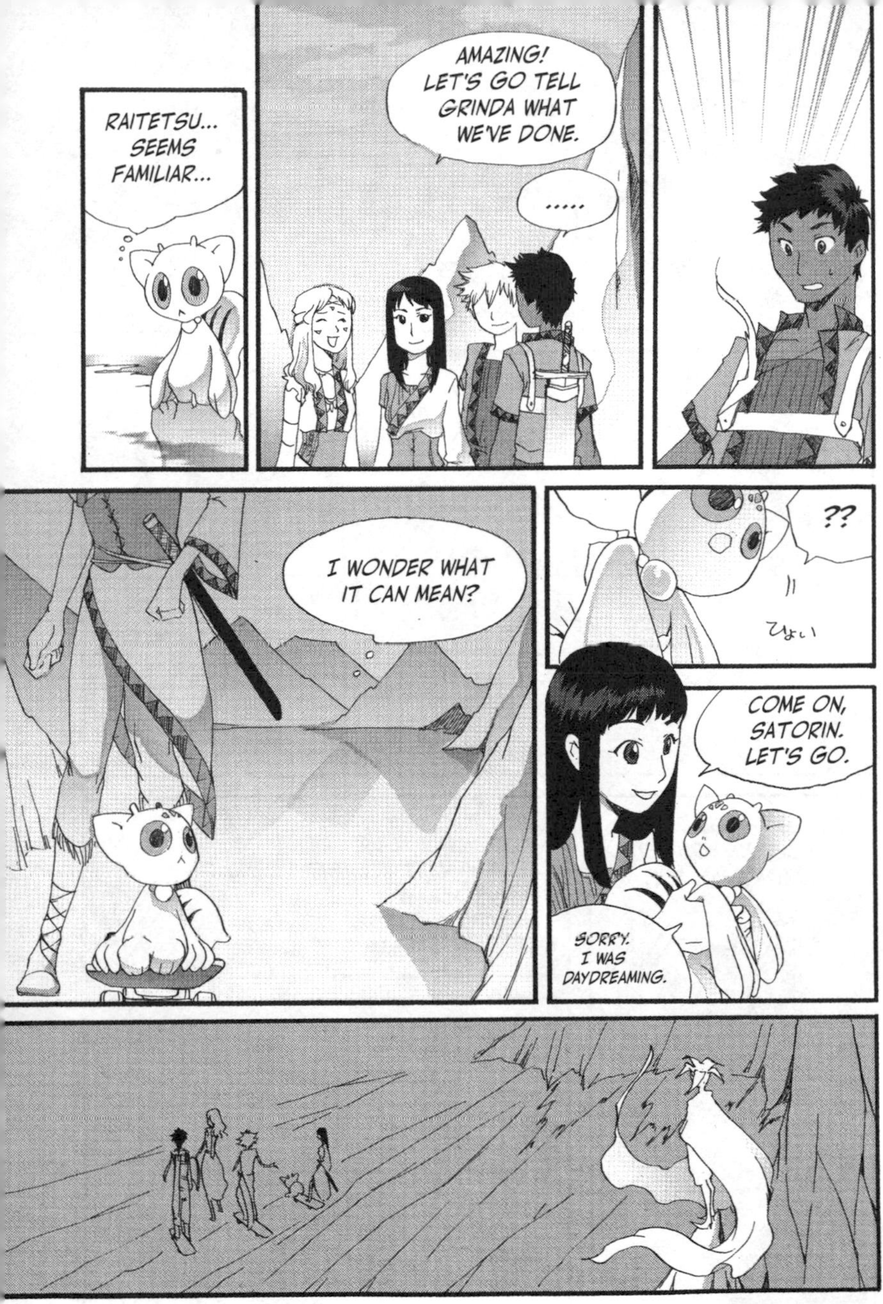
AMAZING! LET'S GO TELL GRINDA WHAT WE'VE DONE.
.....
RAITETSU... SEEMS FAMILIAR...
??
ひょい
COME ON, SATORIN. LET'S GO.
SORRY. I WAS DAYDREAMING.
I WONDER WHAT IT CAN MEAN?

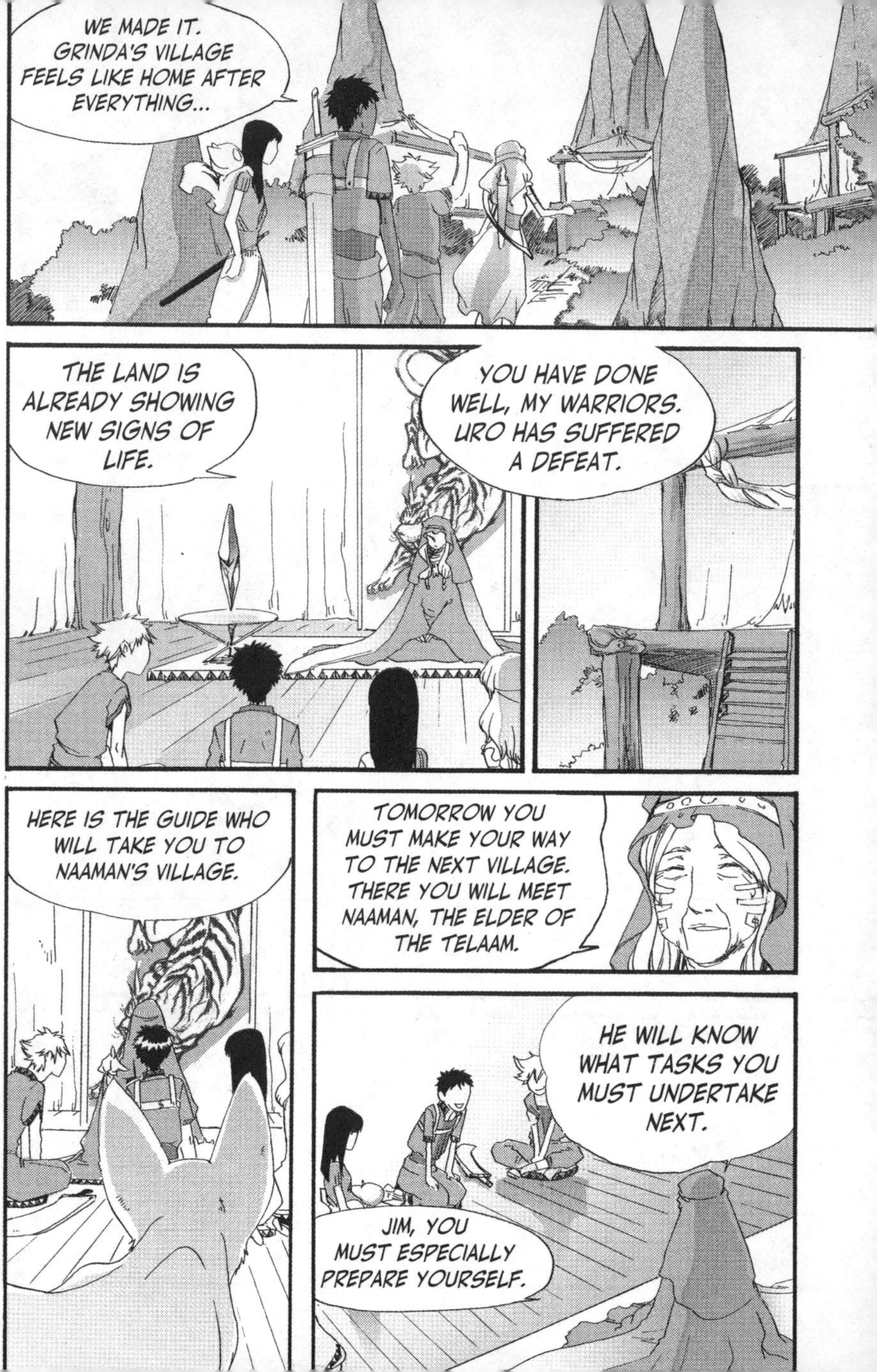
WE MADE IT. GRINDA'S VILLAGE FEELS LIKE HOME AFTER EVERYTHING...
YOU HAVE DONE WELL, MY WARRIORS. URO HAS SUFFERED A DEFEAT.
THE LAND IS ALREADY SHOWING NEW SIGNS OF LIFE.
TOMORROW YOU MUST MAKE YOUR WAY TO THE NEXT VILLAGE. THERE YOU WILL MEET NAAMAN, THE ELDER OF THE TELAAM.
HE WILL KNOW WHAT TASKS YOU MUST UNDERTAKE NEXT.
JIM, YOU MUST ESPECIALLY PREPARE YOURSELF.
HERE IS THE GUIDE WHO WILL TAKE YOU TO NAAMAN'S VILLAGE.

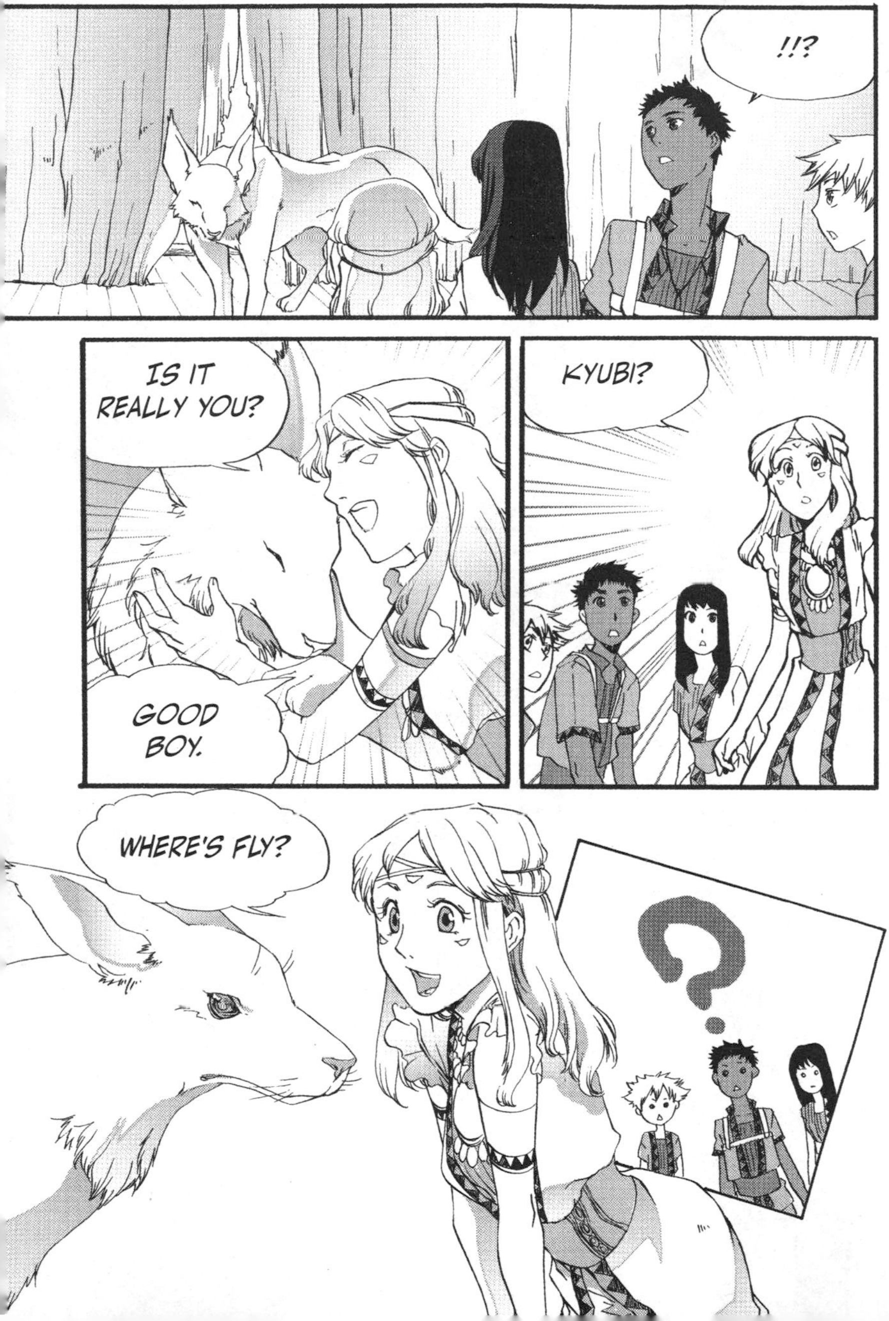
!!?
KYUBI?
IS IT REALLY YOU?
GOOD BOY.
WHERE'S FLY?

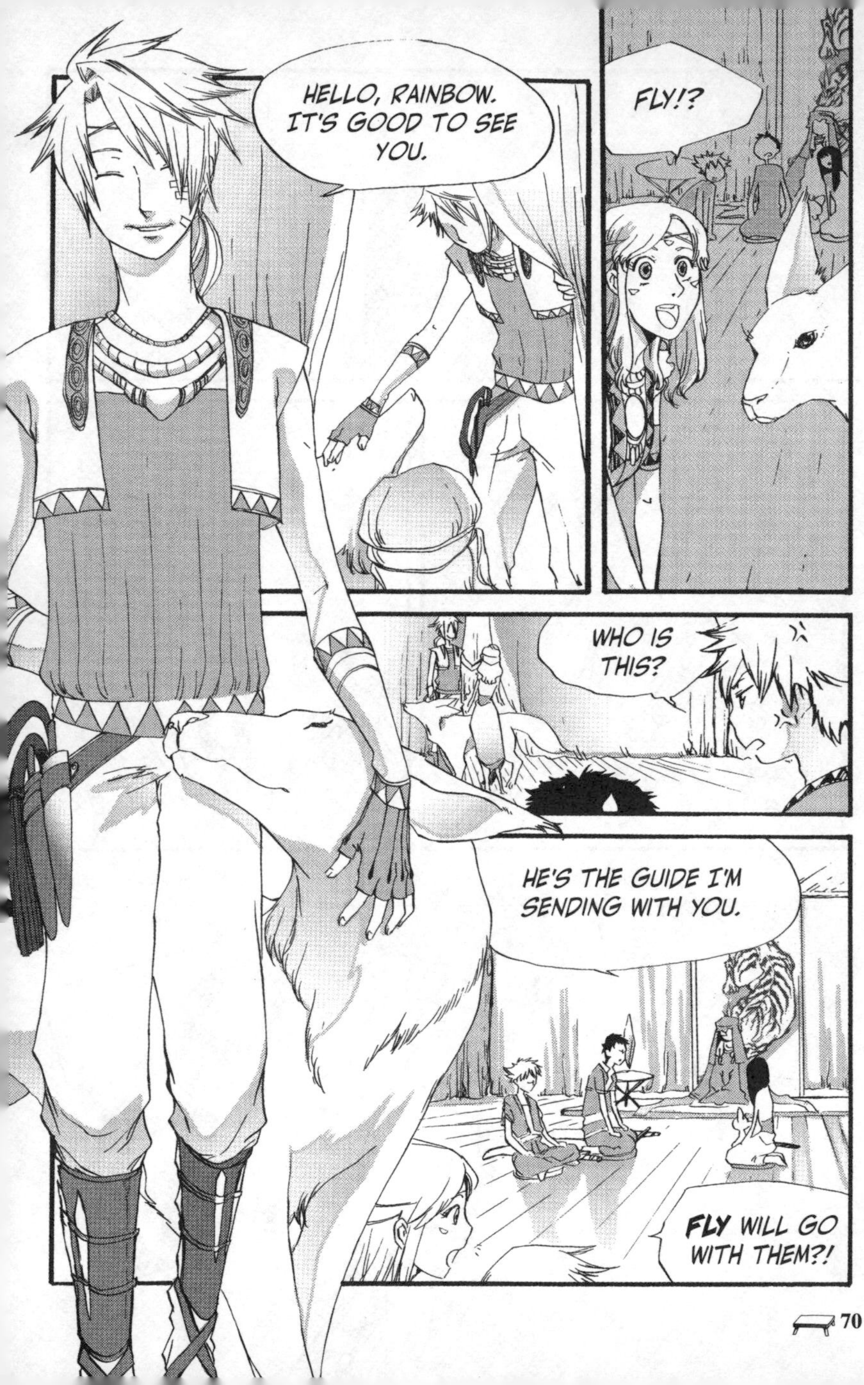
FLY!?
HELLO, RAINBOW. IT'S GOOD TO SEE YOU.
WHO IS THIS?
HE'S THE GUIDE I'M SENDING WITH YOU.
FLY WILL GO WITH THEM?!

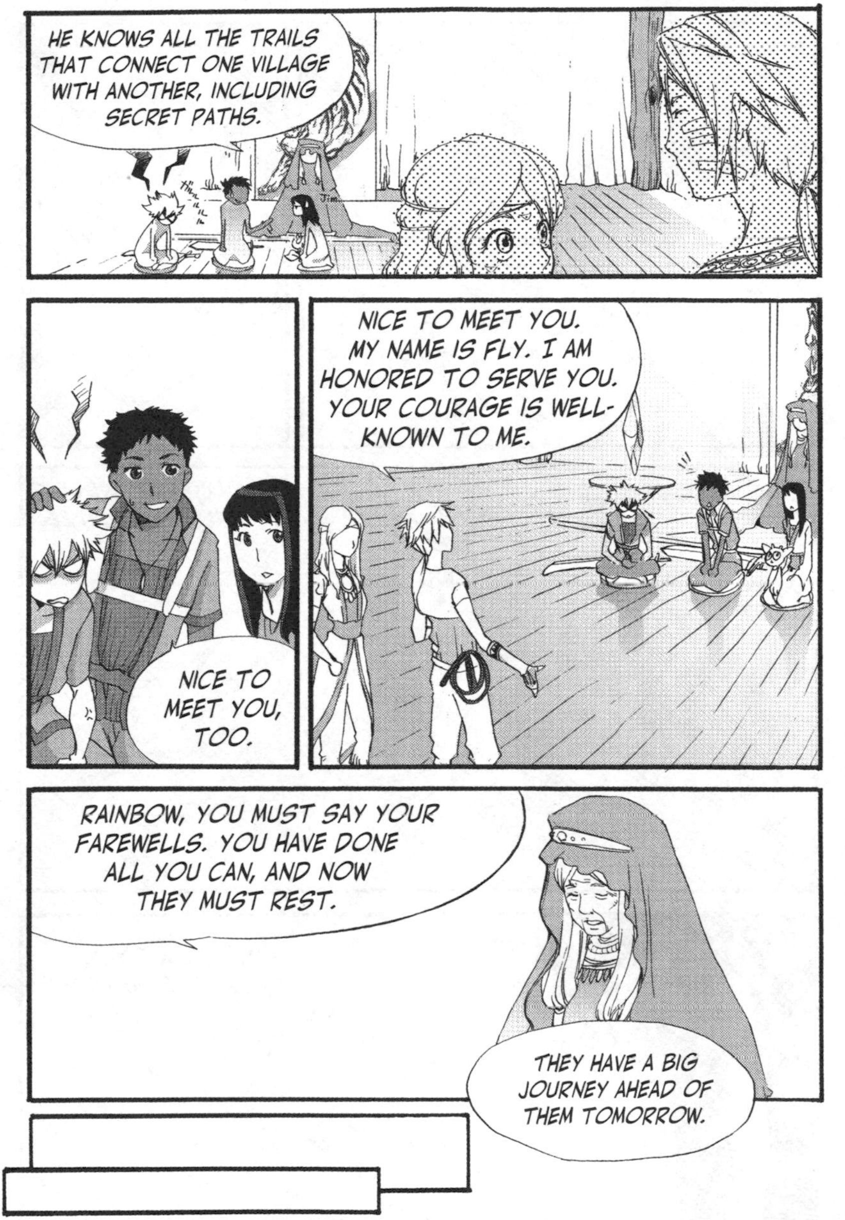
HE KNOWS ALL THE TRAILS THAT CONNECT ONE VILLAGE WITH ANOTHER, INCLUDING SECRET PATHS.
NICE TO MEET YOU. MY NAME IS FLY. I AM HONORED TO SERVE YOU. YOUR COURAGE IS WELL-KNOWN TO ME.
NICE TO MEET YOU, TOO.
RAINBOW, YOU MUST SAY YOUR FAREWELLS. YOU HAVE DONE ALL YOU CAN, AND NOW THEY MUST REST.
THEY HAVE A BIG JOURNEY AHEAD OF THEM TOMORROW.

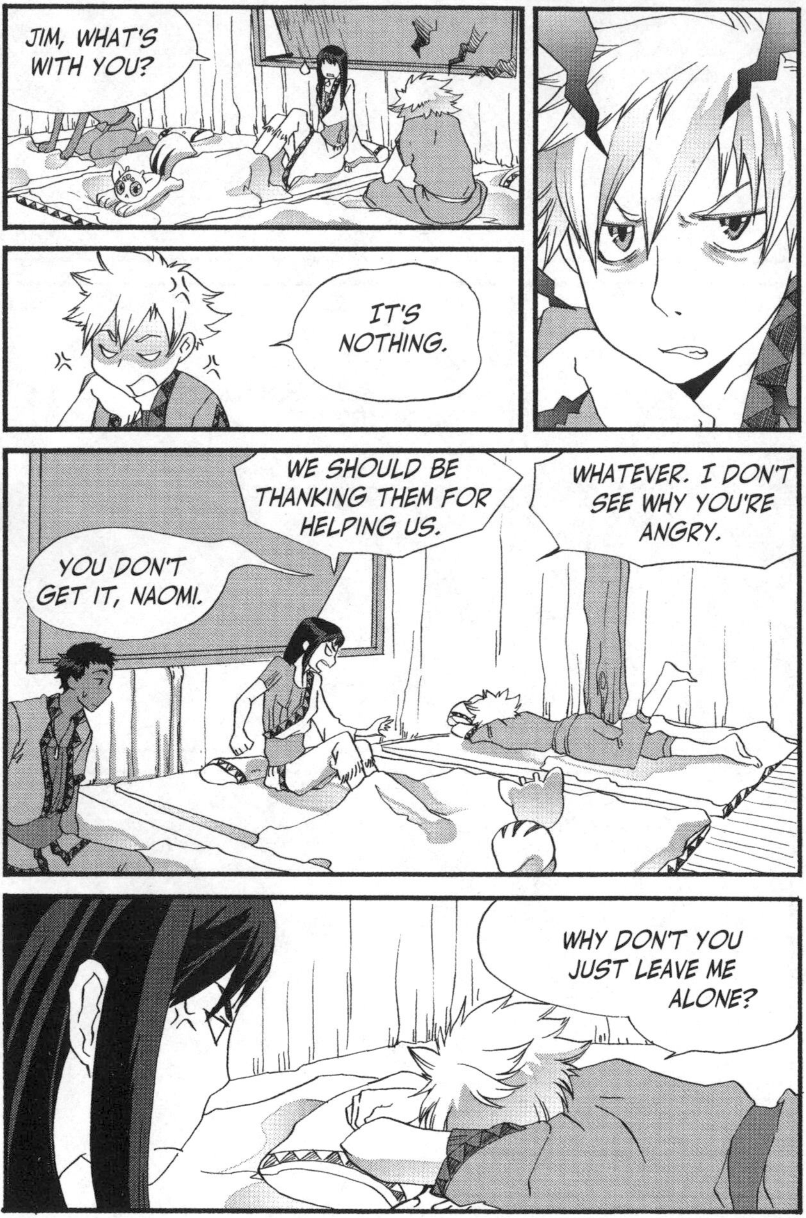
JIM, WHAT'S WITH YOU?
IT'S NOTHING.
WHATEVER. I DON'T SEE WHY YOU'RE ANGRY.
WE SHOULD BE THANKING THEM FOR HELPING US.
YOU DON'T GET IT, NAOMI.
WHY DON'T YOU JUST LEAVE ME ALONE?

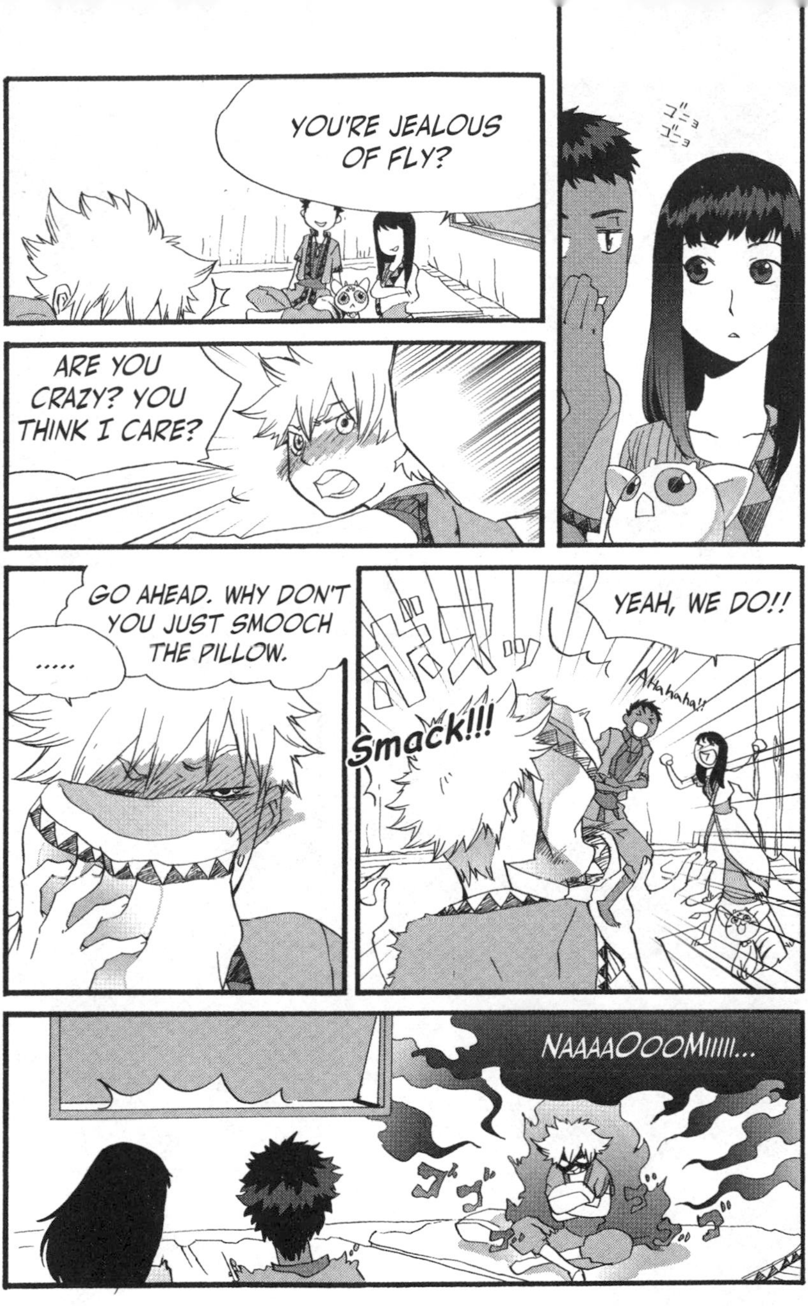
YOU'RE JEALOUS OF FLY?
ARE YOU CRAZY? YOU THINK I CARE?
YEAH, WE DO!!
Smack!!!
Ahahaha!!
GO AHEAD. WHY DON'T YOU JUST SMOOCH THE PILLOW.
.....
NAAAAOOOMIIIII...

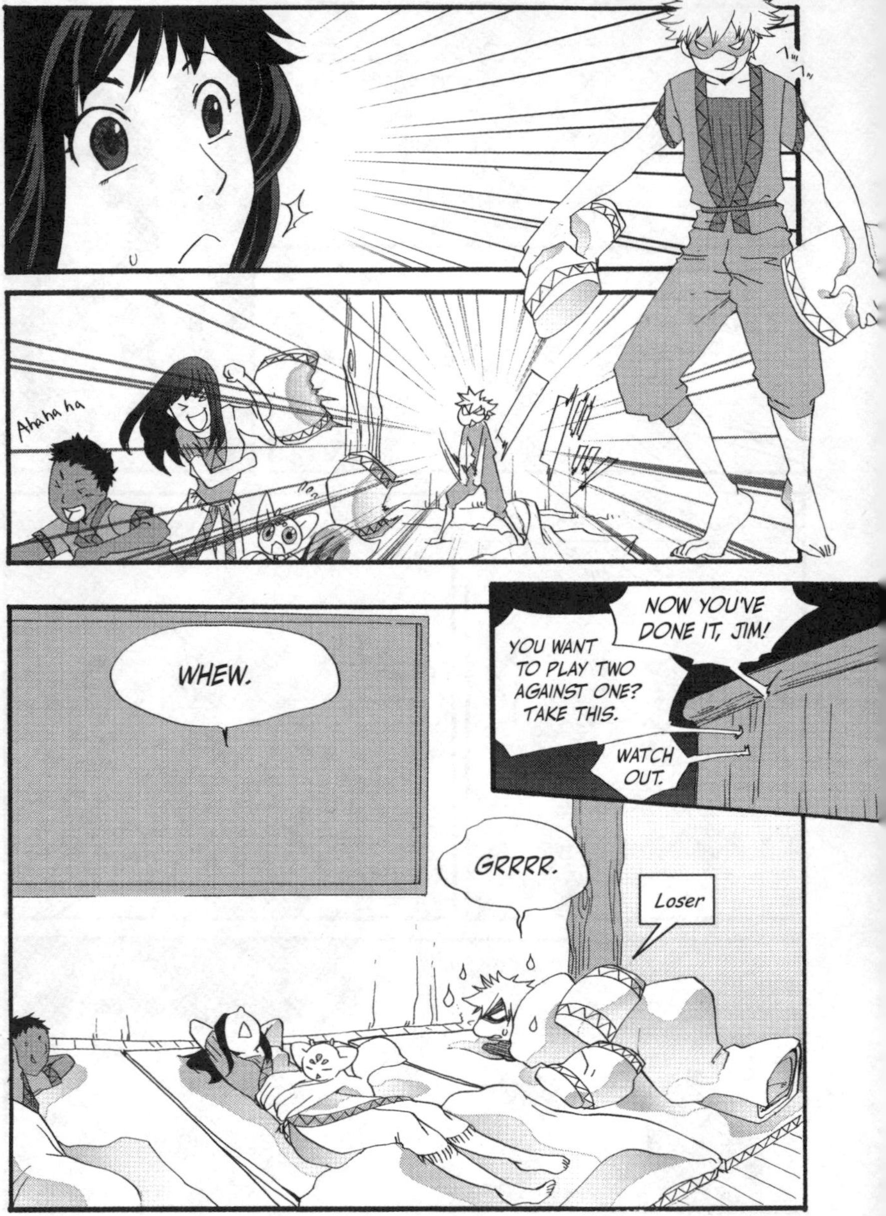
Ahaha ha
NOW YOU'VE DONE IT, JIM!
YOU WANT TO PLAY TWO AGAINST ONE? TAKE THIS.
WATCH OUT.
WHEW.
GRRRR.
Loser

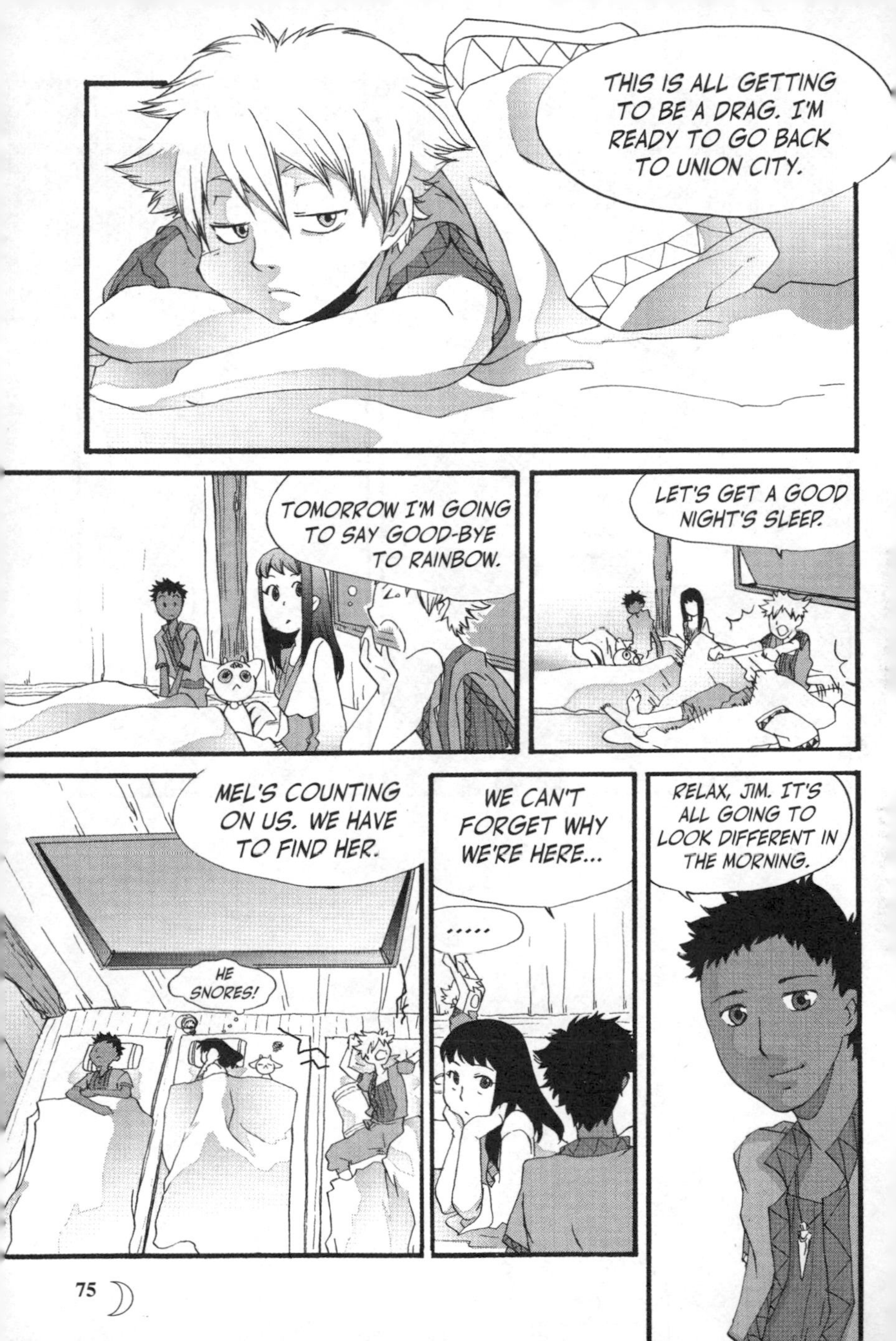
THIS IS ALL GETTING TO BE A DRAG. I'M READY TO GO BACK TO UNION CITY.
LET'S GET A GOOD NIGHT'S SLEEP.
TOMORROW I'M GOING TO SAY GOOD-BYE TO RAINBOW.
RELAX, JIM. IT'S ALL GOING TO LOOK DIFFERENT IN THE MORNING.
WE CAN'T FORGET WHY WE'RE HERE...
.....
MEL'S COUNTING ON US. WE HAVE TO FIND HER.
HE SNORES!

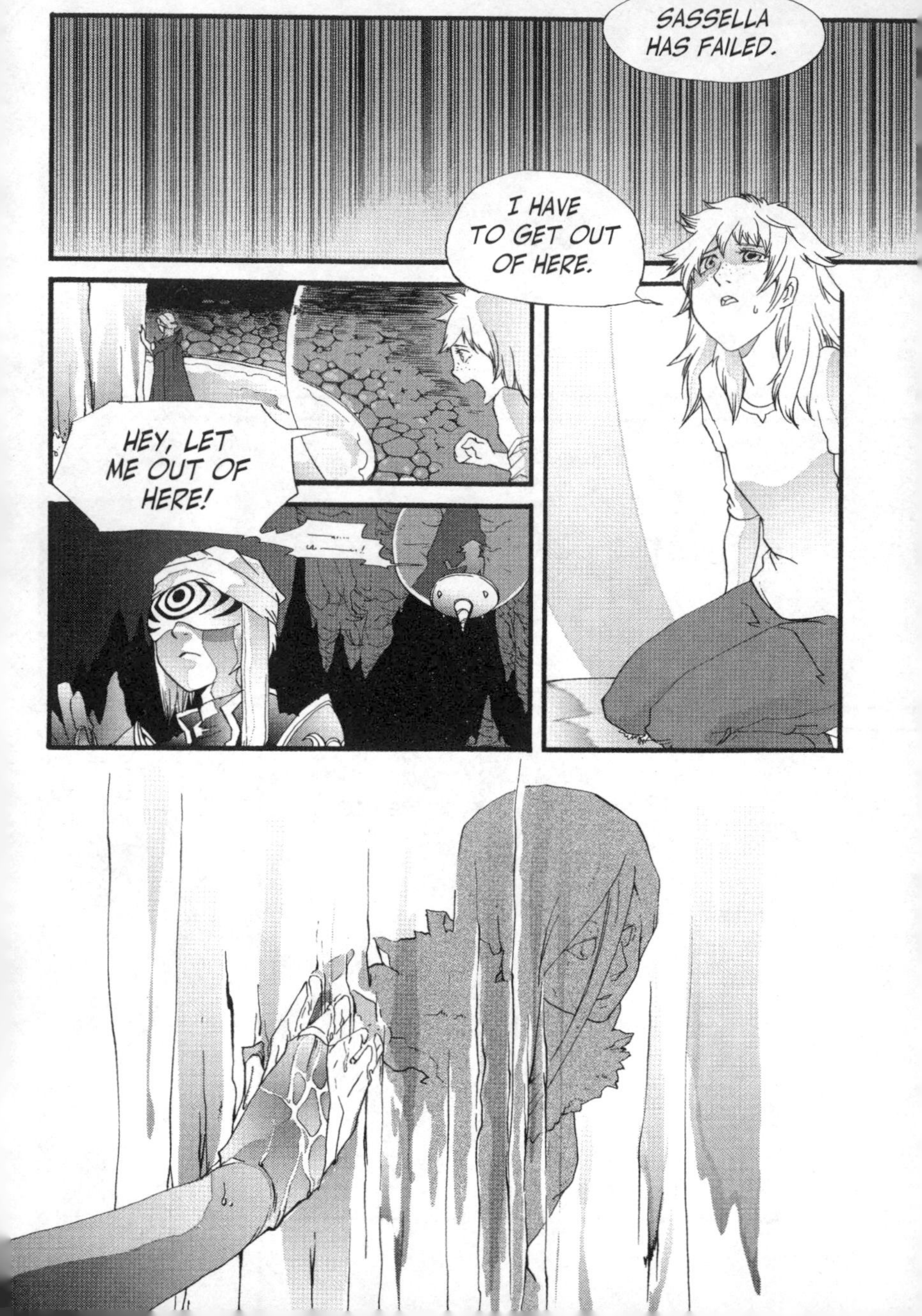
SASSELLA HAS FAILED.
I HAVE TO GET OUT OF HERE.
HEY, LET ME OUT OF HERE!

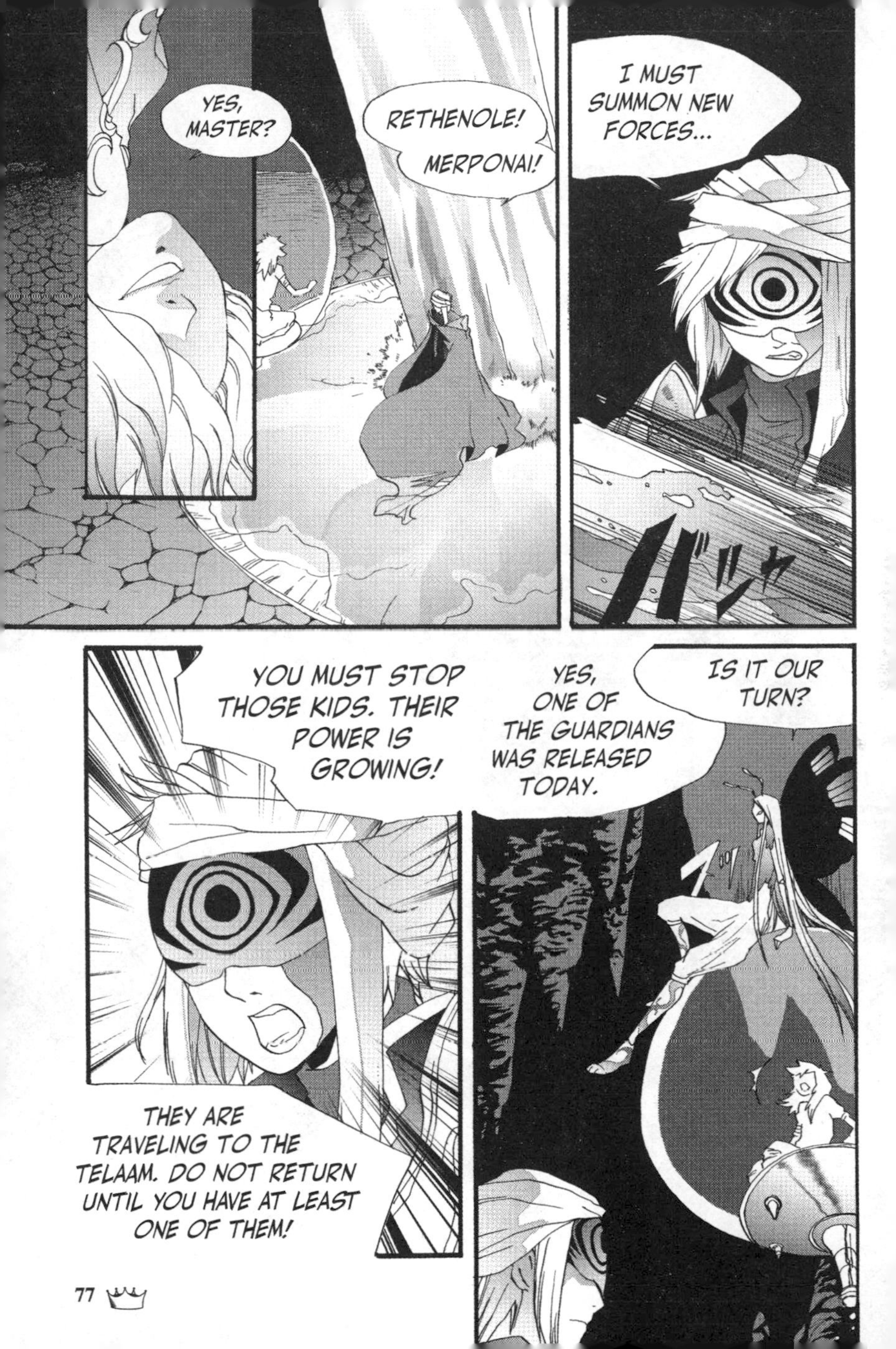
I MUST SUMMON NEW FORCES...
バッ
RETHENOLE!
MERPONAI!
YES, MASTER?
IS IT OUR TURN?
YES, ONE OF THE GUARDIANS WAS RELEASED TODAY.
YOU MUST STOP THOSE KIDS. THEIR POWER IS GROWING!
THEY ARE TRAVELING TO THE TELAAM. DO NOT RETURN UNTIL YOU HAVE AT LEAST ONE OF THEM!

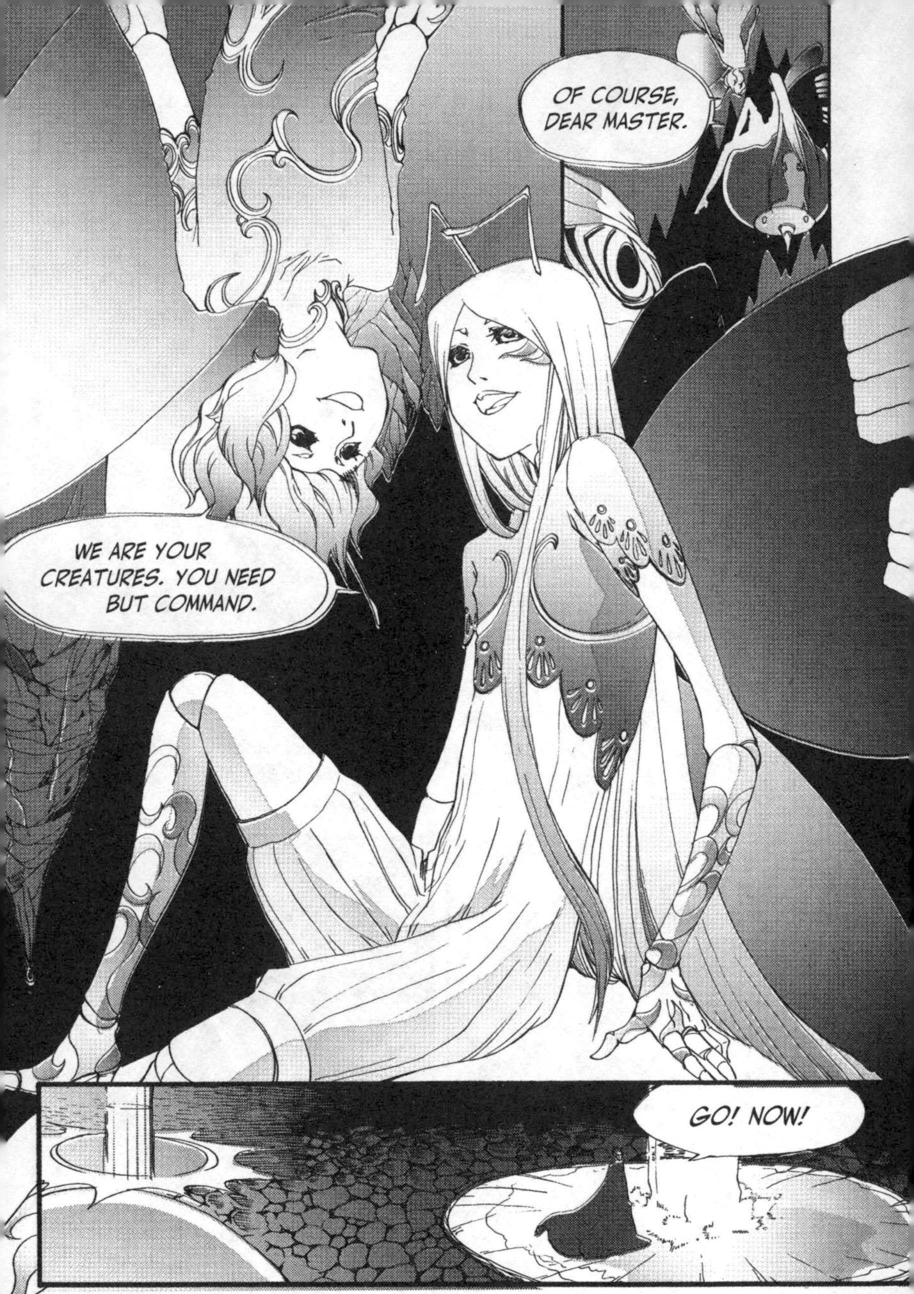
OF COURSE, DEAR MASTER.
WE ARE YOUR CREATURES. YOU NEED BUT COMMAND.
GO! NOW!

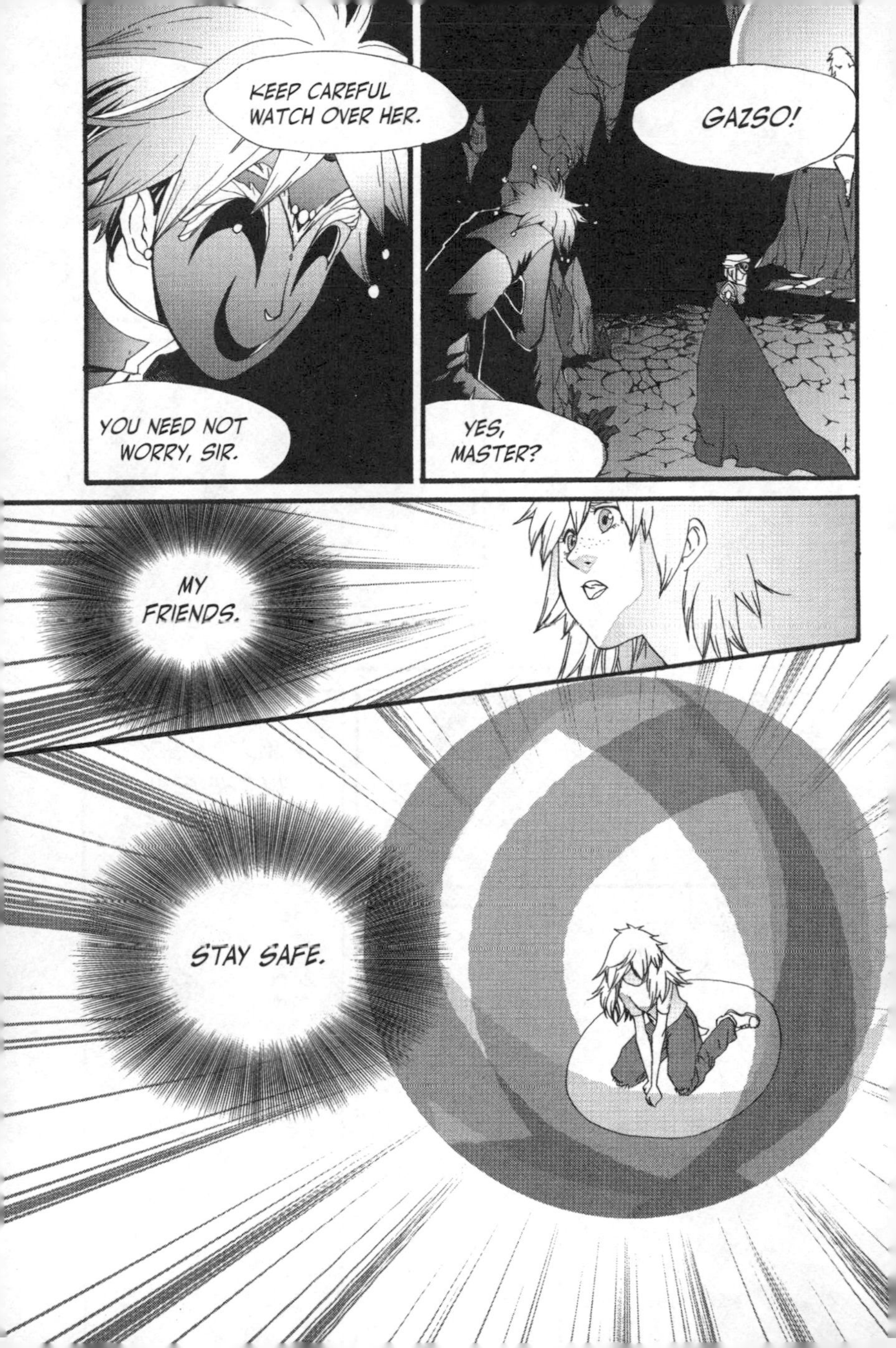
GAZSO!
YES, MASTER?
KEEP CAREFUL WATCH OVER HER.
YOU NEED NOT WORRY, SIR.
MY FRIENDS.
STAY SAFE.

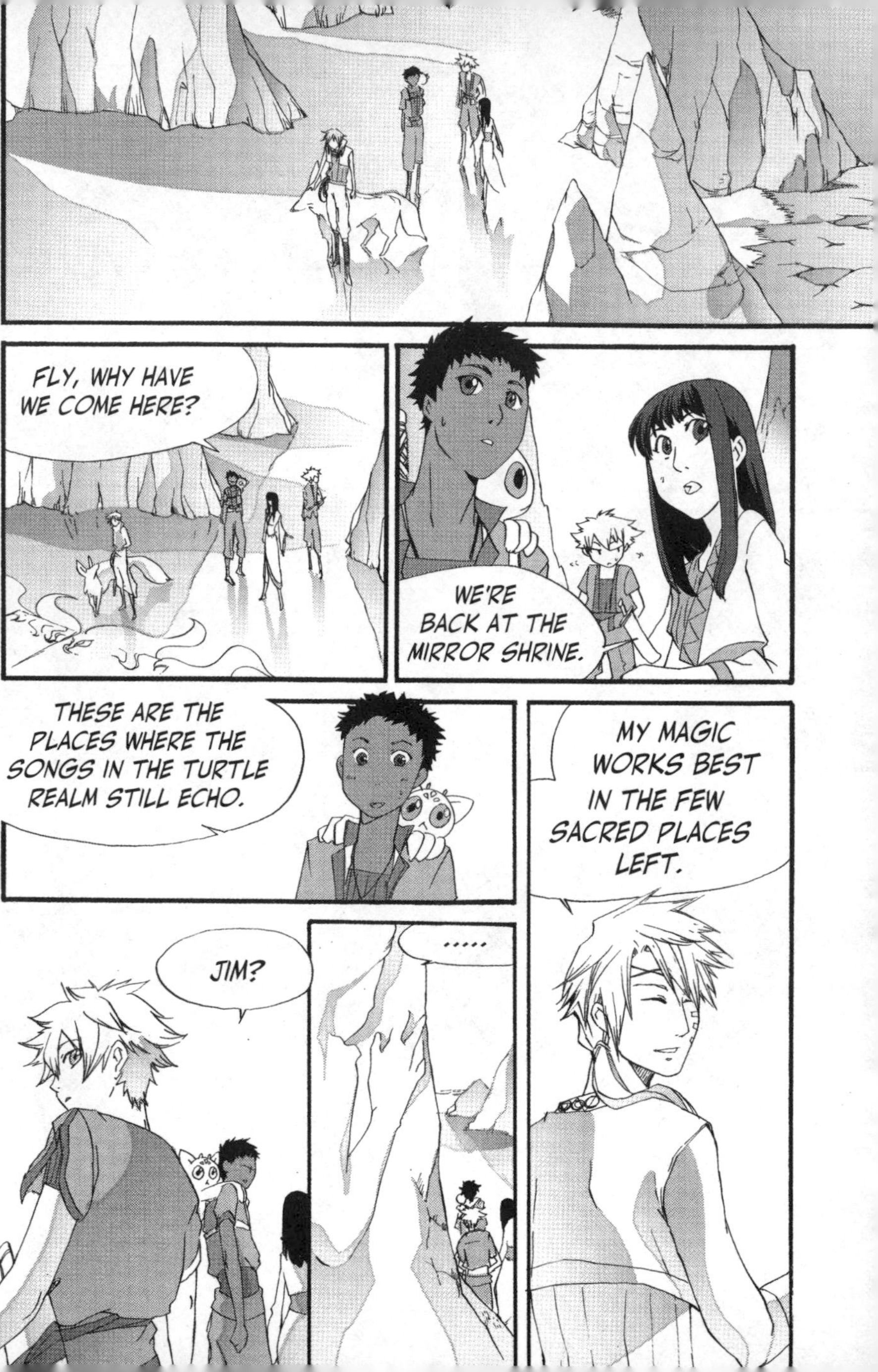
WE'RE BACK AT THE MIRROR SHRINE.
FLY, WHY HAVE WE COME HERE?
MY MAGIC WORKS BEST IN THE FEW SACRED PLACES LEFT.
THESE ARE THE PLACES WHERE THE SONGS IN THE TURTLE REALM STILL ECHO.
......
JIM?

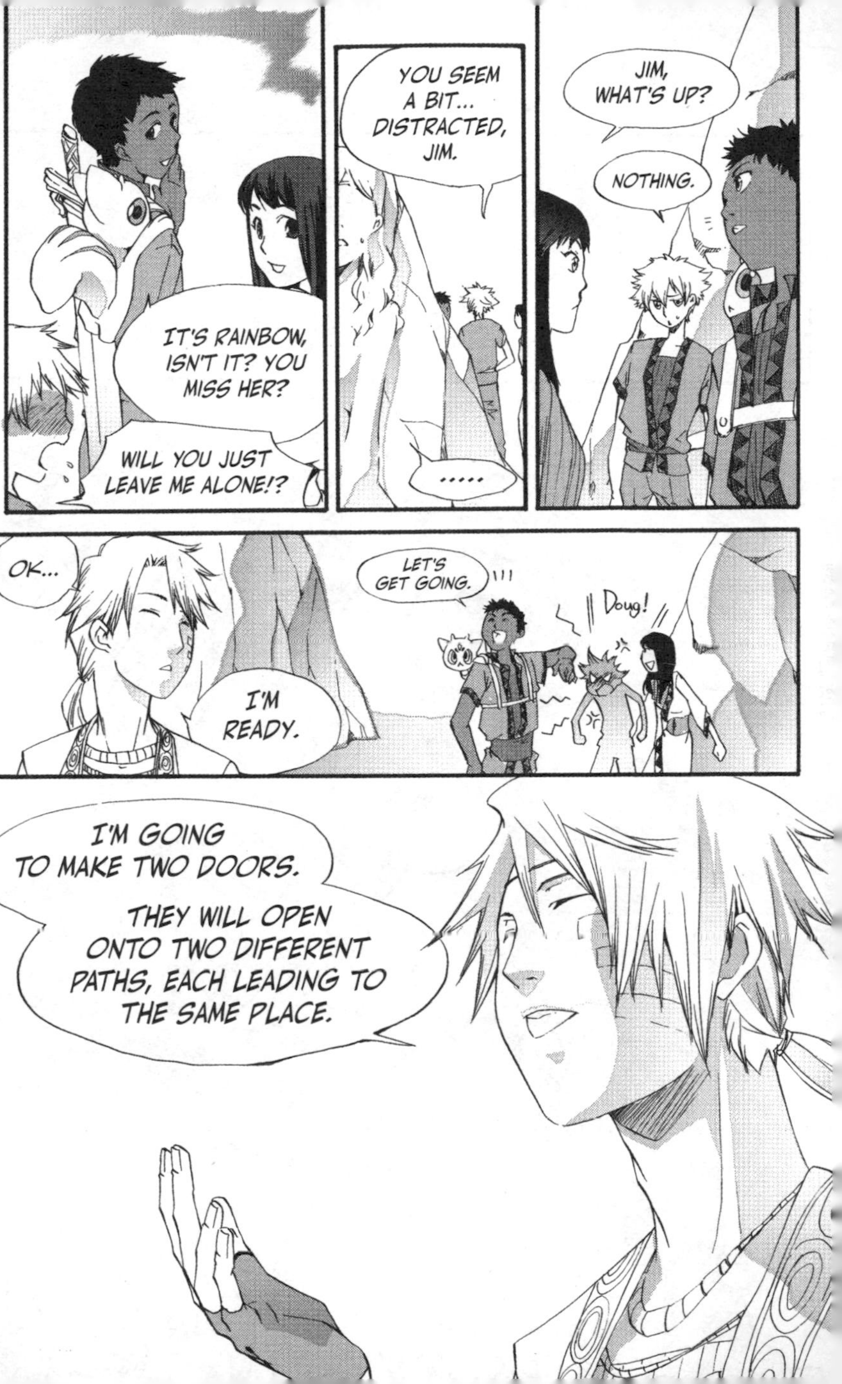
JIM, WHAT'S UP?
NOTHING.
YOU SEEM A BIT... DISTRACTED, JIM.
.....
IT'S RAINBOW, ISN'T IT? YOU MISS HER?
WILL YOU JUST LEAVE ME ALONE!?
LET'S GET GOING.
Doug!
OK...
I'M READY.
I'M GOING TO MAKE TWO DOORS.
THEY WILL OPEN ONTO TWO DIFFERENT PATHS, EACH LEADING TO THE SAME PLACE.

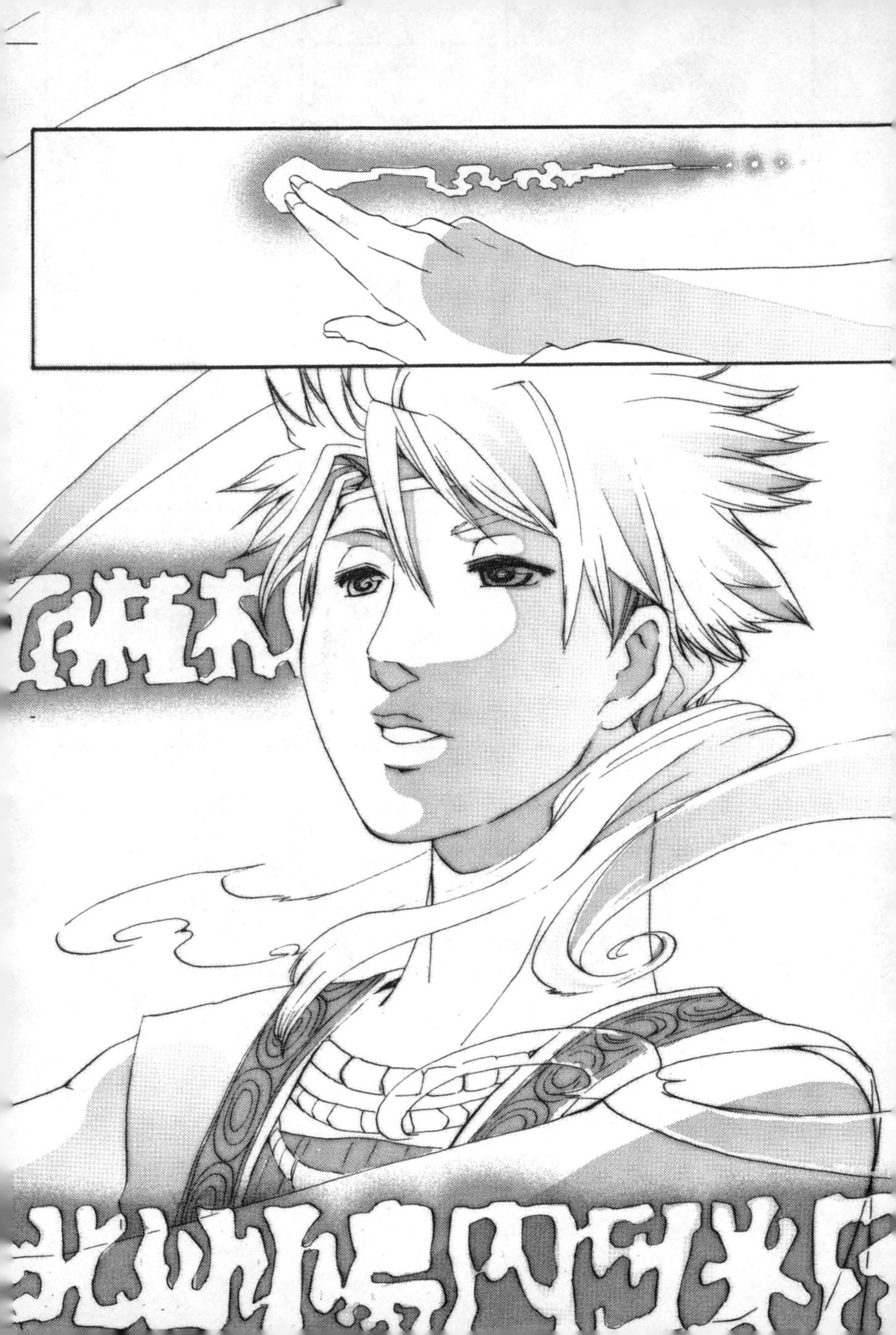

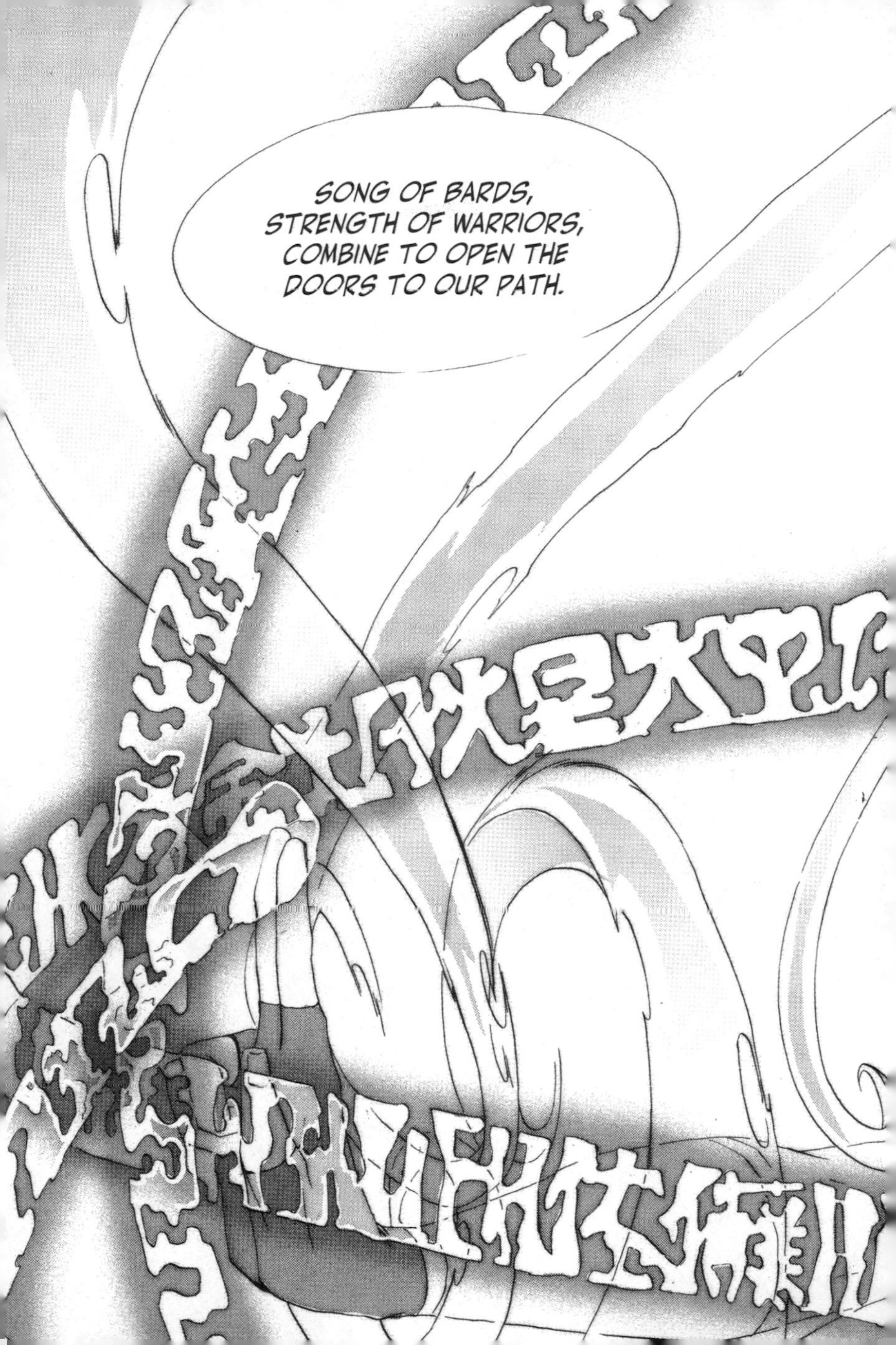
SONG OF BARDS, STRENGTH OF WARRIORS, COMBINE TO OPEN THE DOORS TO OUR PATH.

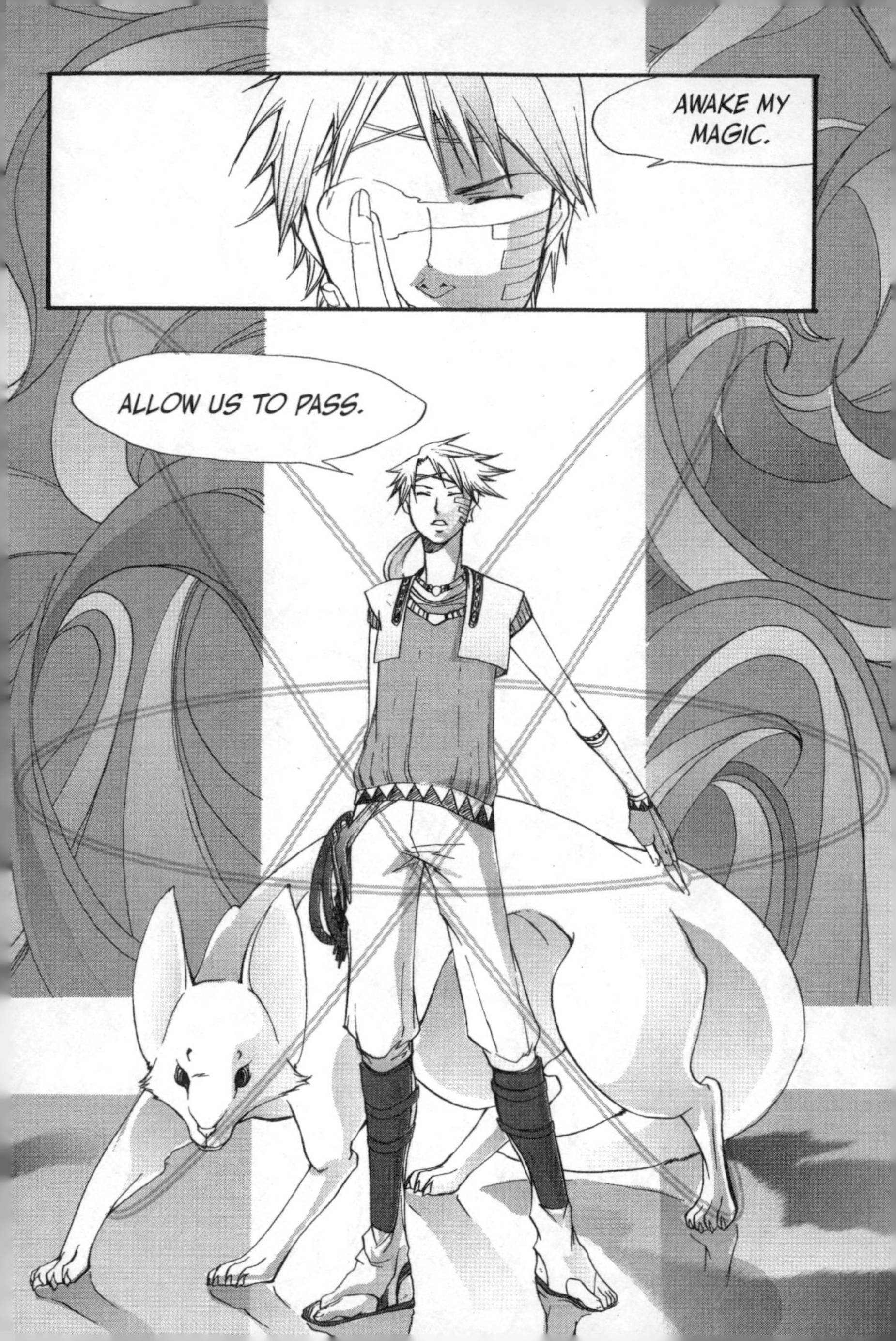
AWAKE MY MAGIC.
ALLOW US TO PASS.

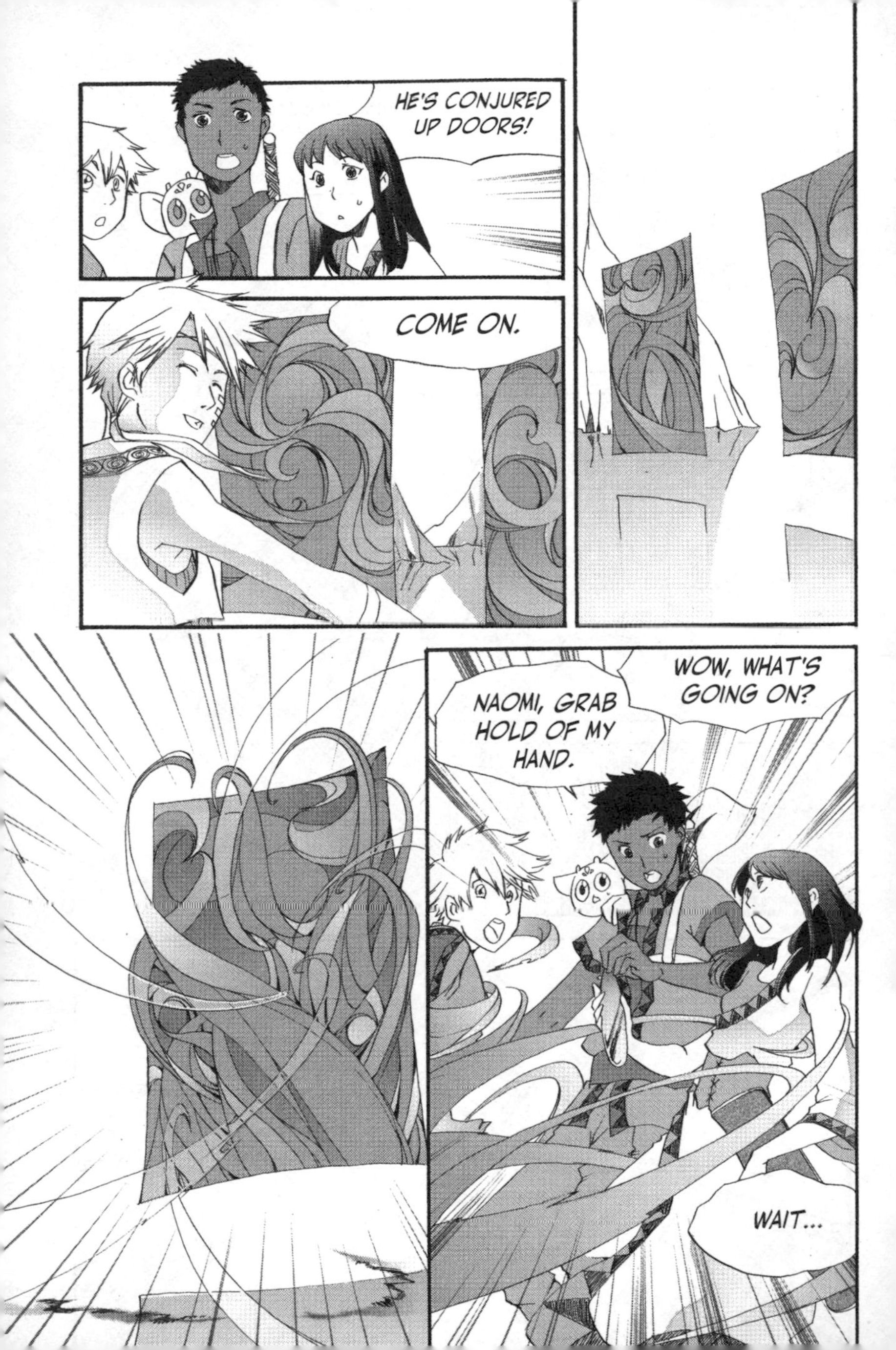
HE'S CONJURED UP DOORS!
COME ON.
WOW, WHAT'S GOING ON?
NAOMI, GRAB HOLD OF MY HAND.
WAIT...

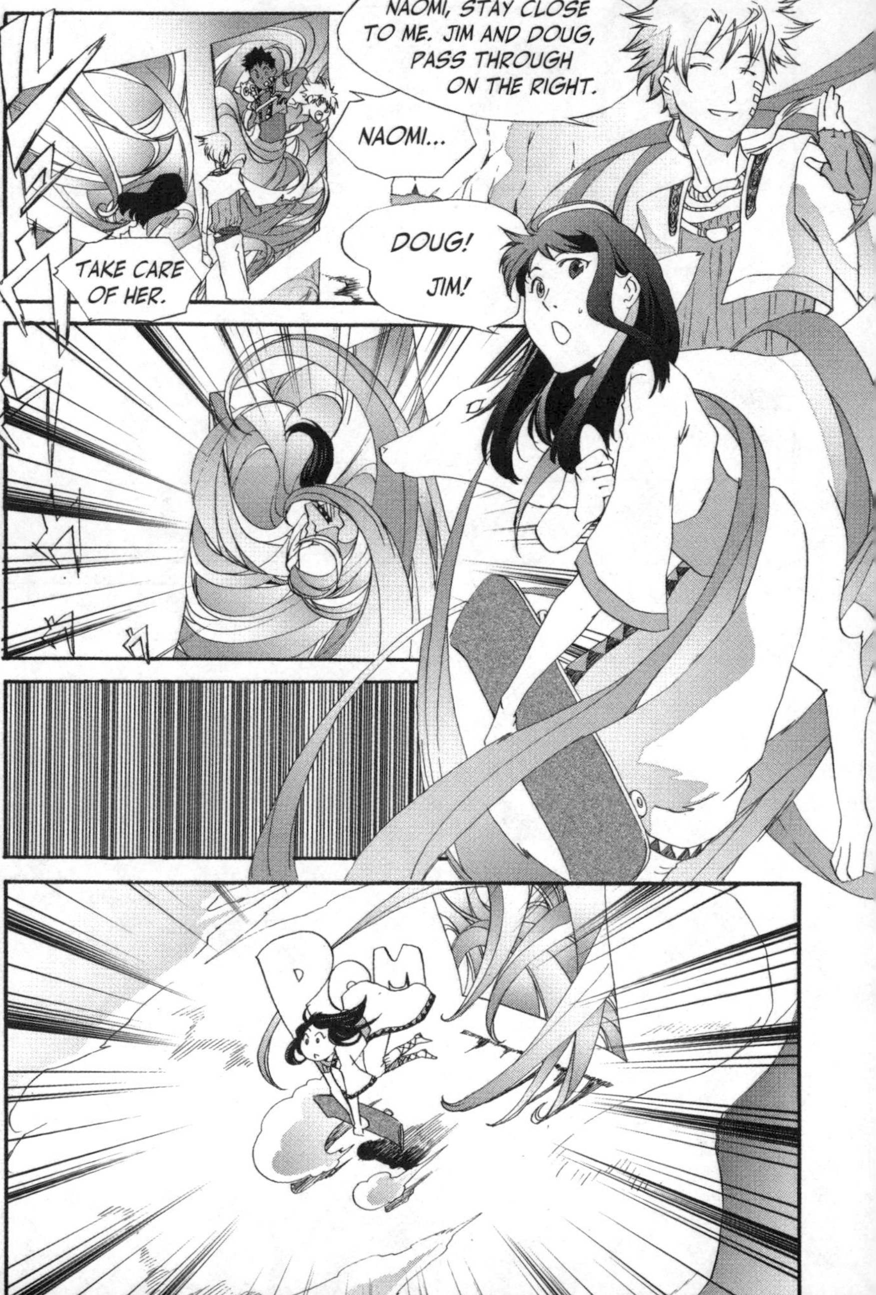
NAOMI, STAY CLOSE TO ME. JIM AND DOUG, PASS THROUGH ON THE RIGHT.
NAOMI...
TAKE CARE OF HER.
DOUG!
JIM!
BOM

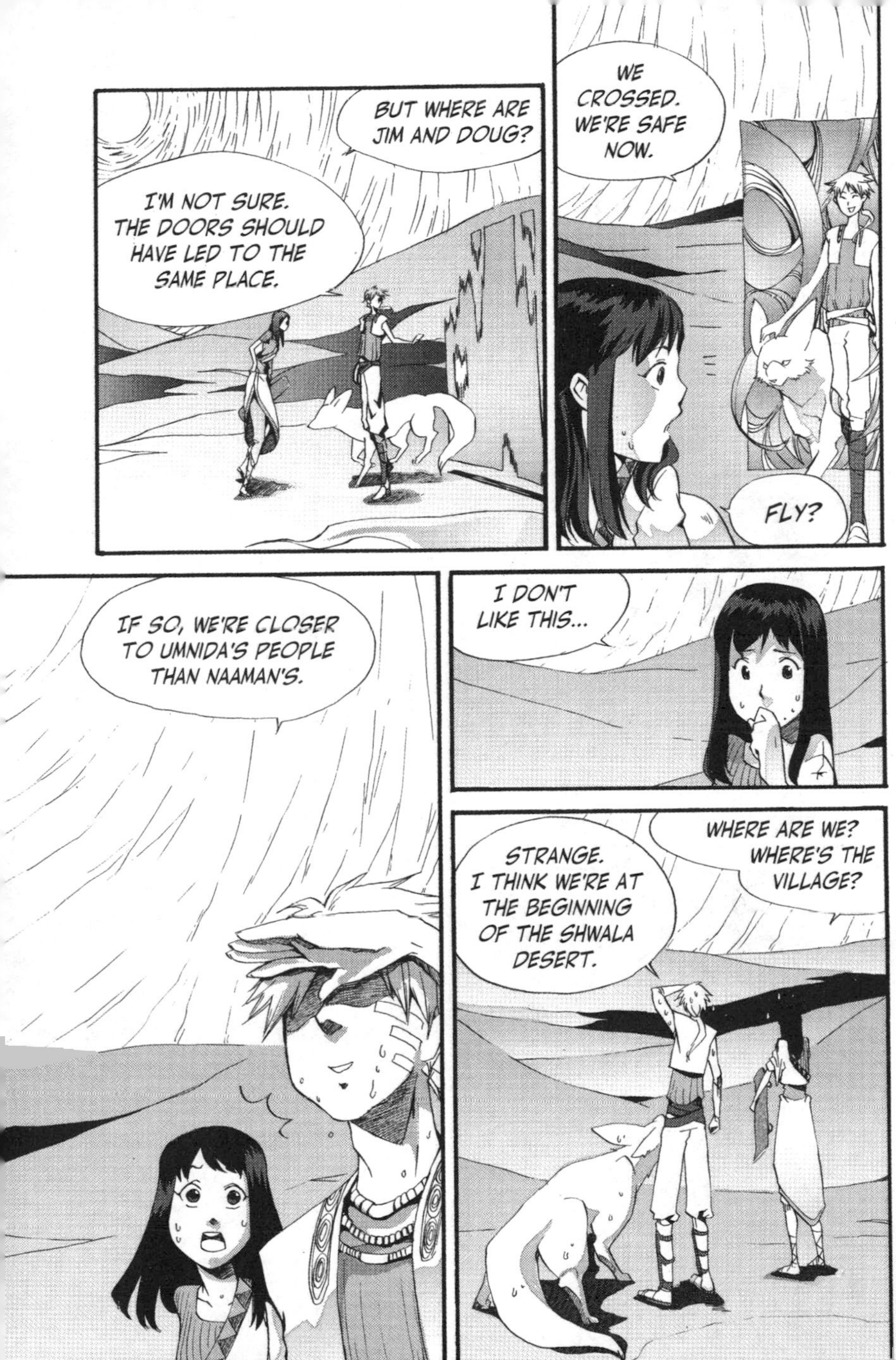
WE CROSSED. WE'RE SAFE NOW.
FLY?
BUT WHERE ARE JIM AND DOUG?
I'M NOT SURE. THE DOORS SHOULD HAVE LED TO THE SAME PLACE.
I DON'T LIKE THIS...
WHERE ARE WE? WHERE'S THE VILLAGE?
STRANGE. I THINK WE'RE AT THE BEGINNING OF THE SHWALA DESERT.
IF SO, WE'RE CLOSER TO UMNIDA'S PEOPLE THAN NAAMAN'S.

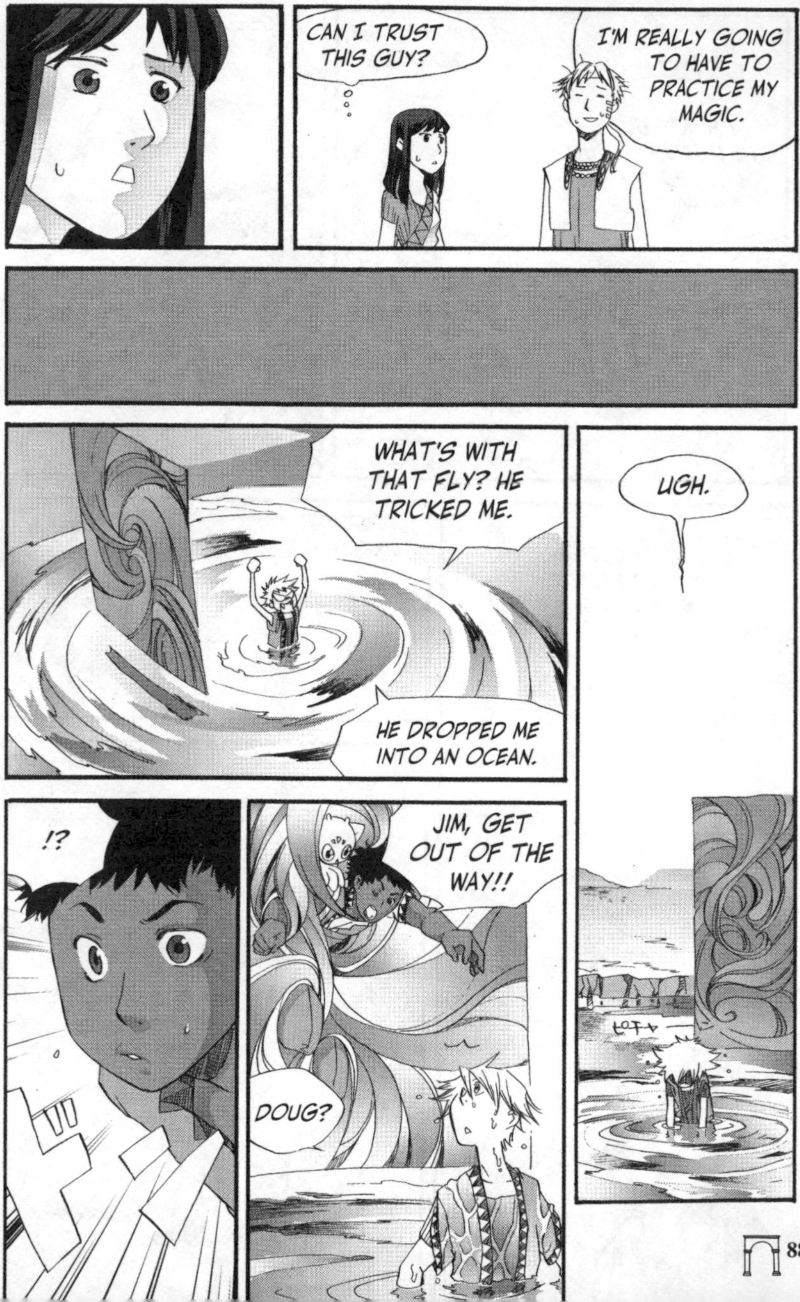
I'M REALLY GOING TO HAVE TO PRACTICE MY MAGIC.
CAN I TRUST THIS GUY?
UGH.
WHAT'S WITH THAT FLY? HE TRICKED ME.
HE DROPPED ME INTO AN OCEAN.
JIM, GET OUT OF THE WAY!!
DOUG?
!?

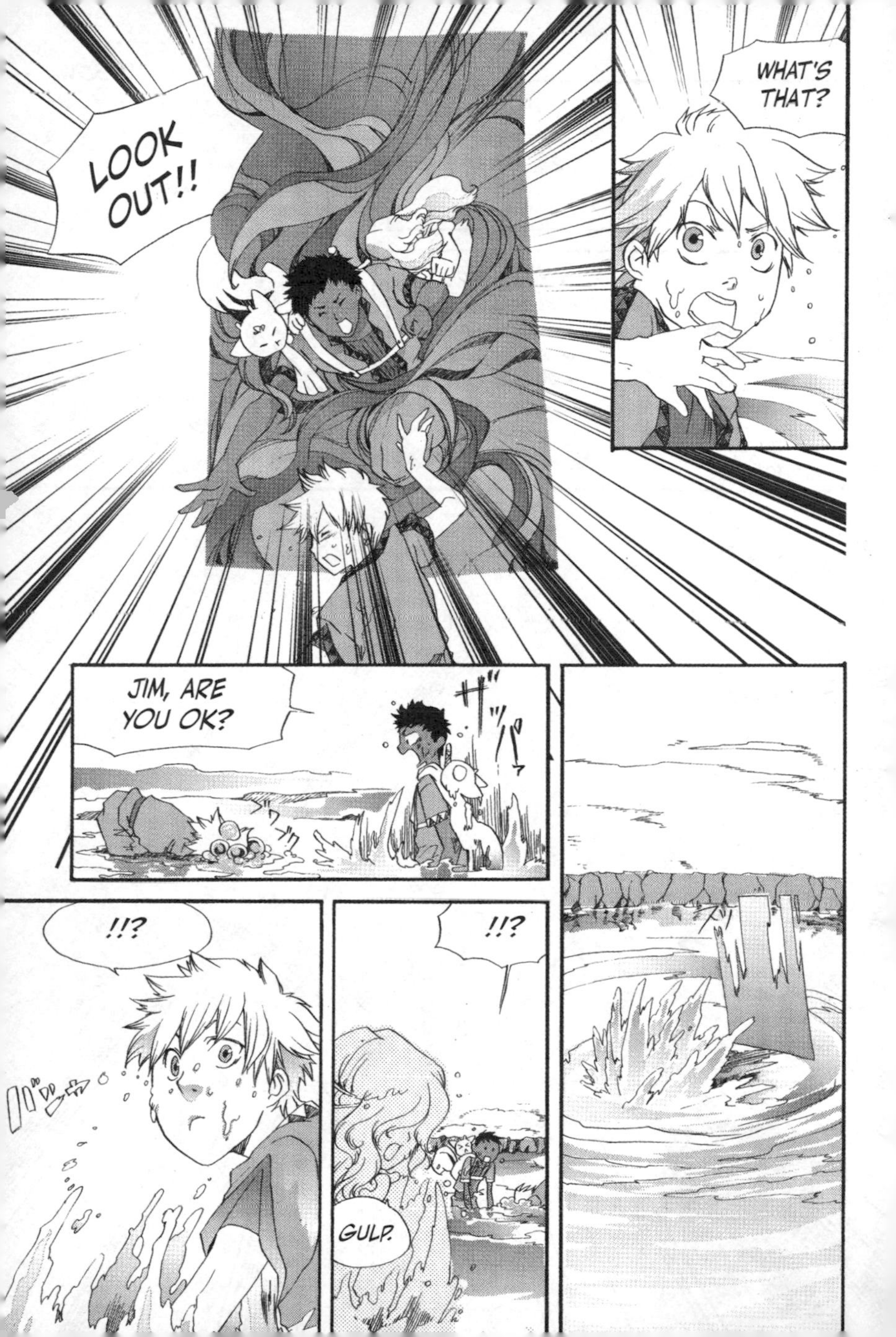
WHAT'S THAT?
LOOK OUT!!
JIM, ARE YOU OK?
!!?
GULP.
!!?

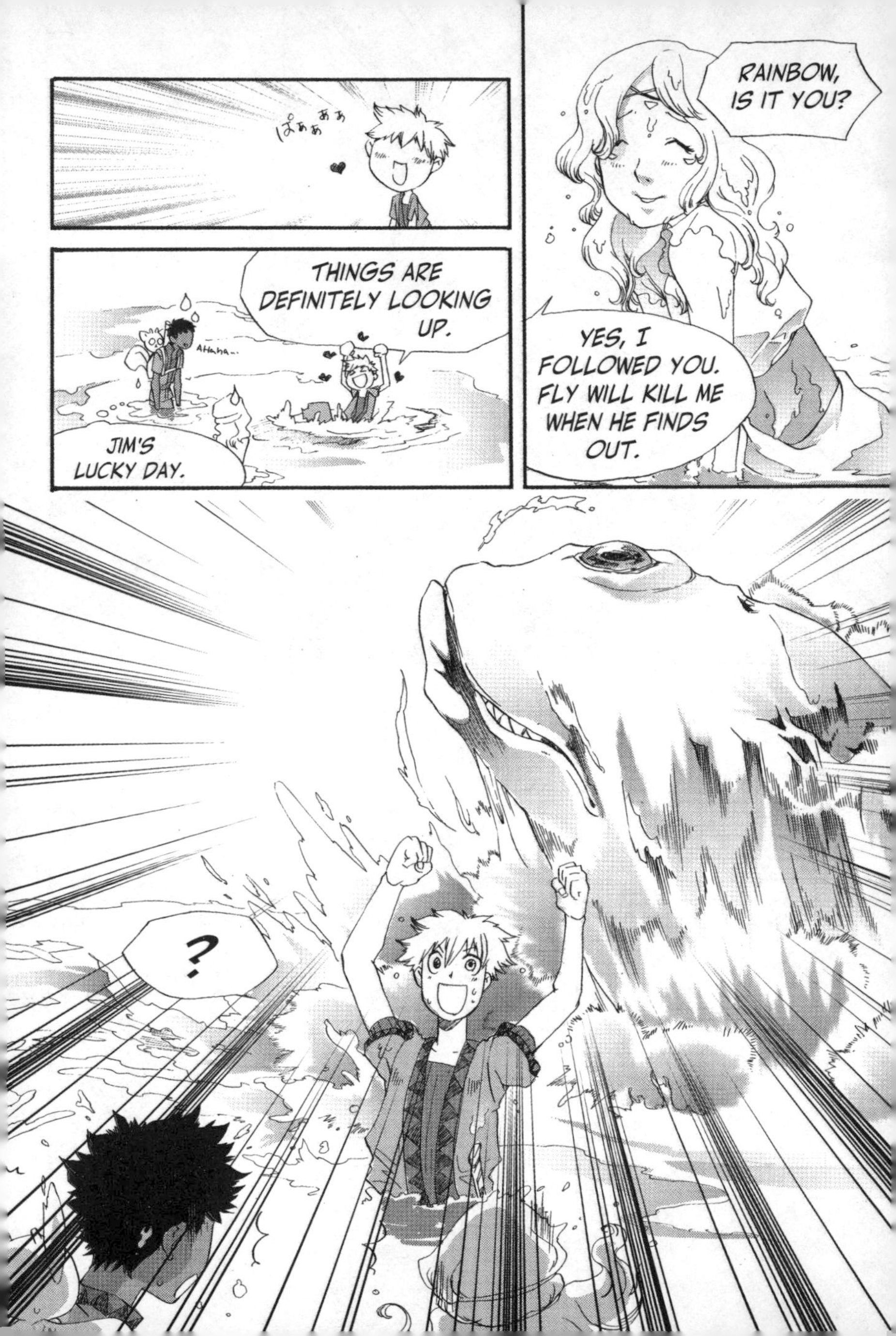
RAINBOW, IS IT YOU?
YES, I FOLLOWED YOU. FLY WILL KILL ME WHEN HE FINDS OUT.
THINGS ARE DEFINITELY LOOKING UP.
AHaha..
JIM'S LUCKY DAY.
?

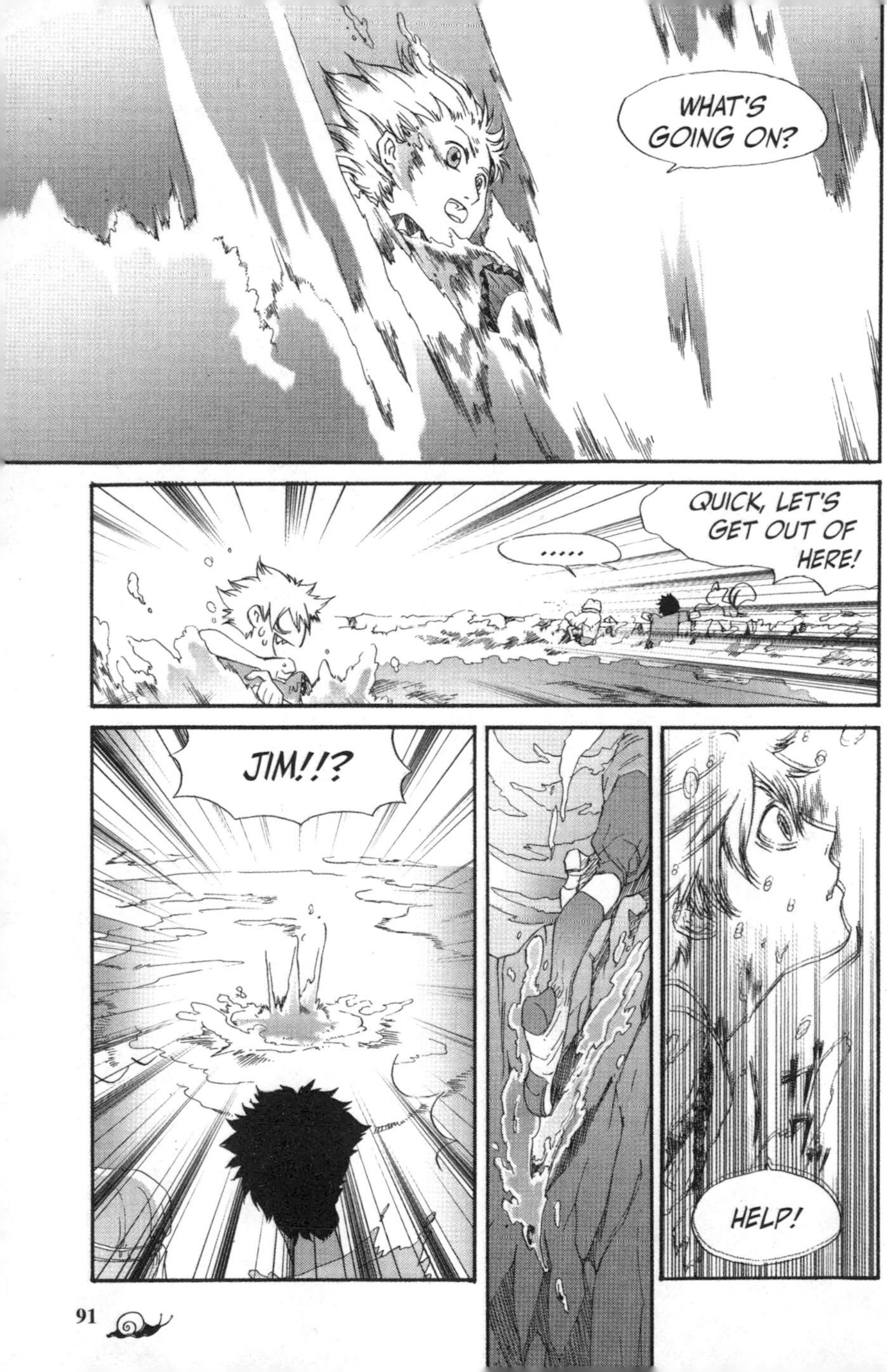
WHAT'S GOING ON?
QUICK, LET'S GET OUT OF HERE!
.....
HELP!
JIM!!?

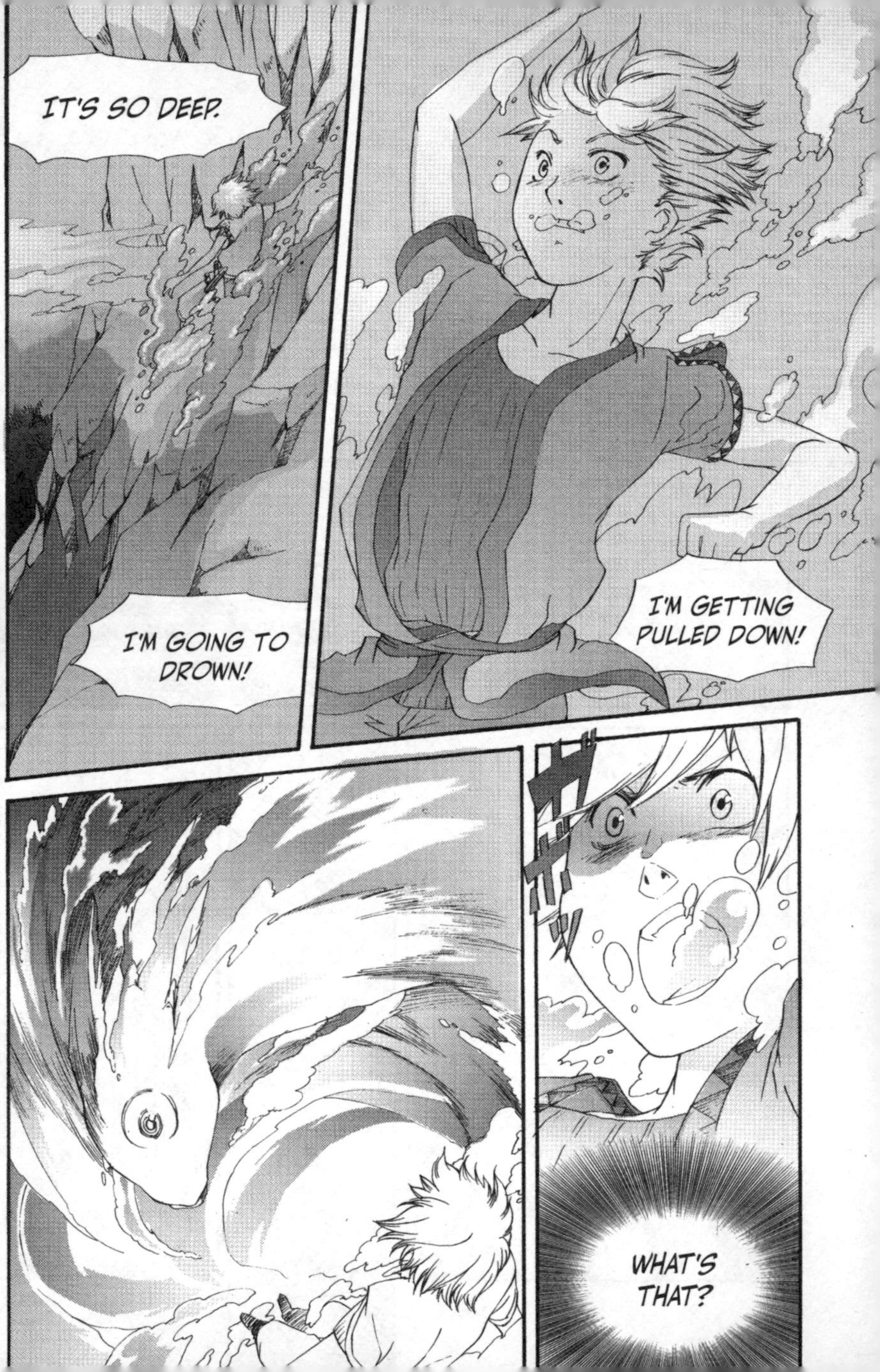
I'M GETTING PULLED DOWN!
IT'S SO DEEP.
I'M GOING TO DROWN!
WHAT'S THAT?

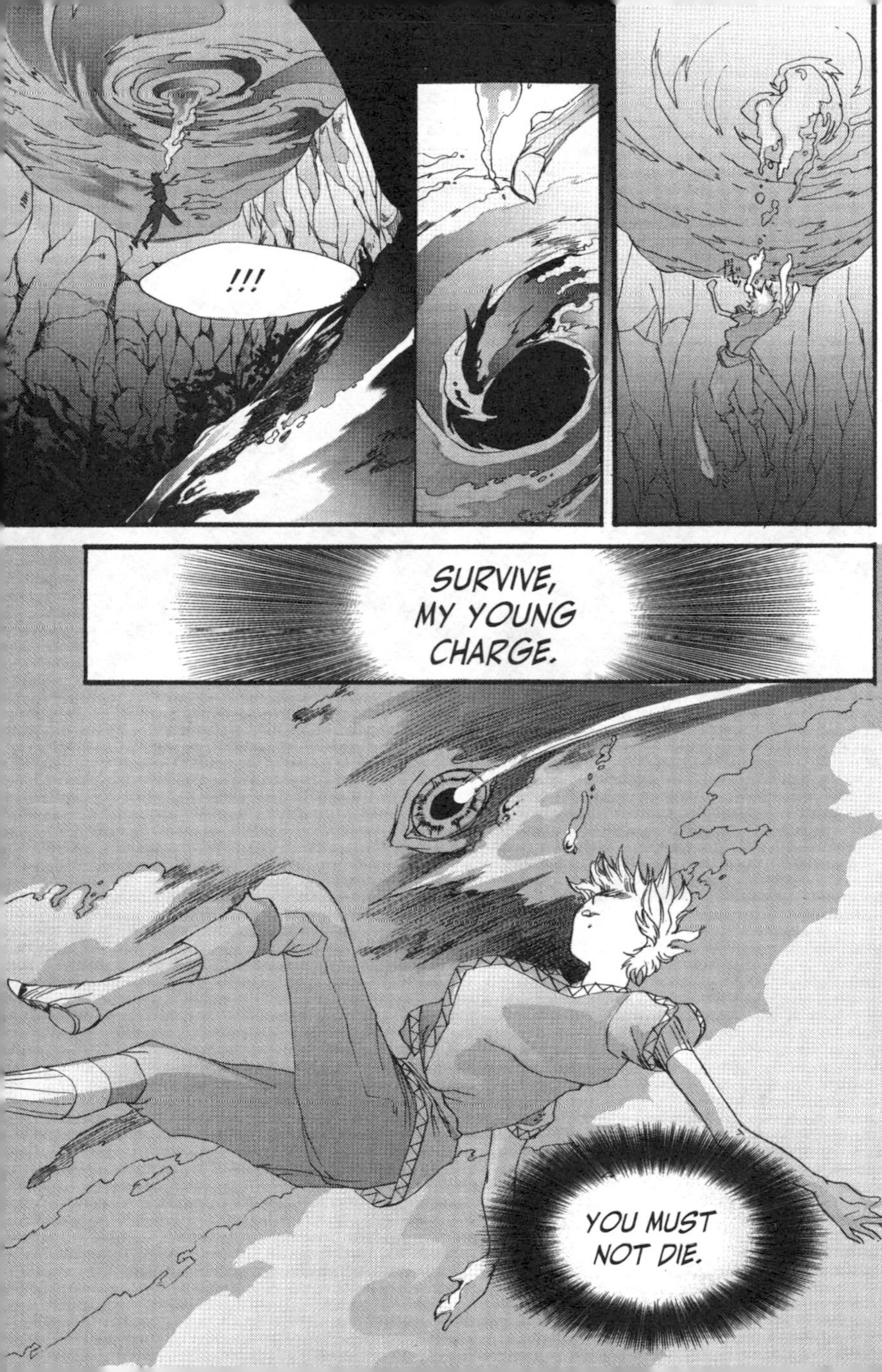
!!!
SURVIVE, MY YOUNG CHARGE.
YOU MUST NOT DIE.

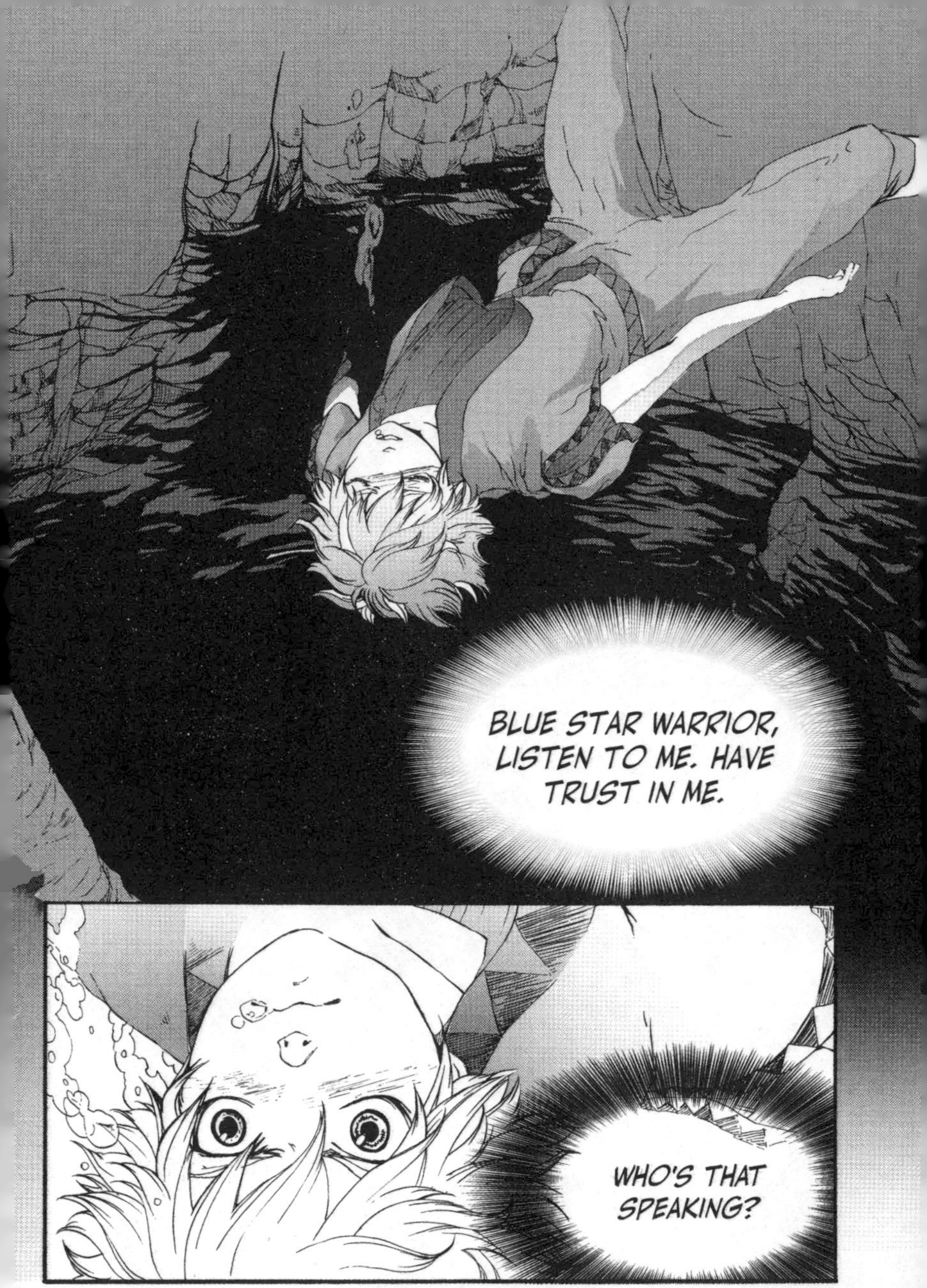
BLUE STAR WARRIOR, LISTEN TO ME. HAVE TRUST IN ME.
WHO'S THAT SPEAKING?

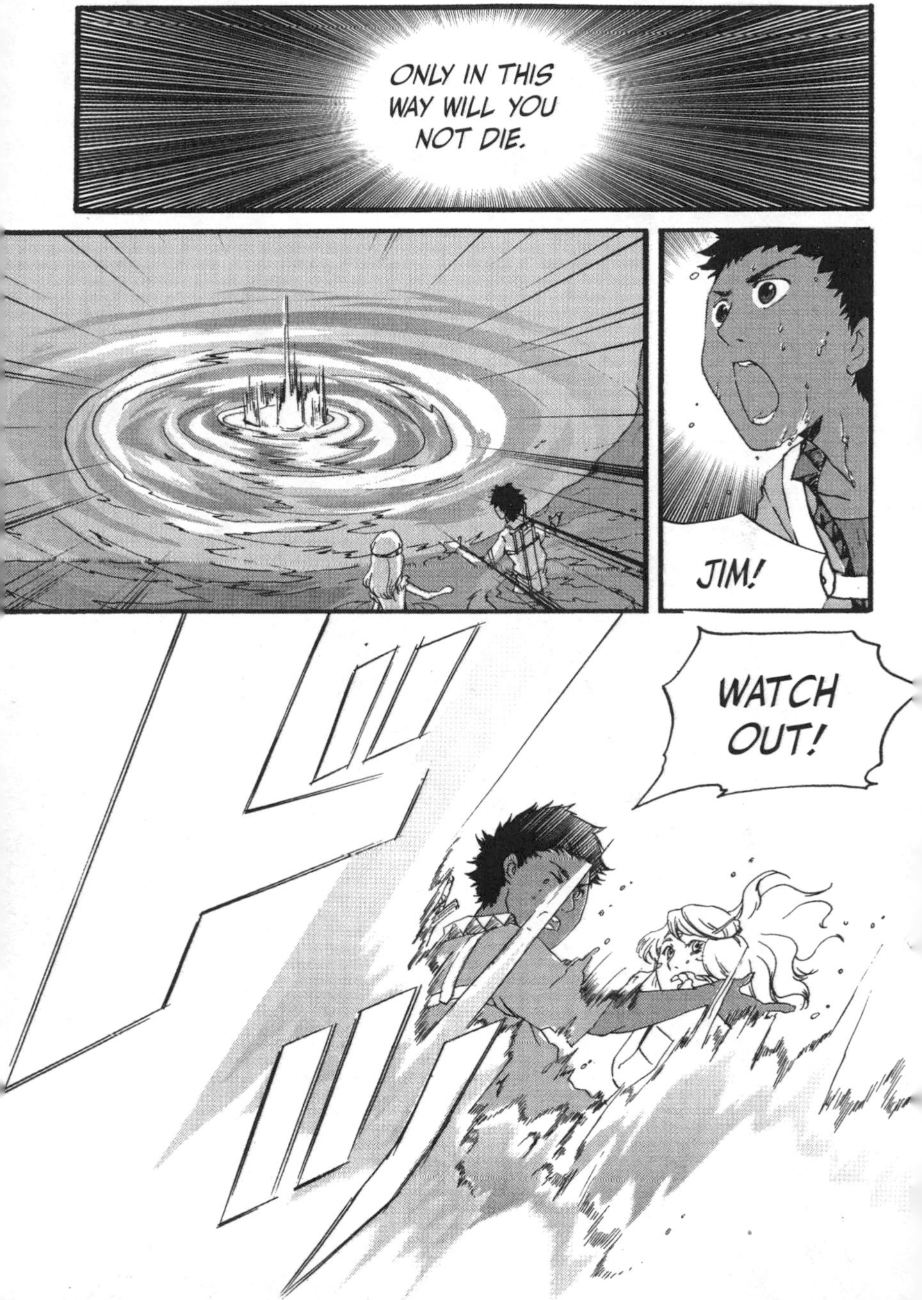
ONLY IN THIS WAY WILL YOU NOT DIE.
JIM!
WATCH OUT!

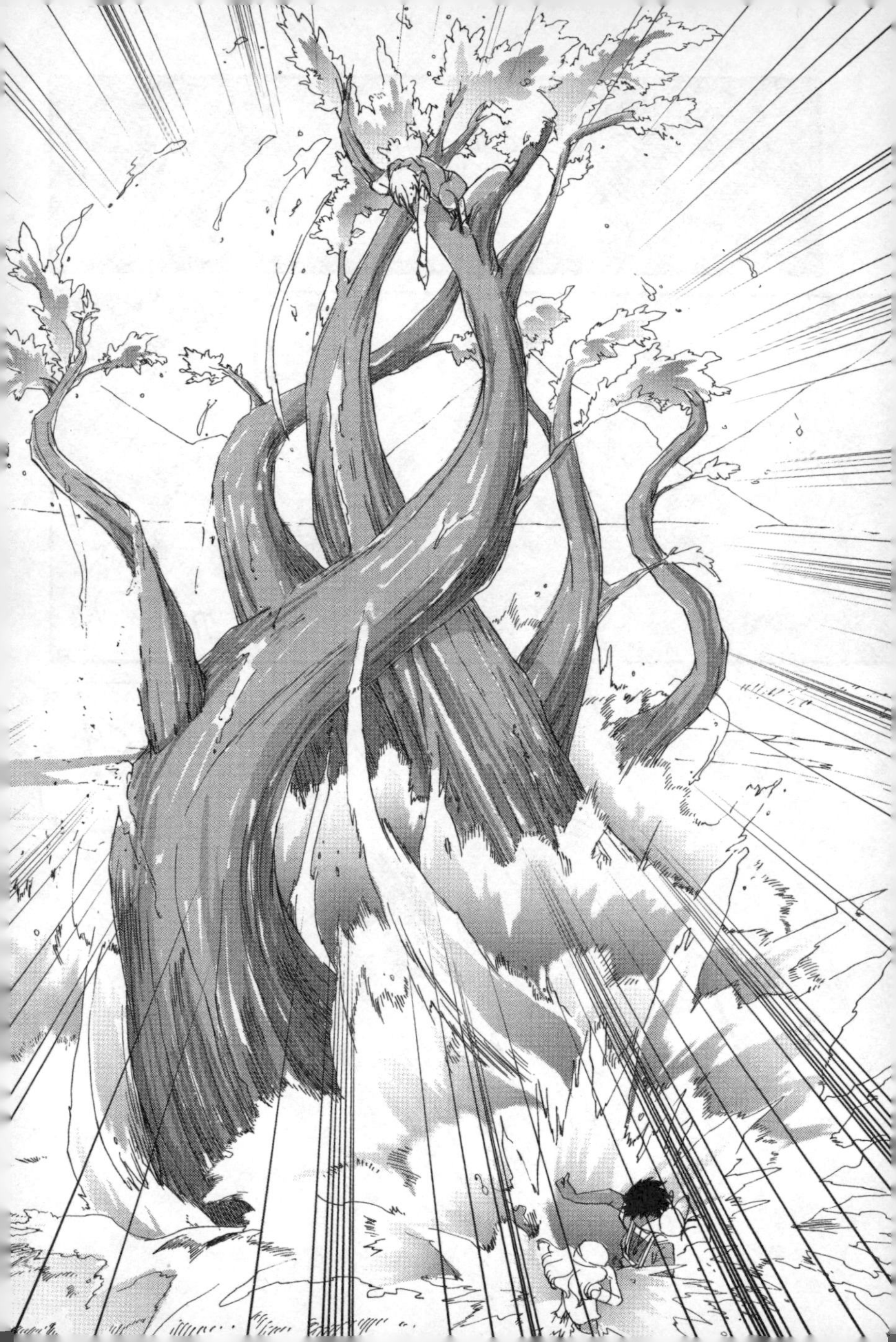

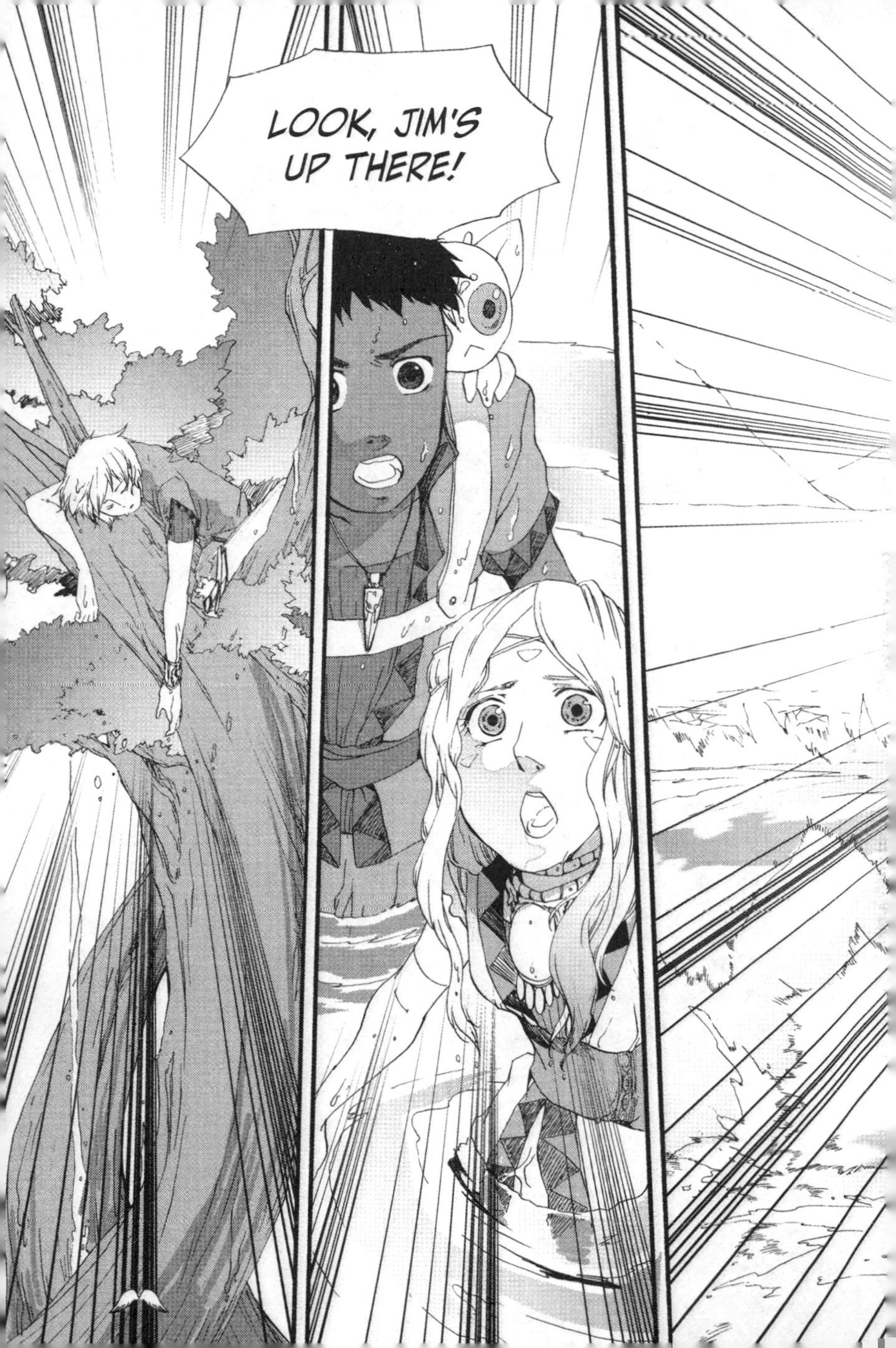
LOOK, JIM'S UP THERE!

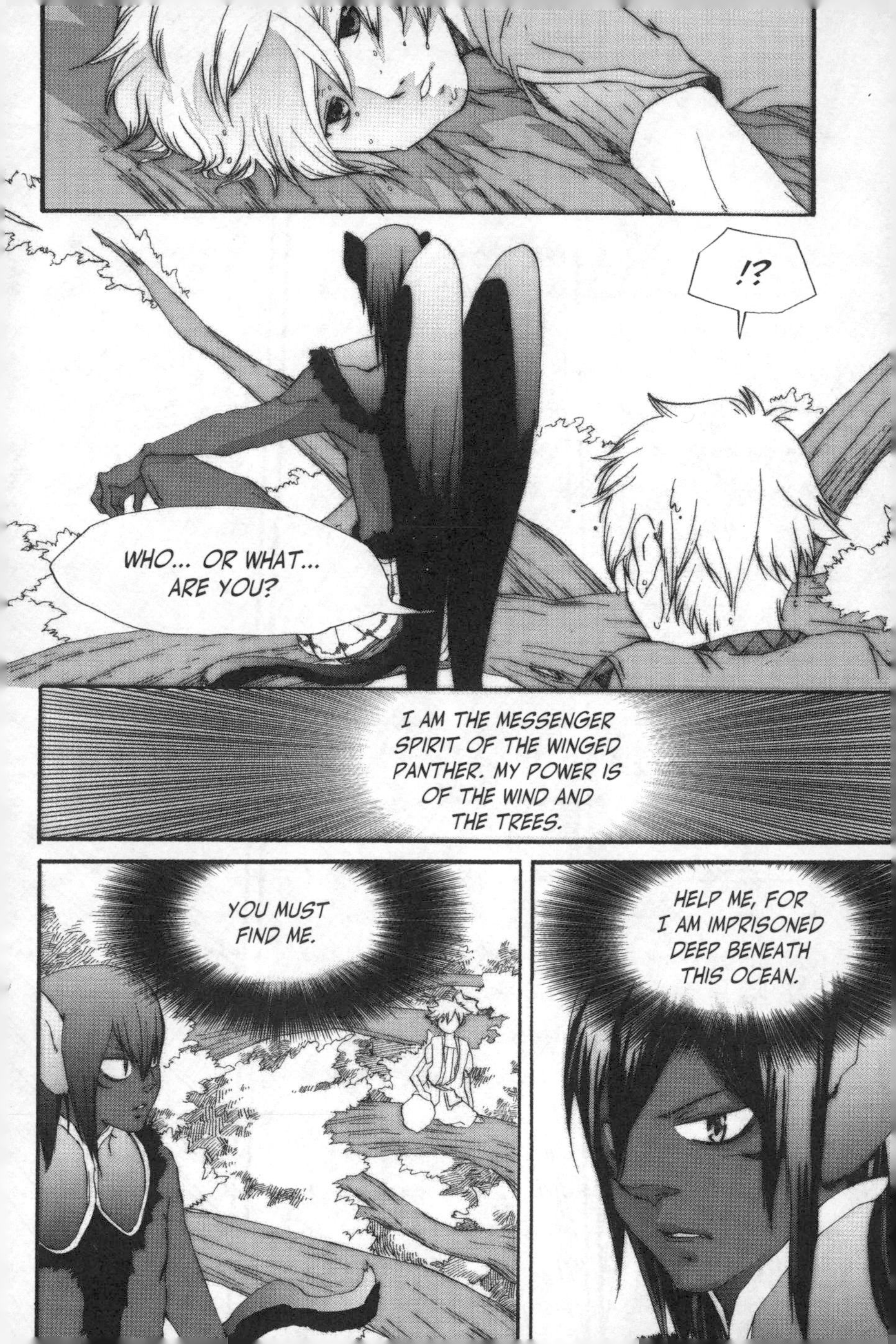
!?
WHO... OR WHAT... ARE YOU?
I AM THE MESSENGER SPIRIT OF THE WINGED PANTHER. MY POWER IS OF THE WIND AND THE TREES.
HELP ME, FOR I AM IMPRISONED DEEP BENEATH THIS OCEAN.
YOU MUST FIND ME.

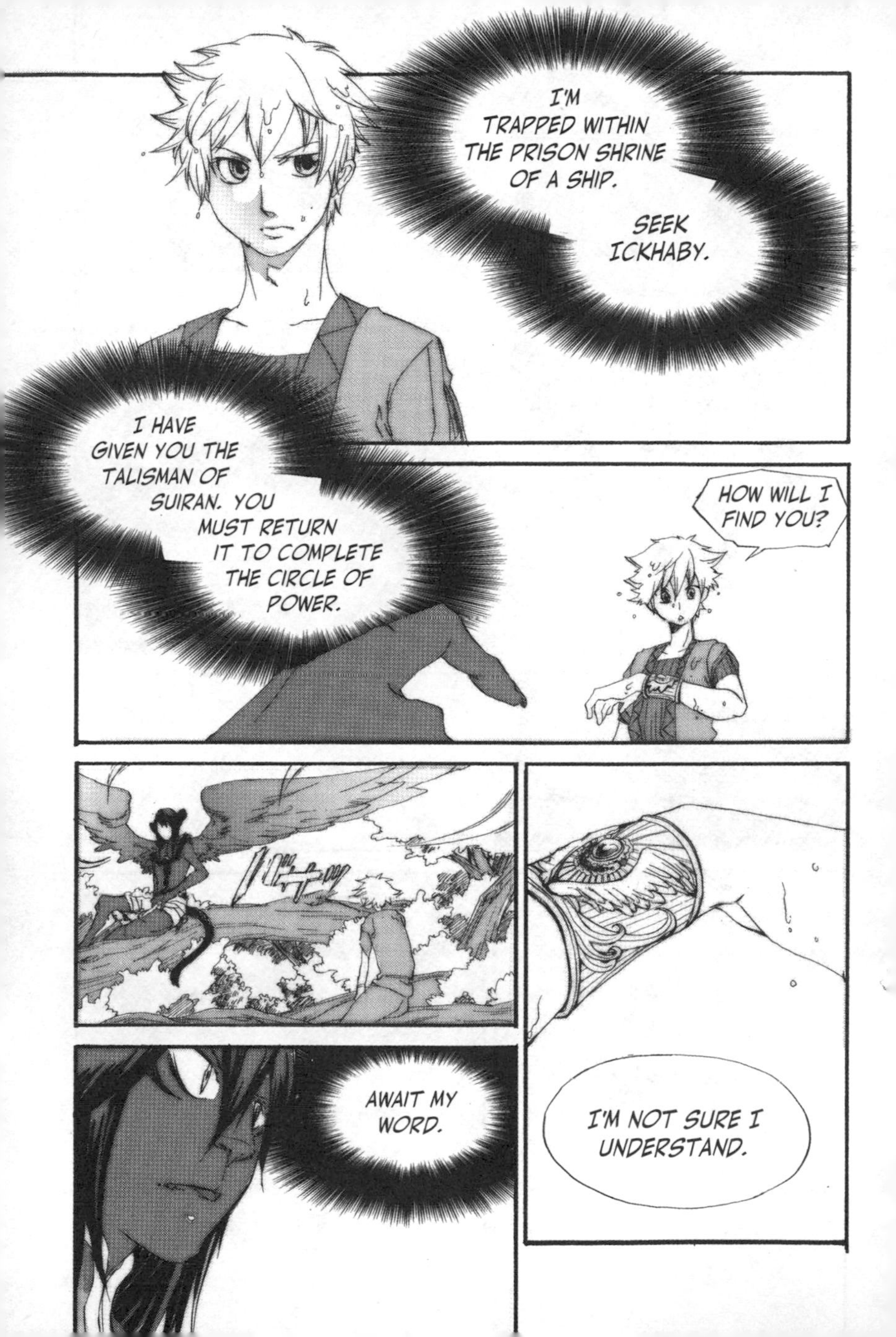
I'M TRAPPED WITHIN THE PRISON SHRINE OF A SHIP.
SEEK ICKHABY.
I HAVE GIVEN YOU THE TALISMAN OF SUIRAN. YOU MUST RETURN IT TO COMPLETE THE CIRCLE OF POWER.
HOW WILL I FIND YOU?
I'M NOT SURE I UNDERSTAND.
AWAIT MY WORD.

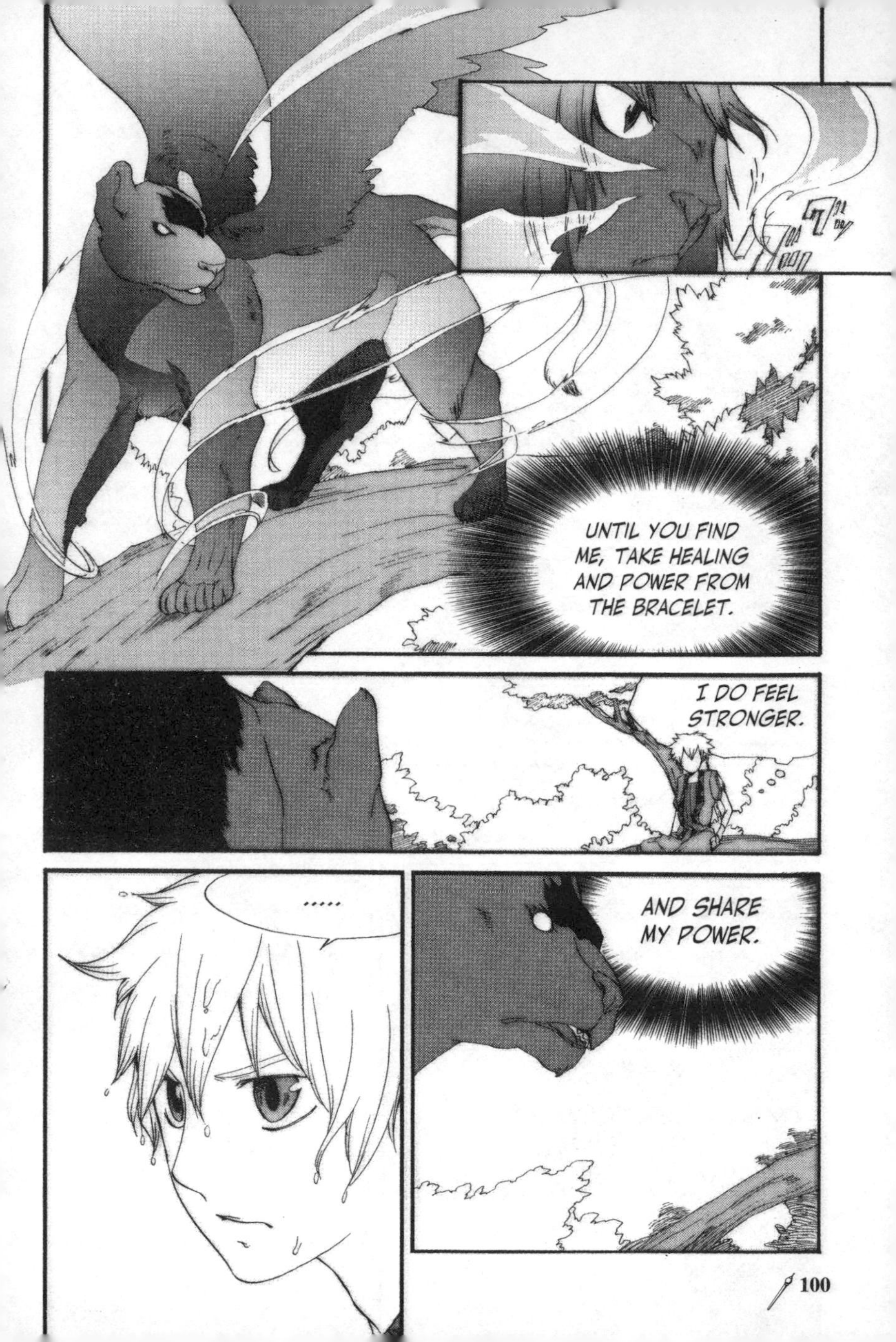
UNTIL YOU FIND ME, TAKE HEALING AND POWER FROM THE BRACELET.
I DO FEEL STRONGER.
AND SHARE MY POWER.
......

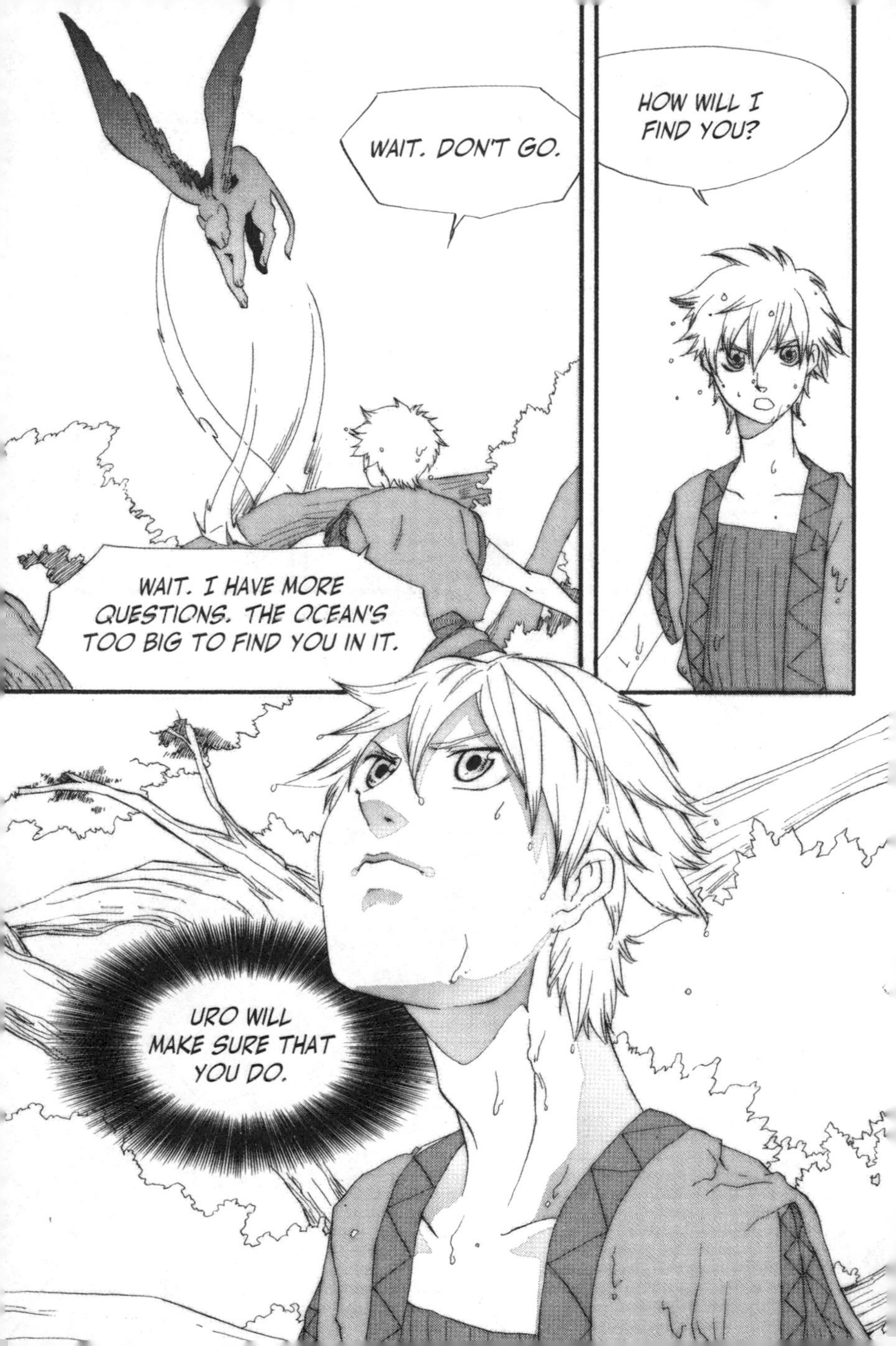
HOW WILL I FIND YOU?
WAIT. DON'T GO.
WAIT. I HAVE MORE QUESTIONS. THE OCEAN'S TOO BIG TO FIND YOU IN IT.
URO WILL MAKE SURE THAT YOU DO.

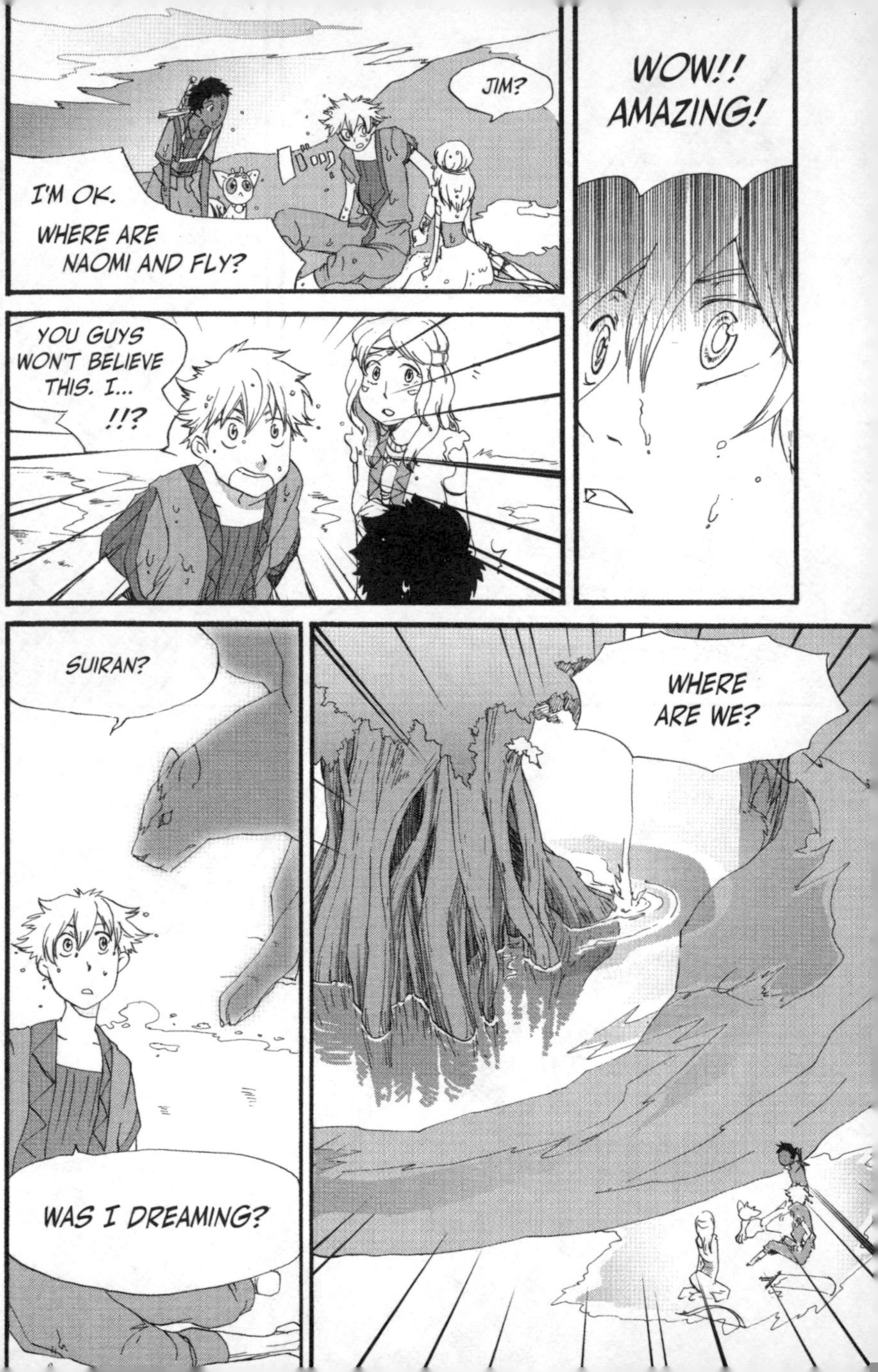
WOW!! AMAZING!
JIM?
I'M OK.
WHERE ARE NAOMI AND FLY?
YOU GUYS WON'T BELIEVE THIS. I...
!!?
WHERE ARE WE?
SUIRAN?
WAS I DREAMING?

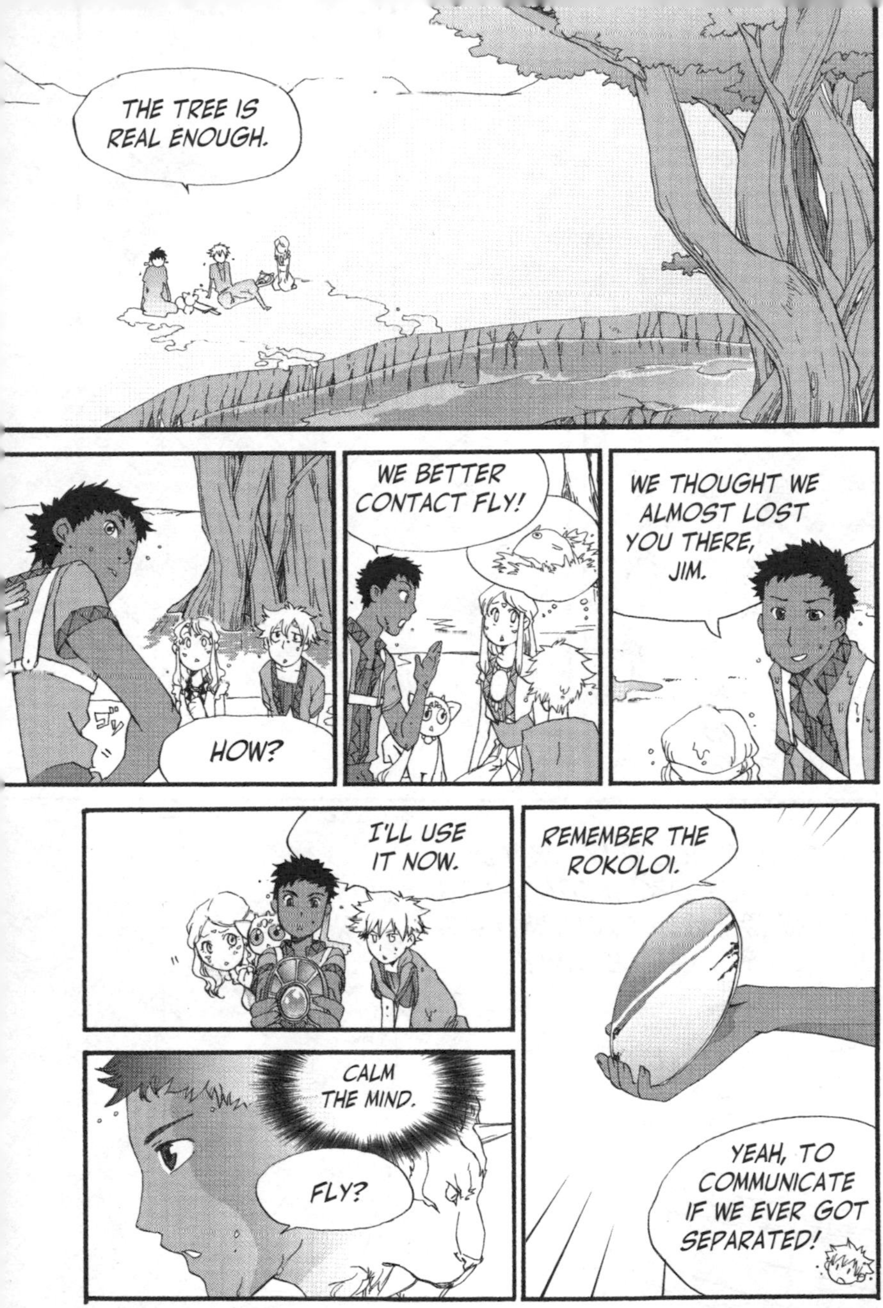
THE TREE IS REAL ENOUGH.
WE THOUGHT WE ALMOST LOST YOU THERE, JIM.
WE BETTER CONTACT FLY!
HOW?
REMEMBER THE ROKOLOI.
YEAH, TO COMMUNICATE IF WE EVER GOT SEPARATED!
I'LL USE IT NOW.
CALM THE MIND.
FLY?

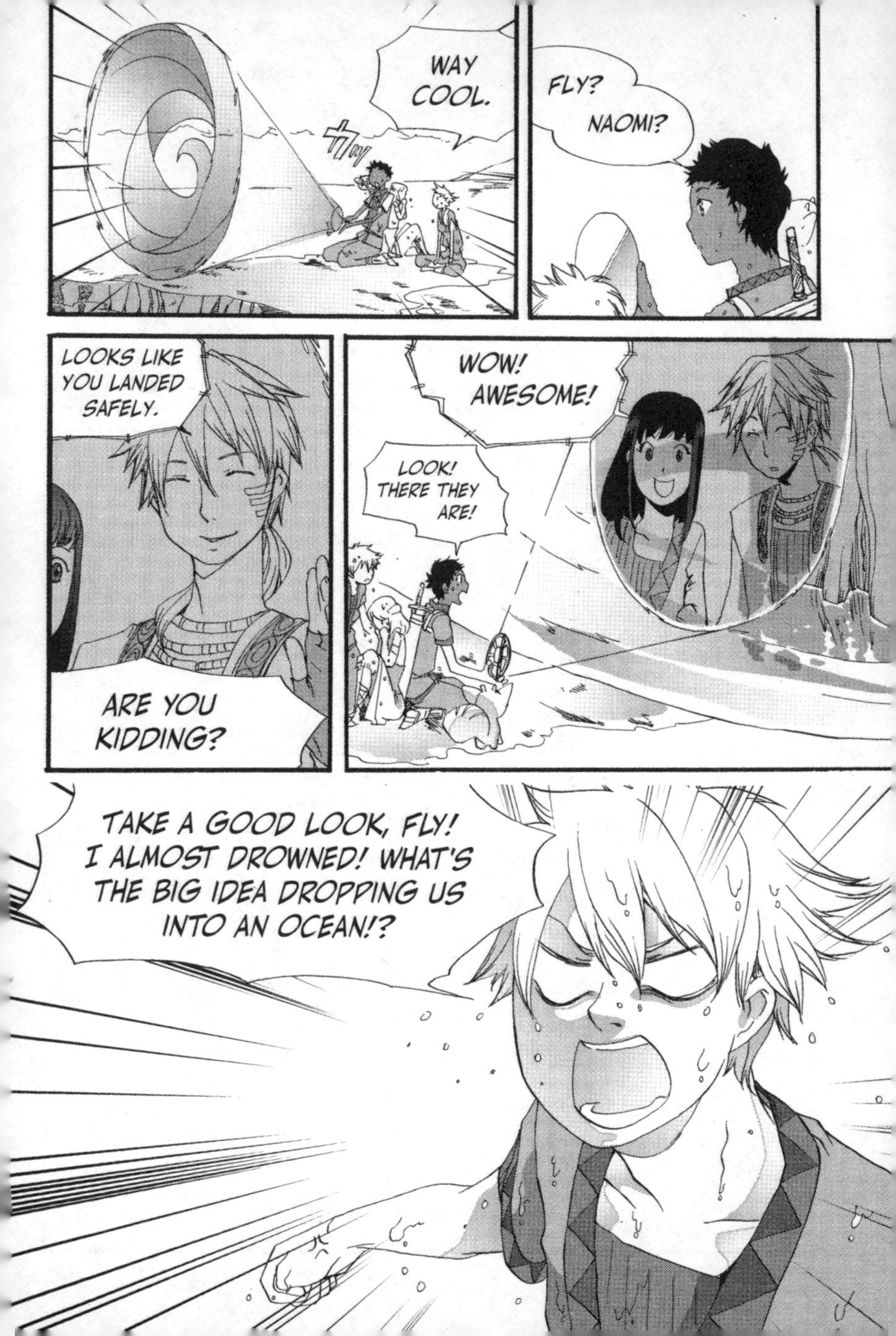
FLY?
NAOMI?
WAY COOL.
カッ
WOW! AWESOME!
LOOK! THERE THEY ARE!
LOOKS LIKE YOU LANDED SAFELY.
ARE YOU KIDDING?
TAKE A GOOD LOOK, FLY! I ALMOST DROWNED! WHAT'S THE BIG IDEA DROPPING US INTO AN OCEAN!?

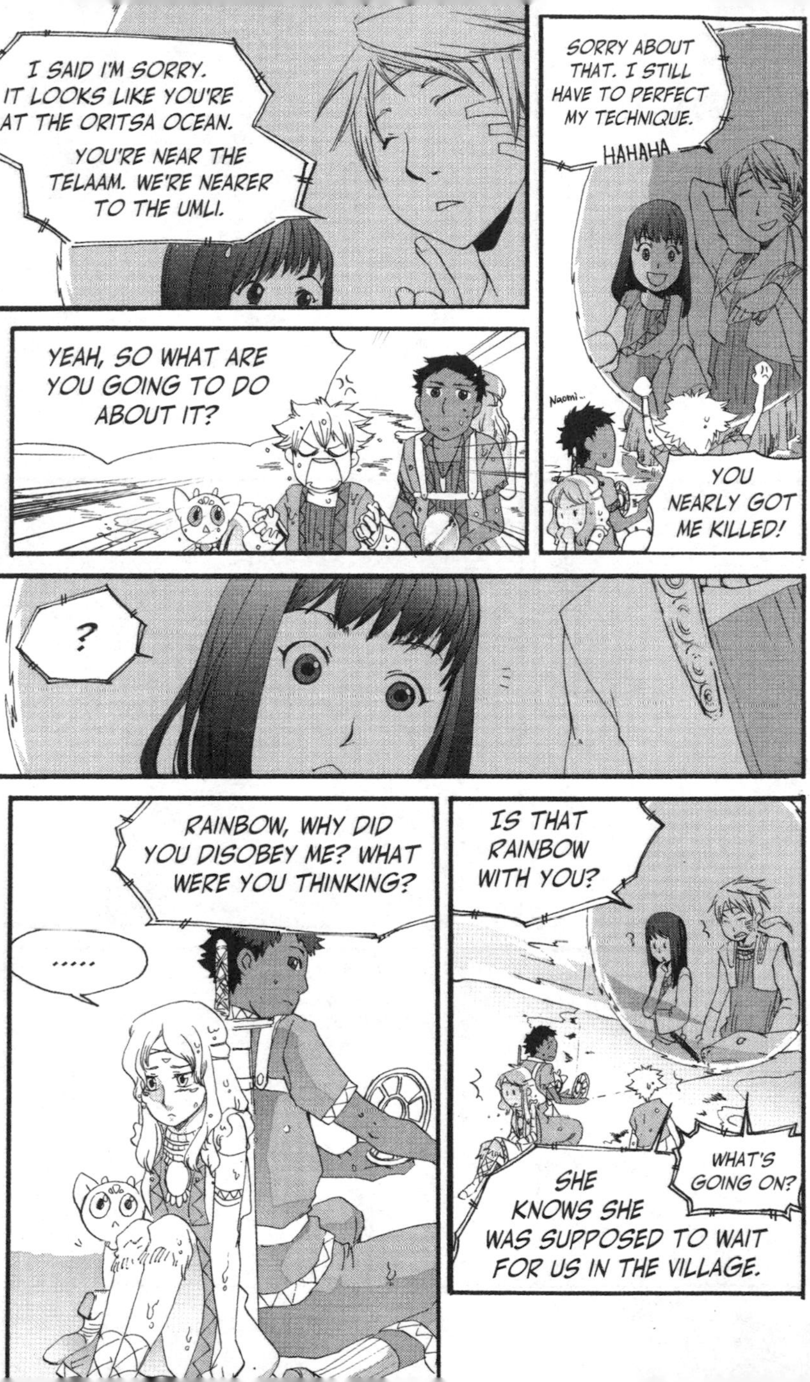
SORRY ABOUT THAT. I STILL HAVE TO PERFECT MY TECHNIQUE.
HAHAHA
Naomi..
YOU NEARLY GOT ME KILLED!
I SAID I'M SORRY. IT LOOKS LIKE YOU'RE AT THE ORITSA OCEAN.
YOU'RE NEAR THE TELAAM. WE'RE NEARER TO THE UMLI.
YEAH, SO WHAT ARE YOU GOING TO DO ABOUT IT?
?
IS THAT RAINBOW WITH YOU?
WHAT'S GOING ON?
SHE KNOWS SHE WAS SUPPOSED TO WAIT FOR US IN THE VILLAGE.
RAINBOW, WHY DID YOU DISOBEY ME? WHAT WERE YOU THINKING?
.....

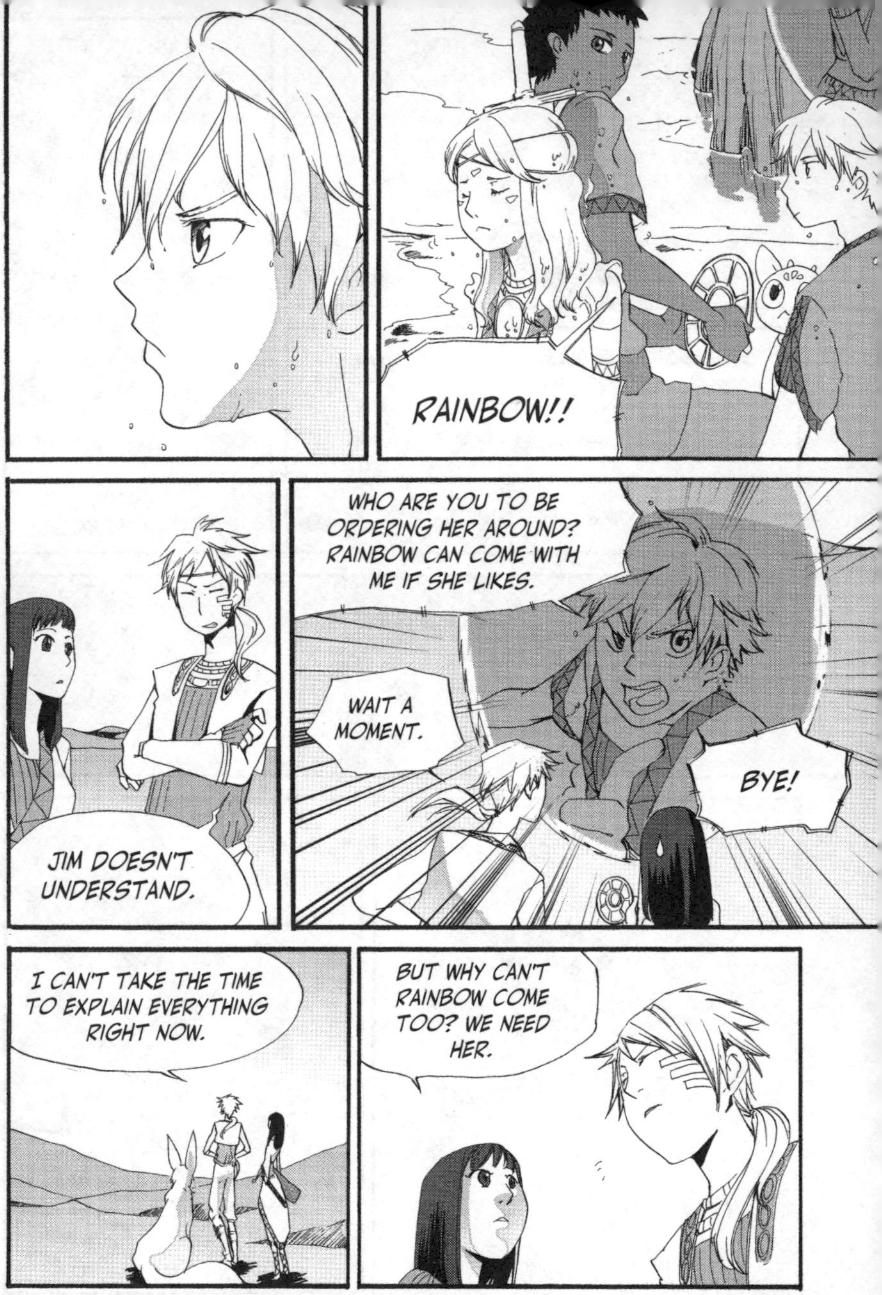
RAINBOW!!
WHO ARE YOU TO BE ORDERING HER AROUND? RAINBOW CAN COME WITH ME IF SHE LIKES.
BYE!
WAIT A MOMENT.
JIM DOESN'T UNDERSTAND.
BUT WHY CAN'T RAINBOW COME TOO? WE NEED HER.
I CAN'T TAKE THE TIME TO EXPLAIN EVERYTHING RIGHT NOW.

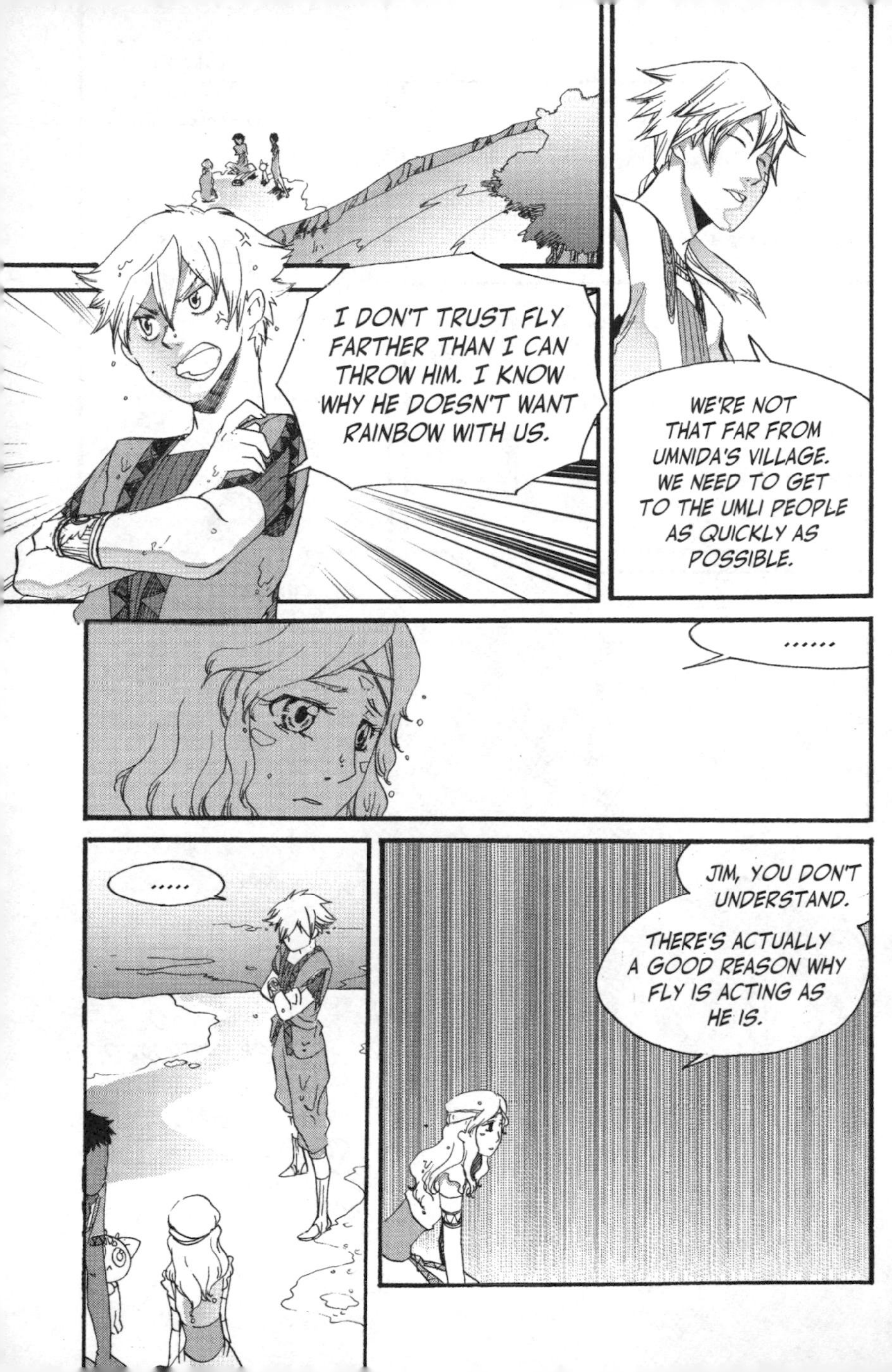
WE'RE NOT THAT FAR FROM UMNIDA'S VILLAGE. WE NEED TO GET TO THE UMLI PEOPLE AS QUICKLY AS POSSIBLE.
I DON'T TRUST FLY FARTHER THAN I CAN THROW HIM. I KNOW WHY HE DOESN'T WANT RAINBOW WITH US.
......
JIM, YOU DON'T UNDERSTAND.
THERE'S ACTUALLY A GOOD REASON WHY FLY IS ACTING AS HE IS.
.....

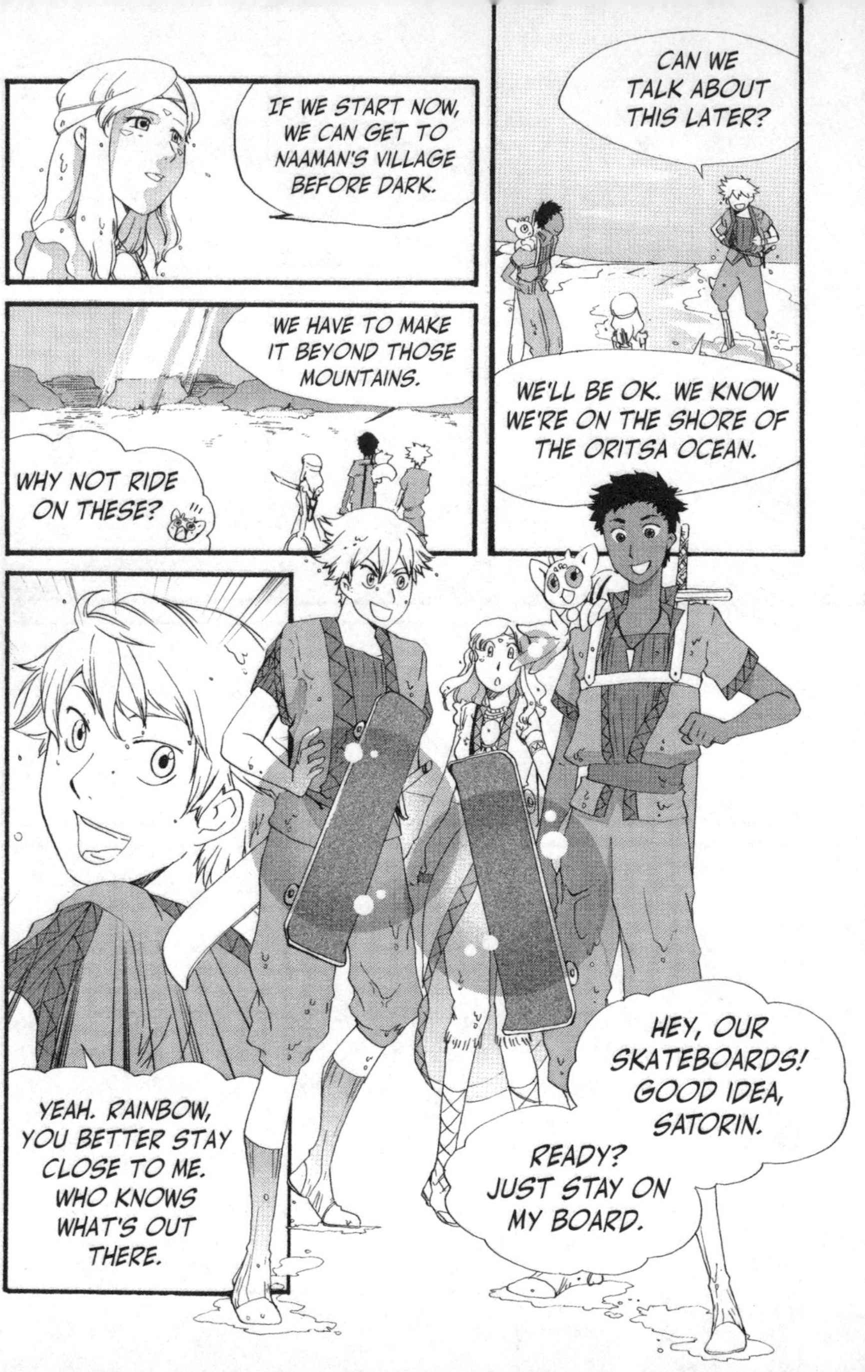
CAN WE TALK ABOUT THIS LATER?
WE'LL BE OK. WE KNOW WE'RE ON THE SHORE OF THE ORITSA OCEAN.
IF WE START NOW, WE CAN GET TO NAAMAN'S VILLAGE BEFORE DARK.
WE HAVE TO MAKE IT BEYOND THOSE MOUNTAINS.
WHY NOT RIDE ON THESE?
HEY, OUR SKATEBOARDS! GOOD IDEA, SATORIN.
READY? JUST STAY ON MY BOARD.
YEAH. RAINBOW, YOU BETTER STAY CLOSE TO ME. WHO KNOWS WHAT'S OUT THERE.

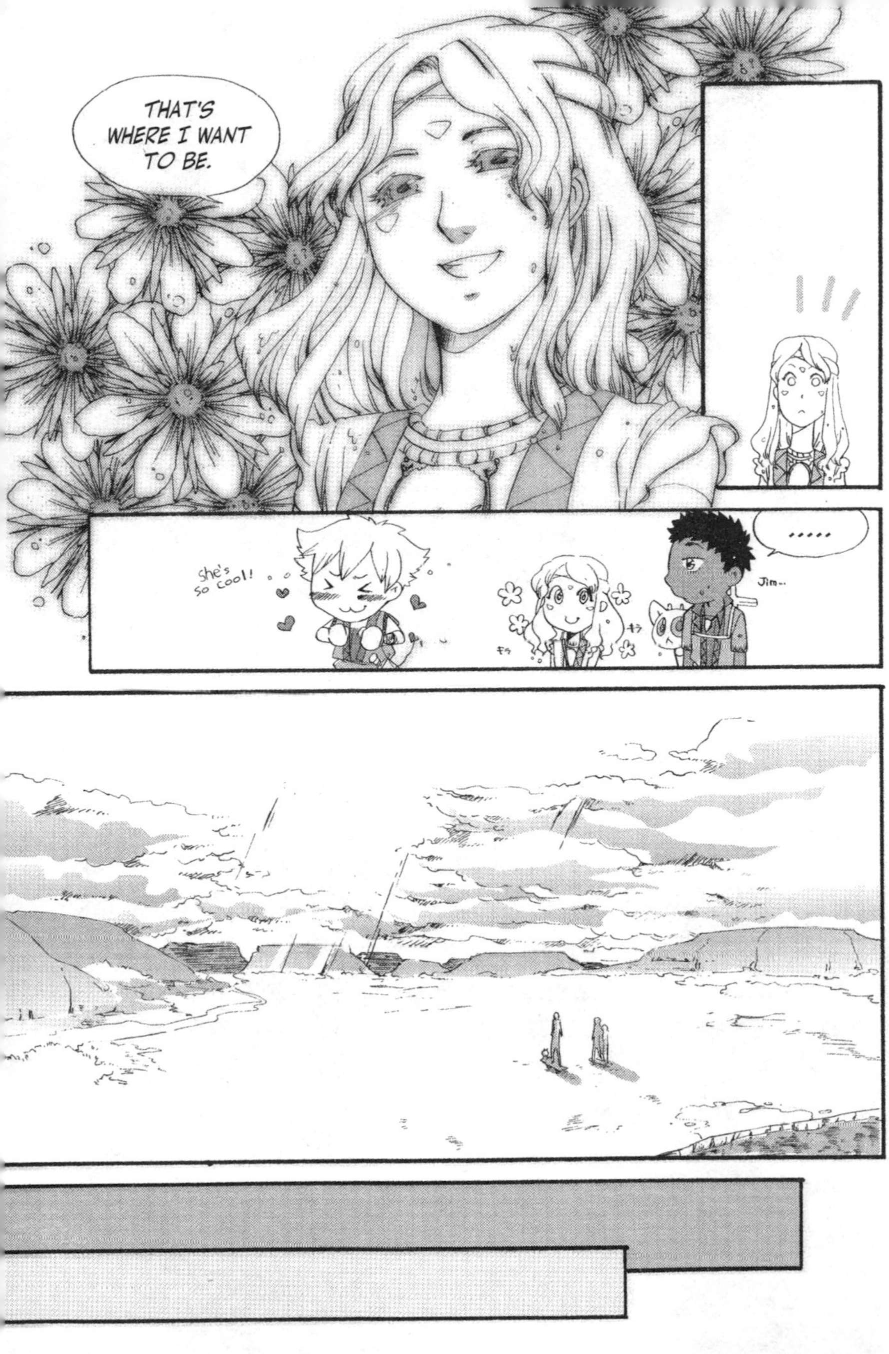
THAT'S WHERE I WANT TO BE.
......
Jim...
she's so cool!

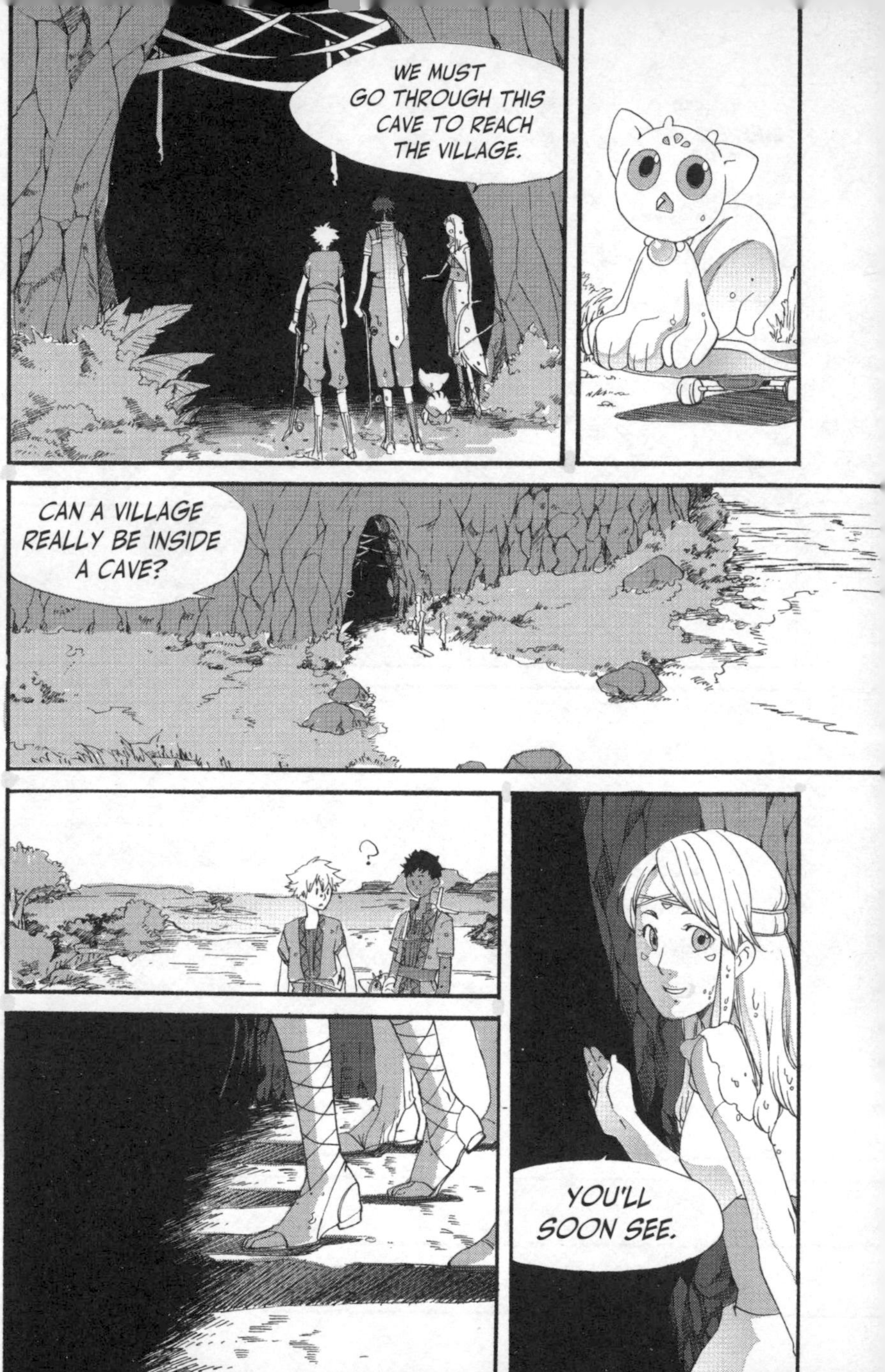
WE MUST GO THROUGH THIS CAVE TO REACH THE VILLAGE.
CAN A VILLAGE REALLY BE INSIDE A CAVE?
YOU'LL SOON SEE.
?

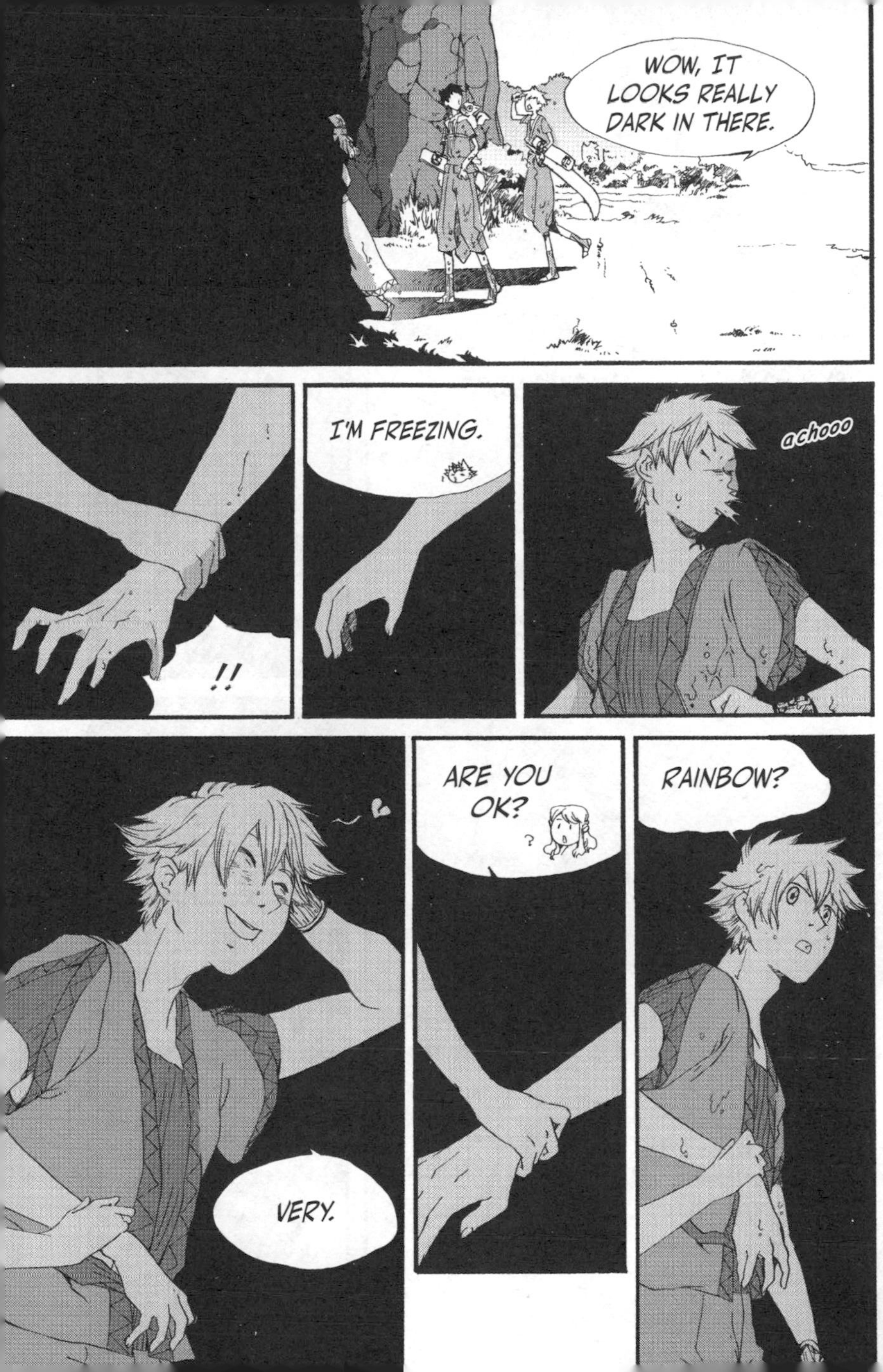
WOW, IT LOOKS REALLY DARK IN THERE.
!!
I'M FREEZING.
achooo
ARE YOU OK?
?
RAINBOW?
VERY.

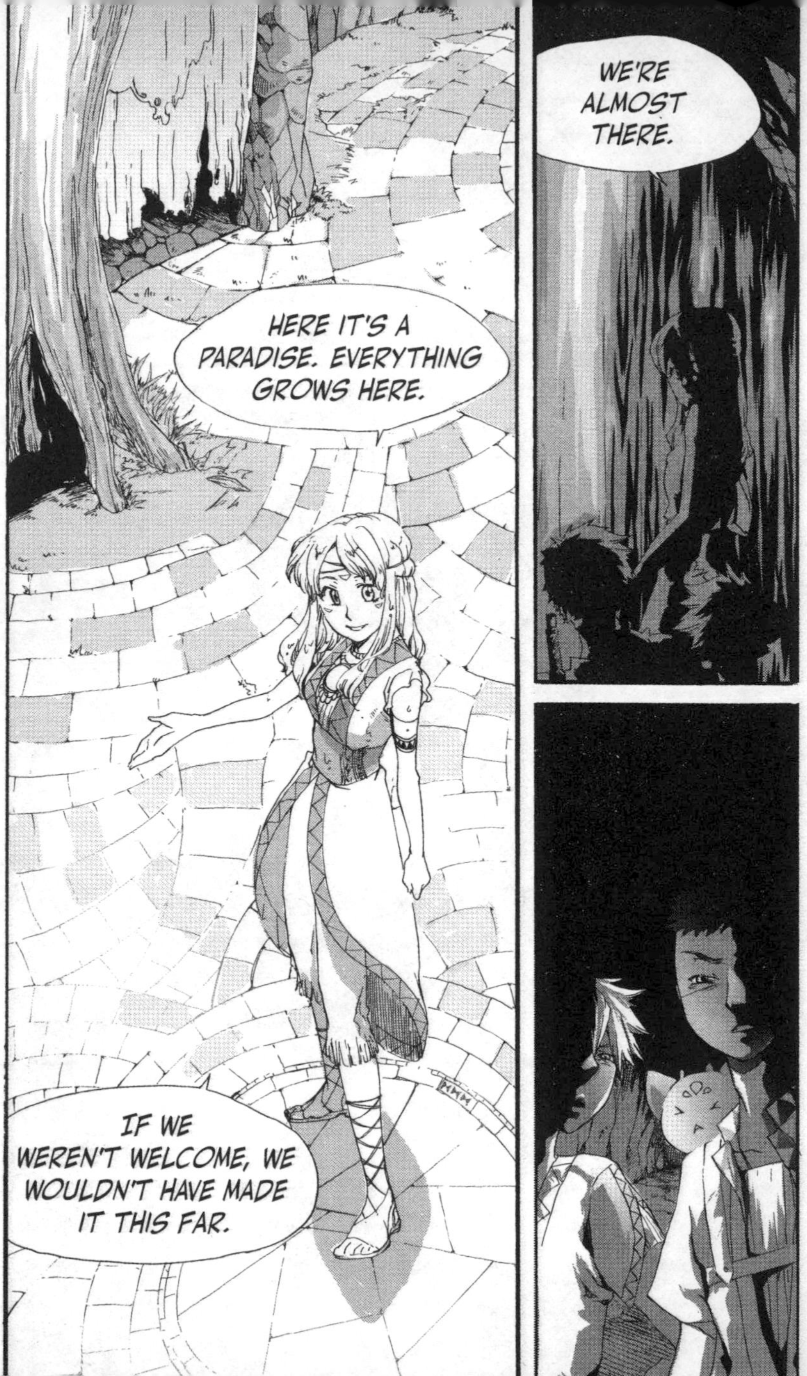
HERE IT'S A PARADISE. EVERYTHING GROWS HERE.
IF WE WEREN'T WELCOME, WE WOULDN'T HAVE MADE IT THIS FAR.
WE'RE ALMOST THERE.

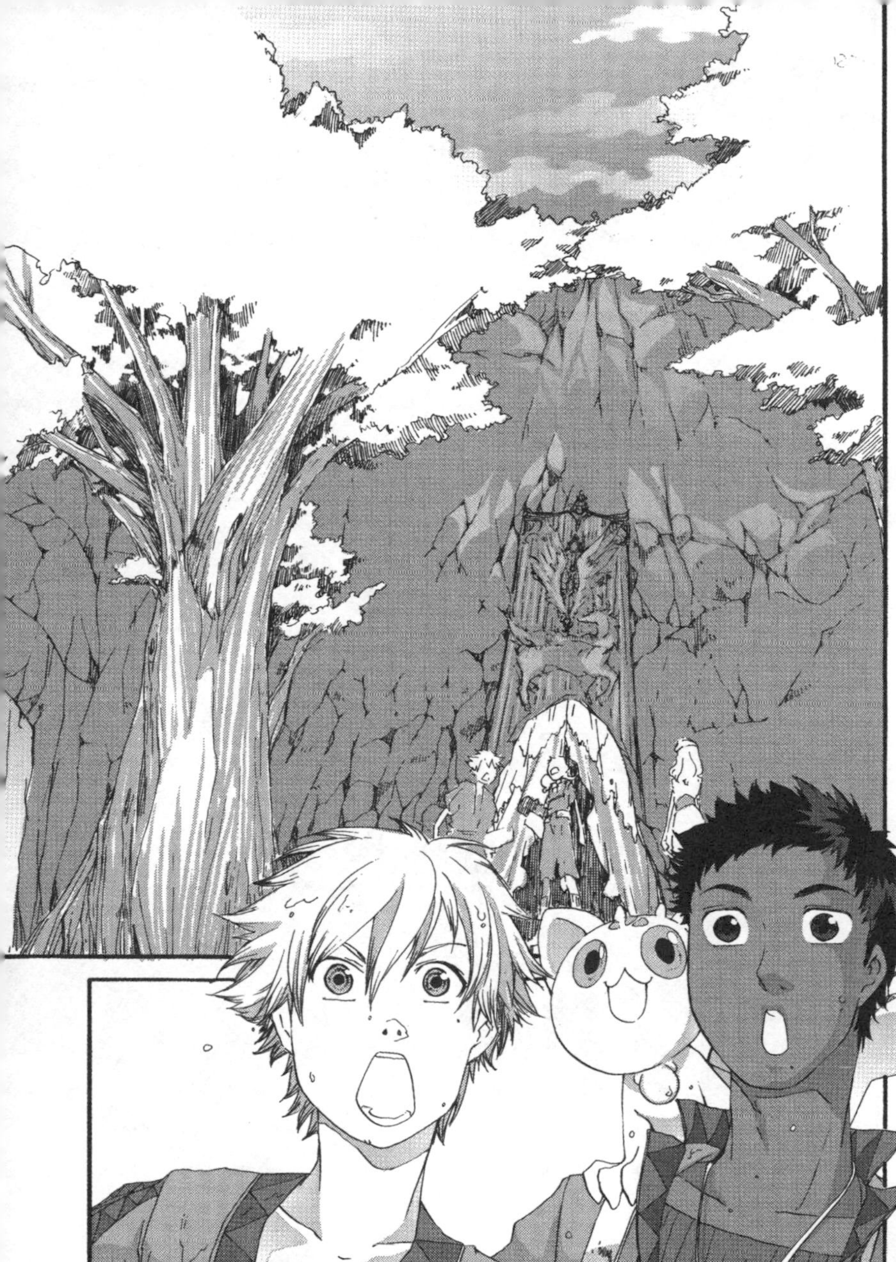

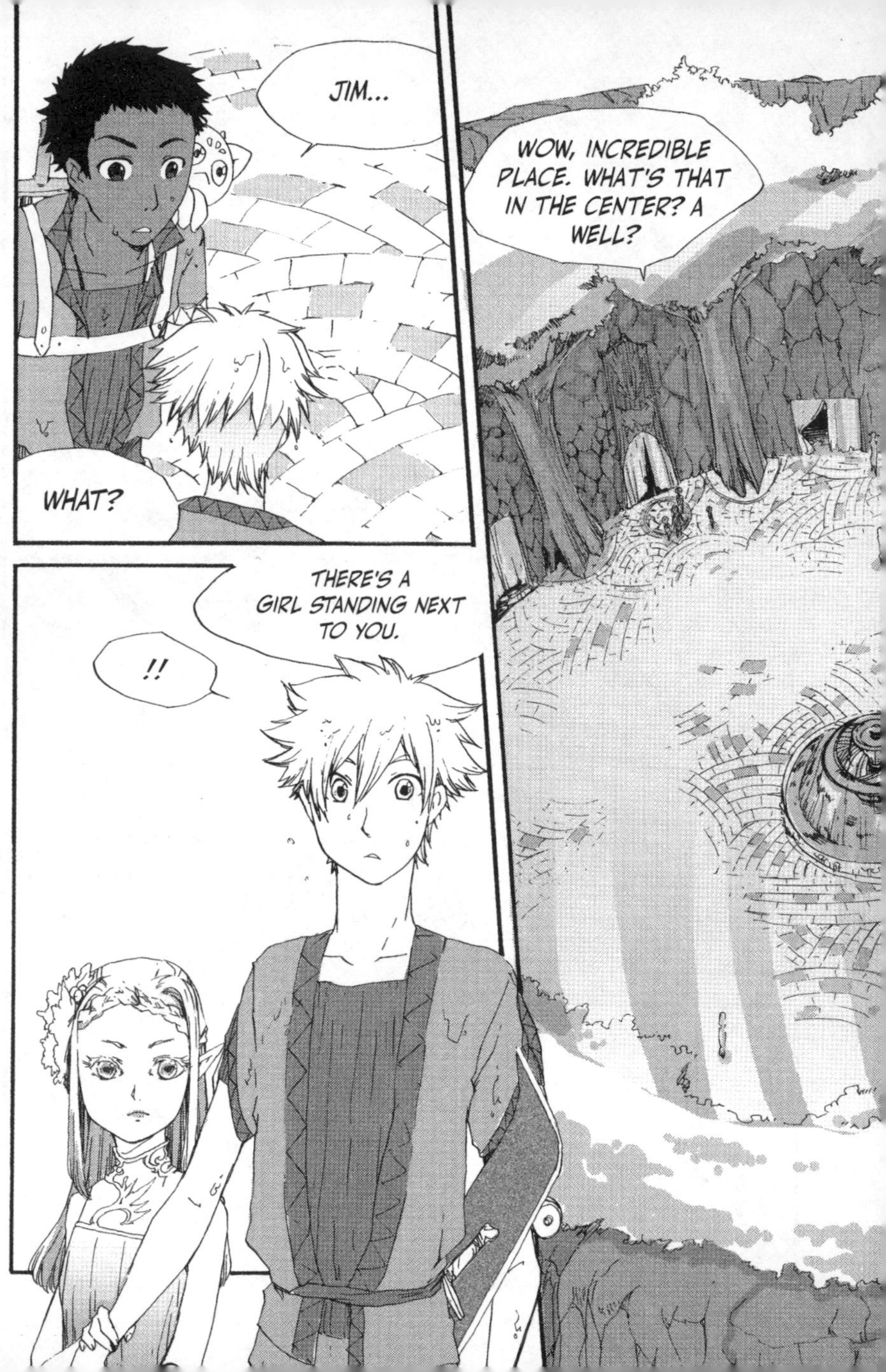
JIM...
WHAT?
WOW, INCREDIBLE PLACE. WHAT'S THAT IN THE CENTER? A WELL?
THERE'S A GIRL STANDING NEXT TO YOU.
!!

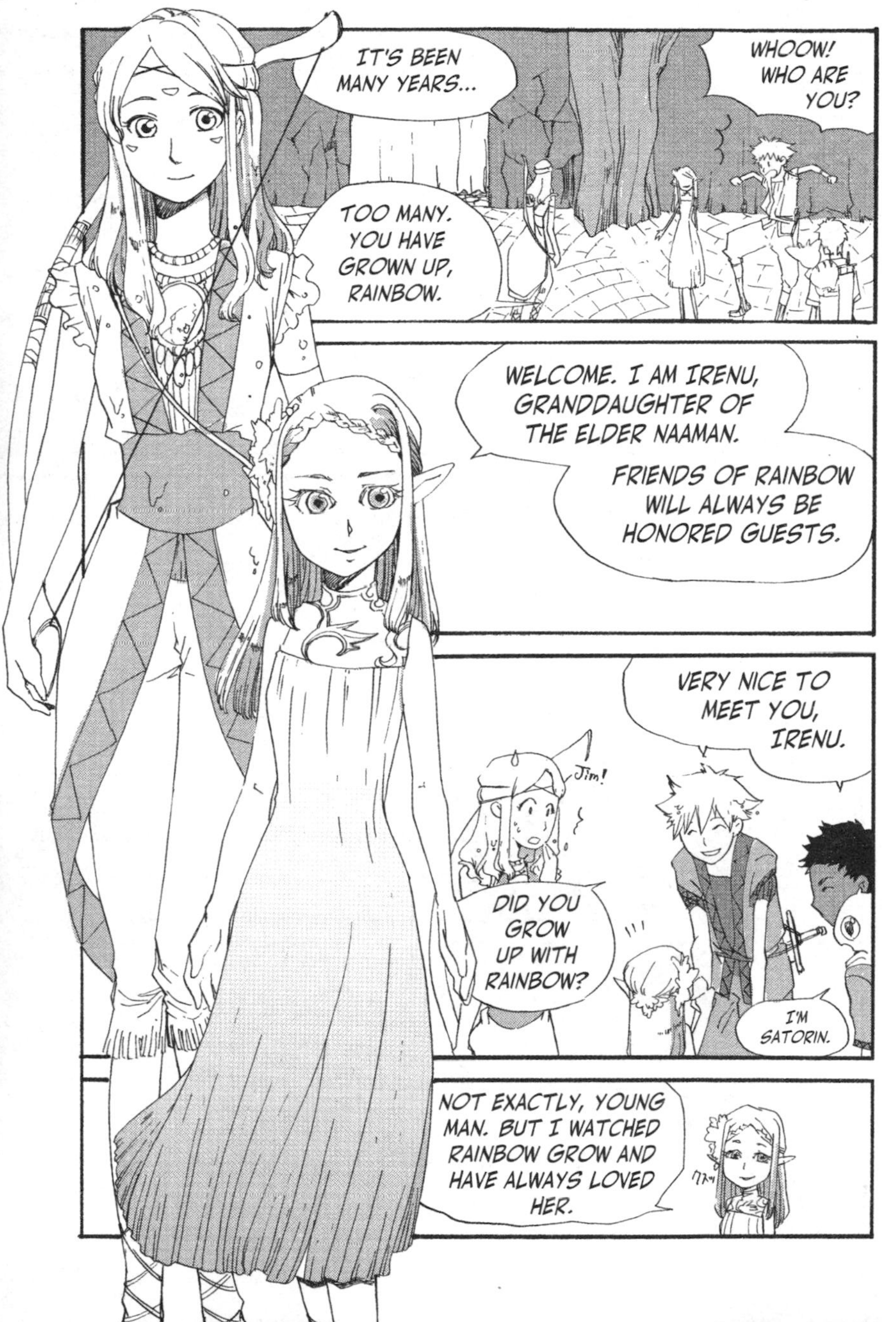
WHOOW! WHO ARE YOU?
IT'S BEEN MANY YEARS...
TOO MANY. YOU HAVE GROWN UP, RAINBOW.
WELCOME. I AM IRENU, GRANDDAUGHTER OF THE ELDER NAAMAN.
FRIENDS OF RAINBOW WILL ALWAYS BE HONORED GUESTS.
VERY NICE TO MEET YOU, IRENU.
Jim!
I'M SATORIN.
DID YOU GROW UP WITH RAINBOW?
NOT EXACTLY, YOUNG MAN. BUT I WATCHED RAINBOW GROW AND HAVE ALWAYS LOVED HER.
クスッ

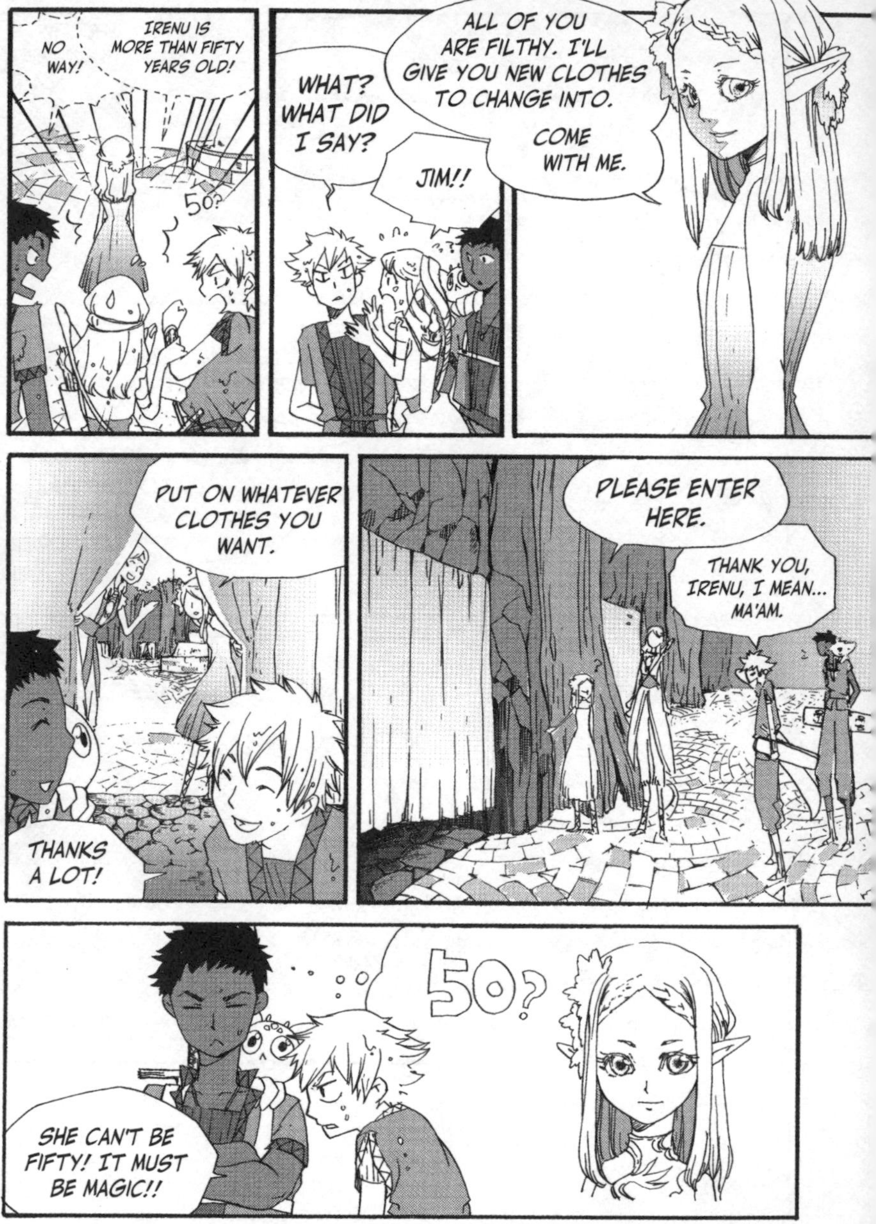

NO WAY!
IRENU IS MORE THAN FIFTY YEARS OLD!
50?
WHAT? WHAT DID I SAY?
JIM!!
ALL OF YOU ARE FILTHY. I'LL GIVE YOU NEW CLOTHES TO CHANGE INTO.
COME WITH ME.
PUT ON WHATEVER CLOTHES YOU WANT.
THANKS A LOT!
PLEASE ENTER HERE.
THANK YOU, IRENU, I MEAN... MA'AM.
50?
SHE CAN'T BE FIFTY! IT MUST BE MAGIC!!

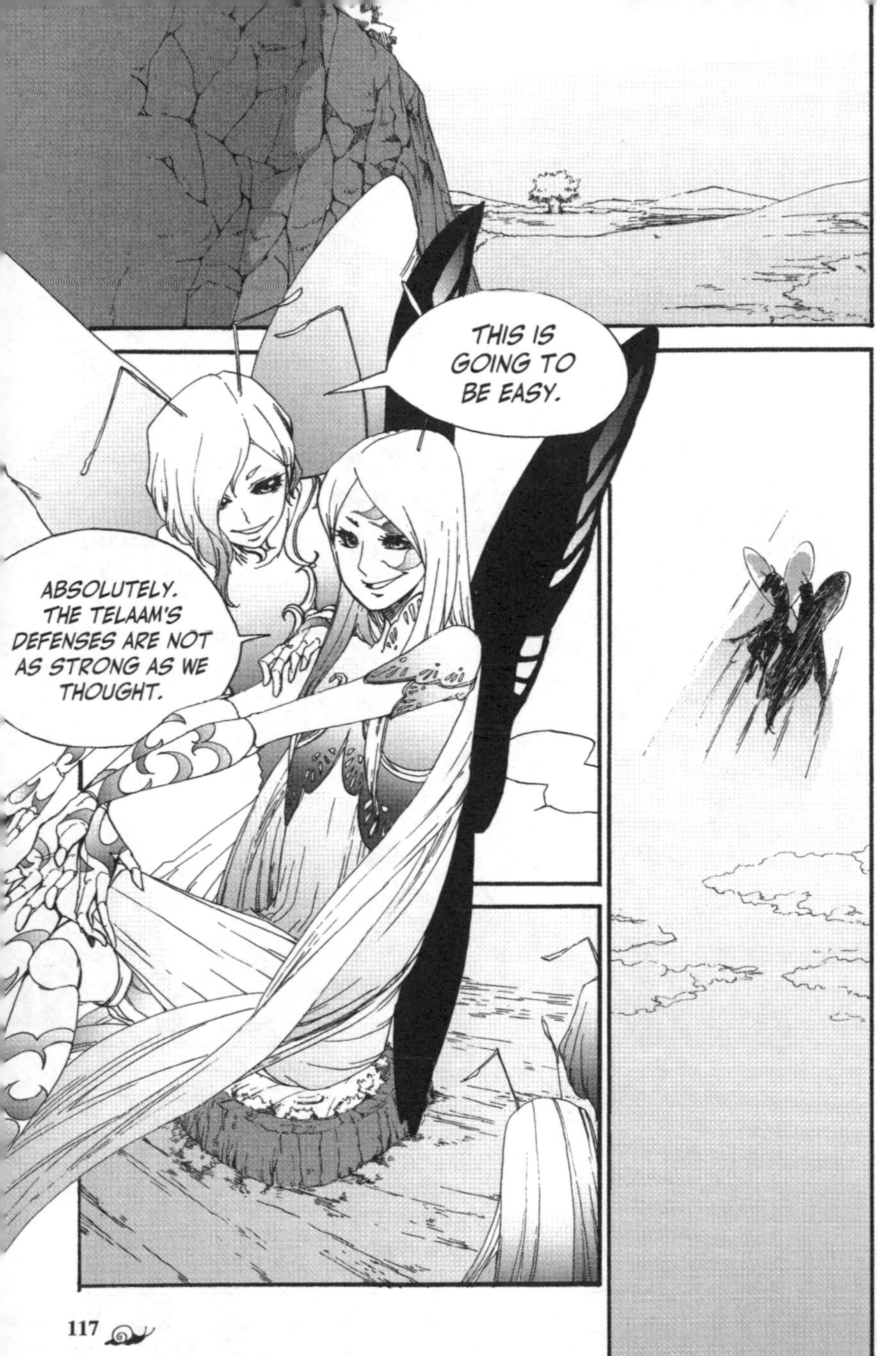
THIS IS GOING TO BE EASY.
ABSOLUTELY. THE TELAAM'S DEFENSES ARE NOT AS STRONG AS WE THOUGHT.

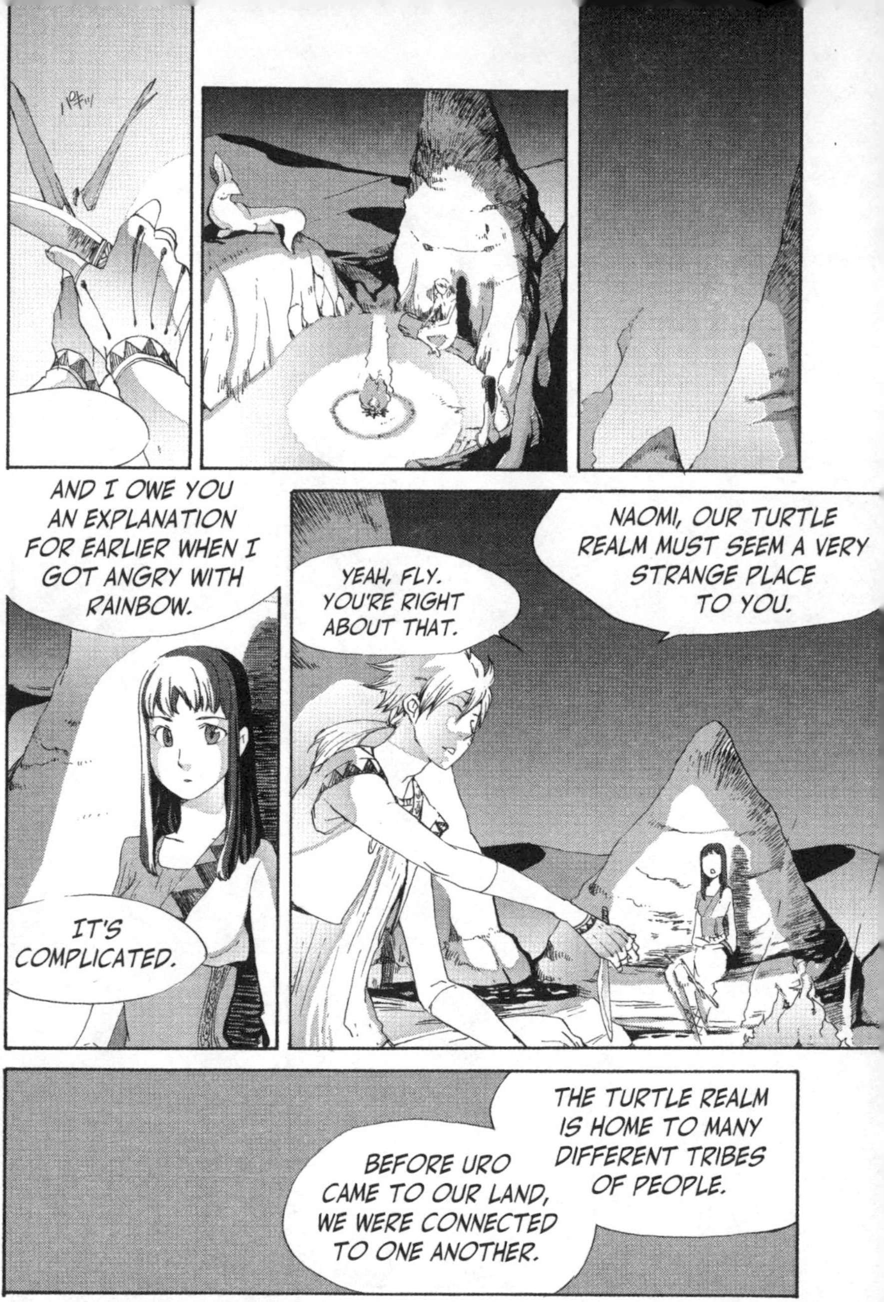
NAOMI, OUR TURTLE REALM MUST SEEM A VERY STRANGE PLACE TO YOU.
YEAH, FLY. YOU'RE RIGHT ABOUT THAT.
AND I OWE YOU AN EXPLANATION FOR EARLIER WHEN I GOT ANGRY WITH RAINBOW.
IT'S COMPLICATED.
THE TURTLE REALM IS HOME TO MANY DIFFERENT TRIBES OF PEOPLE.
BEFORE URO CAME TO OUR LAND, WE WERE CONNECTED TO ONE ANOTHER.

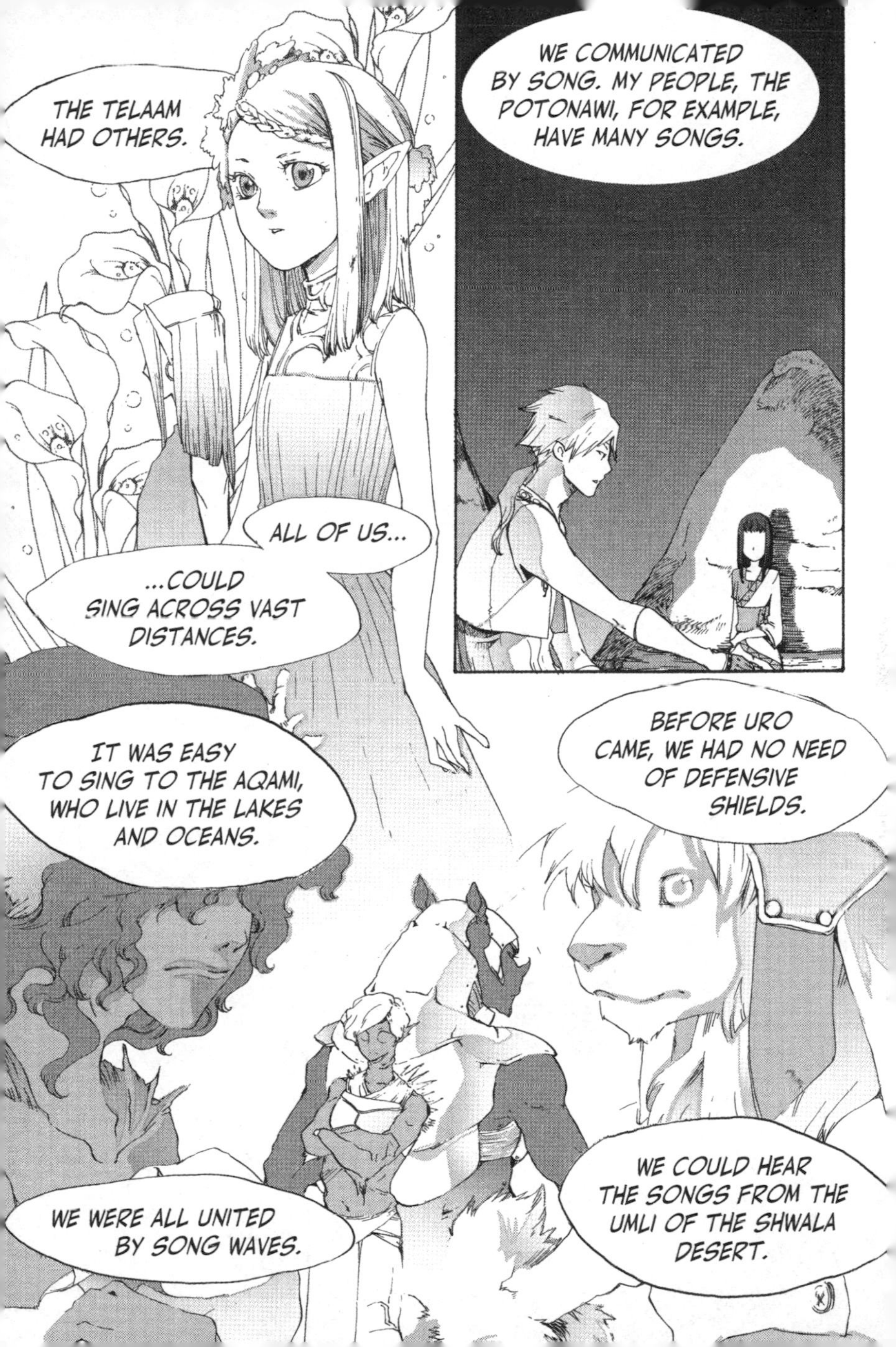
WE COMMUNICATED BY SONG. MY PEOPLE, THE POTONAWI, FOR EXAMPLE, HAVE MANY SONGS.
THE TELAAM HAD OTHERS.
ALL OF US...
...COULD SING ACROSS VAST DISTANCES.
BEFORE URO CAME, WE HAD NO NEED OF DEFENSIVE SHIELDS.
IT WAS EASY TO SING TO THE AQAMI, WHO LIVE IN THE LAKES AND OCEANS.
WE COULD HEAR THE SONGS FROM THE UMLI OF THE SHWALA DESERT.
WE WERE ALL UNITED BY SONG WAVES.

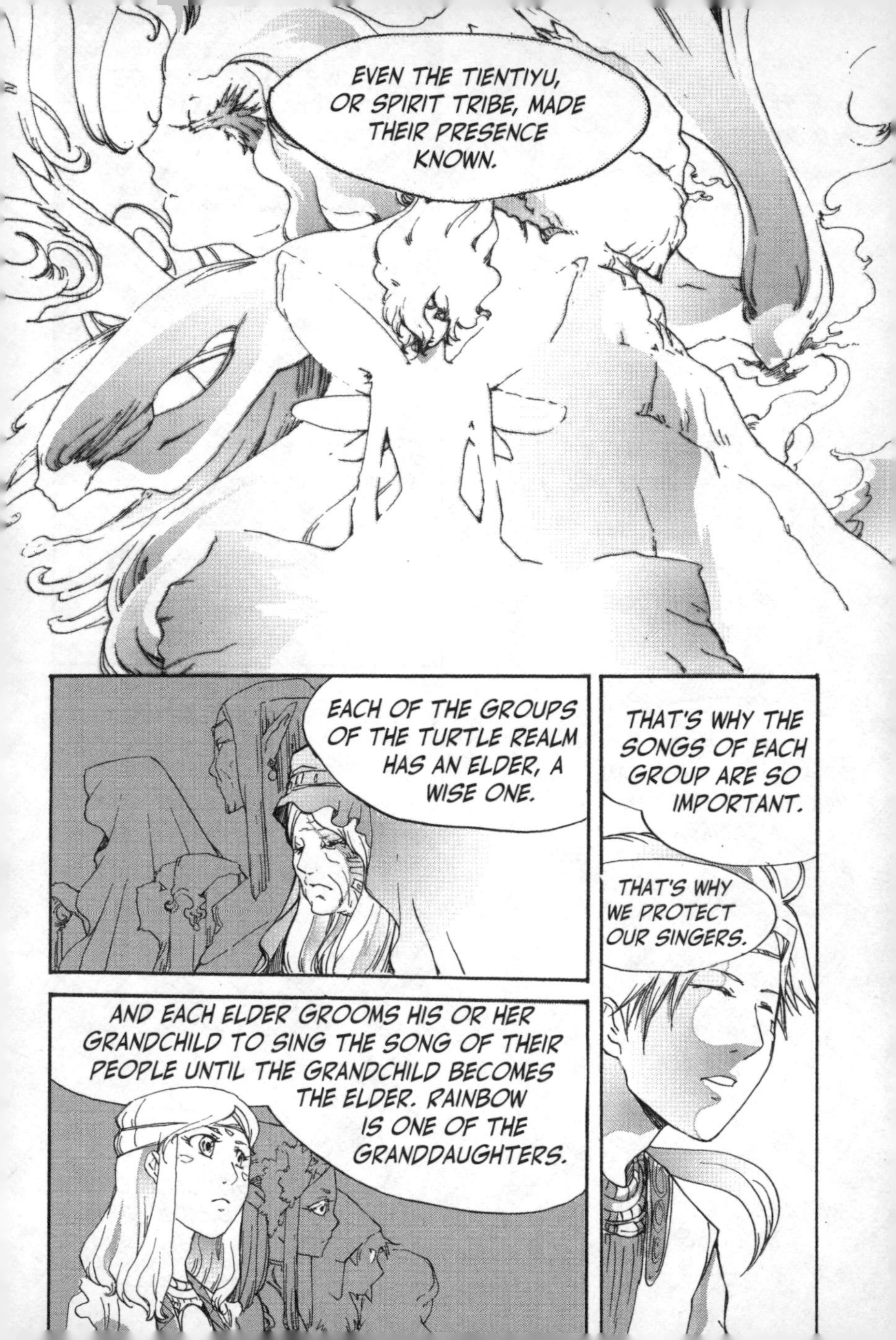
EVEN THE TIENTIYU, OR SPIRIT TRIBE, MADE THEIR PRESENCE KNOWN.
THAT'S WHY THE SONGS OF EACH GROUP ARE SO IMPORTANT.
THAT'S WHY WE PROTECT OUR SINGERS.
EACH OF THE GROUPS OF THE TURTLE REALM HAS AN ELDER, A WISE ONE.
AND EACH ELDER GROOMS HIS OR HER GRANDCHILD TO SING THE SONG OF THEIR PEOPLE UNTIL THE GRANDCHILD BECOMES THE ELDER. RAINBOW IS ONE OF THE GRANDDAUGHTERS.

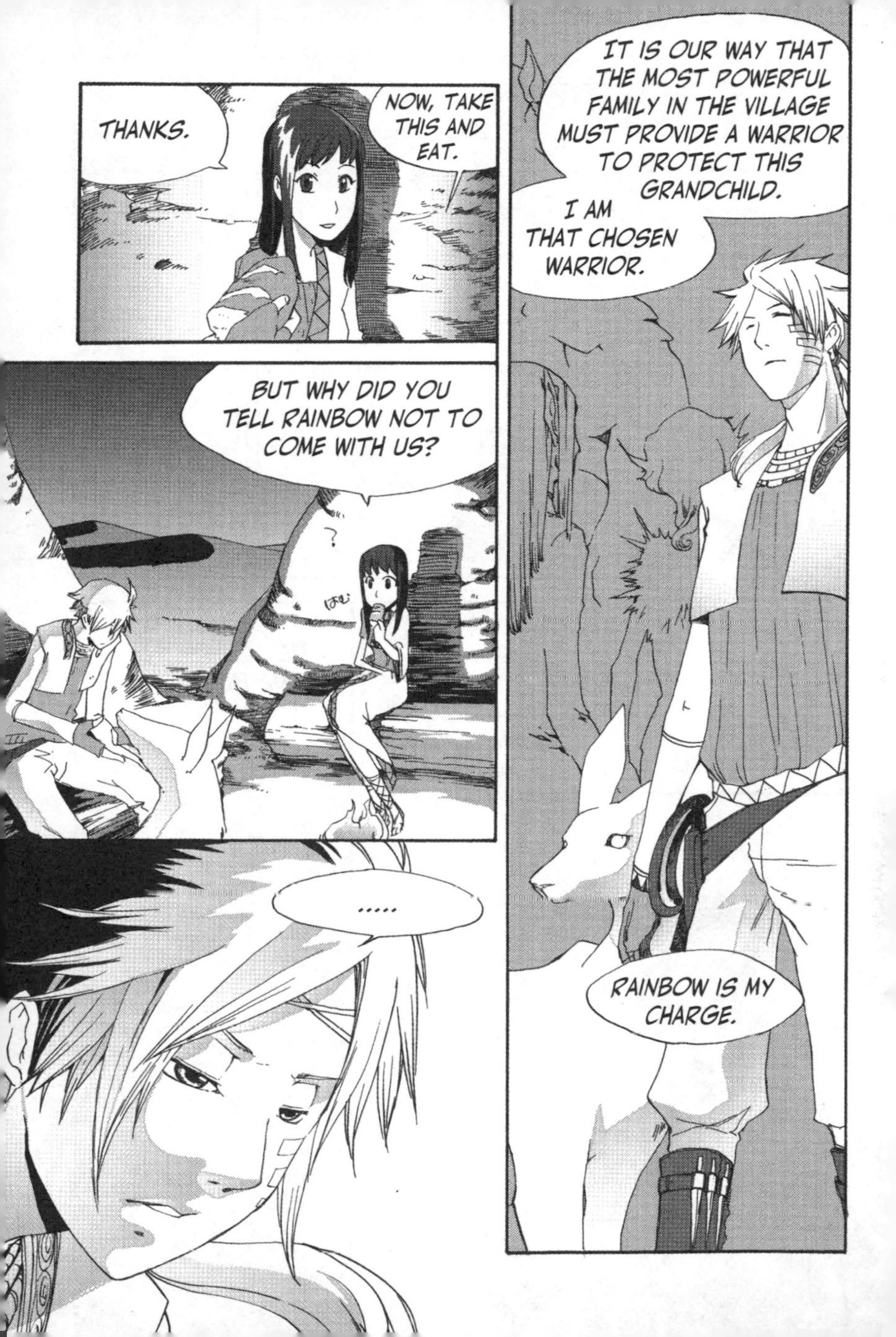
THANKS.
NOW, TAKE THIS AND EAT.
BUT WHY DID YOU TELL RAINBOW NOT TO COME WITH US?
?
.....
IT IS OUR WAY THAT THE MOST POWERFUL FAMILY IN THE VILLAGE MUST PROVIDE A WARRIOR TO PROTECT THIS GRANDCHILD.
I AM THAT CHOSEN WARRIOR.
RAINBOW IS MY CHARGE.

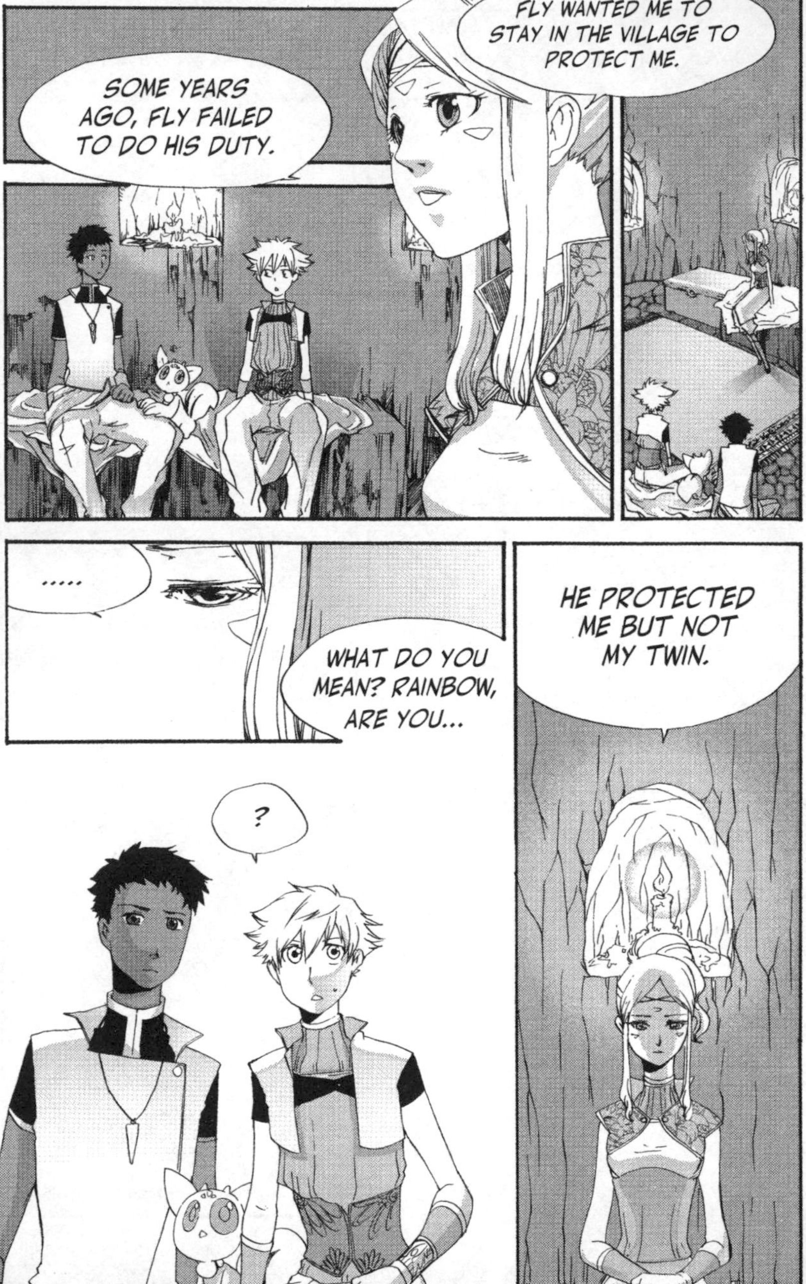
SOME YEARS AGO, FLY FAILED TO DO HIS DUTY.
FLY WANTED ME TO STAY IN THE VILLAGE TO PROTECT ME.
.....
WHAT DO YOU MEAN? RAINBOW, ARE YOU...
HE PROTECTED ME BUT NOT MY TWIN.
?

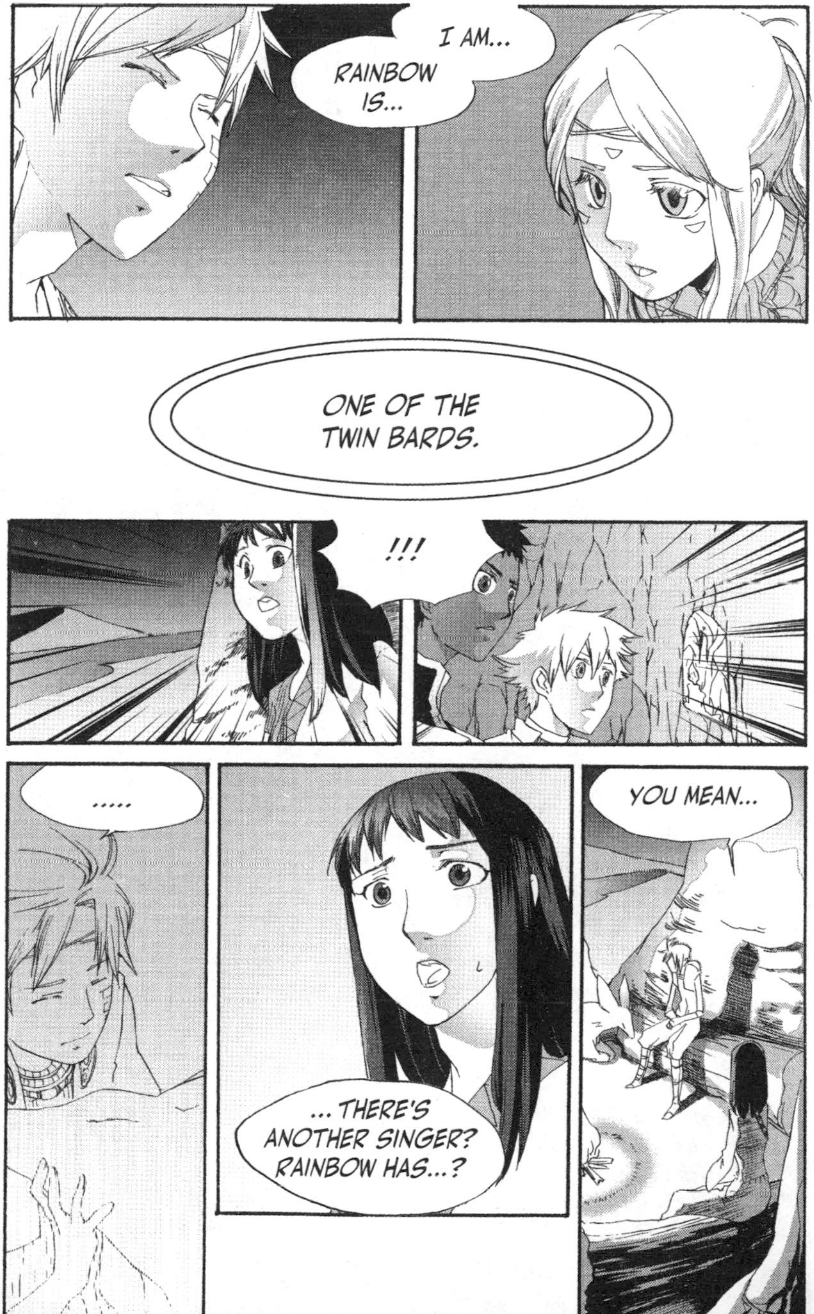
I AM... RAINBOW IS...
ONE OF THE TWIN BARDS.
!!!
YOU MEAN...
... THERE'S ANOTHER SINGER? RAINBOW HAS...?
......

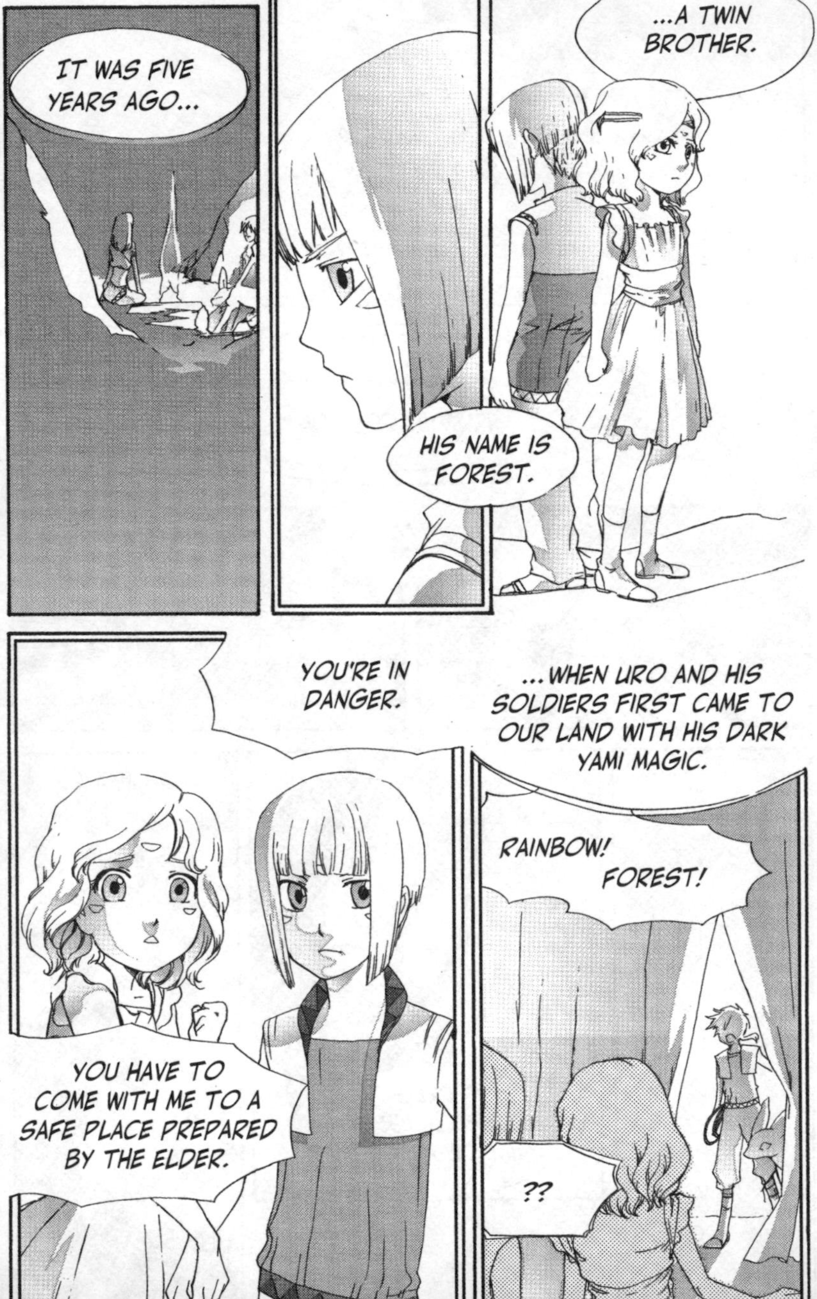
...A TWIN BROTHER.
HIS NAME IS FOREST.
IT WAS FIVE YEARS AGO...
...WHEN URO AND HIS SOLDIERS FIRST CAME TO OUR LAND WITH HIS DARK YAMI MAGIC.
RAINBOW! FOREST!
??
YOU'RE IN DANGER.
YOU HAVE TO COME WITH ME TO A SAFE PLACE PREPARED BY THE ELDER.

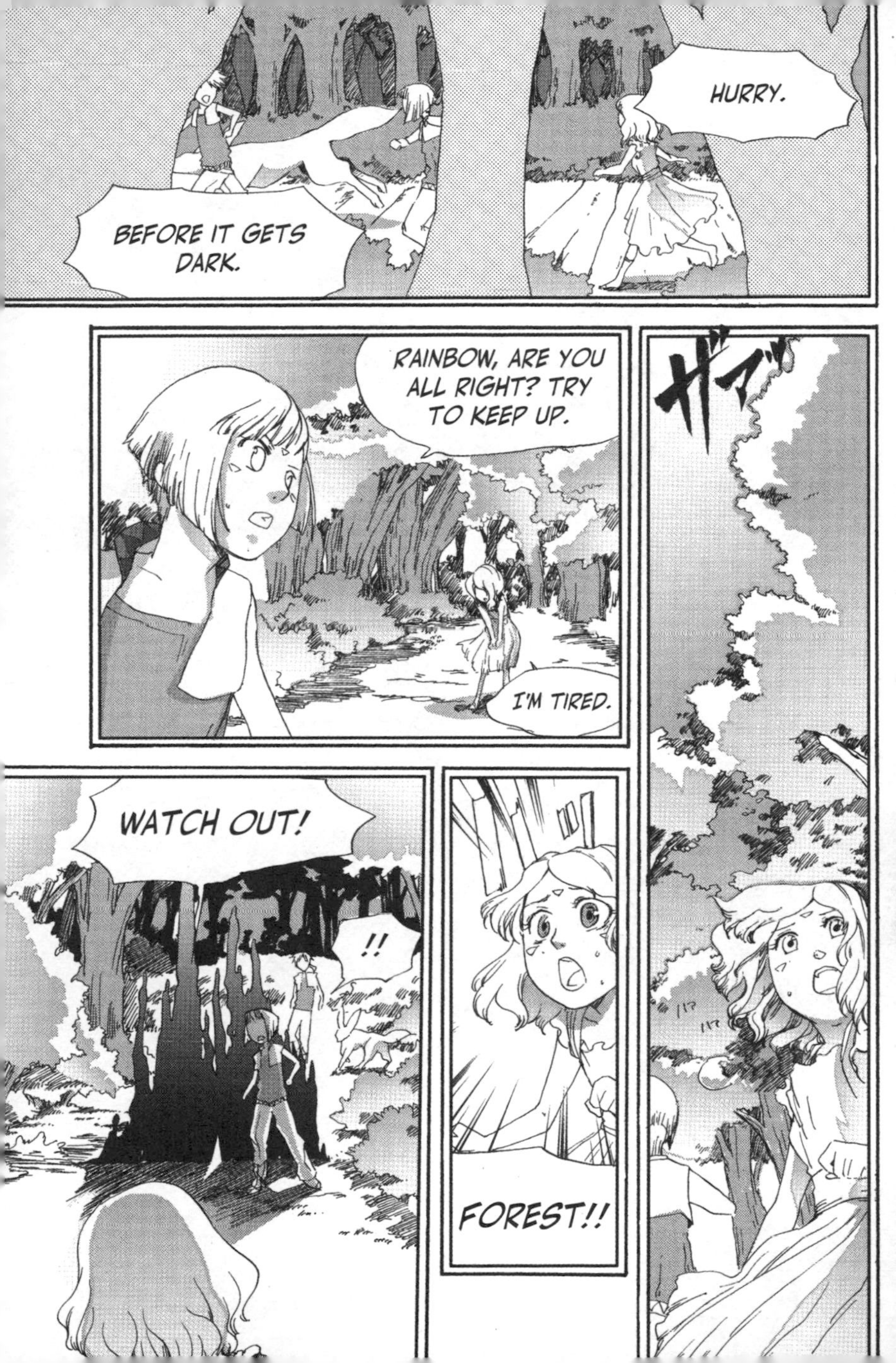
HURRY.
BEFORE IT GETS DARK.
ザア゙
RAINBOW, ARE YOU ALL RIGHT? TRY TO KEEP UP.
I'M TIRED.
FOREST!!
WATCH OUT!
!!

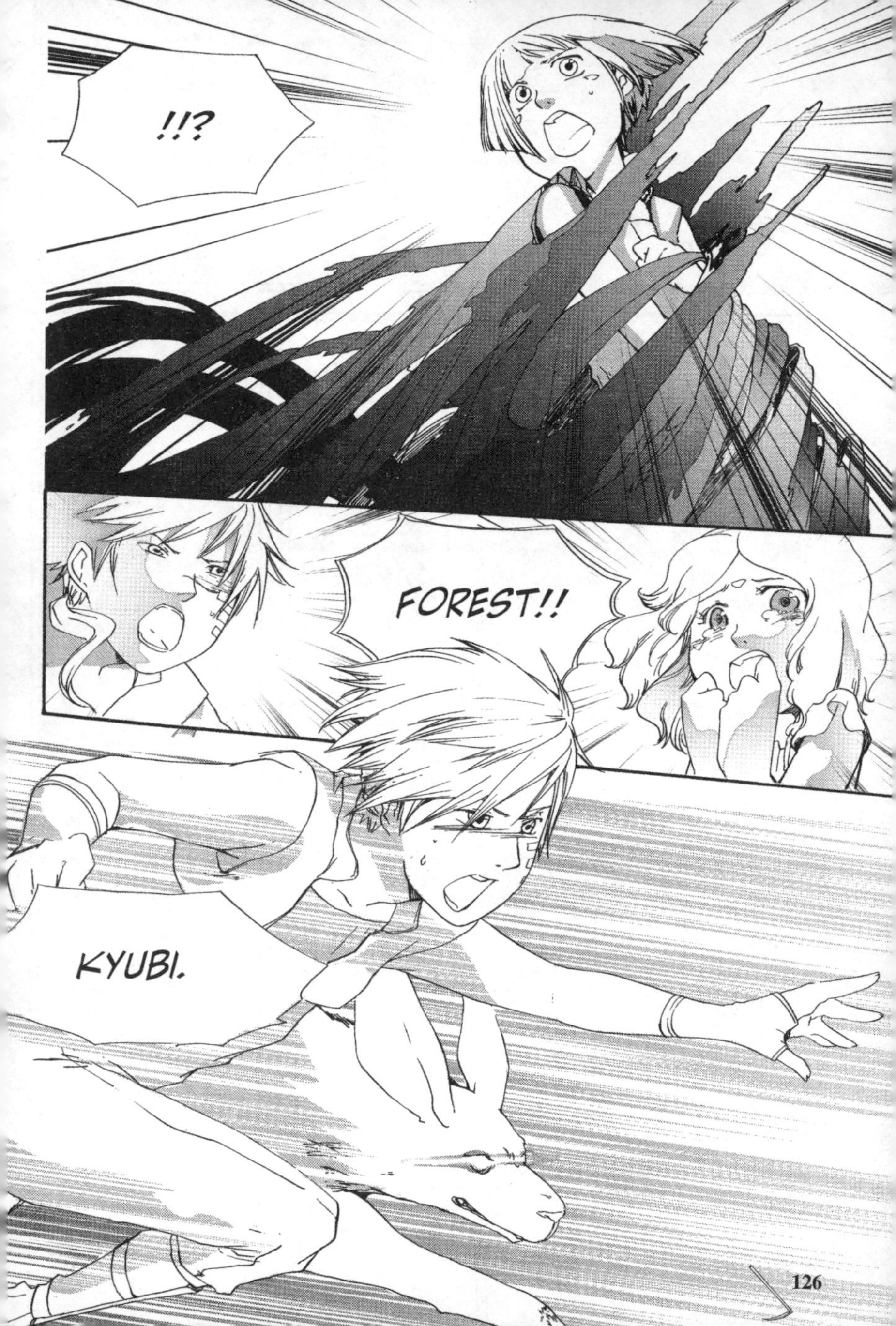
!!?
FOREST!!
KYUBI.

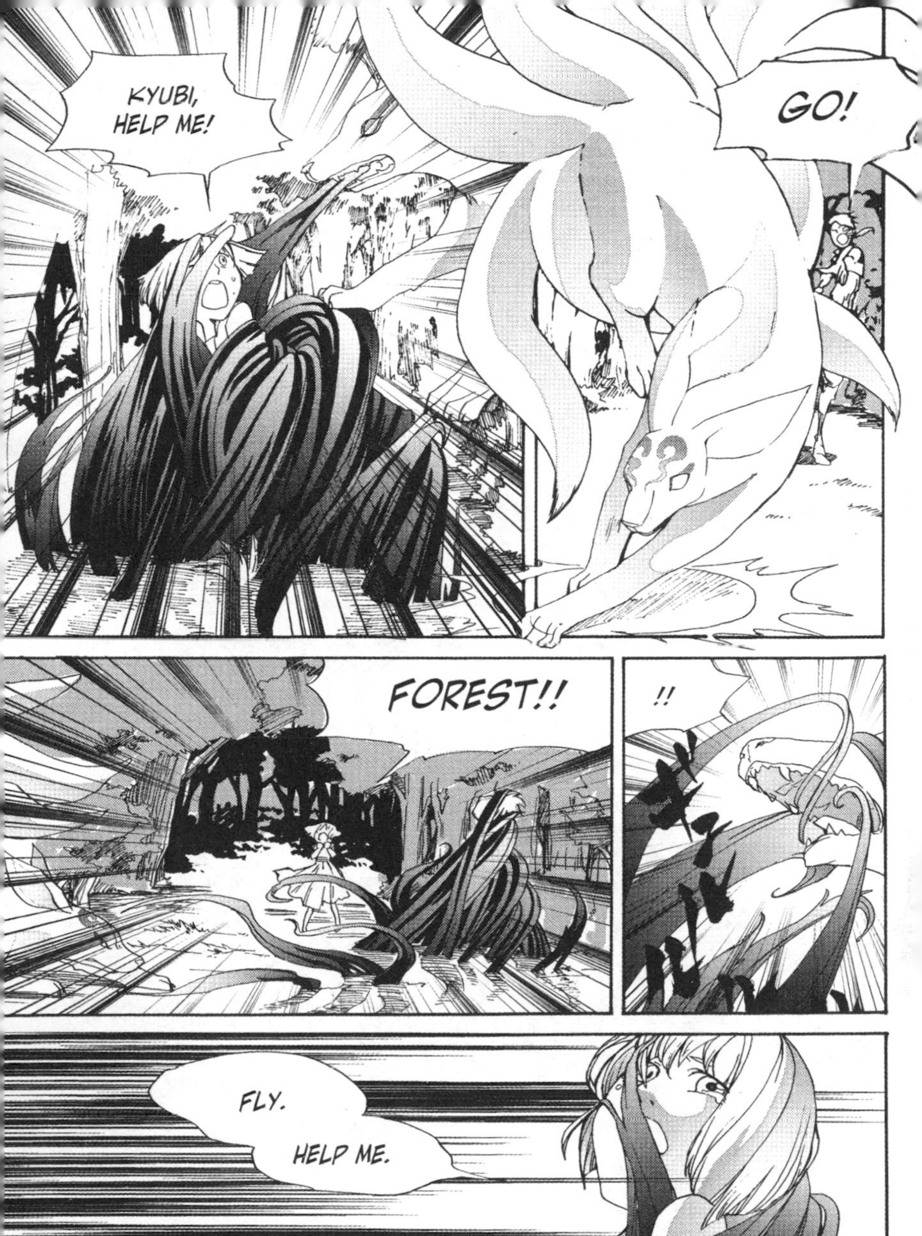
GO!
KYUBI, HELP ME!
!!
FOREST!!
FLY.
HELP ME.

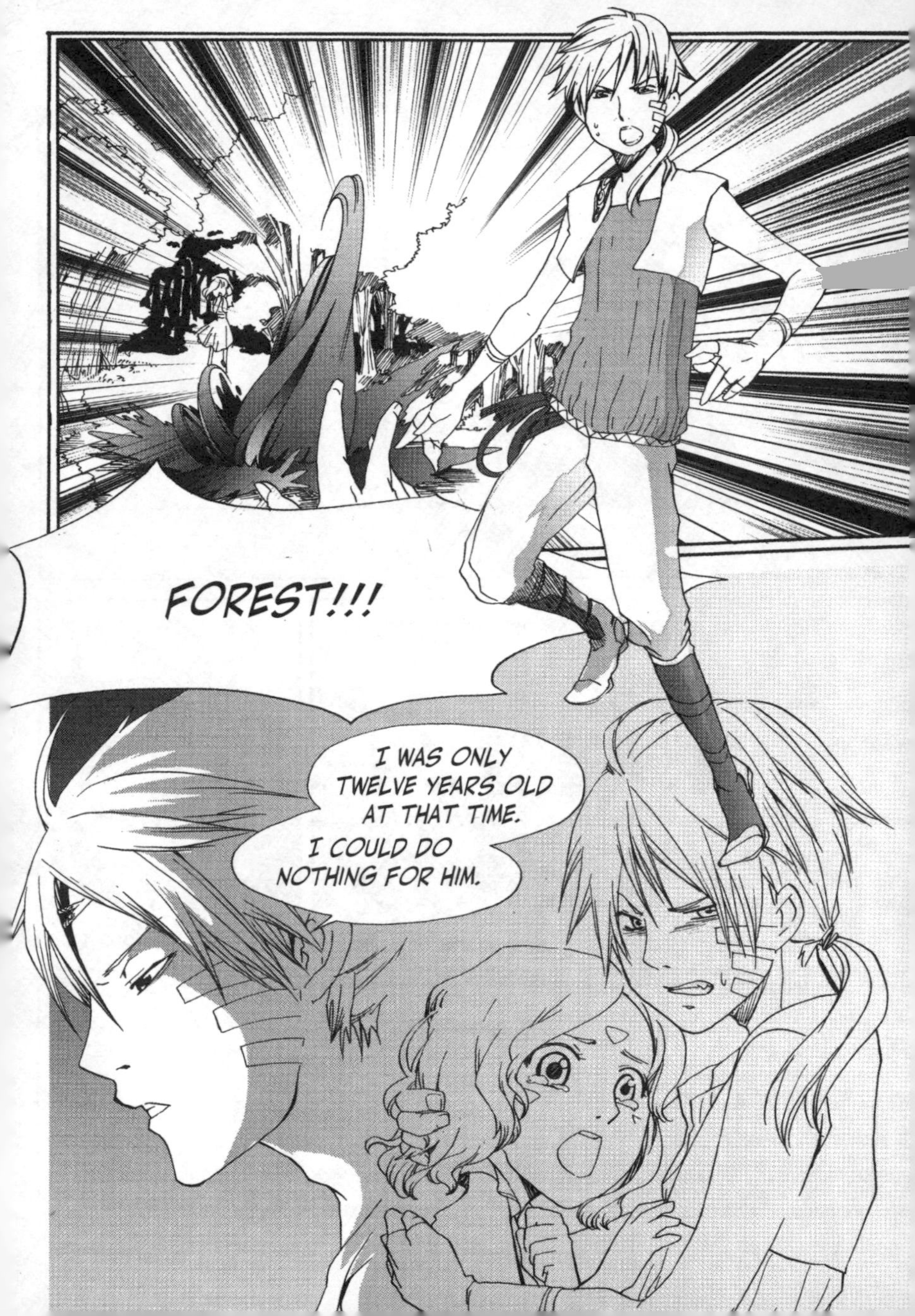
FOREST!!!
I WAS ONLY TWELVE YEARS OLD AT THAT TIME.
I COULD DO NOTHING FOR HIM.

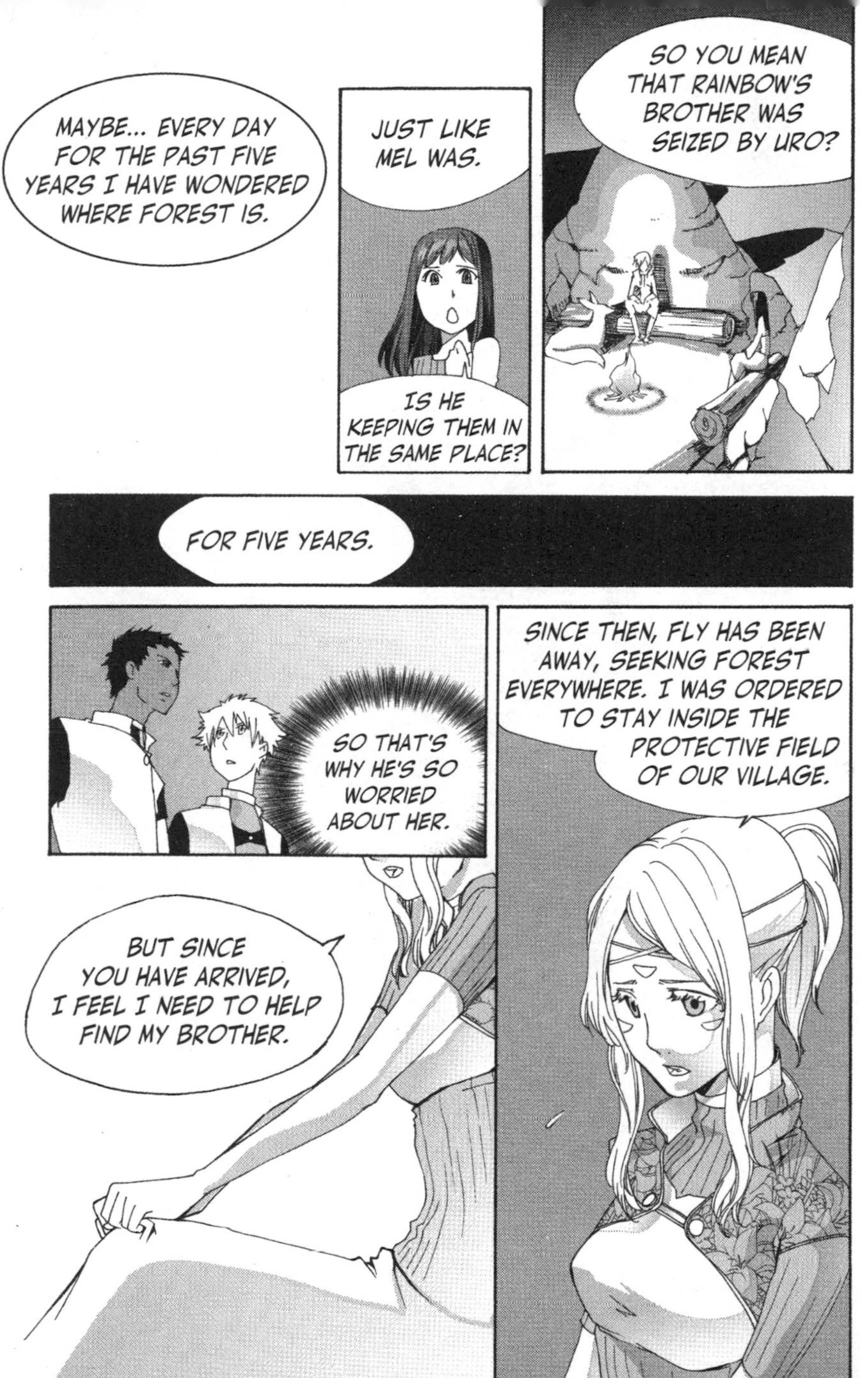
SO YOU MEAN THAT RAINBOW'S BROTHER WAS SEIZED BY URO?
JUST LIKE MEL WAS.
IS HE KEEPING THEM IN THE SAME PLACE?
MAYBE... EVERY DAY FOR THE PAST FIVE YEARS I HAVE WONDERED WHERE FOREST IS.
FOR FIVE YEARS.
SINCE THEN, FLY HAS BEEN AWAY, SEEKING FOREST EVERYWHERE. I WAS ORDERED TO STAY INSIDE THE PROTECTIVE FIELD OF OUR VILLAGE.
SO THAT'S WHY HE'S SO WORRIED ABOUT HER.
BUT SINCE YOU HAVE ARRIVED, I FEEL I NEED TO HELP FIND MY BROTHER.

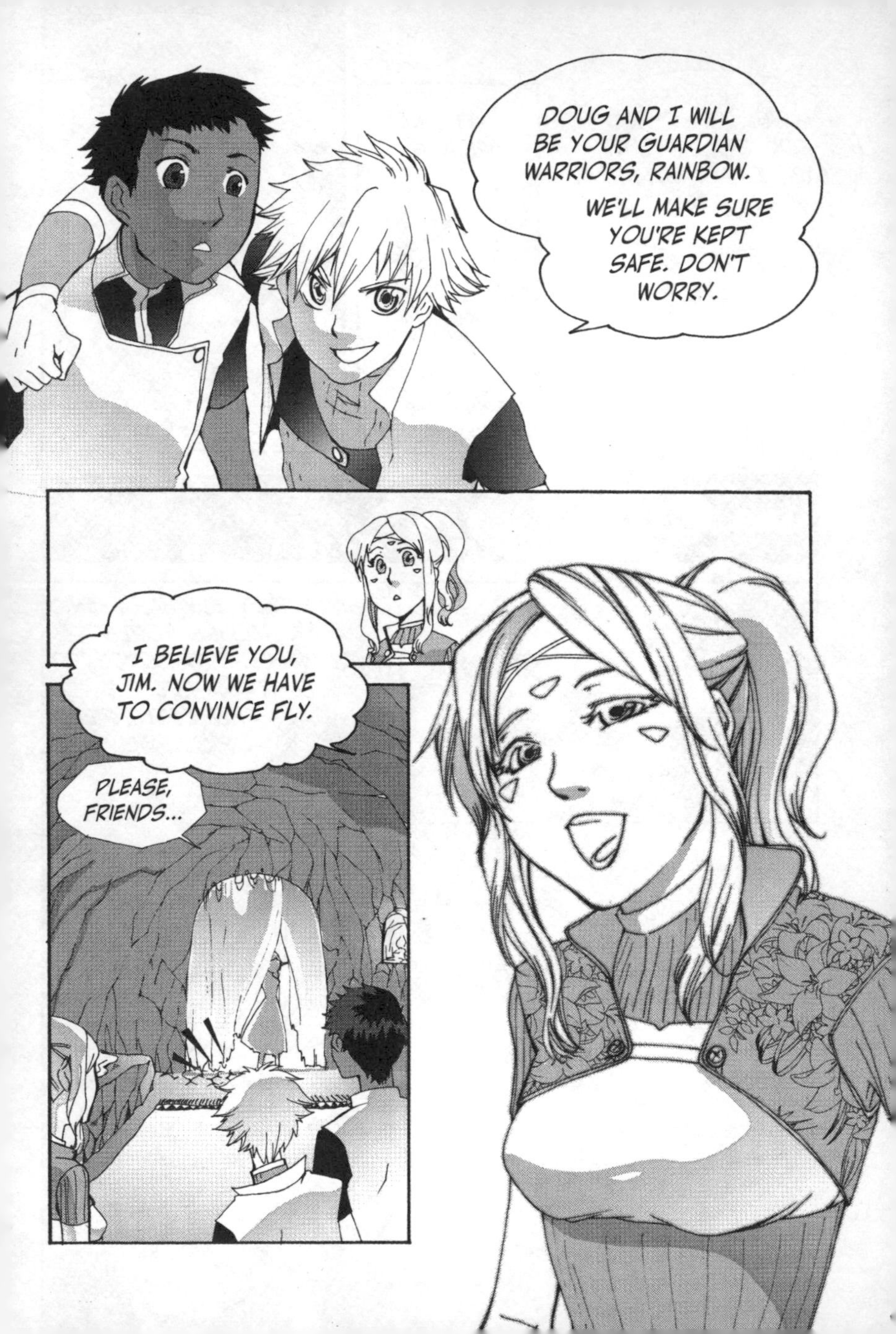
DOUG AND I WILL BE YOUR GUARDIAN WARRIORS, RAINBOW.
WE'LL MAKE SURE YOU'RE KEPT SAFE. DON'T WORRY.
I BELIEVE YOU, JIM. NOW WE HAVE TO CONVINCE FLY.
PLEASE, FRIENDS...

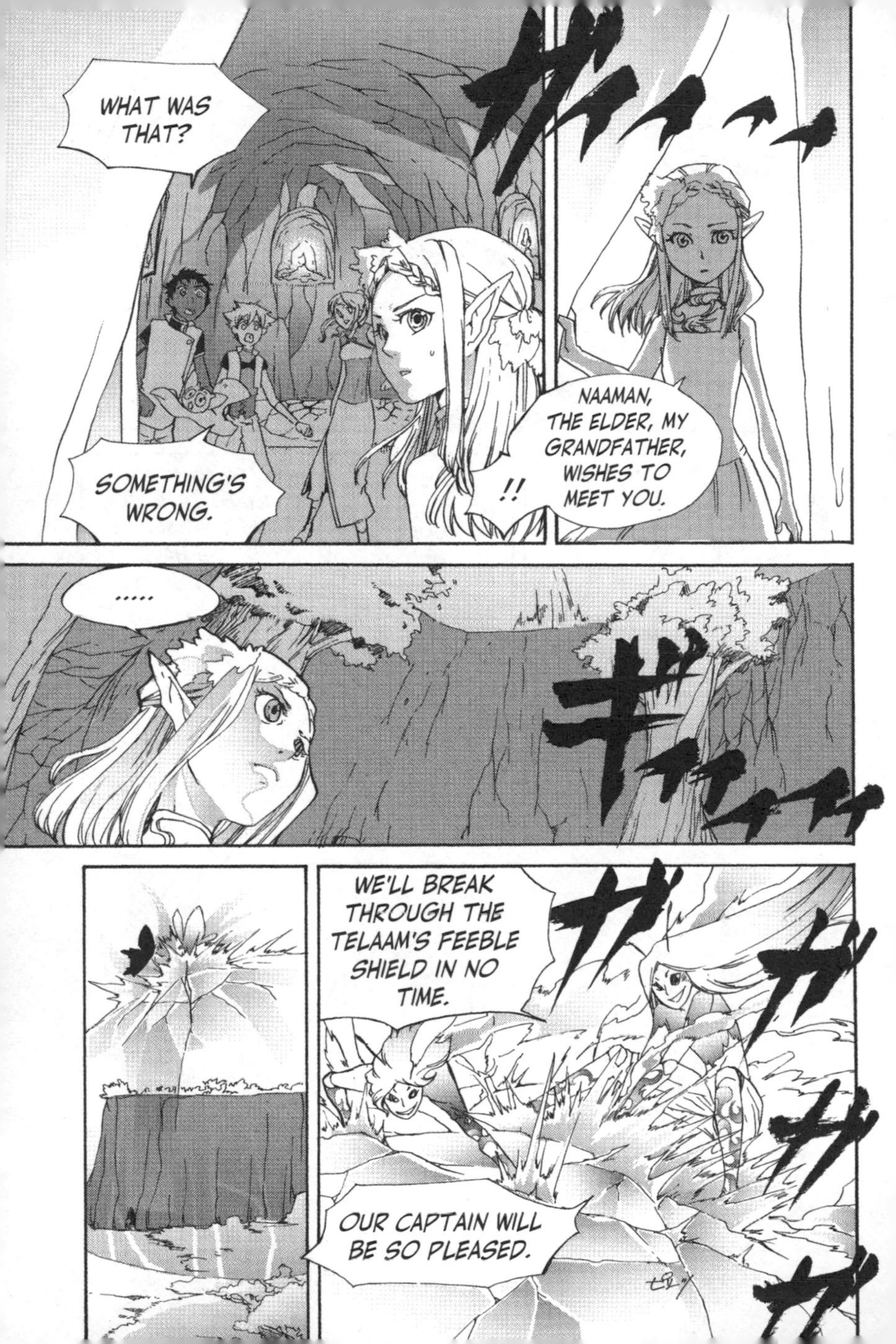
NAAMAN, THE ELDER, MY GRANDFATHER, WISHES TO MEET YOU.
WHAT WAS THAT?
!!
SOMETHING'S WRONG.
.....
WE'LL BREAK THROUGH THE TELAAM'S FEEBLE SHIELD IN NO TIME.
OUR CAPTAIN WILL BE SO PLEASED.

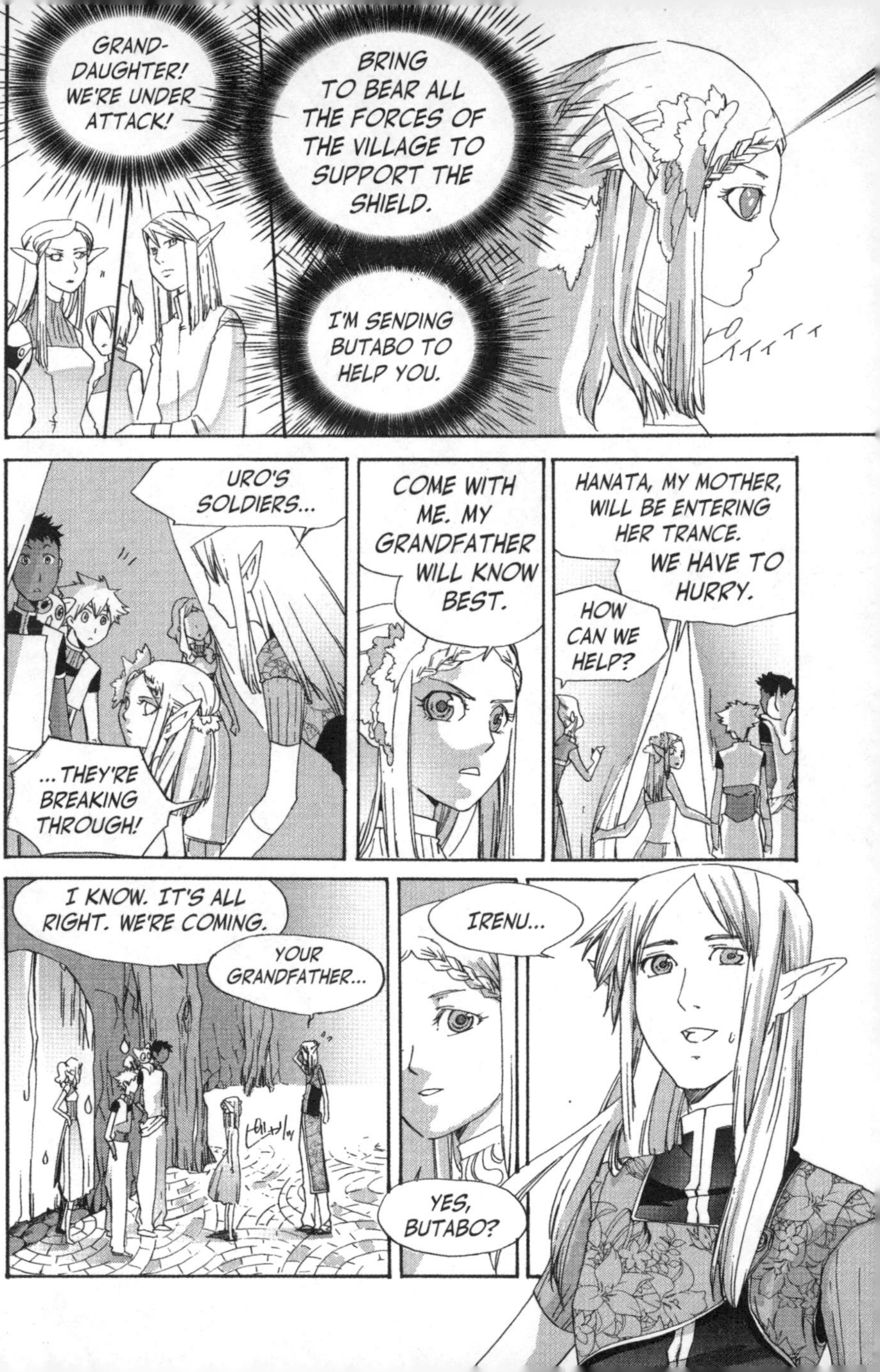
GRAND-DAUGHTER! WE'RE UNDER ATTACK!
BRING TO BEAR ALL THE FORCES OF THE VILLAGE TO SUPPORT THE SHIELD.
I'M SENDING BUTABO TO HELP YOU.
URO'S SOLDIERS...
...THEY'RE BREAKING THROUGH!
COME WITH ME. MY GRANDFATHER WILL KNOW BEST.
HANATA, MY MOTHER, WILL BE ENTERING HER TRANCE.
WE HAVE TO HURRY.
HOW CAN WE HELP?
I KNOW. IT'S ALL RIGHT. WE'RE COMING.
YOUR GRANDFATHER...
IRENU...
YES, BUTABO?

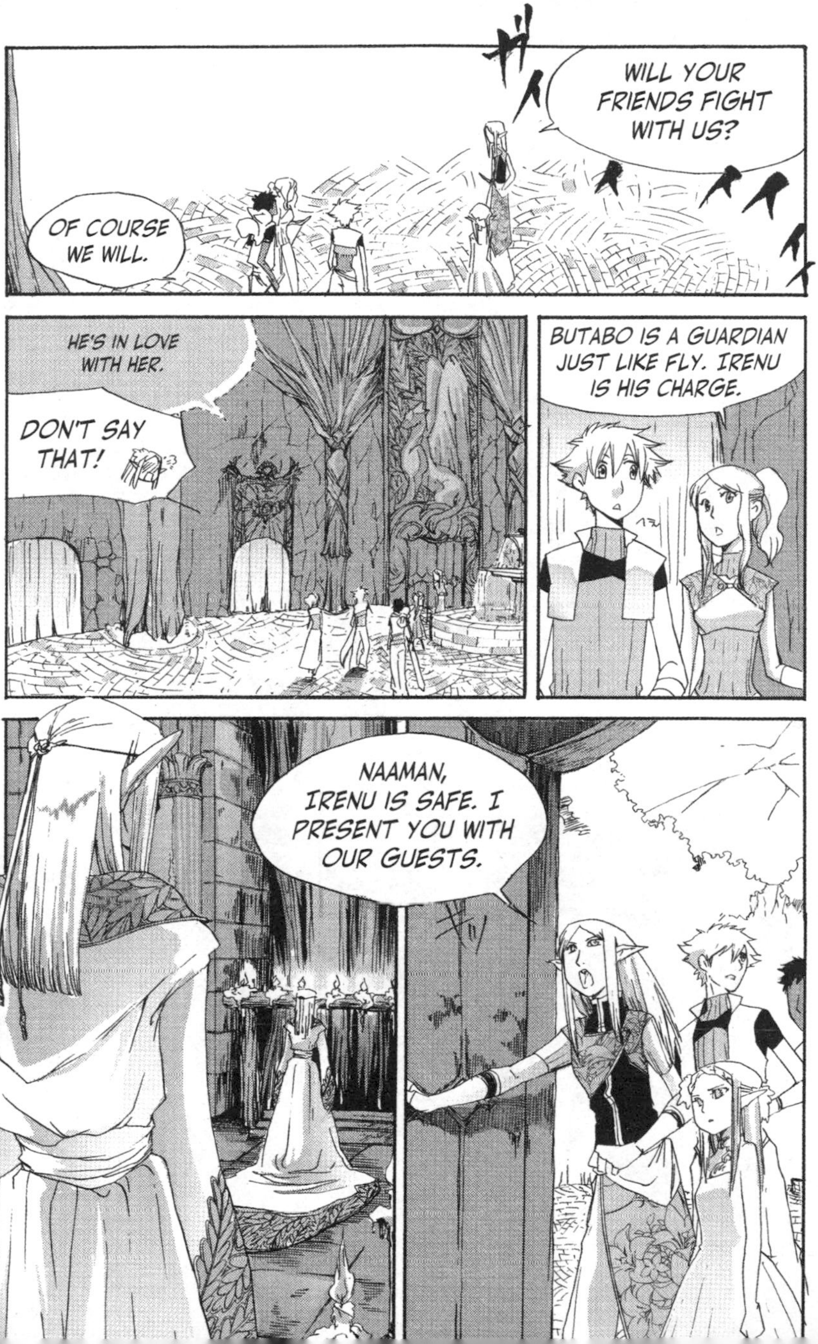
WILL YOUR FRIENDS FIGHT WITH US?
OF COURSE WE WILL.
BUTABO IS A GUARDIAN JUST LIKE FLY. IRENU IS HIS CHARGE.
HE'S IN LOVE WITH HER.
DON'T SAY THAT!
NAAMAN, IRENU IS SAFE. I PRESENT YOU WITH OUR GUESTS.

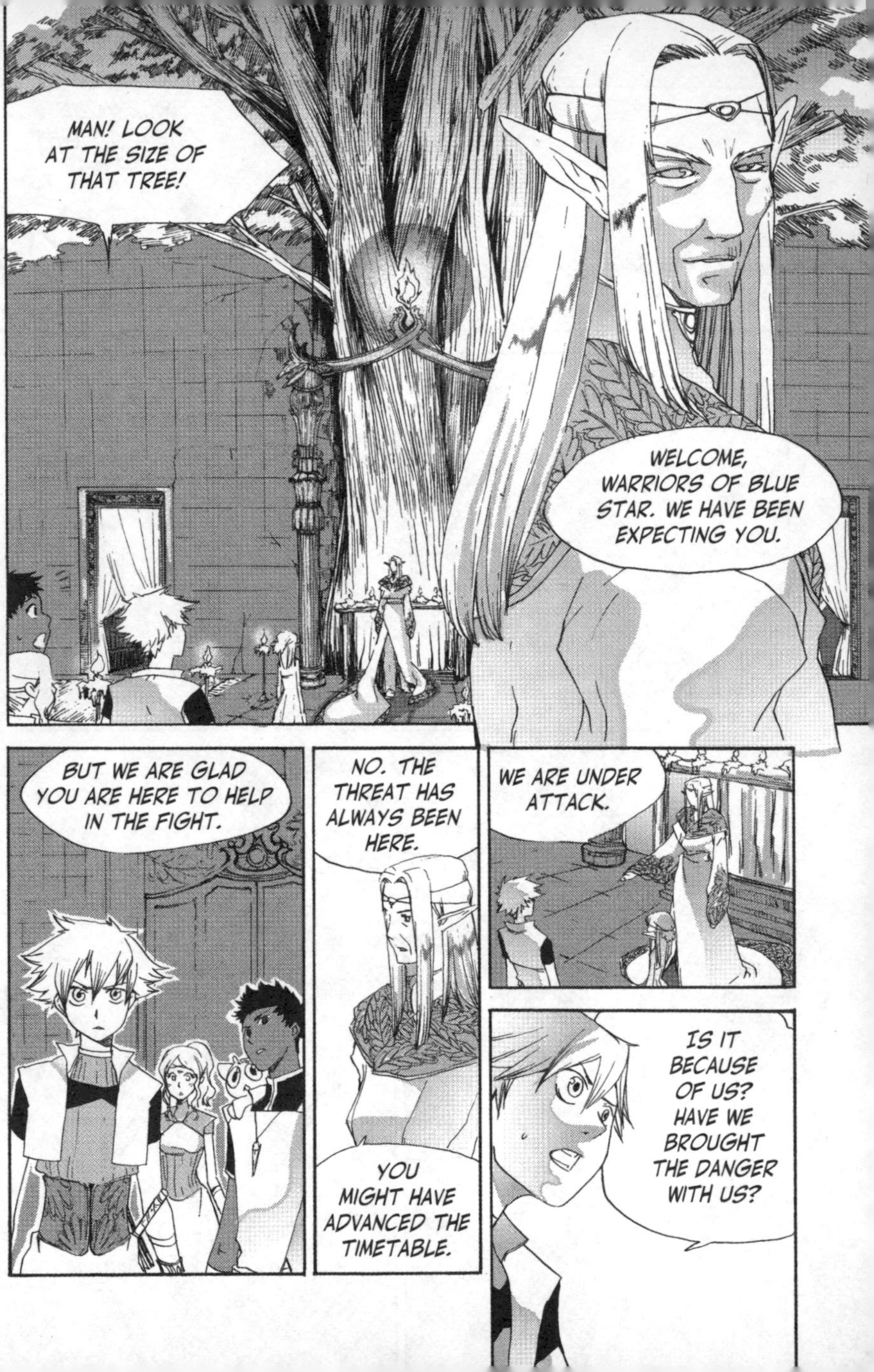
MAN! LOOK AT THE SIZE OF THAT TREE!
WELCOME, WARRIORS OF BLUE STAR. WE HAVE BEEN EXPECTING YOU.
WE ARE UNDER ATTACK.
IS IT BECAUSE OF US? HAVE WE BROUGHT THE DANGER WITH US?
NO. THE THREAT HAS ALWAYS BEEN HERE.
YOU MIGHT HAVE ADVANCED THE TIMETABLE.
BUT WE ARE GLAD YOU ARE HERE TO HELP IN THE FIGHT.

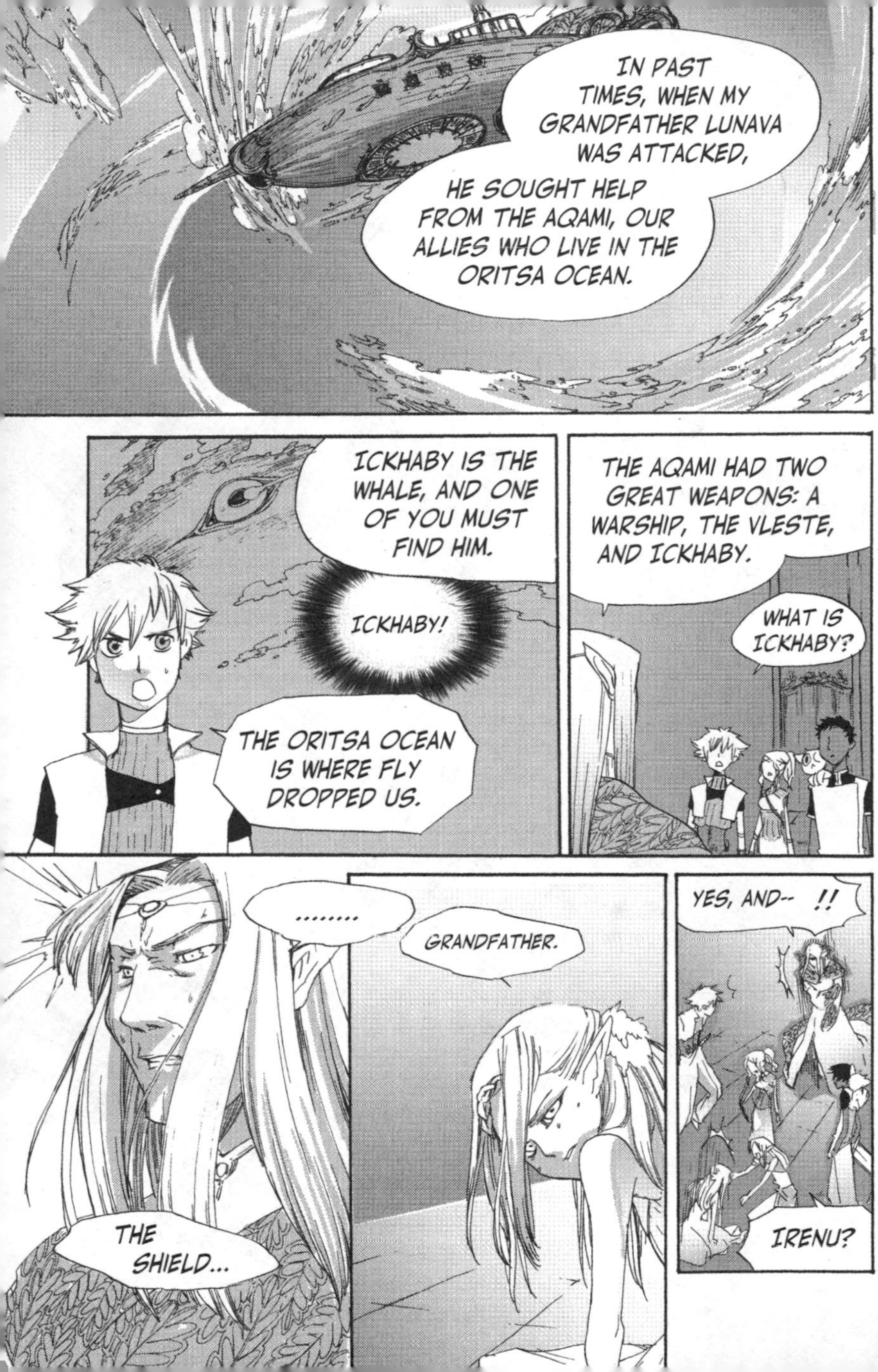

IN PAST TIMES, WHEN MY GRANDFATHER LUNAVA WAS ATTACKED,
HE SOUGHT HELP FROM THE AQAMI, OUR ALLIES WHO LIVE IN THE ORITSA OCEAN.
THE AQAMI HAD TWO GREAT WEAPONS: A WARSHIP, THE VLESTE, AND ICKHABY.
WHAT IS ICKHABY?
ICKHABY IS THE WHALE, AND ONE OF YOU MUST FIND HIM.
ICKHABY!
THE ORITSA OCEAN IS WHERE FLY DROPPED US.
YES, AND-- !!
IRENU?
GRANDFATHER.
....
THE SHIELD...

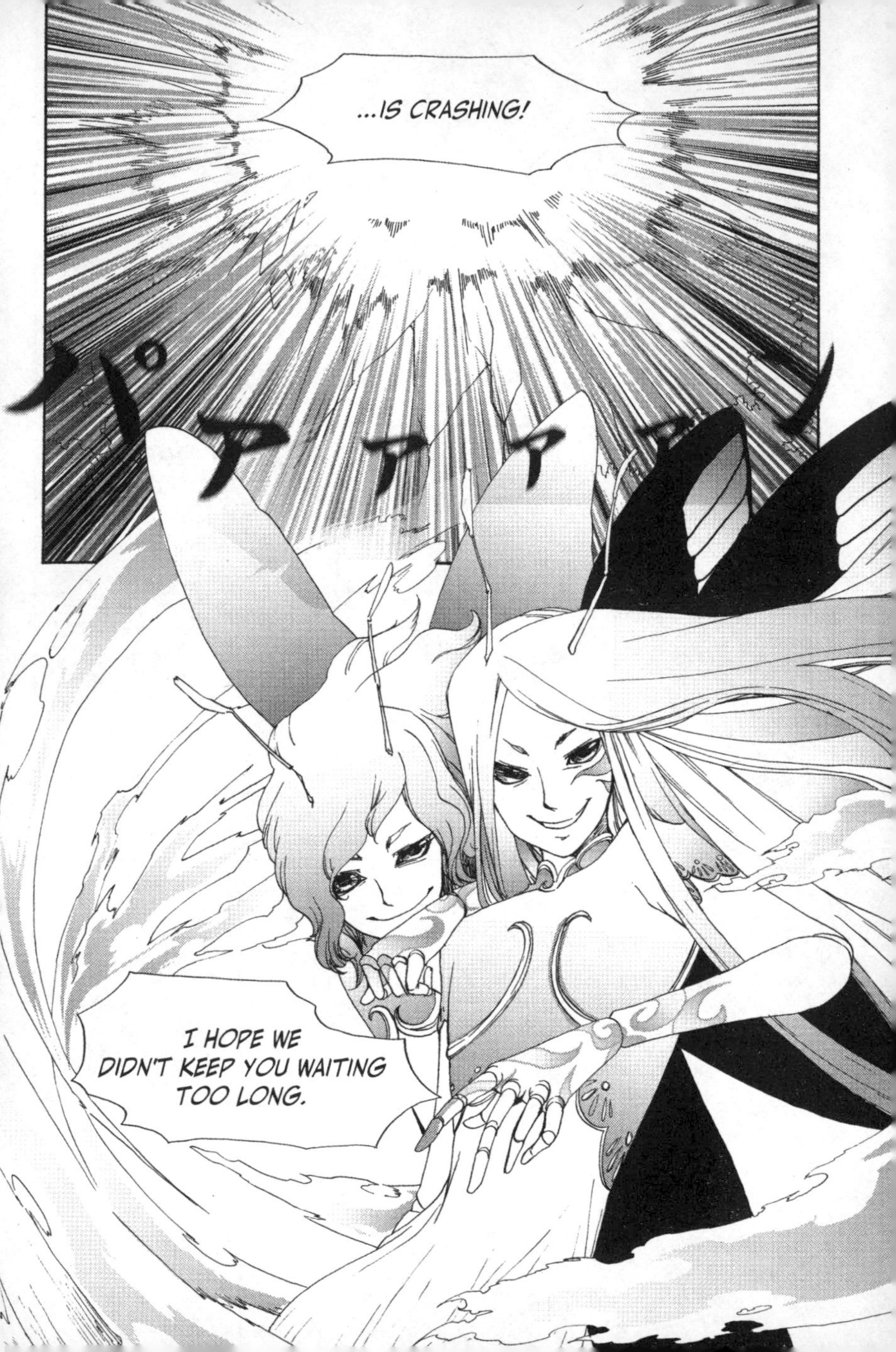
...IS CRASHING!
パアアアン
I HOPE WE DIDN'T KEEP YOU WAITING TOO LONG.

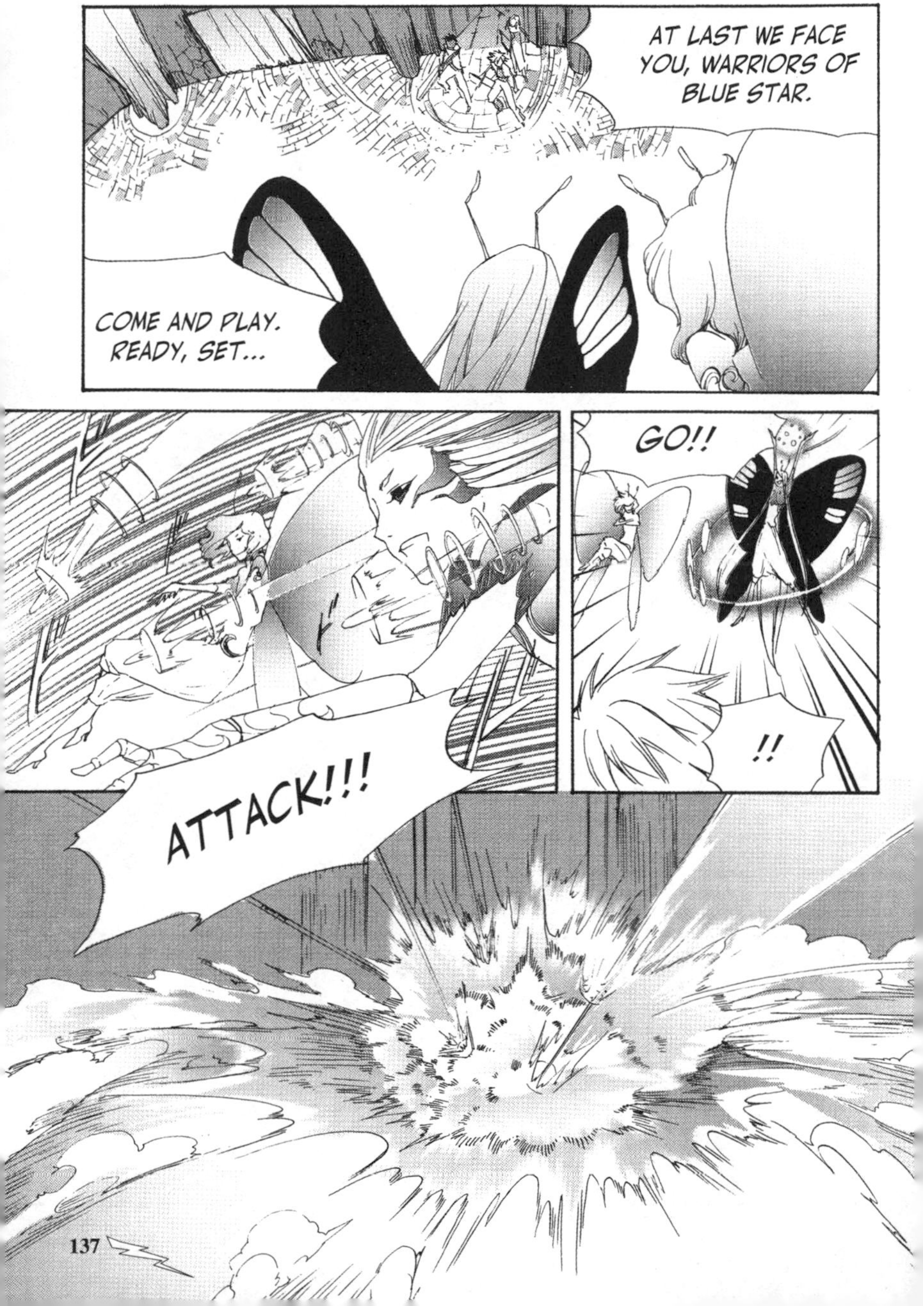
AT LAST WE FACE YOU, WARRIORS OF BLUE STAR.
COME AND PLAY. READY, SET...
GO!!
!!
ATTACK!!!

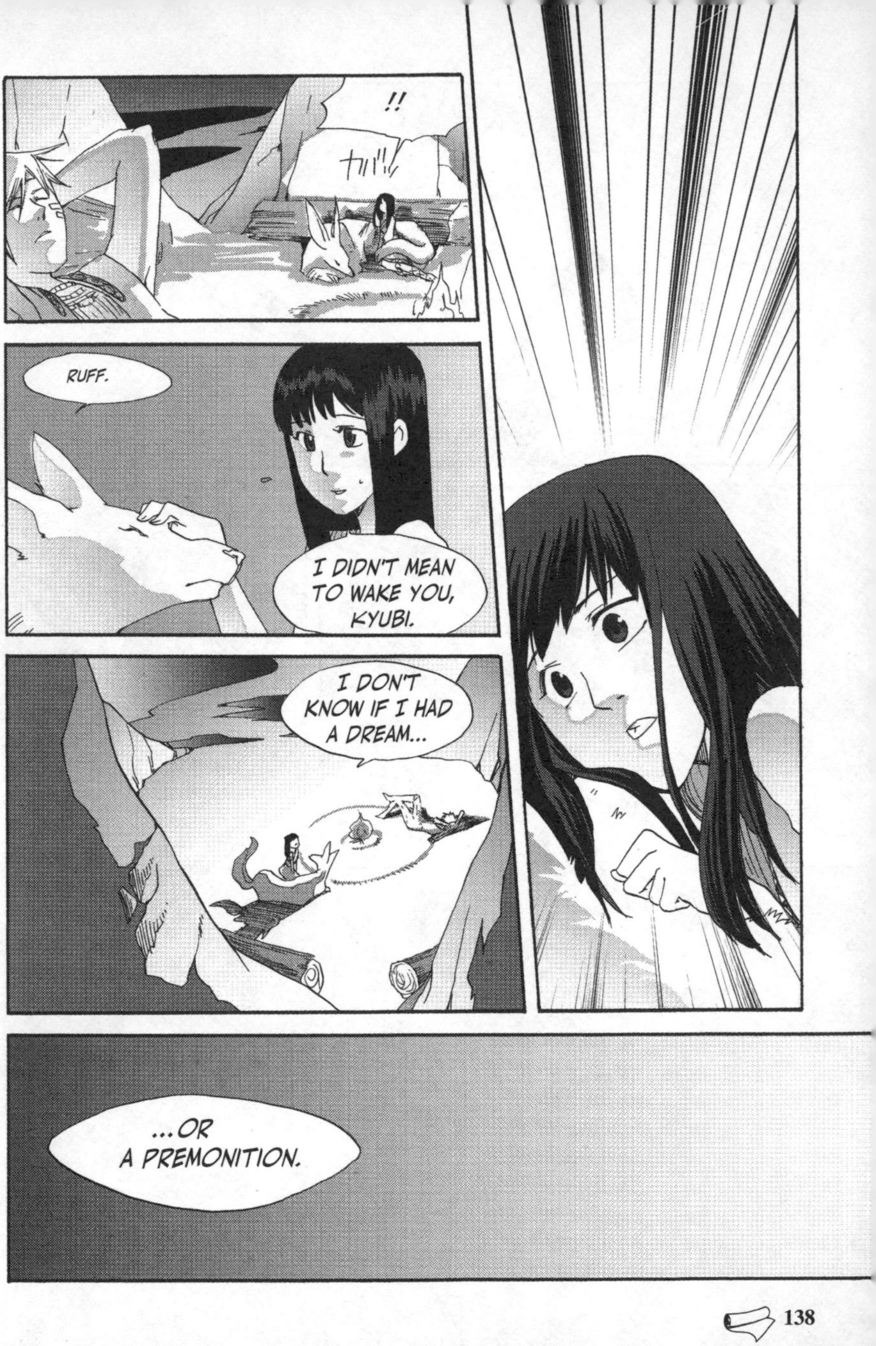
!!
RUFF.
I DIDN'T MEAN TO WAKE YOU, KYUBI.
I DON'T KNOW IF I HAD A DREAM...
...OR A PREMONITION.

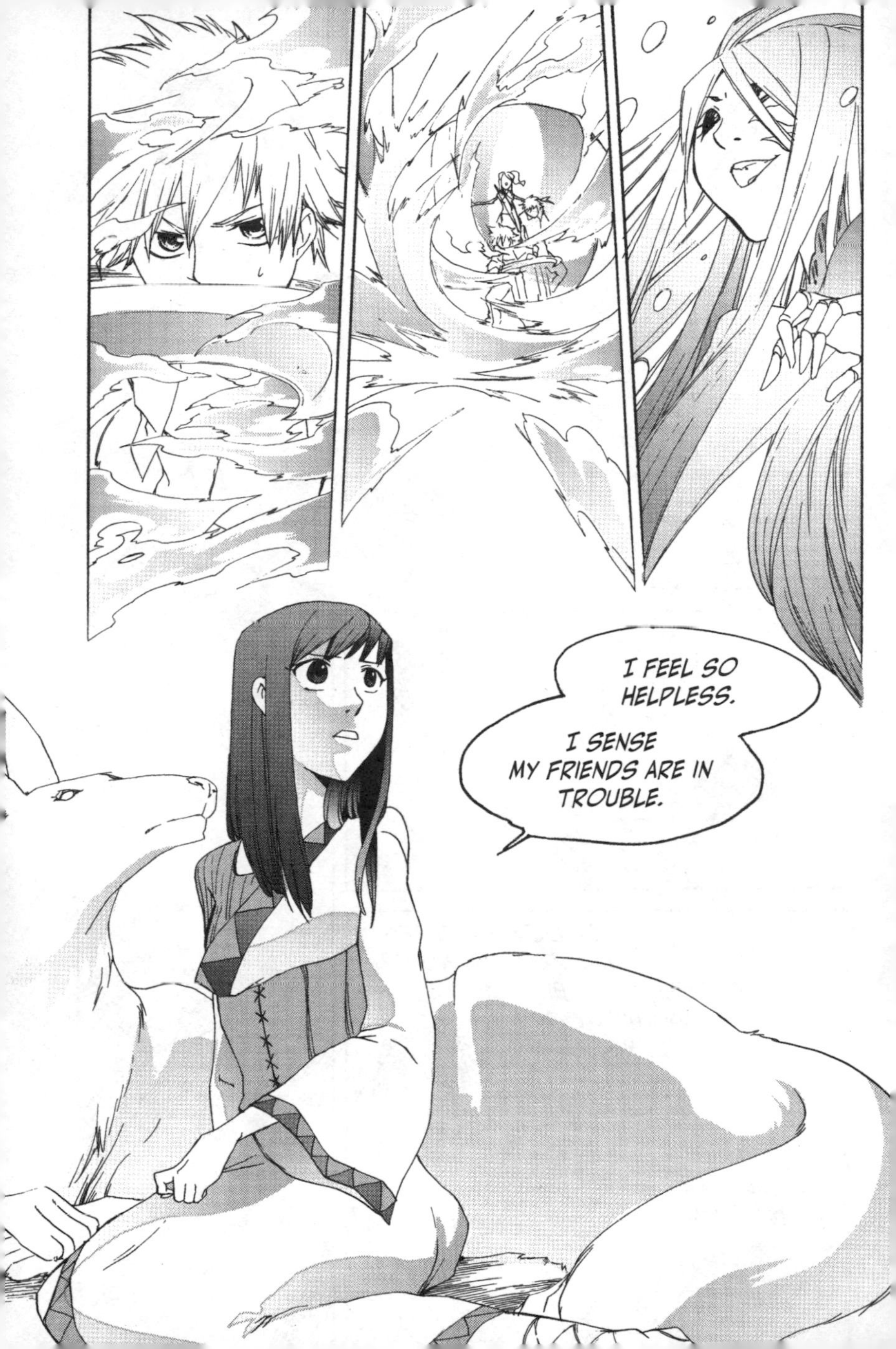
I FEEL SO HELPLESS.
I SENSE MY FRIENDS ARE IN TROUBLE.

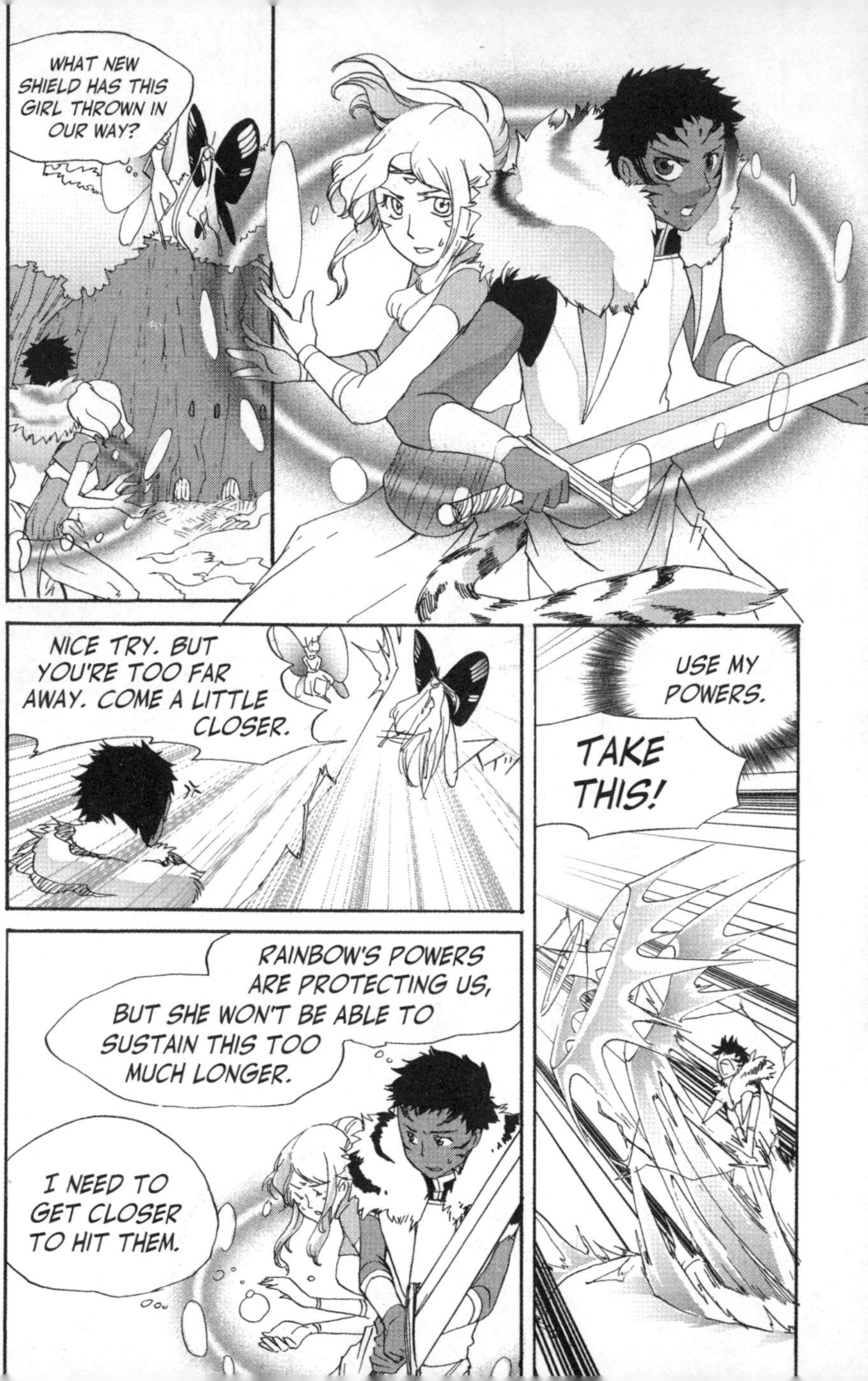
WHAT NEW SHIELD HAS THIS GIRL THROWN IN OUR WAY?
USE MY POWERS.
TAKE THIS!
NICE TRY. BUT YOU'RE TOO FAR AWAY. COME A LITTLE CLOSER.
RAINBOW'S POWERS ARE PROTECTING US, BUT SHE WON'T BE ABLE TO SUSTAIN THIS TOO MUCH LONGER.
I NEED TO GET CLOSER TO HIT THEM.

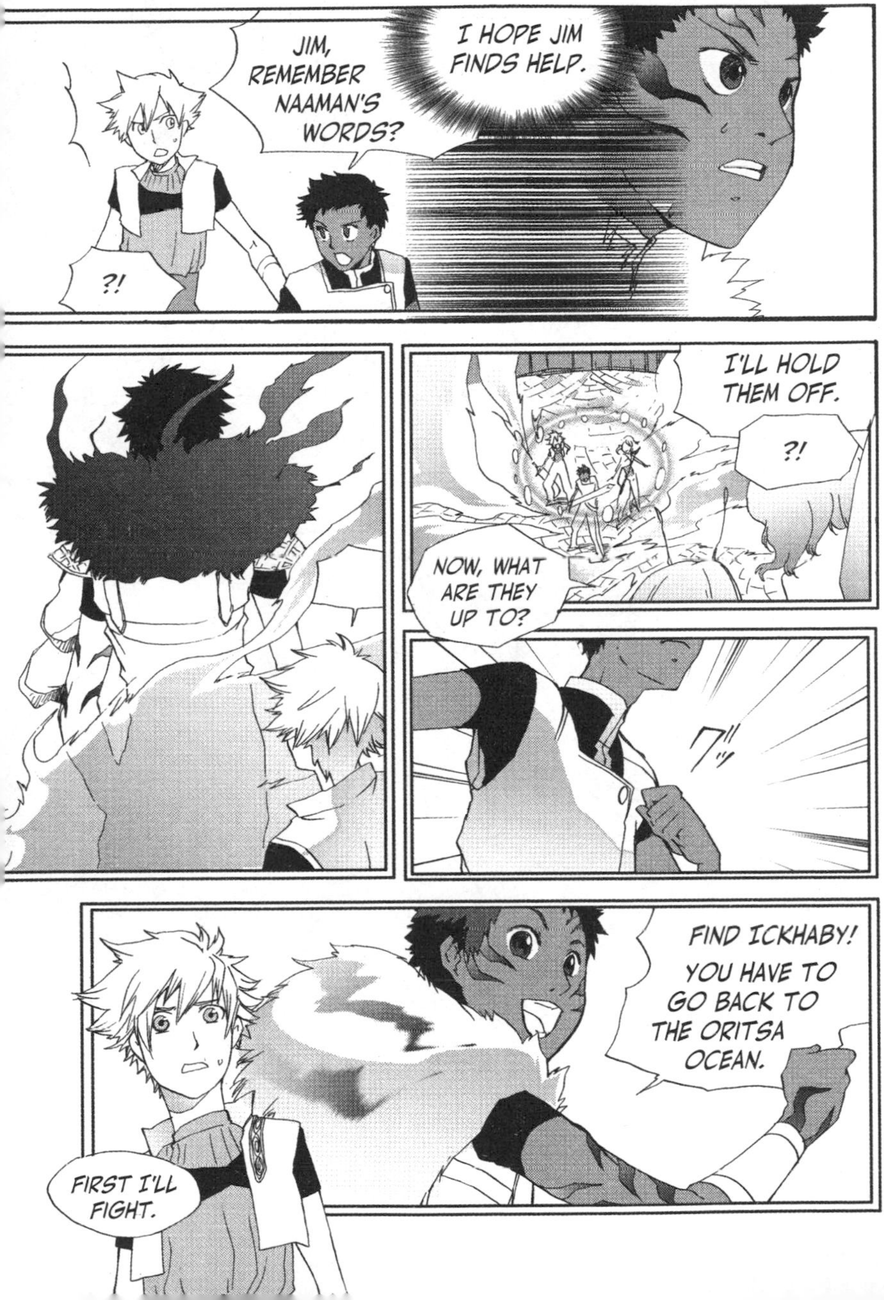
I HOPE JIM FINDS HELP.
JIM, REMEMBER NAAMAN'S WORDS?
?!
I'LL HOLD THEM OFF.
?!
NOW, WHAT ARE THEY UP TO?
グッ
FIND ICKHABY! YOU HAVE TO GO BACK TO THE ORITSA OCEAN.
FIRST I'LL FIGHT.

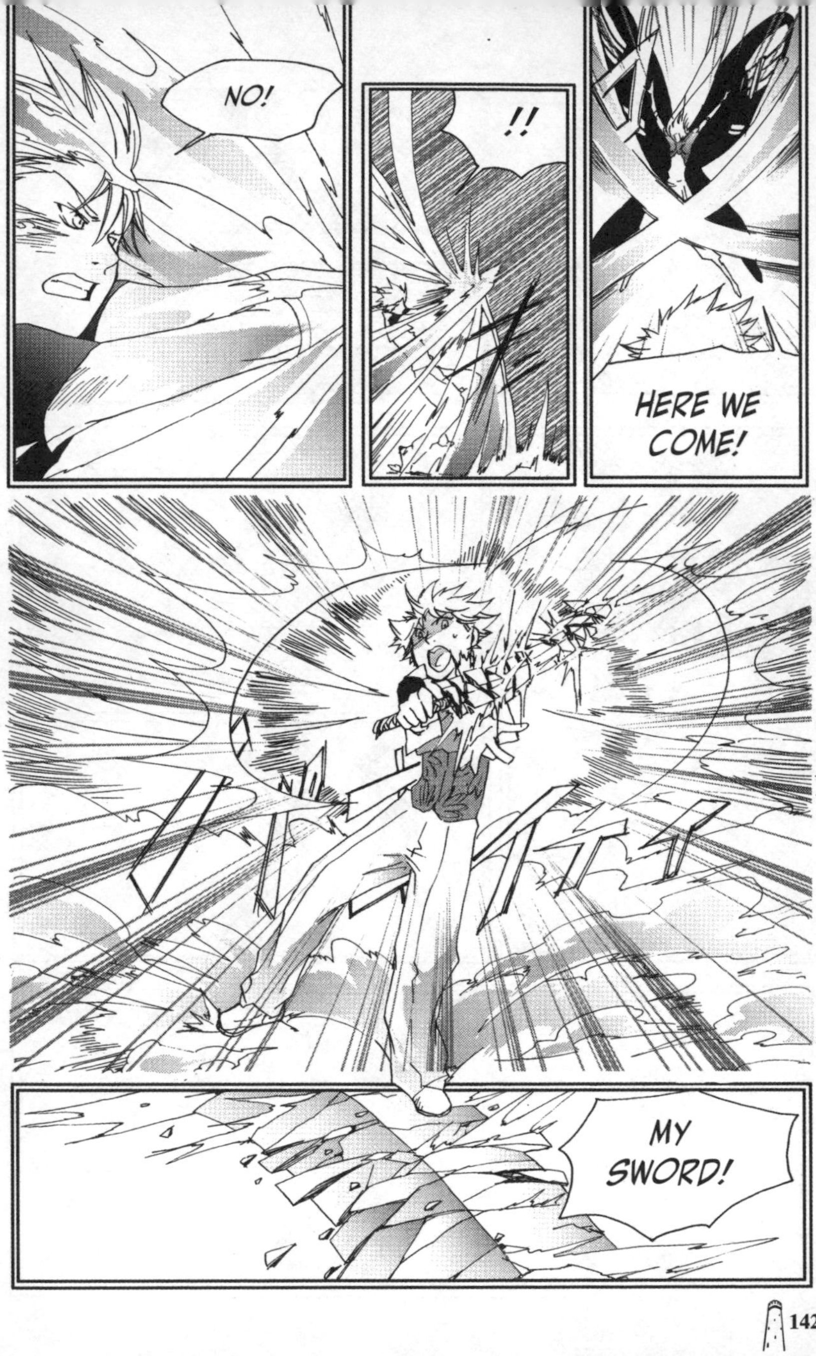
HERE WE COME!
!!
NO!
MY SWORD!

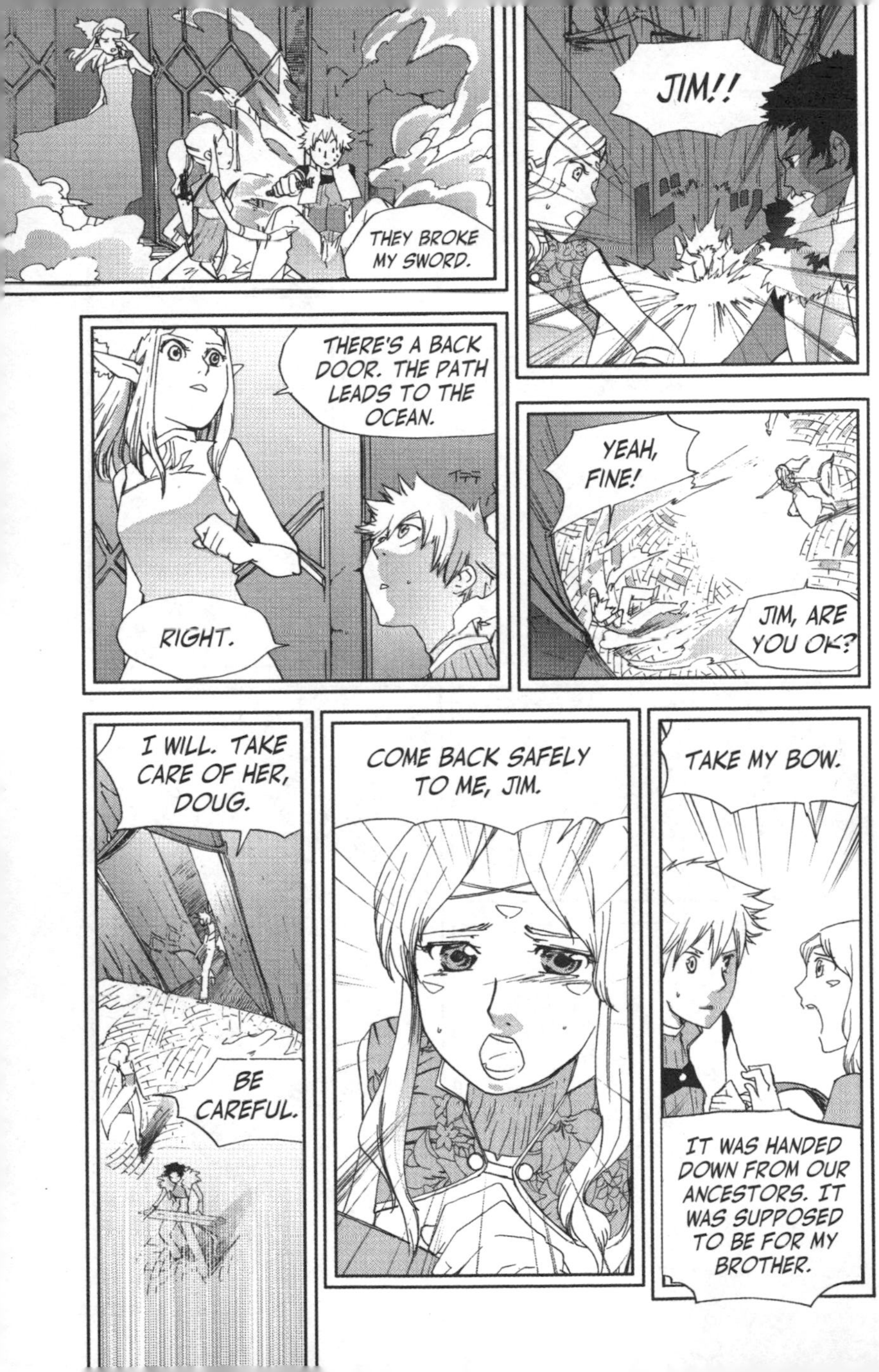
JIM!!
THEY BROKE MY SWORD.
JIM, ARE YOU OK?
YEAH, FINE!
THERE'S A BACK DOOR. THE PATH LEADS TO THE OCEAN.
RIGHT.
TAKE MY BOW.
IT WAS HANDED DOWN FROM OUR ANCESTORS. IT WAS SUPPOSED TO BE FOR MY BROTHER.
COME BACK SAFELY TO ME, JIM.
I WILL. TAKE CARE OF HER, DOUG.
BE CAREFUL.

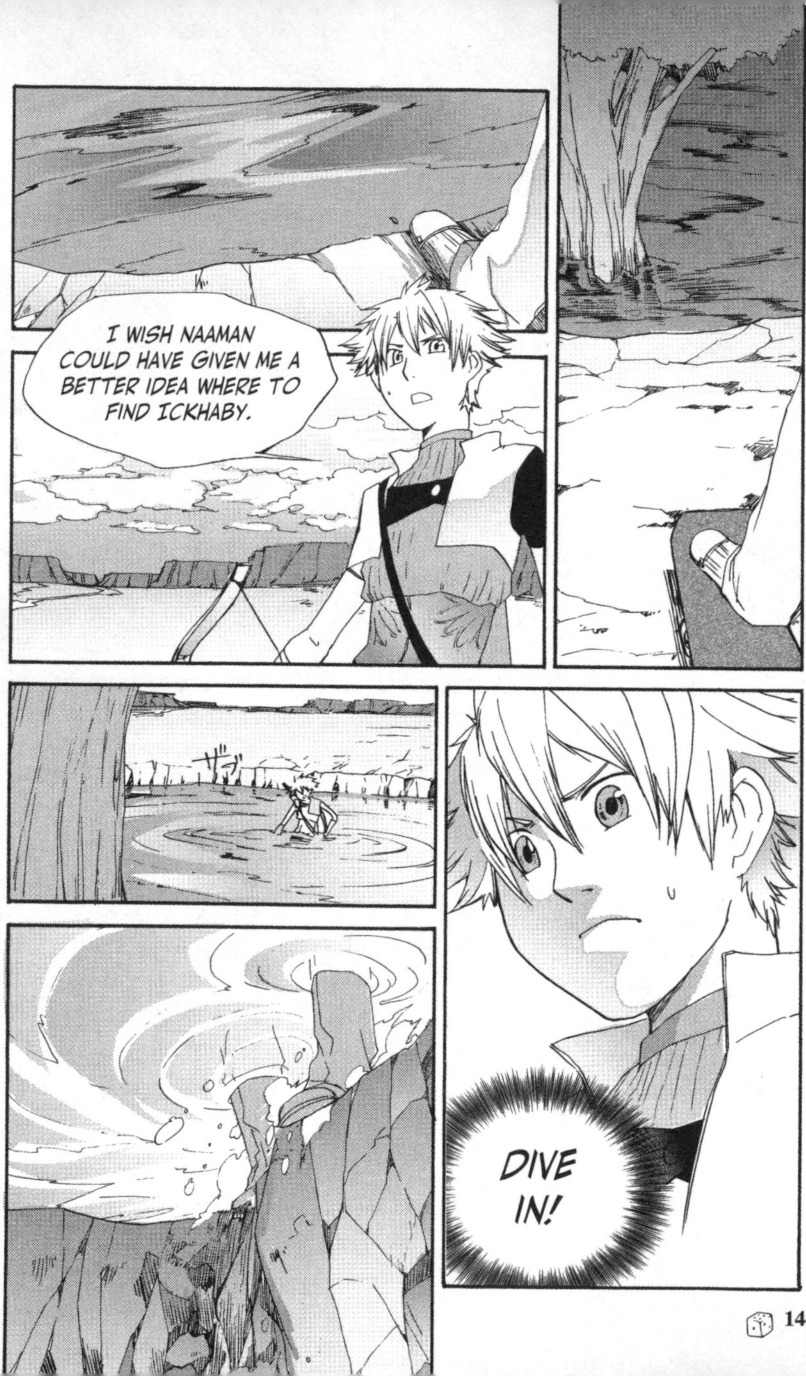
I WISH NAAMAN COULD HAVE GIVEN ME A BETTER IDEA WHERE TO FIND ICKHABY.
DIVE IN!
ザブ

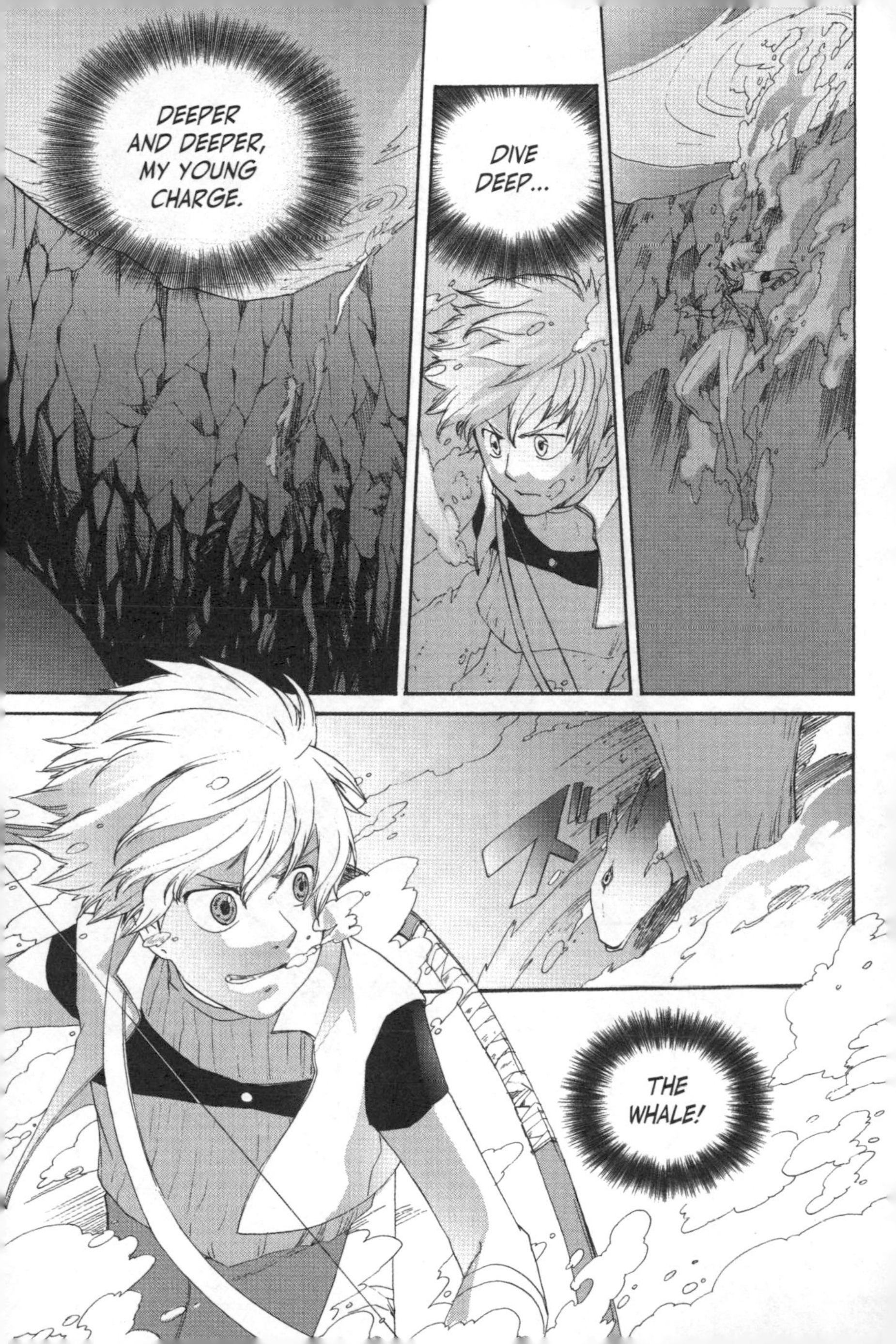
DIVE DEEP...
DEEPER AND DEEPER, MY YOUNG CHARGE.
THE WHALE!

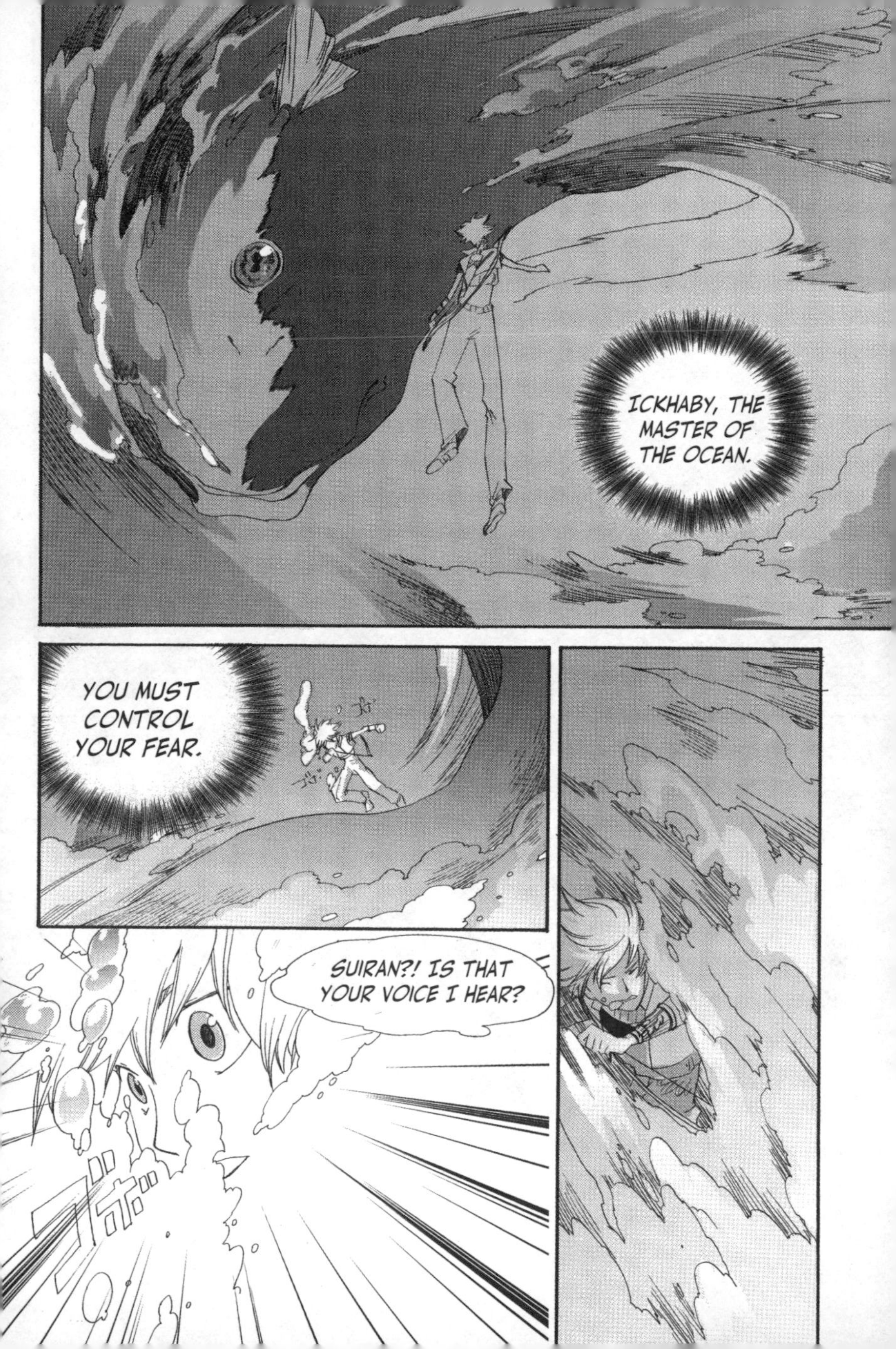
ICKHABY, THE MASTER OF THE OCEAN.
YOU MUST CONTROL YOUR FEAR.
SUIRAN?! IS THAT YOUR VOICE I HEAR?

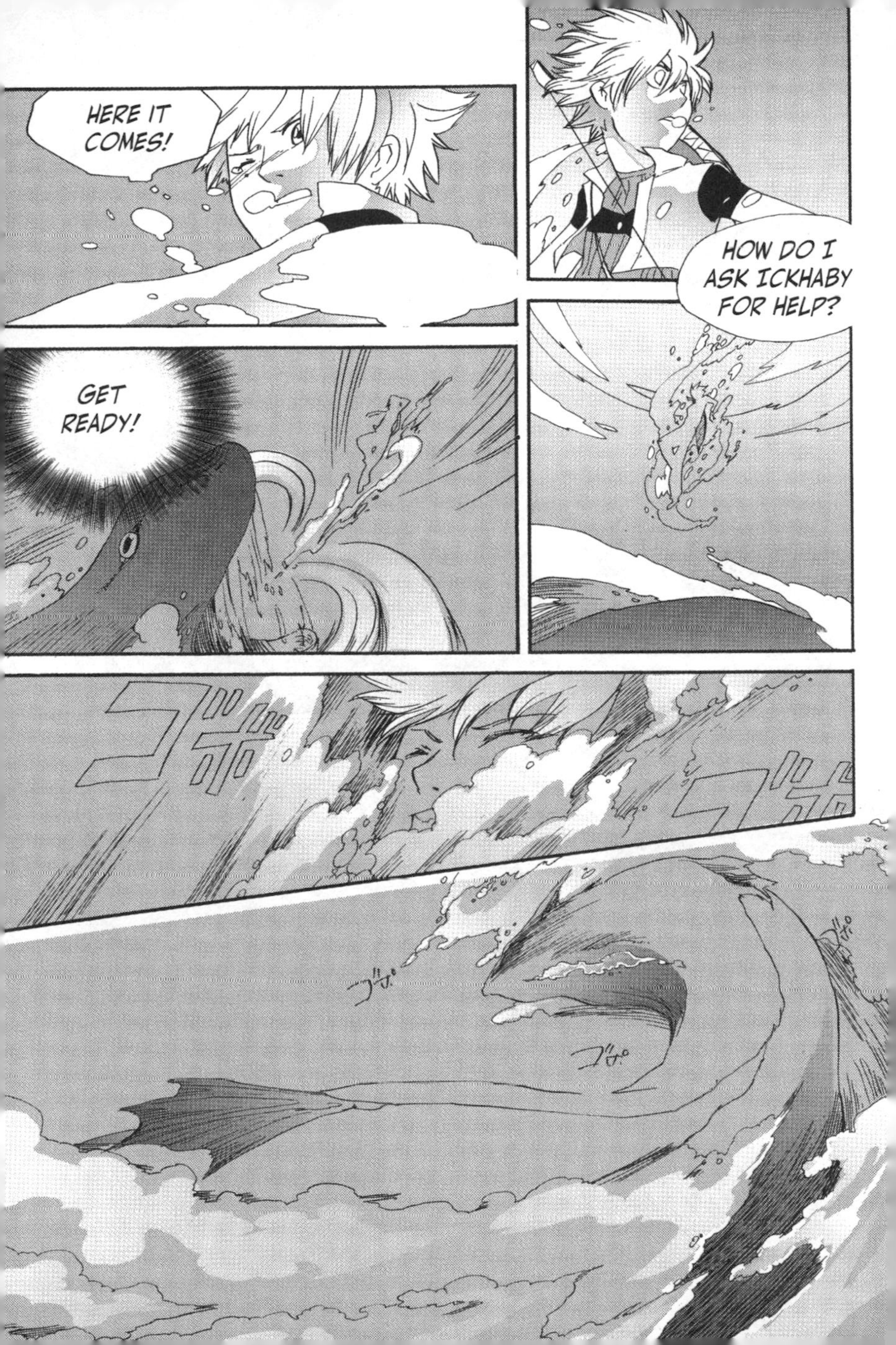
HOW DO I ASK ICKHABY FOR HELP?
HERE IT COMES!
GET READY!

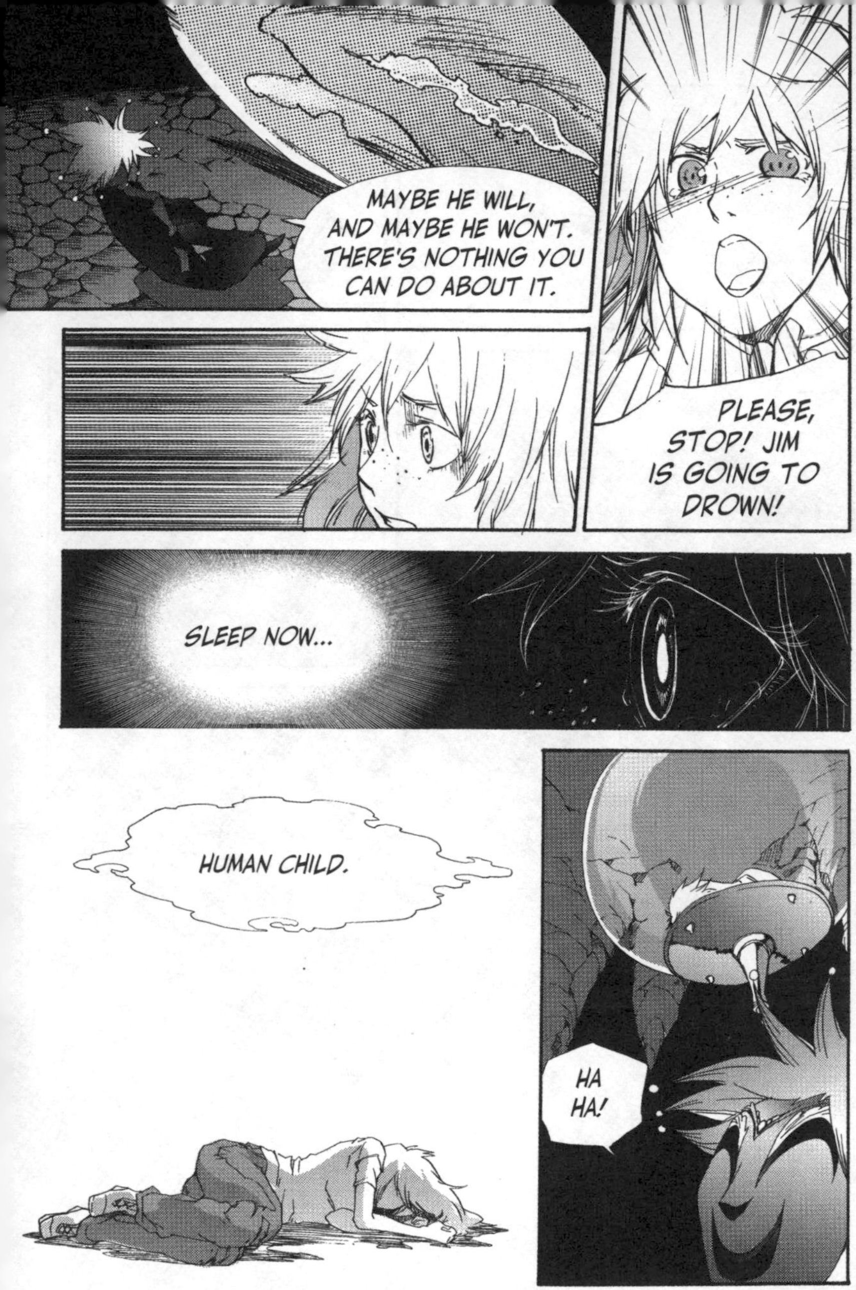
PLEASE, STOP! JIM IS GOING TO DROWN!
MAYBE HE WILL, AND MAYBE HE WON'T. THERE'S NOTHING YOU CAN DO ABOUT IT.
SLEEP NOW...
HA HA!
HUMAN CHILD.

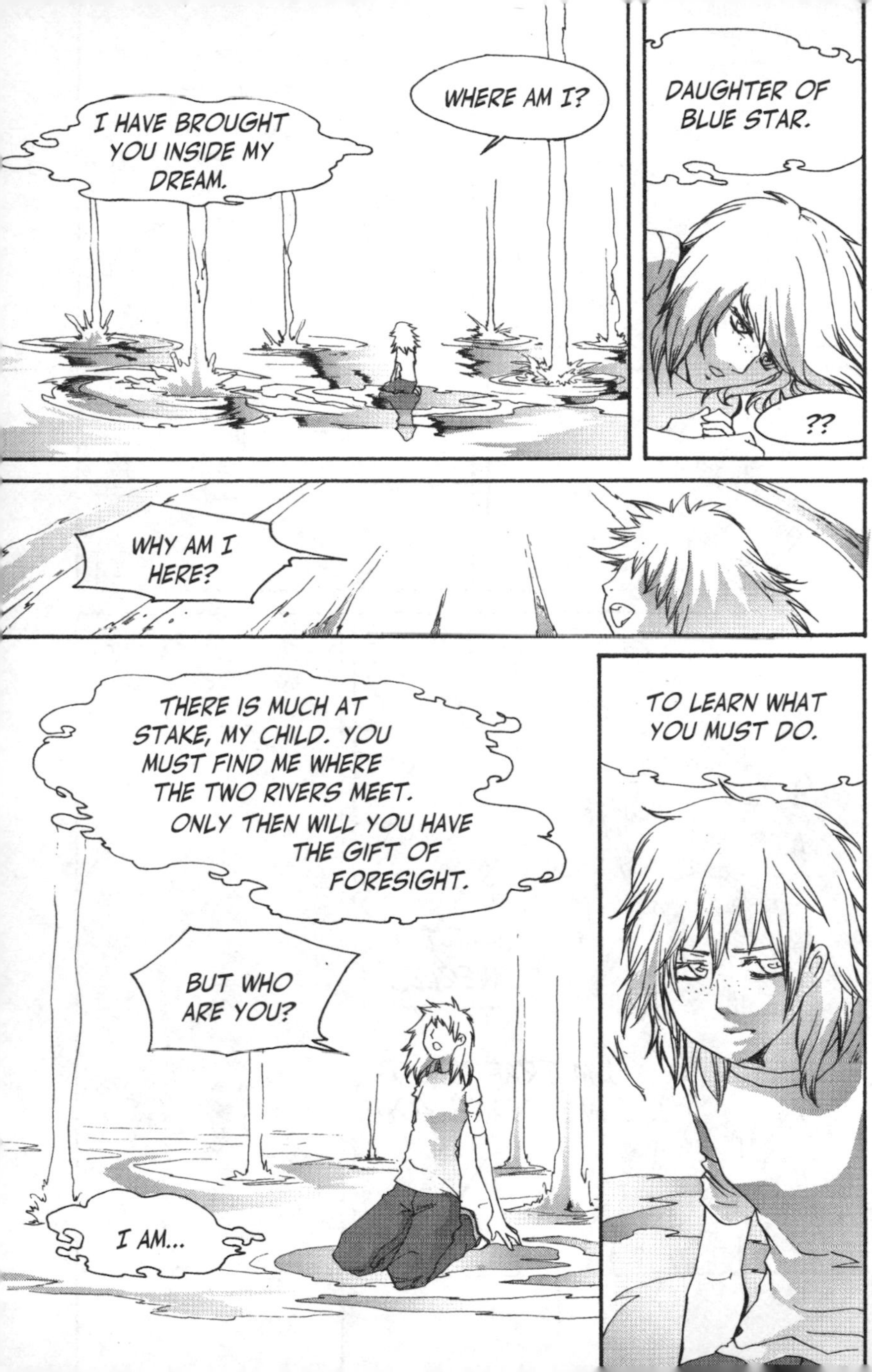
DAUGHTER OF BLUE STAR.
??
WHERE AM I?
I HAVE BROUGHT YOU INSIDE MY DREAM.
WHY AM I HERE?
TO LEARN WHAT YOU MUST DO.
THERE IS MUCH AT STAKE, MY CHILD. YOU MUST FIND ME WHERE THE TWO RIVERS MEET. ONLY THEN WILL YOU HAVE THE GIFT OF FORESIGHT.
BUT WHO ARE YOU?
I AM...

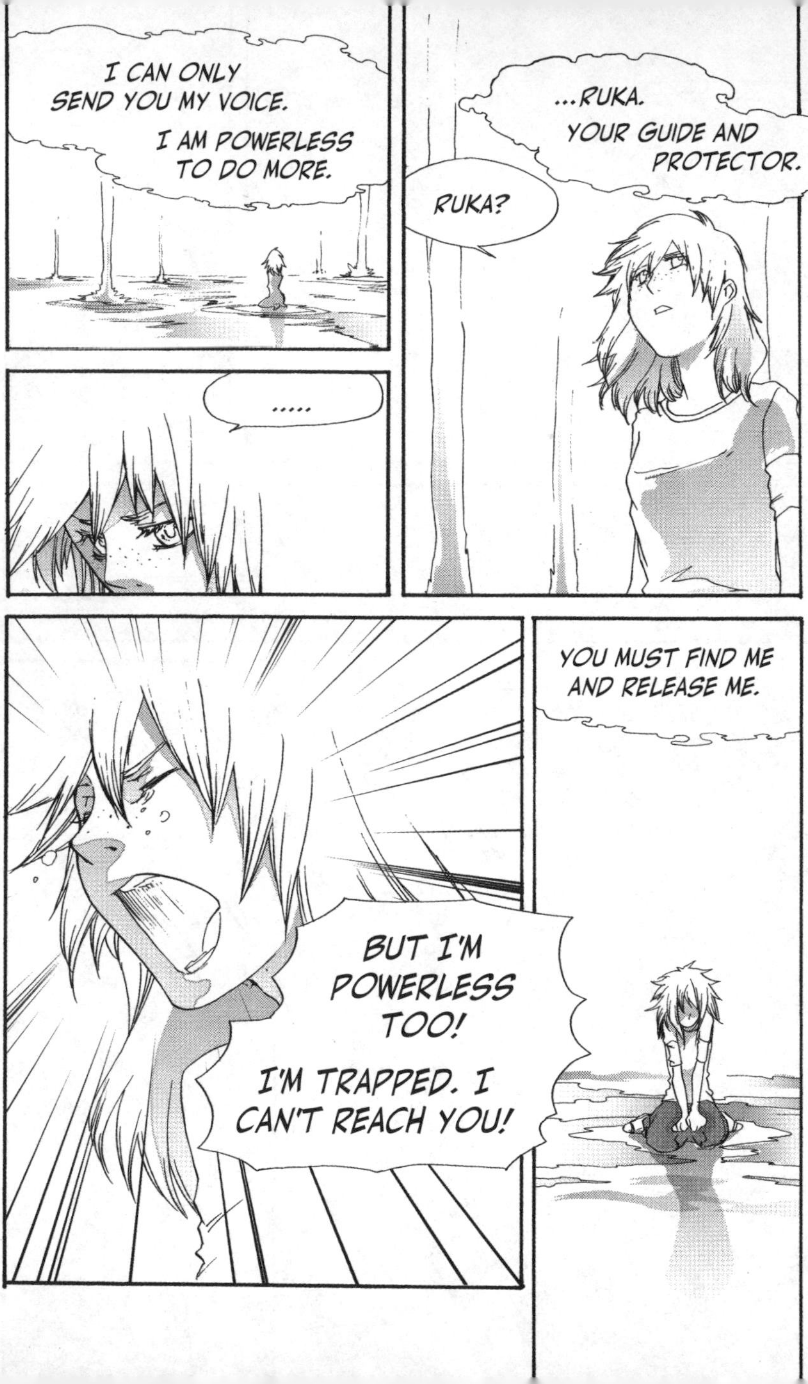
...RUKA. YOUR GUIDE AND PROTECTOR.
RUKA?
I CAN ONLY SEND YOU MY VOICE.
I AM POWERLESS TO DO MORE.
.....
YOU MUST FIND ME AND RELEASE ME.
BUT I'M POWERLESS TOO!
I'M TRAPPED. I CAN'T REACH YOU!

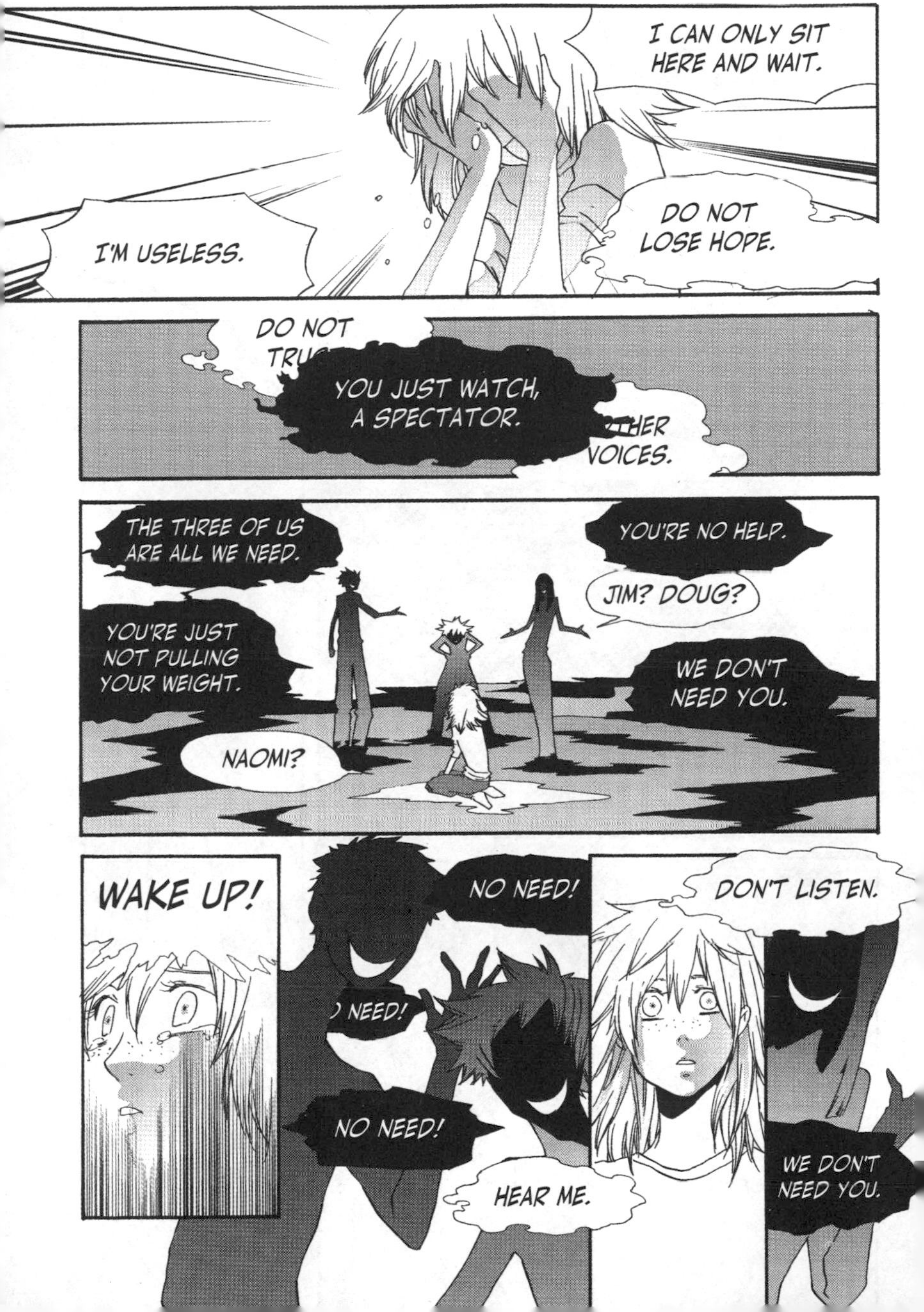

I CAN ONLY SIT HERE AND WAIT.
DO NOT LOSE HOPE.
I'M USELESS.
DO NOT TRU
YOU JUST WATCH, A SPECTATOR.
THER VOICES.
YOU'RE NO HELP.
JIM? DOUG?
WE DON'T NEED YOU.
THE THREE OF US ARE ALL WE NEED.
YOU'RE JUST NOT PULLING YOUR WEIGHT.
NAOMI?
DON'T LISTEN.
WE DON'T NEED YOU.
NO NEED!
NEED!
NO NEED!
HEAR ME.
WAKE UP!

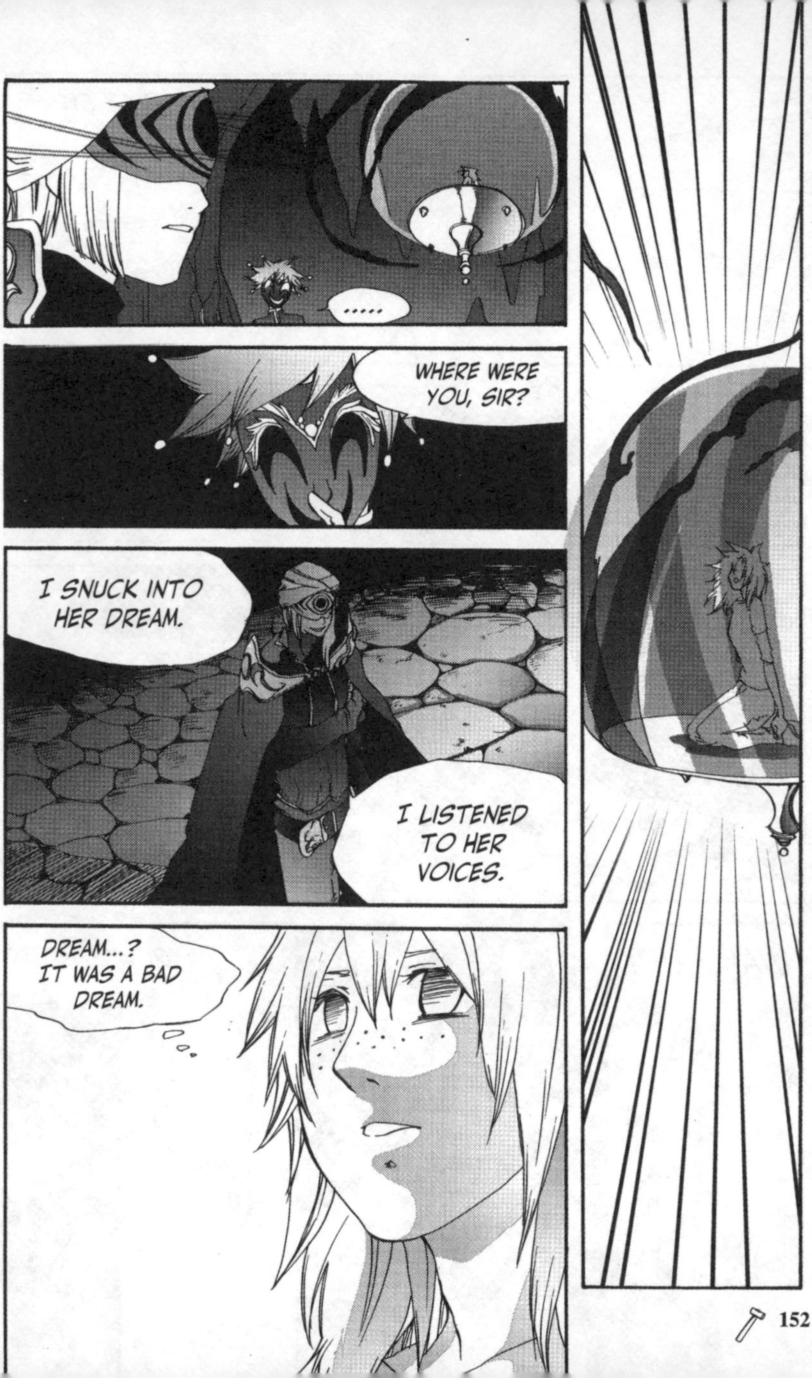
......
WHERE WERE YOU, SIR?
I SNUCK INTO HER DREAM.
I LISTENED TO HER VOICES.
DREAM...? IT WAS A BAD DREAM.

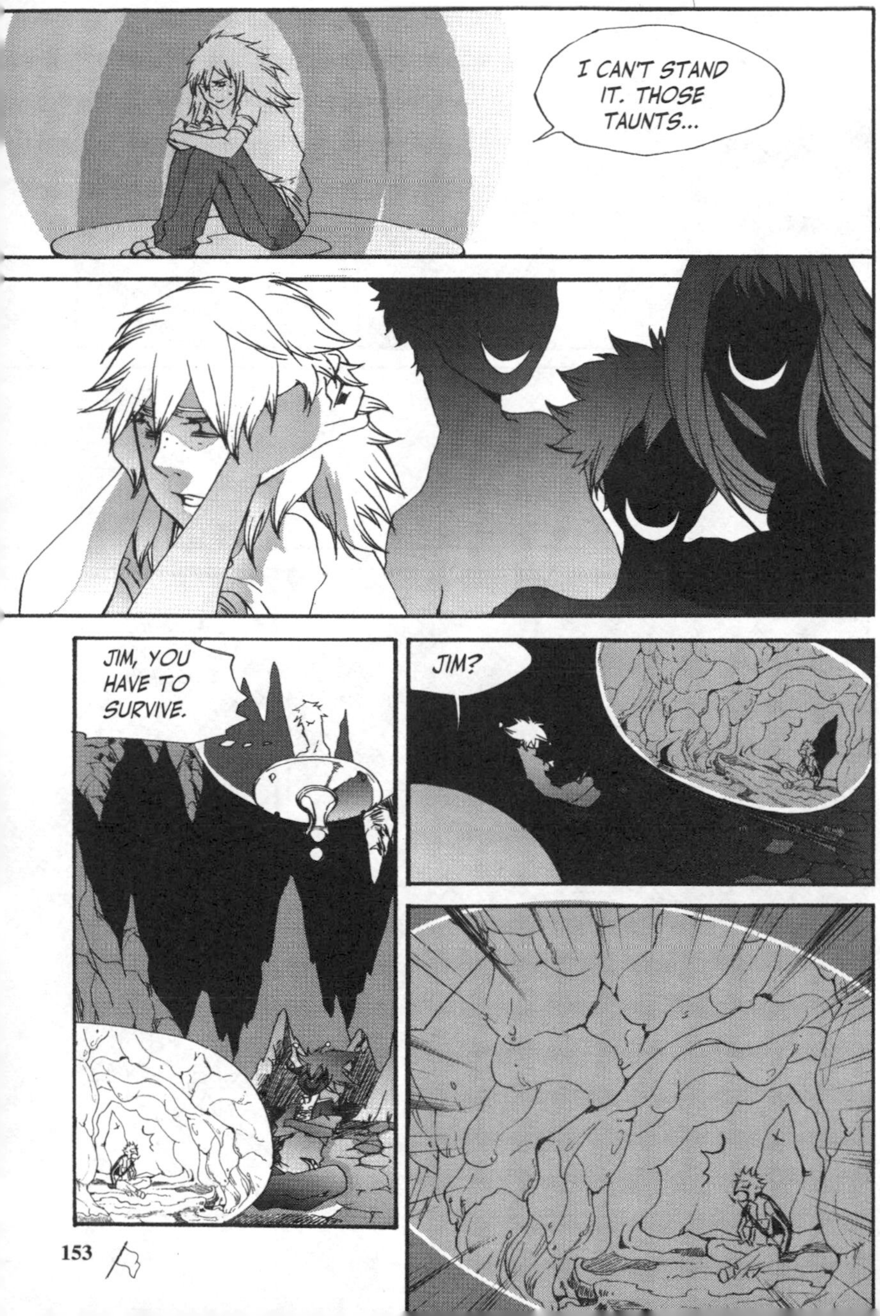
I CAN'T STAND IT. THOSE TAUNTS...
JIM?
JIM, YOU HAVE TO SURVIVE.

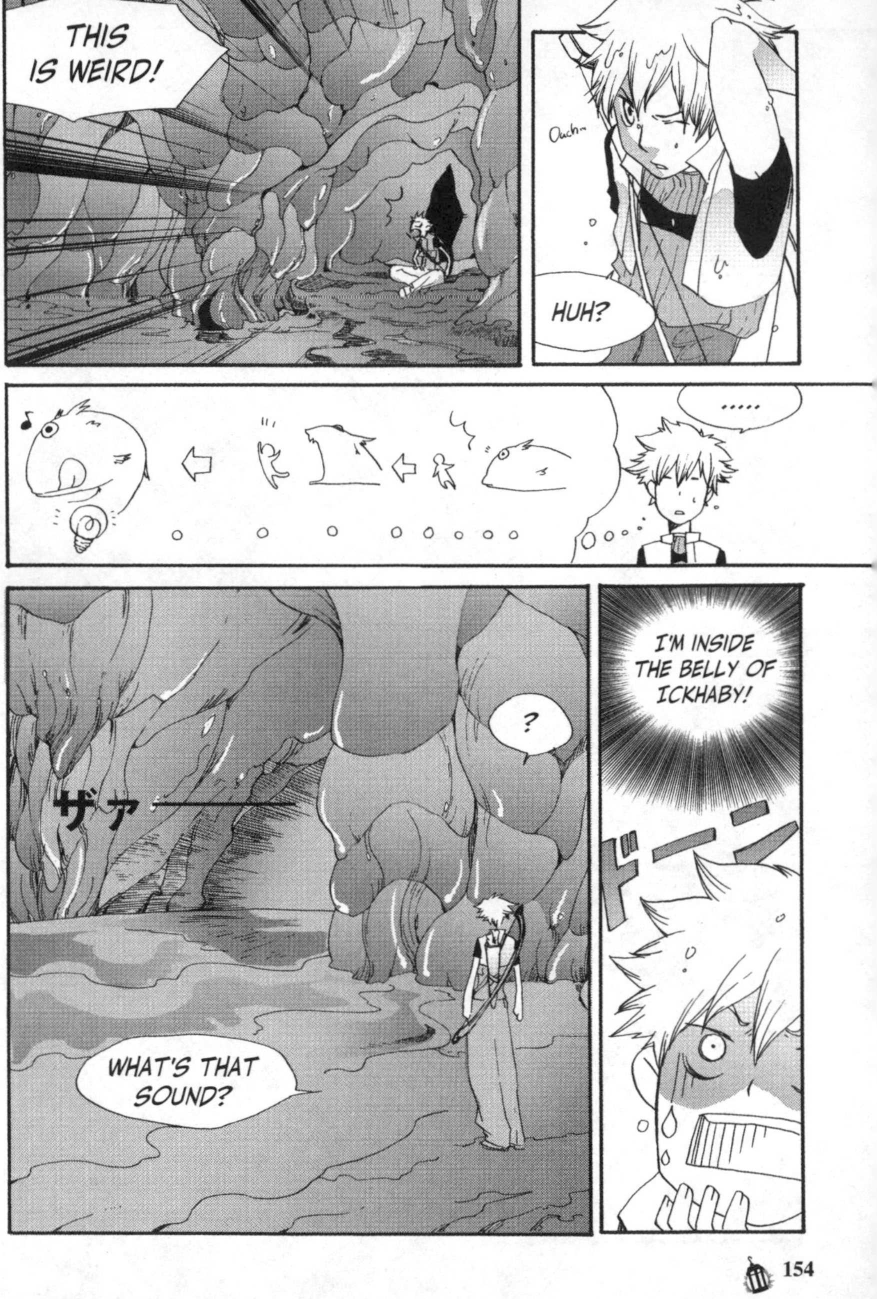
Ouch~
HUH?
THIS IS WEIRD!
......
I'M INSIDE THE BELLY OF ICKHABY!
ドーン
?
ザァ
WHAT'S THAT SOUND?

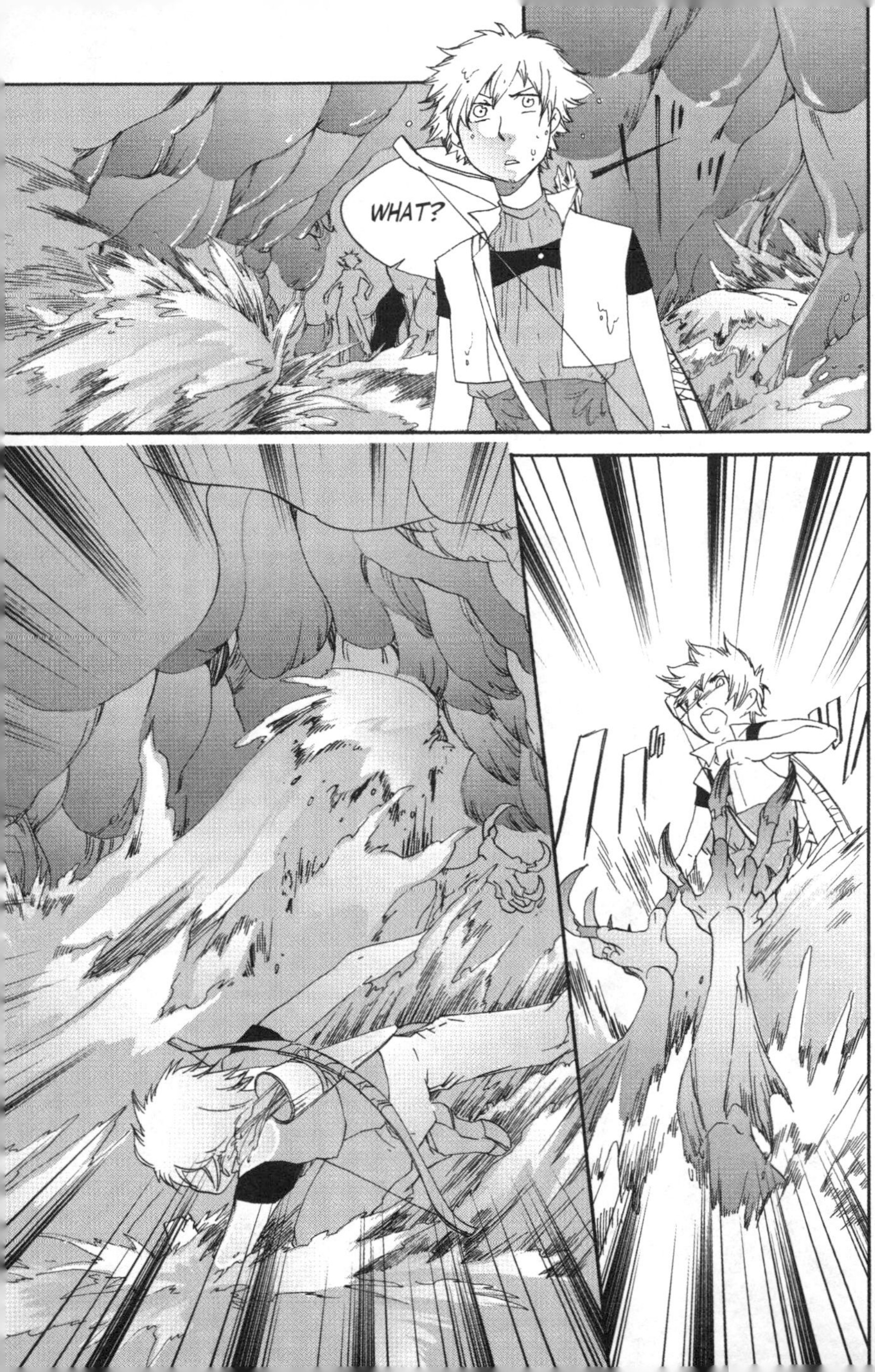
WHAT?

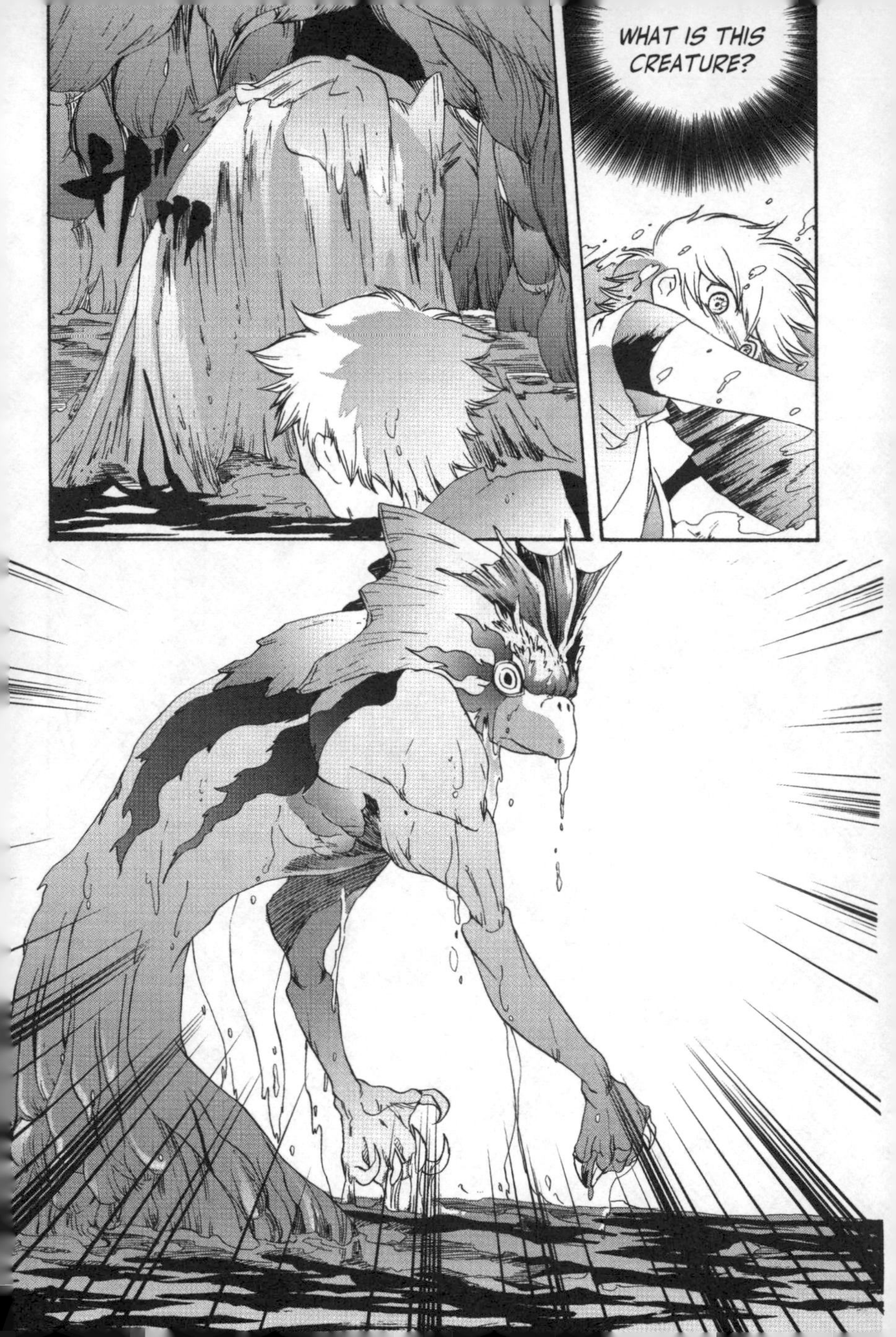
WHAT IS THIS CREATURE?

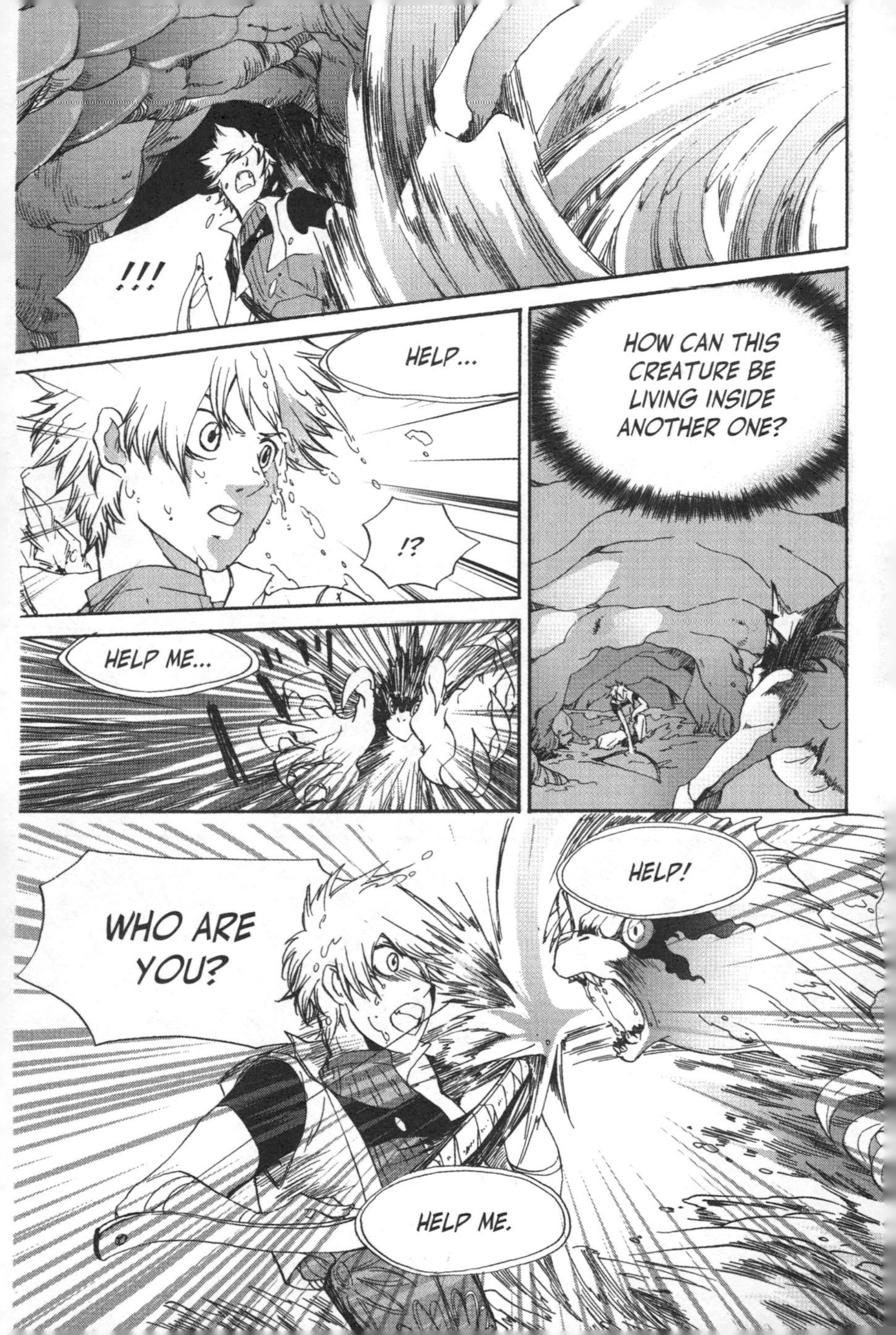
!!!
HOW CAN THIS CREATURE BE LIVING INSIDE ANOTHER ONE?
HELP...
!?
HELP ME...
HELP!
WHO ARE YOU?
HELP ME.

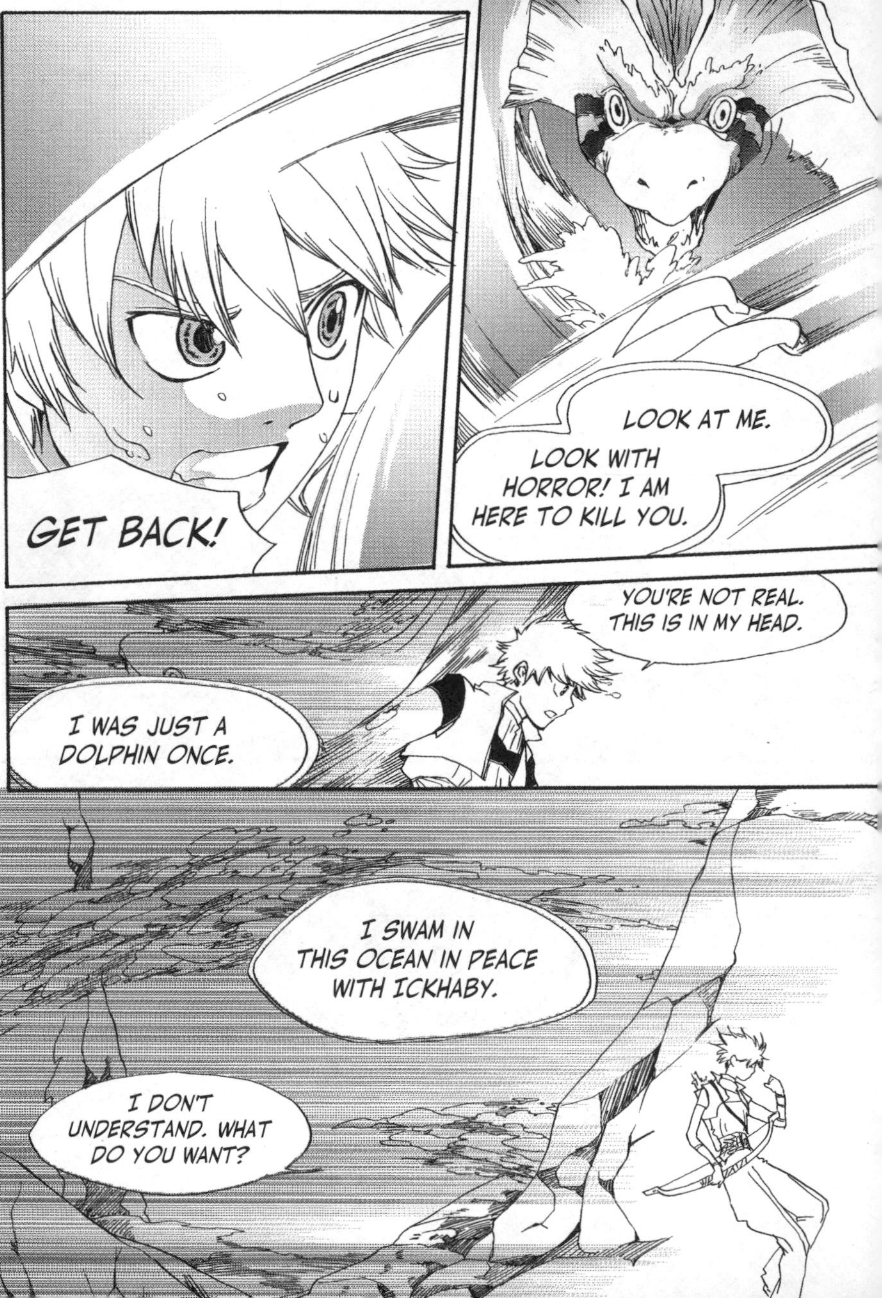
LOOK AT ME.
LOOK WITH HORROR! I AM HERE TO KILL YOU.
GET BACK!
YOU'RE NOT REAL. THIS IS IN MY HEAD.
I WAS JUST A DOLPHIN ONCE.
I SWAM IN THIS OCEAN IN PEACE WITH ICKHABY.
I DON'T UNDERSTAND. WHAT DO YOU WANT?

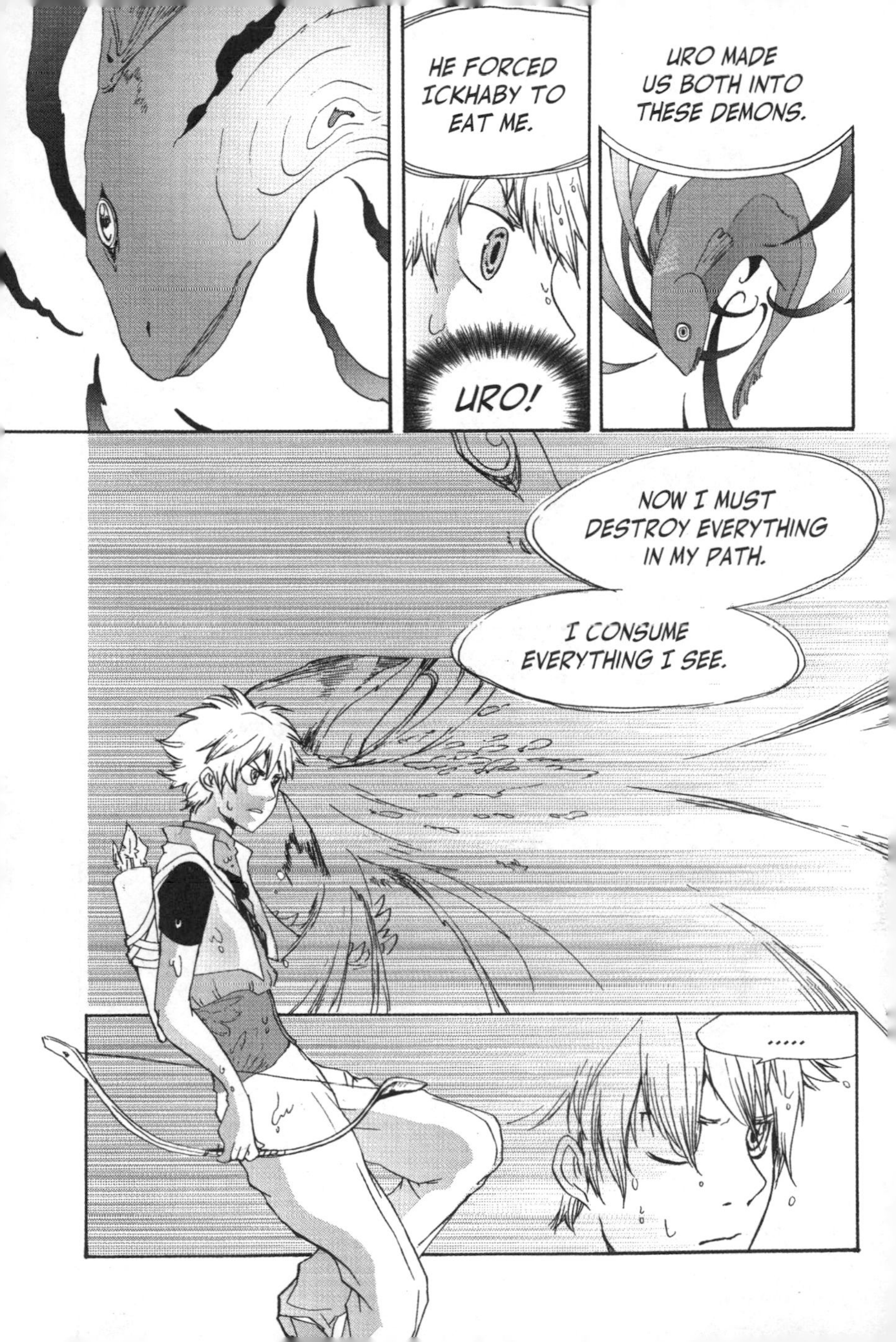
URO MADE US BOTH INTO THESE DEMONS.
HE FORCED ICKHABY TO EAT ME.
URO!
NOW I MUST DESTROY EVERYTHING IN MY PATH.
I CONSUME EVERYTHING I SEE.
.....

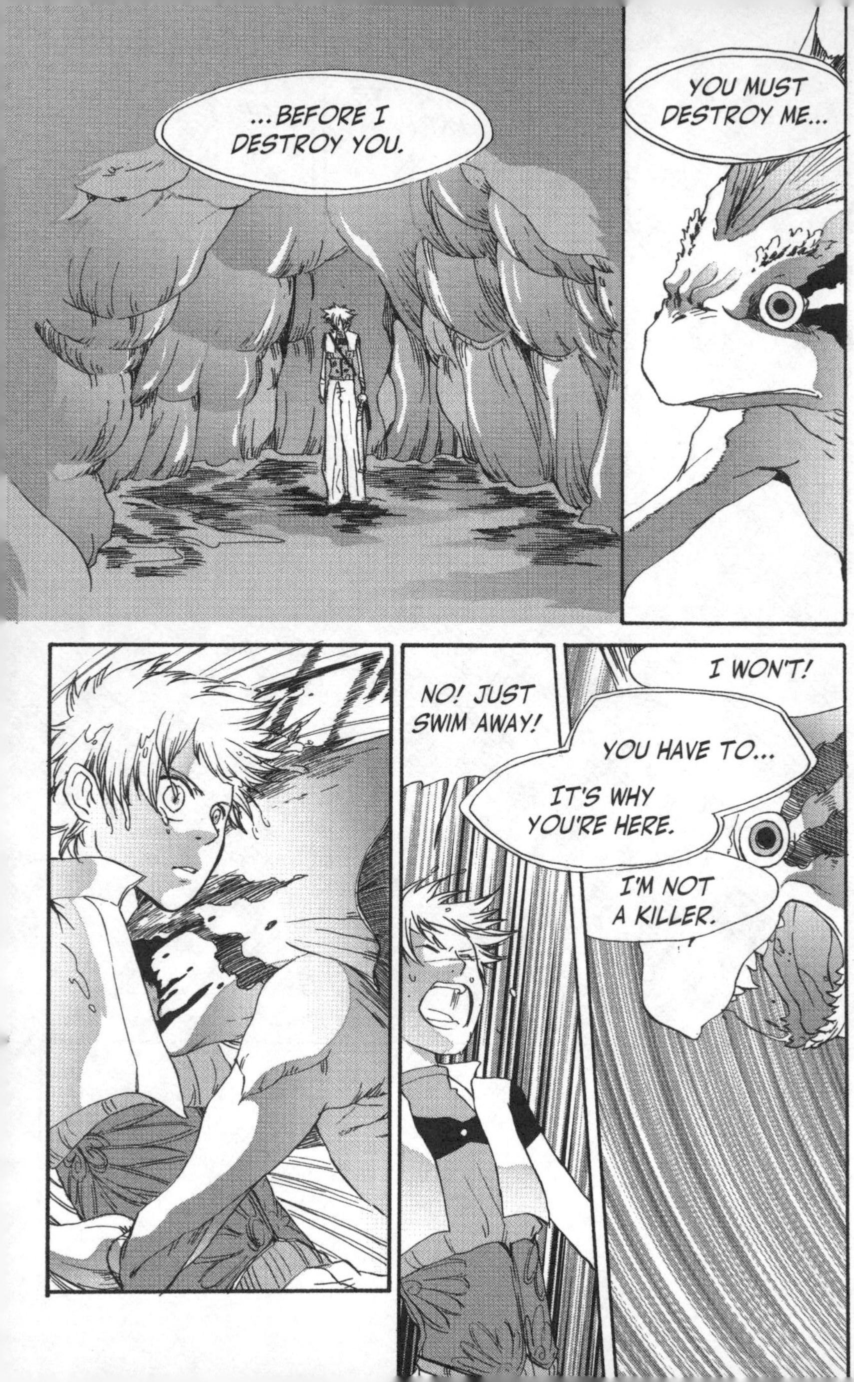
YOU MUST DESTROY ME...
...BEFORE I DESTROY YOU.
I WON'T!
NO! JUST SWIM AWAY!
YOU HAVE TO...
IT'S WHY YOU'RE HERE.
I'M NOT A KILLER.

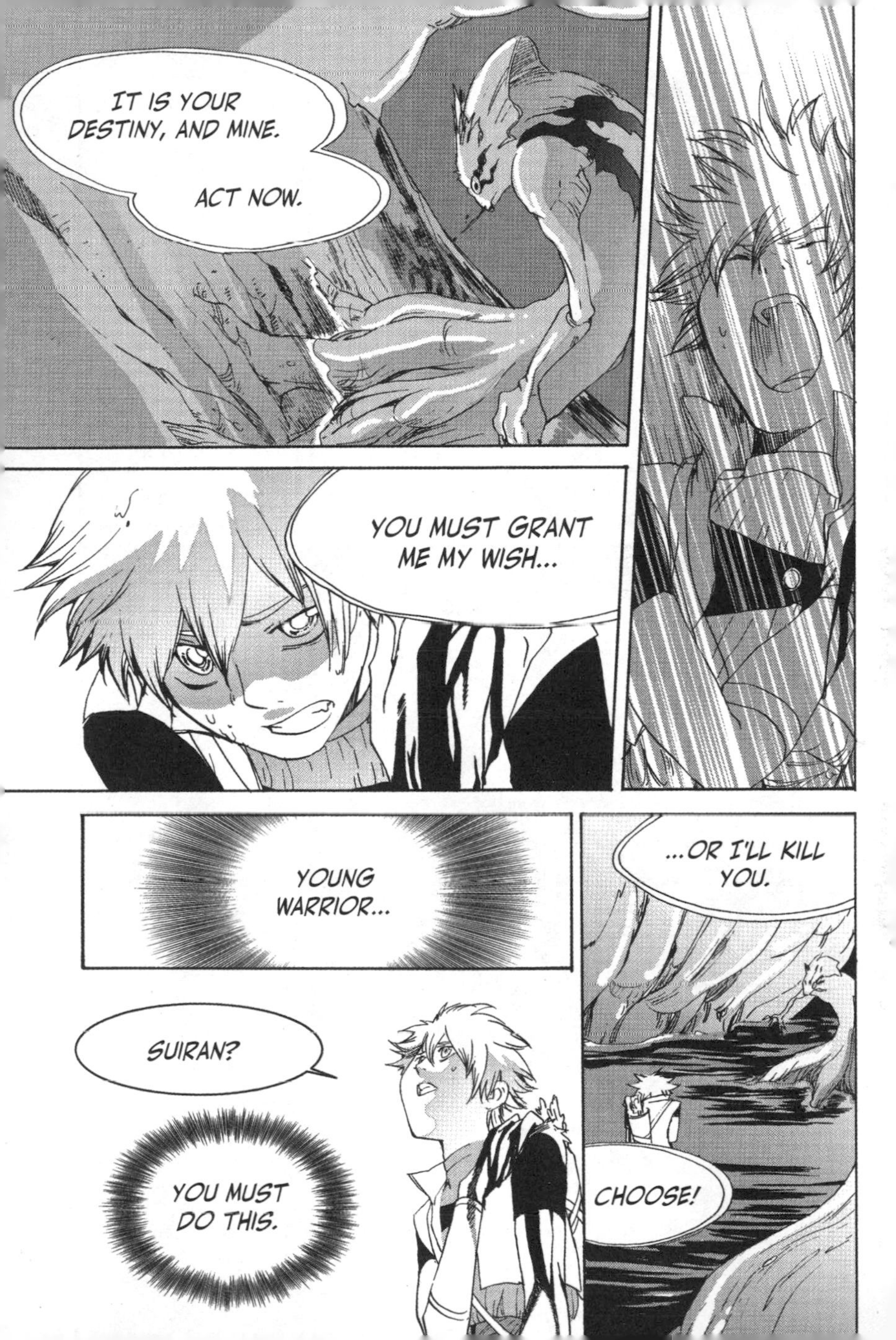

IT IS YOUR DESTINY, AND MINE.
ACT NOW.
YOU MUST GRANT ME MY WISH...
...OR I'LL KILL YOU.
CHOOSE!
YOUNG WARRIOR...
SUIRAN?
YOU MUST DO THIS.

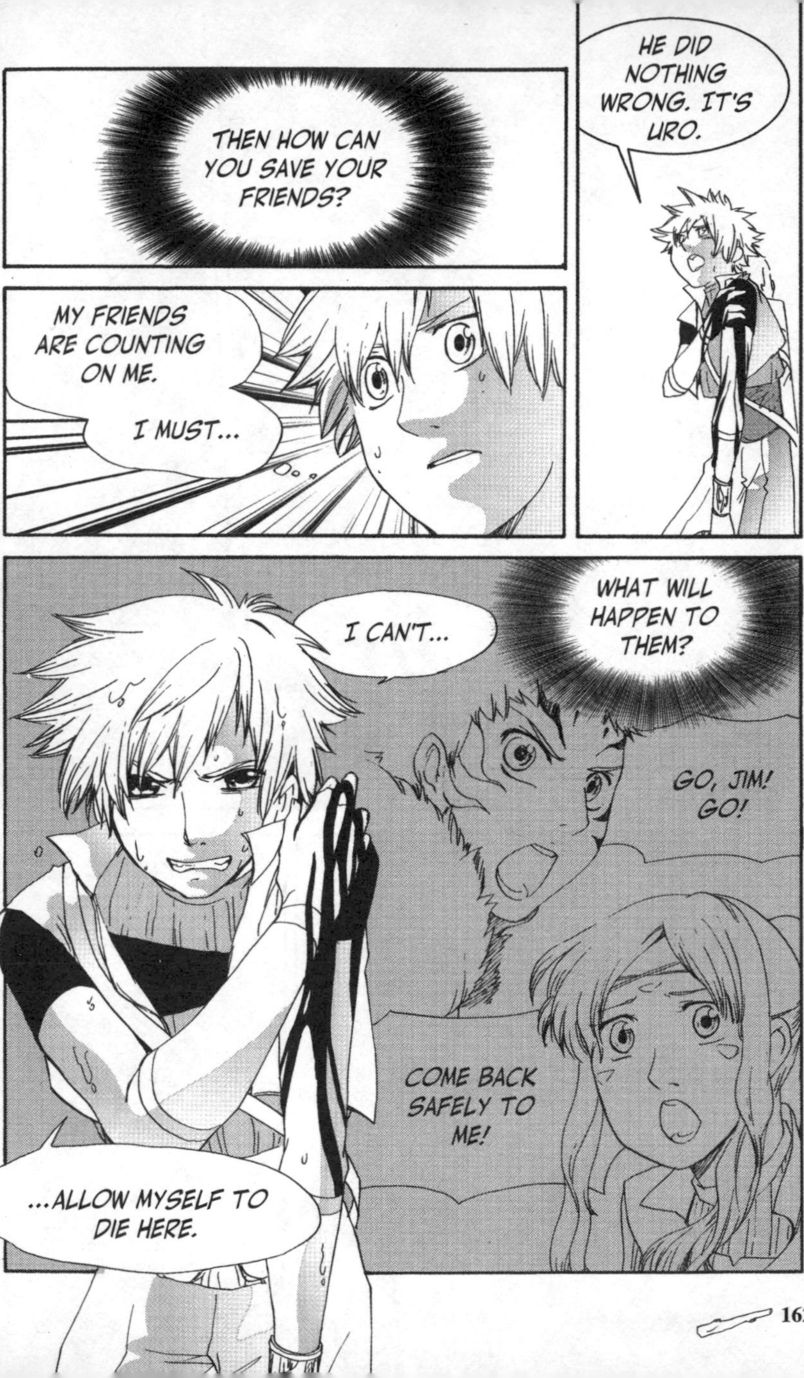
HE DID NOTHING WRONG. IT'S URO.
THEN HOW CAN YOU SAVE YOUR FRIENDS?
MY FRIENDS ARE COUNTING ON ME.
I MUST...
WHAT WILL HAPPEN TO THEM?
I CAN'T...
GO, JIM! GO!
COME BACK SAFELY TO ME!
...ALLOW MYSELF TO DIE HERE.

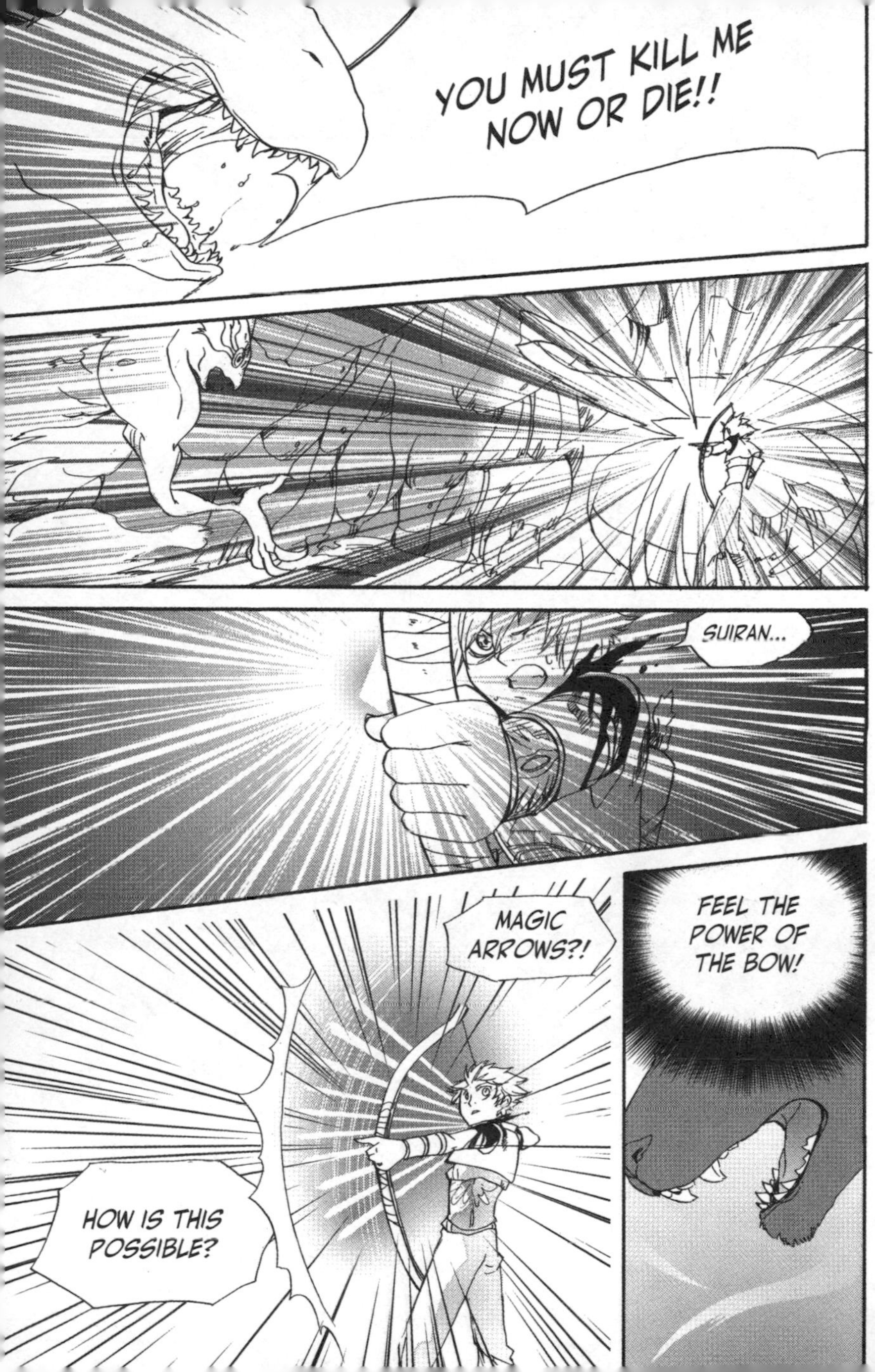
YOU MUST KILL ME NOW OR DIE!!
SUIRAN...
FEEL THE POWER OF THE BOW!
MAGIC ARROWS?!
HOW IS THIS POSSIBLE?

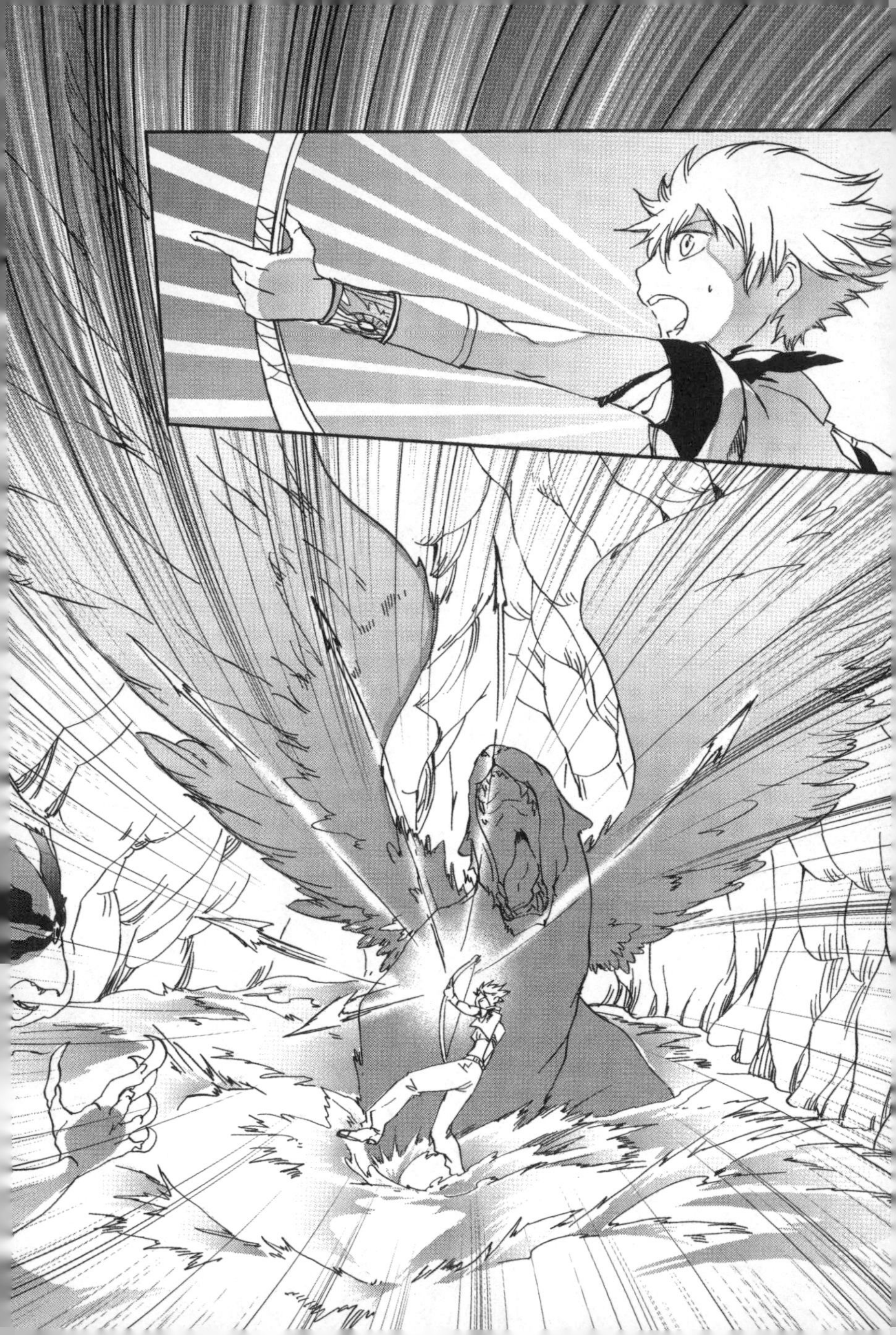

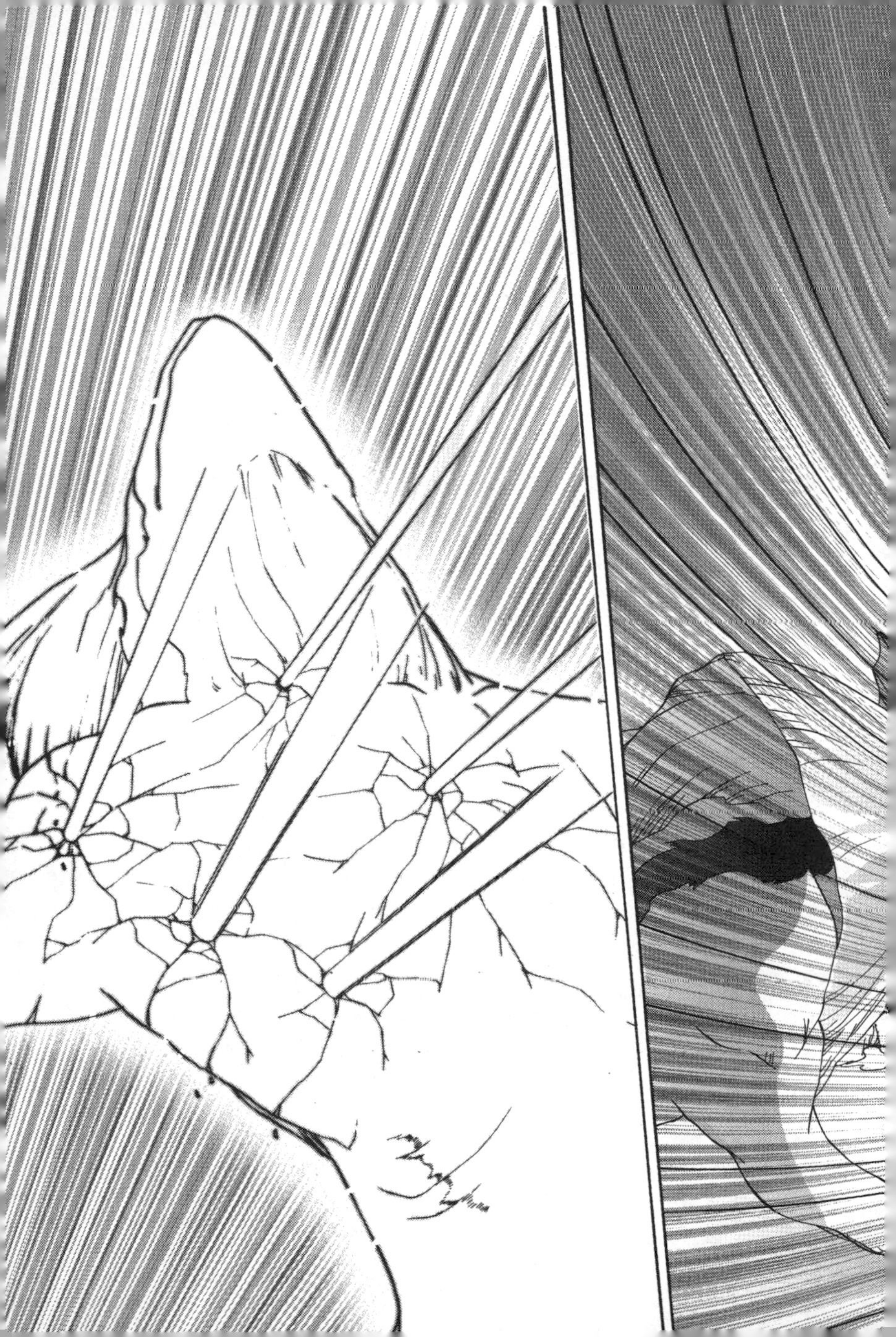

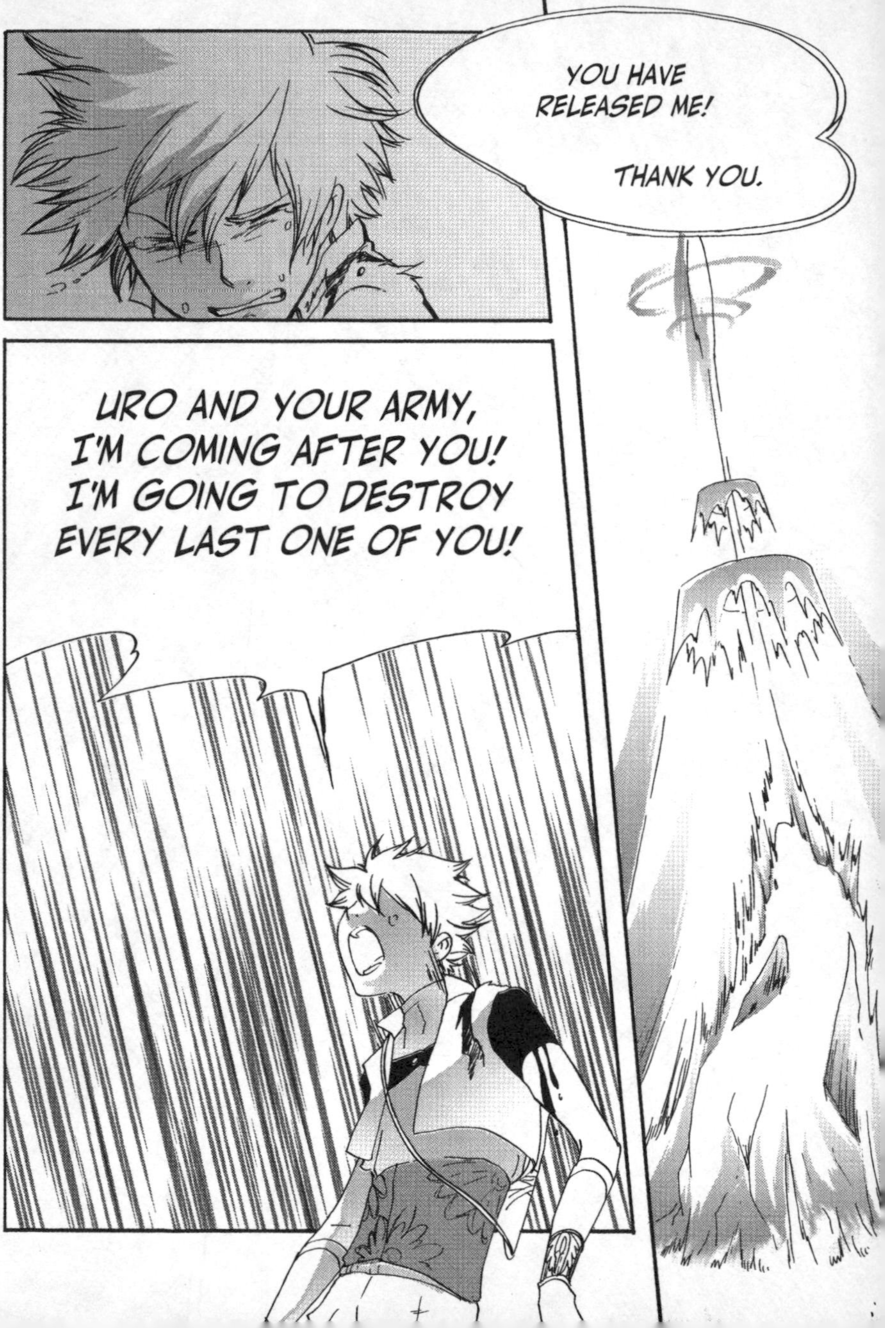
YOU HAVE RELEASED ME! THANK YOU.
URO AND YOUR ARMY, I'M COMING AFTER YOU! I'M GOING TO DESTROY EVERY LAST ONE OF YOU!

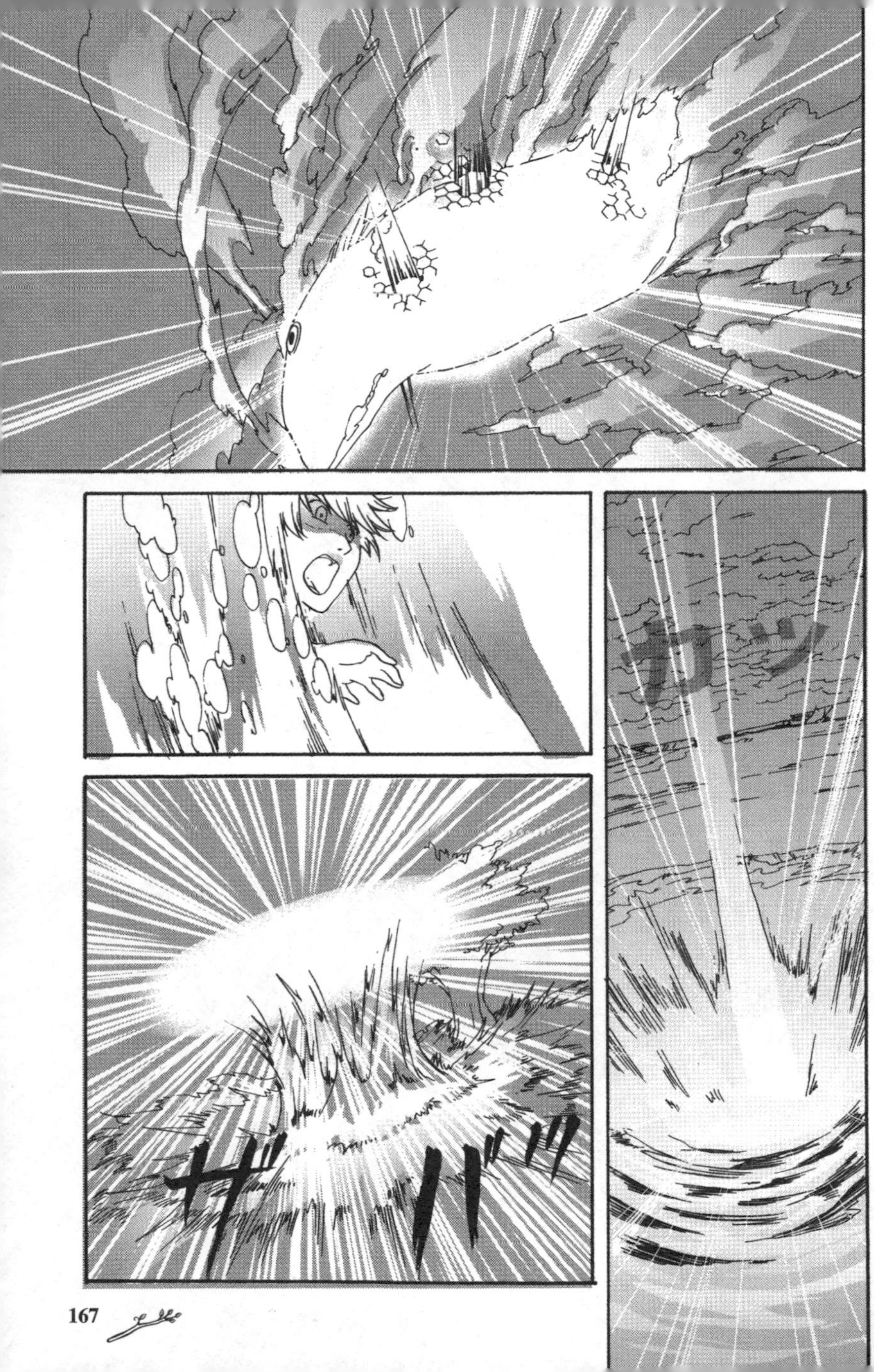
ガッ
ザバ

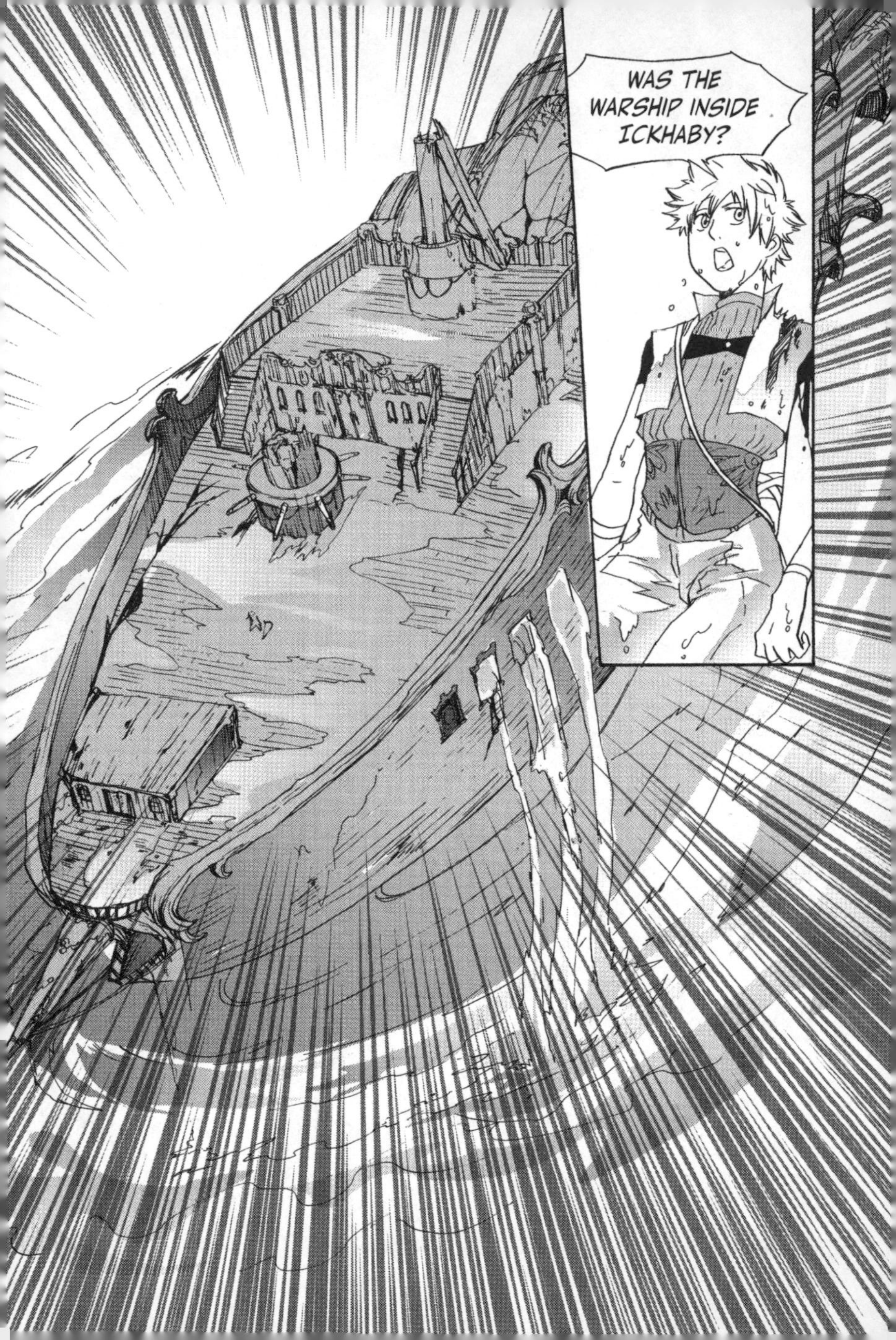
WAS THE WARSHIP INSIDE ICKHABY?

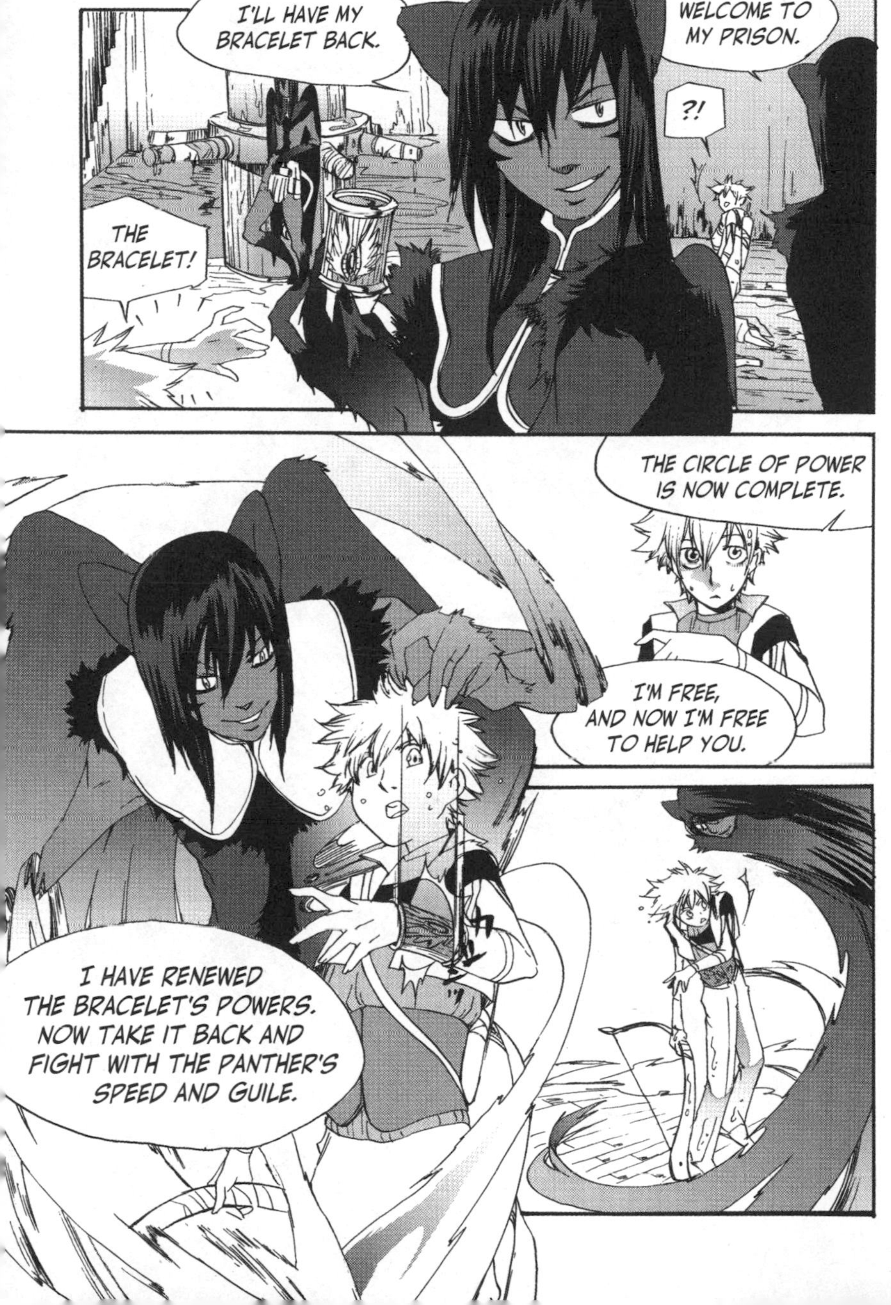
WELCOME TO MY PRISON.
I'LL HAVE MY BRACELET BACK.
?!
THE BRACELET!
THE CIRCLE OF POWER IS NOW COMPLETE.
I'M FREE, AND NOW I'M FREE TO HELP YOU.
I HAVE RENEWED THE BRACELET'S POWERS. NOW TAKE IT BACK AND FIGHT WITH THE PANTHER'S SPEED AND GUILE.

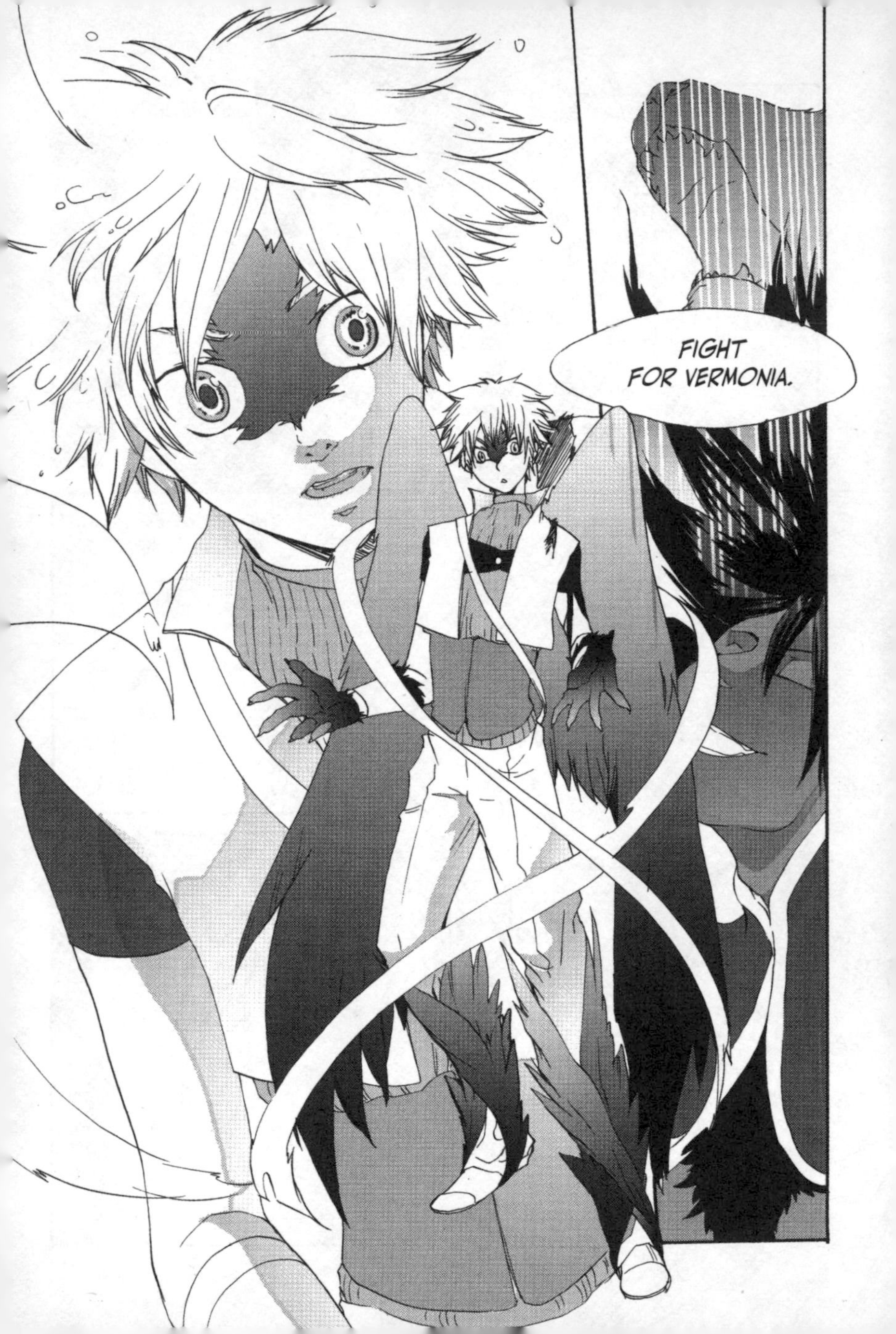
FIGHT
FOR VERMONIA.

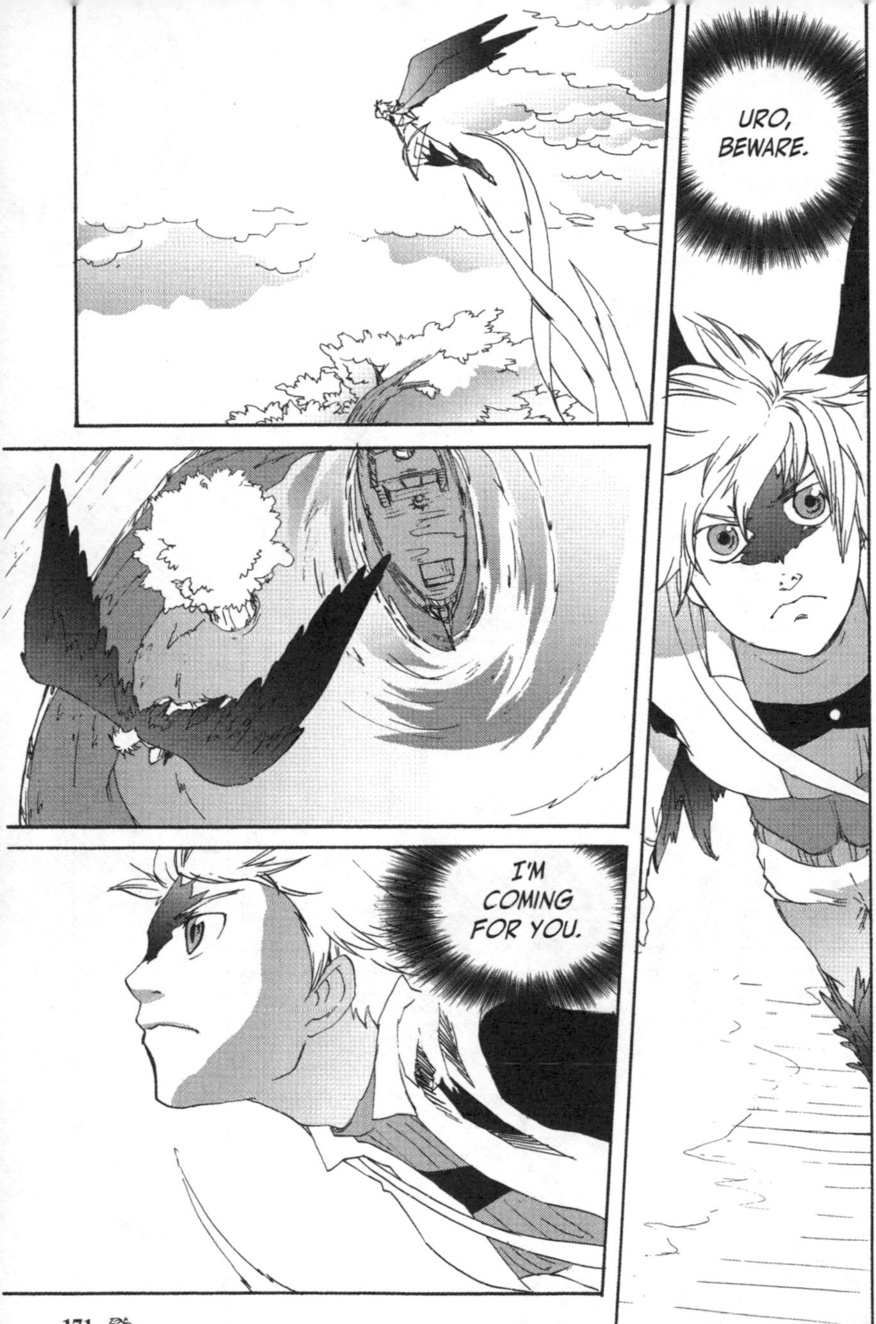
URO, BEWARE.
I'M COMING FOR YOU.

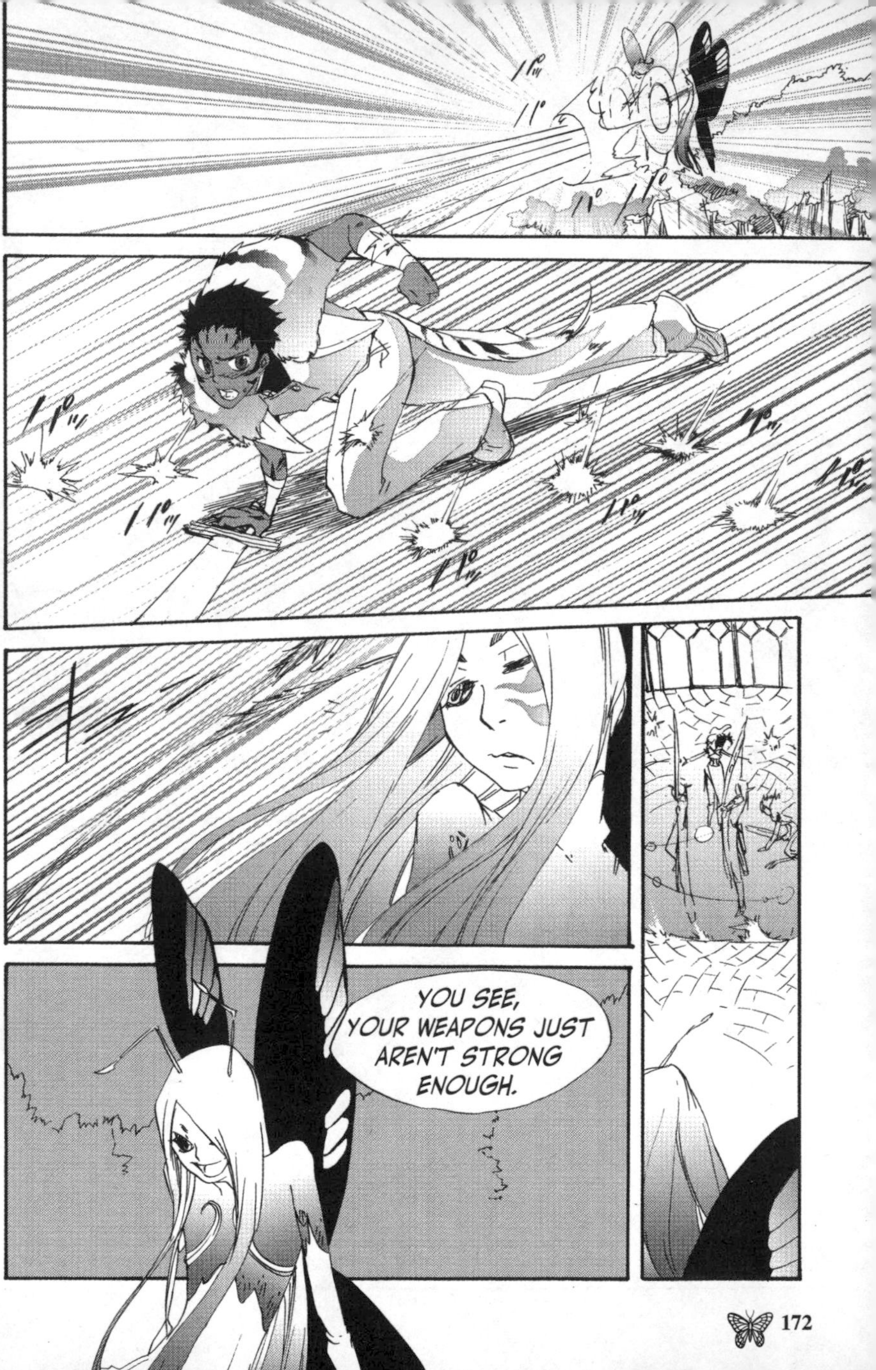
YOU SEE, YOUR WEAPONS JUST AREN'T STRONG ENOUGH.

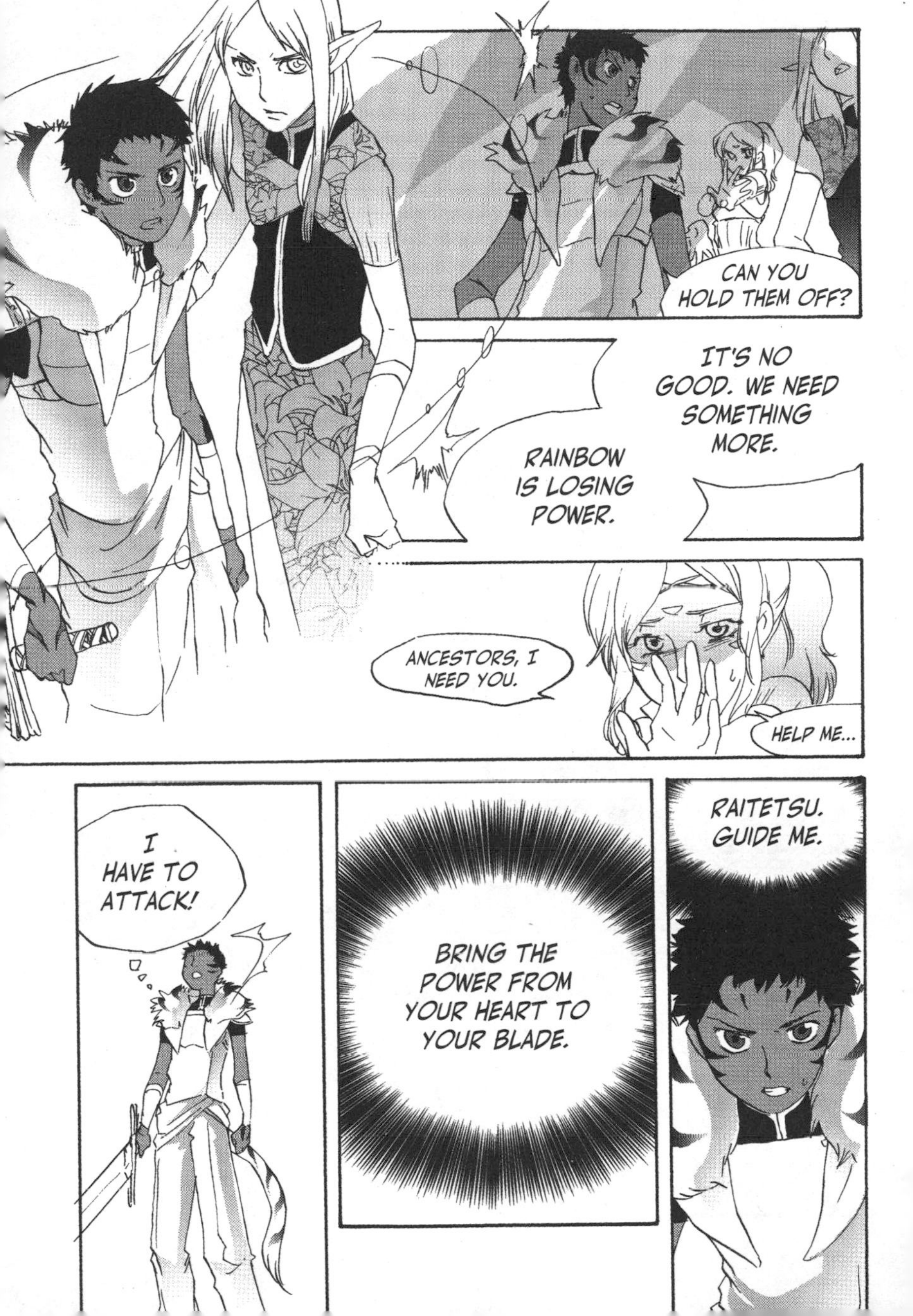
CAN YOU HOLD THEM OFF?
IT'S NO GOOD. WE NEED SOMETHING MORE.
RAINBOW IS LOSING POWER.
ANCESTORS, I NEED YOU.
HELP ME...
RAITETSU. GUIDE ME.
BRING THE POWER FROM YOUR HEART TO YOUR BLADE.
I HAVE TO ATTACK!

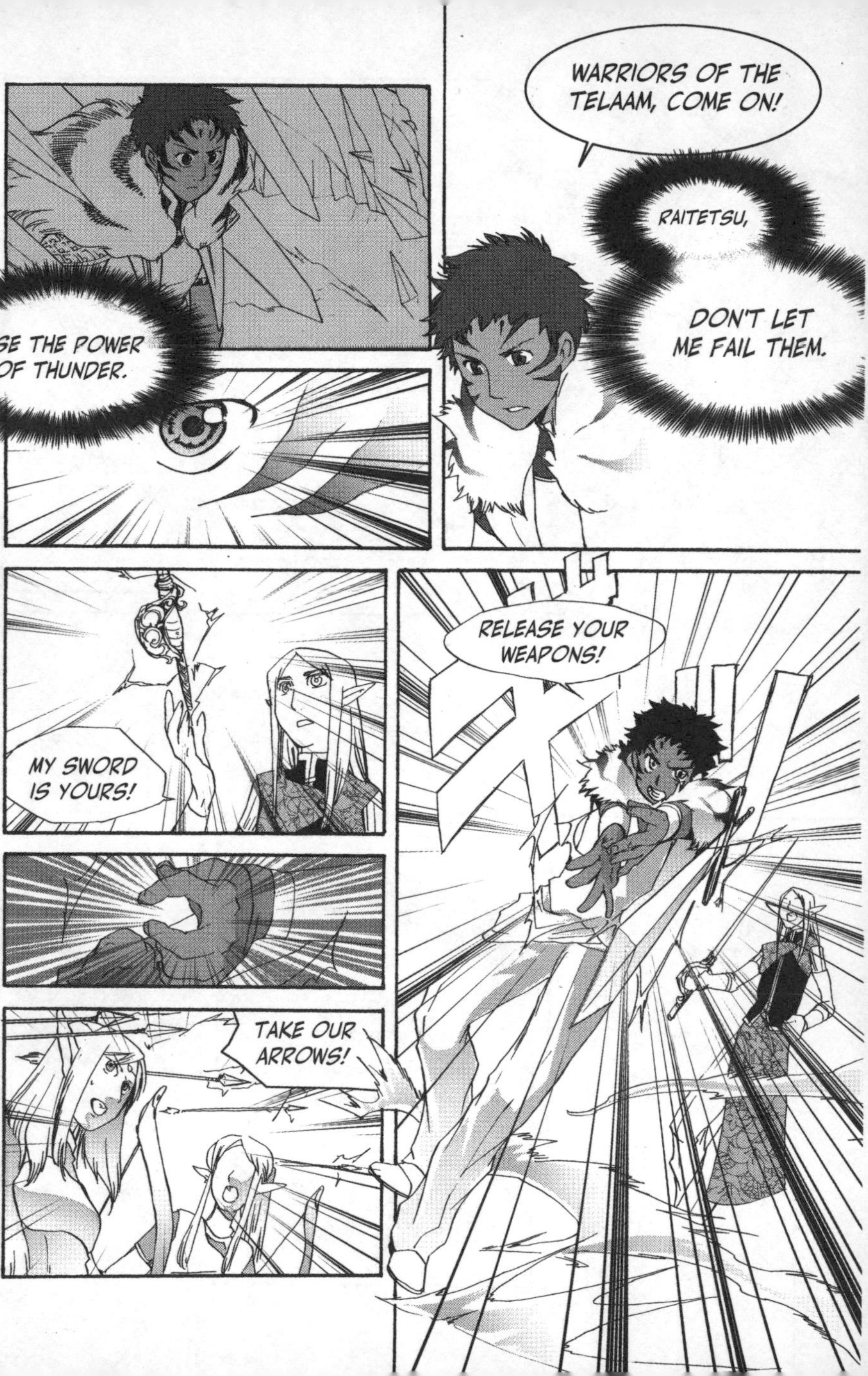
WARRIORS OF THE TELAAM, COME ON!
RAITETSU,
DON'T LET ME FAIL THEM.
USE THE POWER OF THUNDER.
RELEASE YOUR WEAPONS!
MY SWORD IS YOURS!
TAKE OUR ARROWS!

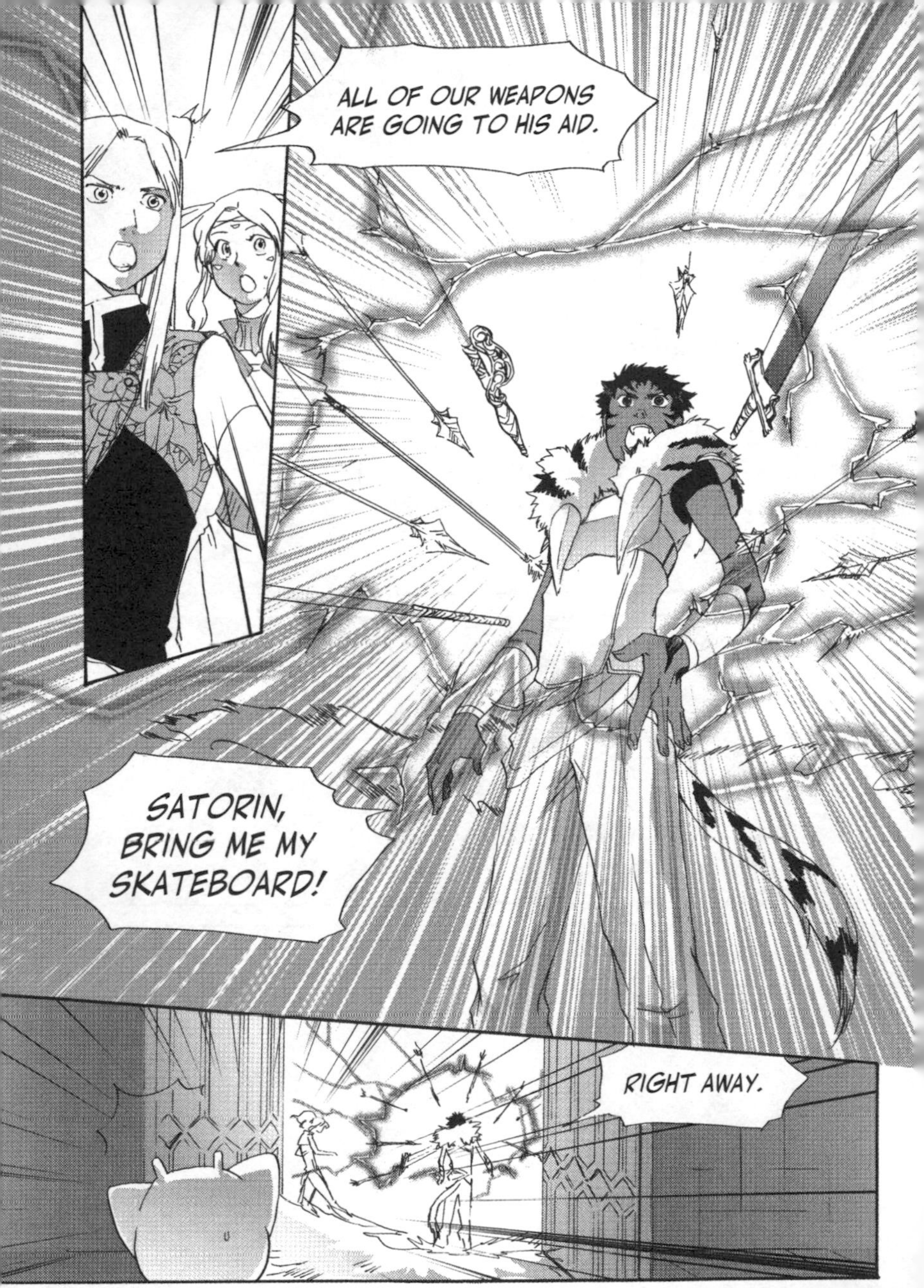
ALL OF OUR WEAPONS ARE GOING TO HIS AID.
SATORIN, BRING ME MY SKATEBOARD!
RIGHT AWAY.

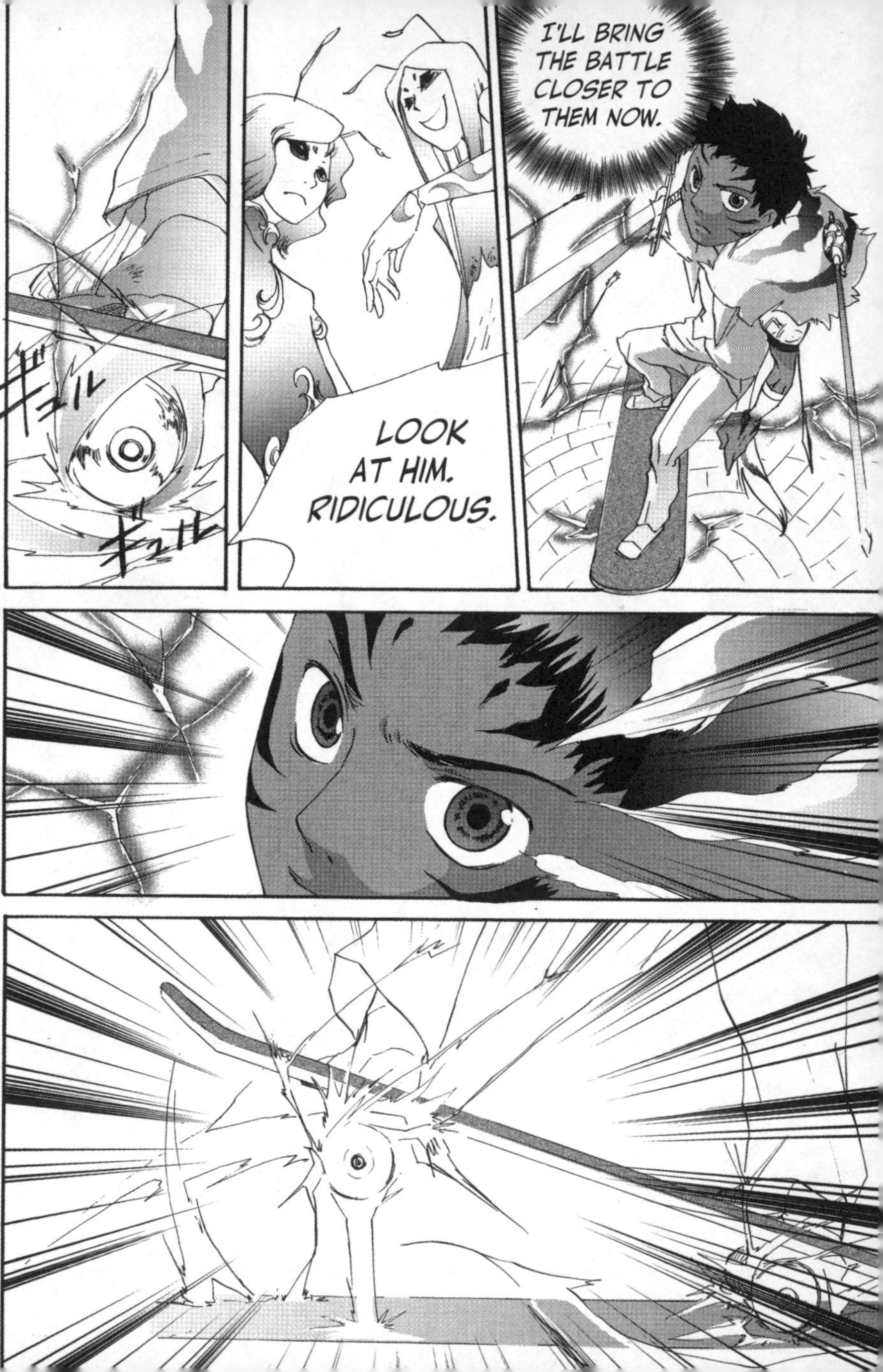
I'LL BRING THE BATTLE CLOSER TO THEM NOW.
LOOK AT HIM. RIDICULOUS.
ギュル
ギュル

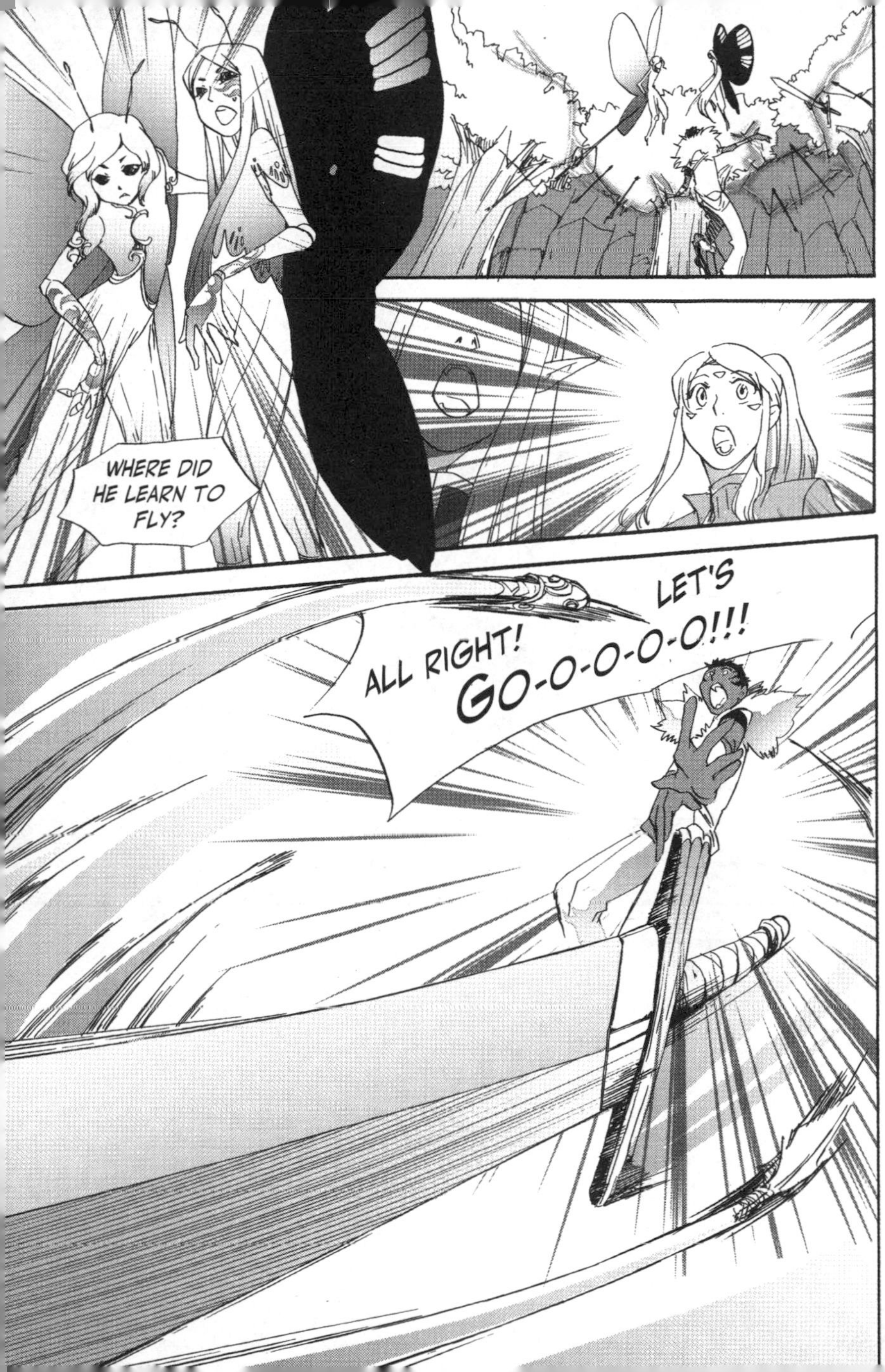
WHERE DID HE LEARN TO FLY?
ALL RIGHT! LET'S GO-O-O-O-O-O!!!

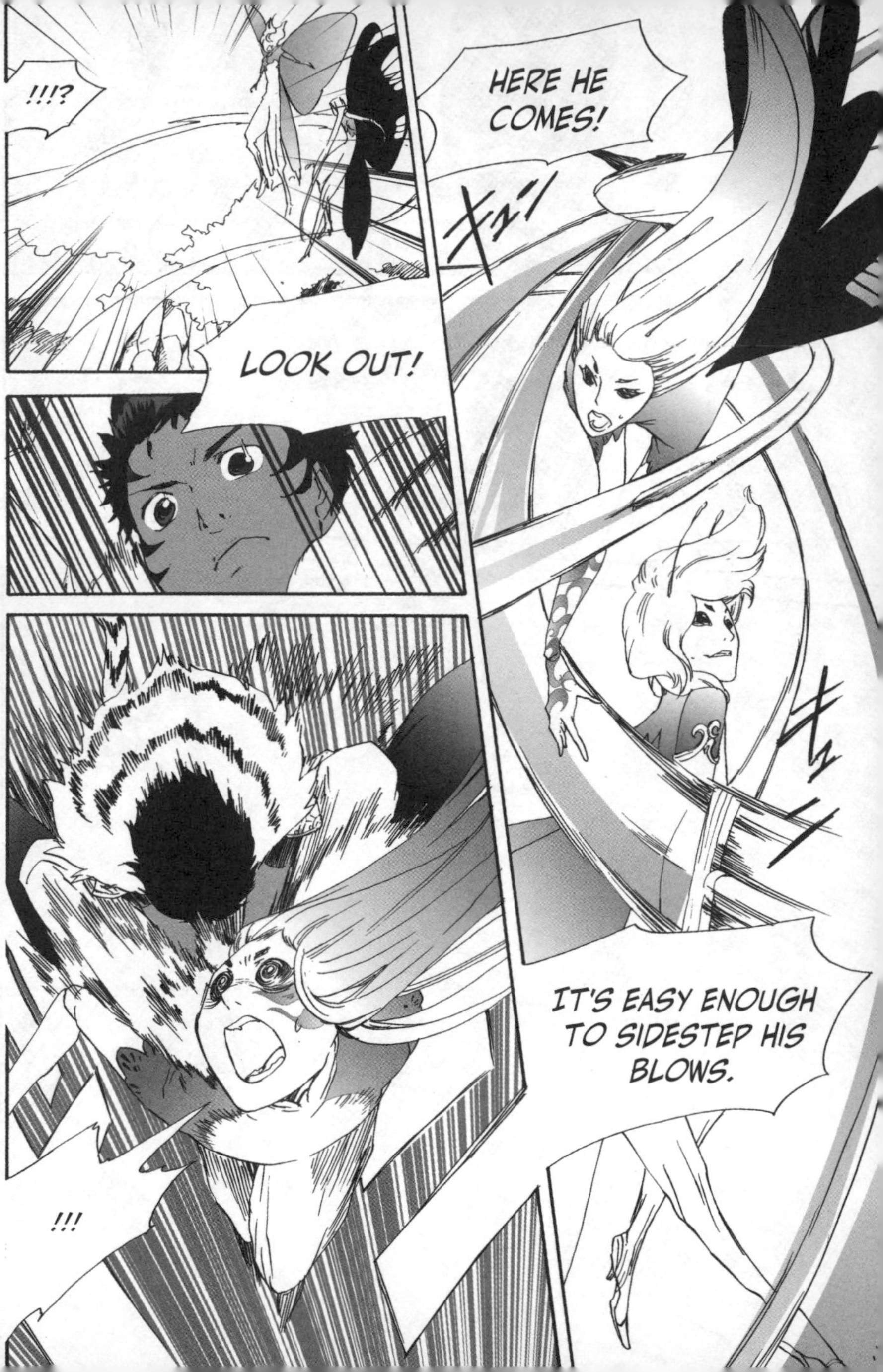
HERE HE COMES!
IT'S EASY ENOUGH TO SIDESTEP HIS BLOWS.
!!!?
LOOK OUT!
!!!

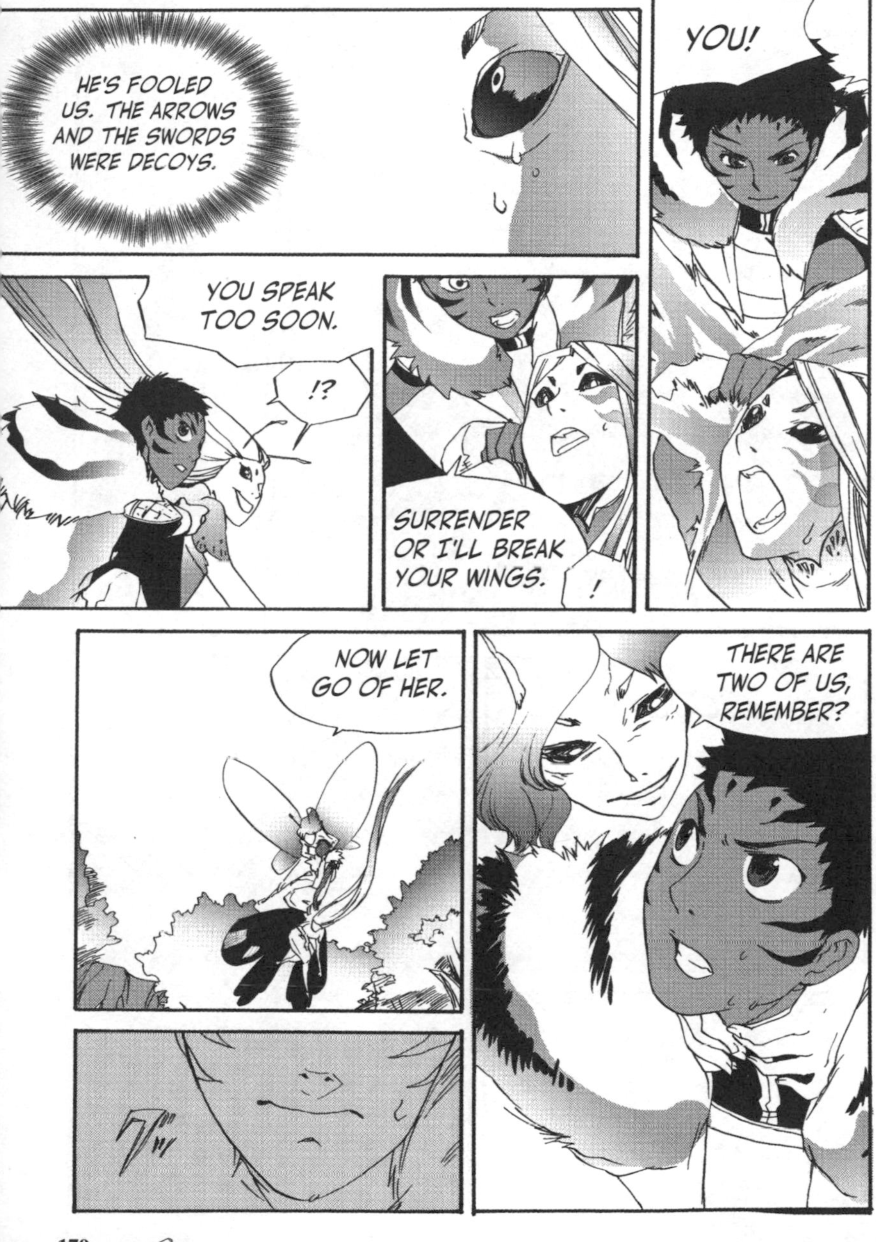
YOU!
HE'S FOOLED US. THE ARROWS AND THE SWORDS WERE DECOYS.
SURRENDER OR I'LL BREAK YOUR WINGS.
!
YOU SPEAK TOO SOON.
!?
THERE ARE TWO OF US, REMEMBER?
NOW LET GO OF HER.

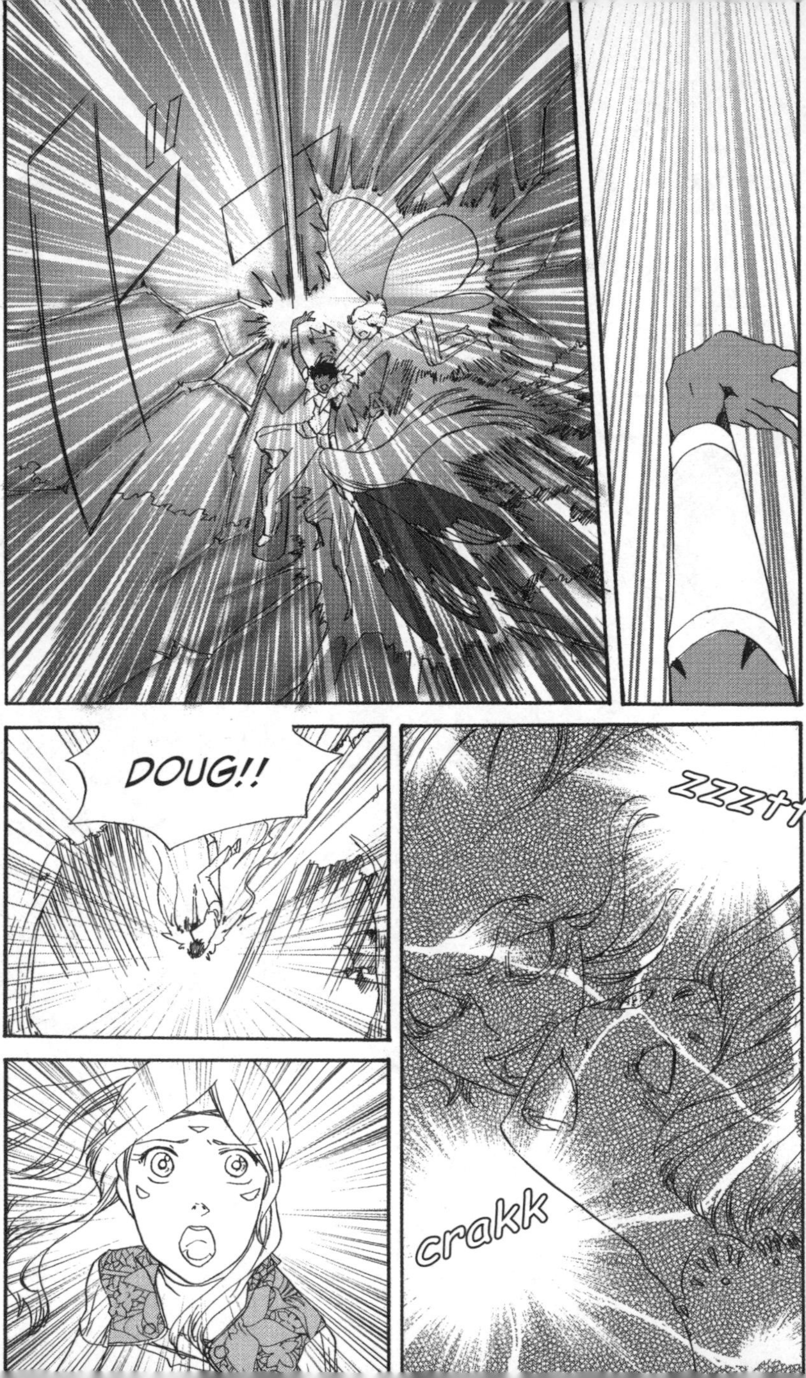
ZZZttt
crakk
DOUG!!

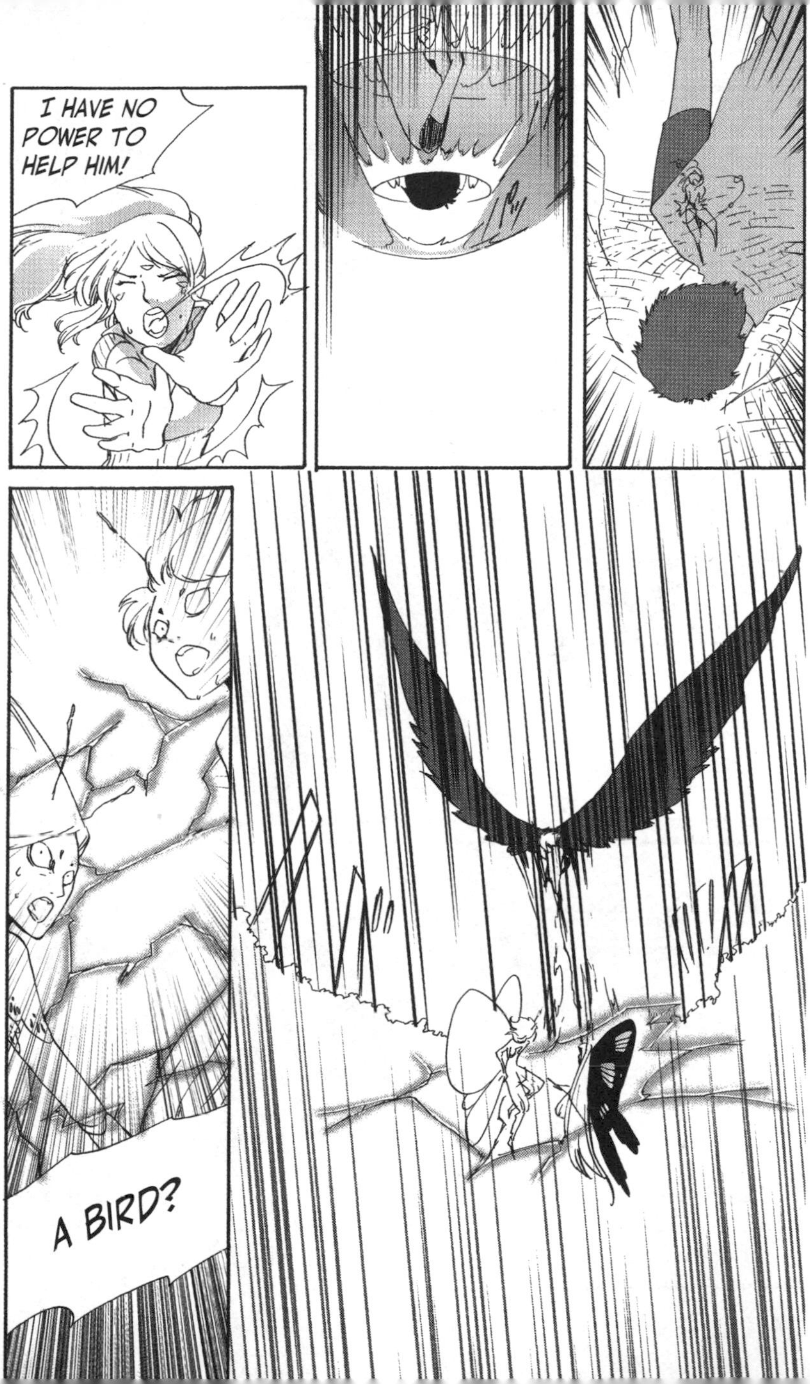
I HAVE NO POWER TO HELP HIM!
A BIRD?

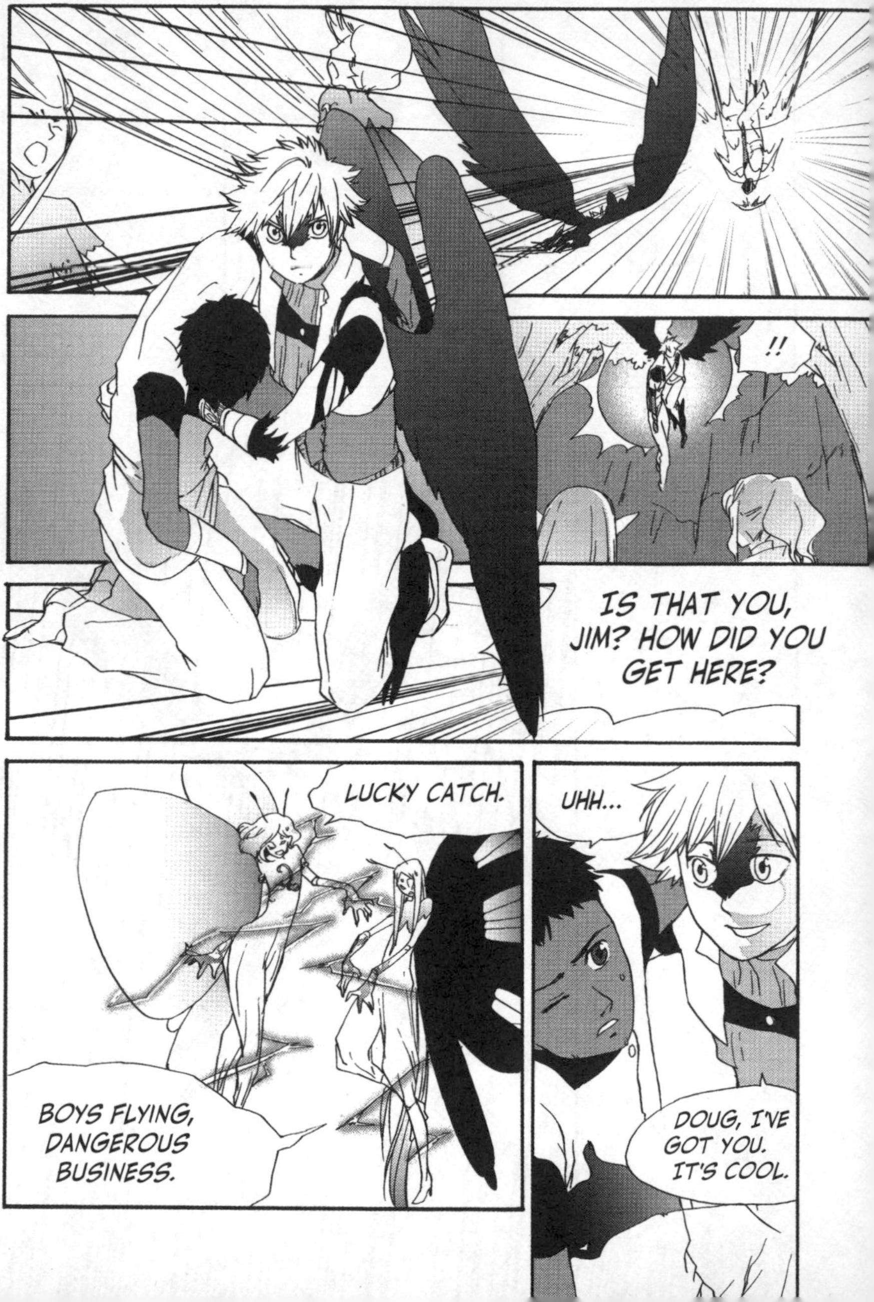
!!
IS THAT YOU, JIM? HOW DID YOU GET HERE?
UHH...
DOUG, I'VE GOT YOU. IT'S COOL.
LUCKY CATCH.
BOYS FLYING, DANGEROUS BUSINESS.

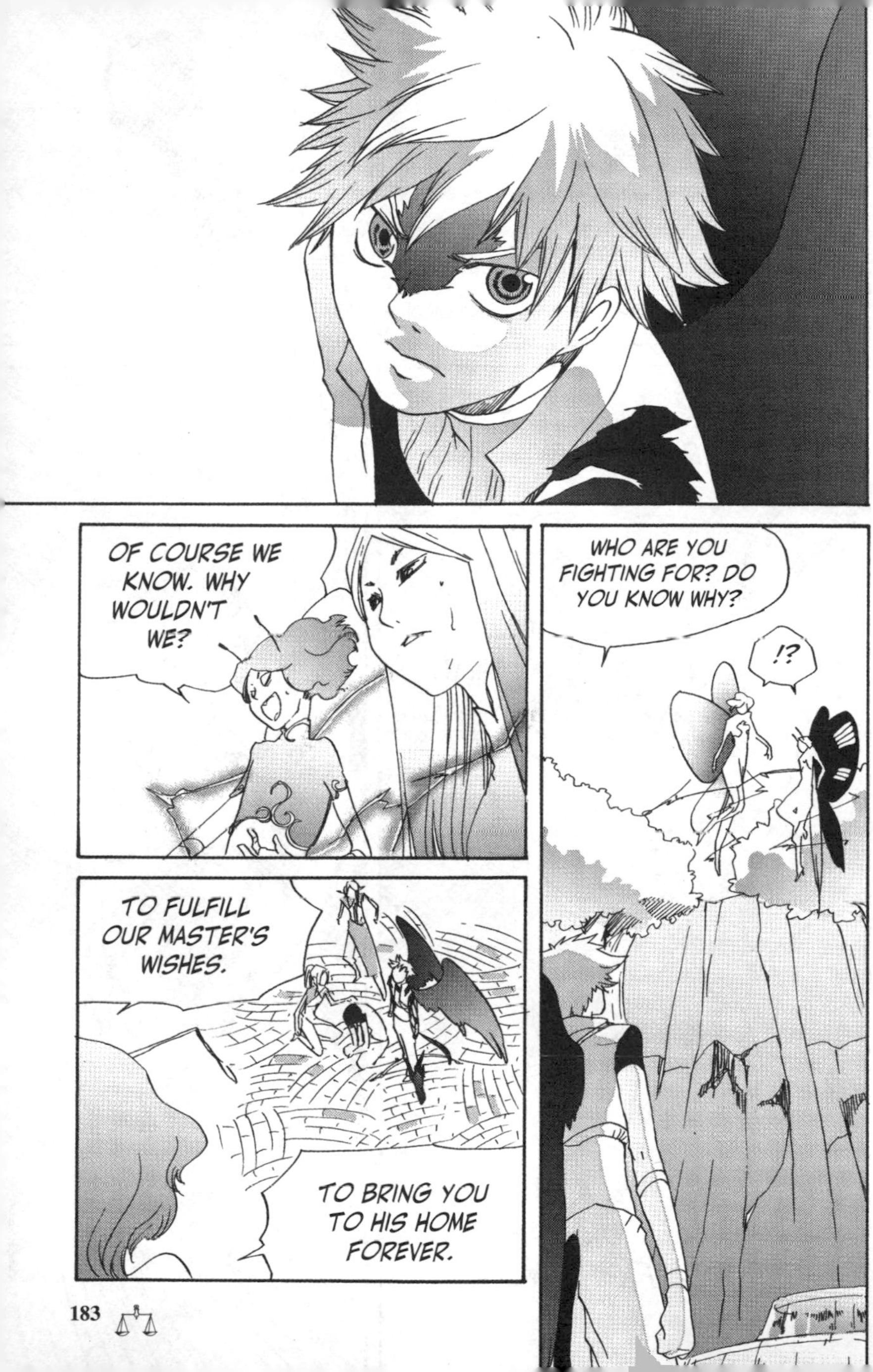
WHO ARE YOU FIGHTING FOR? DO YOU KNOW WHY?
!?
OF COURSE WE KNOW. WHY WOULDN'T WE?
TO FULFILL OUR MASTER'S WISHES.
TO BRING YOU TO HIS HOME FOREVER.

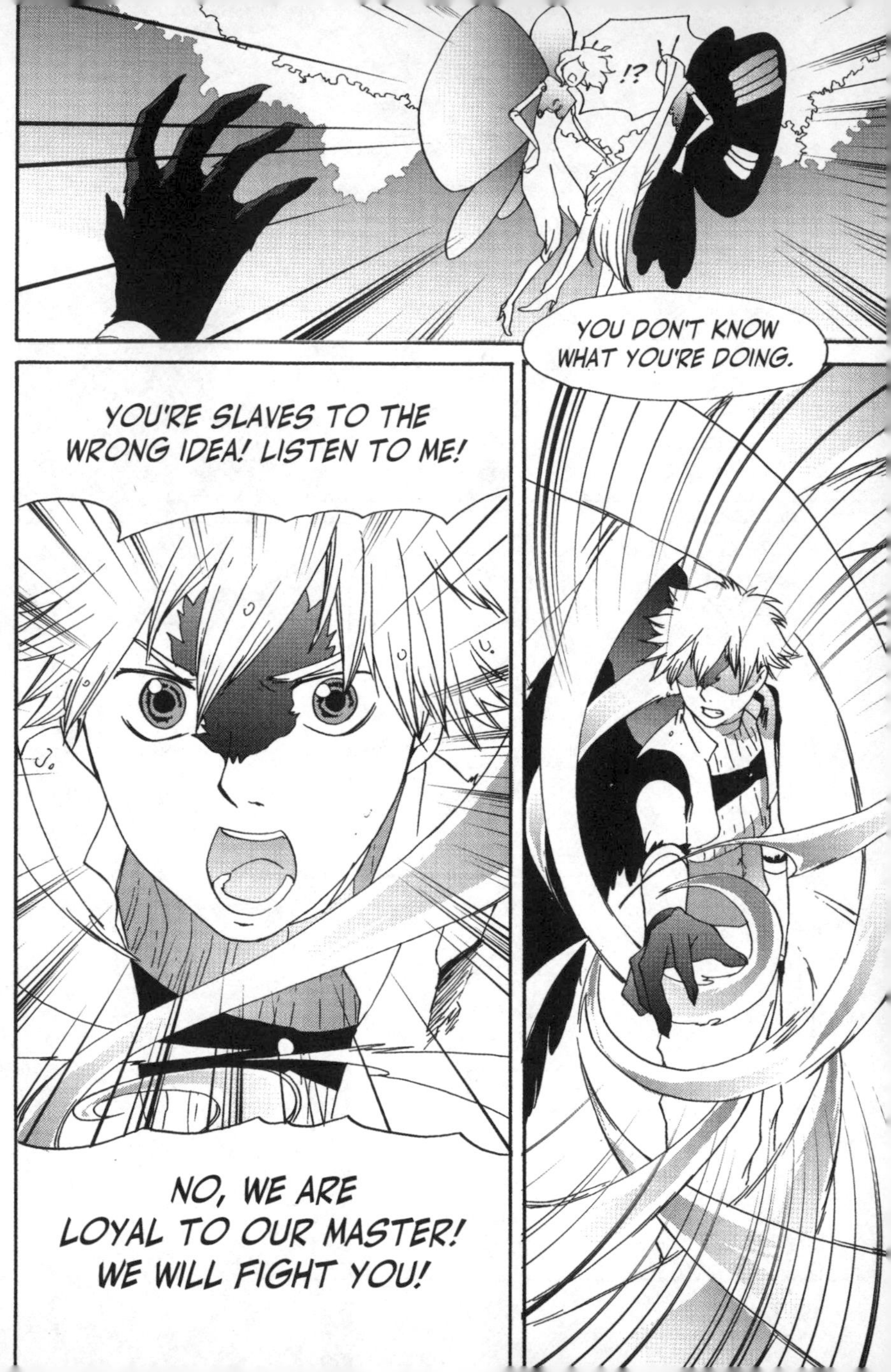
!?
YOU DON'T KNOW WHAT YOU'RE DOING.
YOU'RE SLAVES TO THE WRONG IDEA! LISTEN TO ME!
NO, WE ARE LOYAL TO OUR MASTER! WE WILL FIGHT YOU!

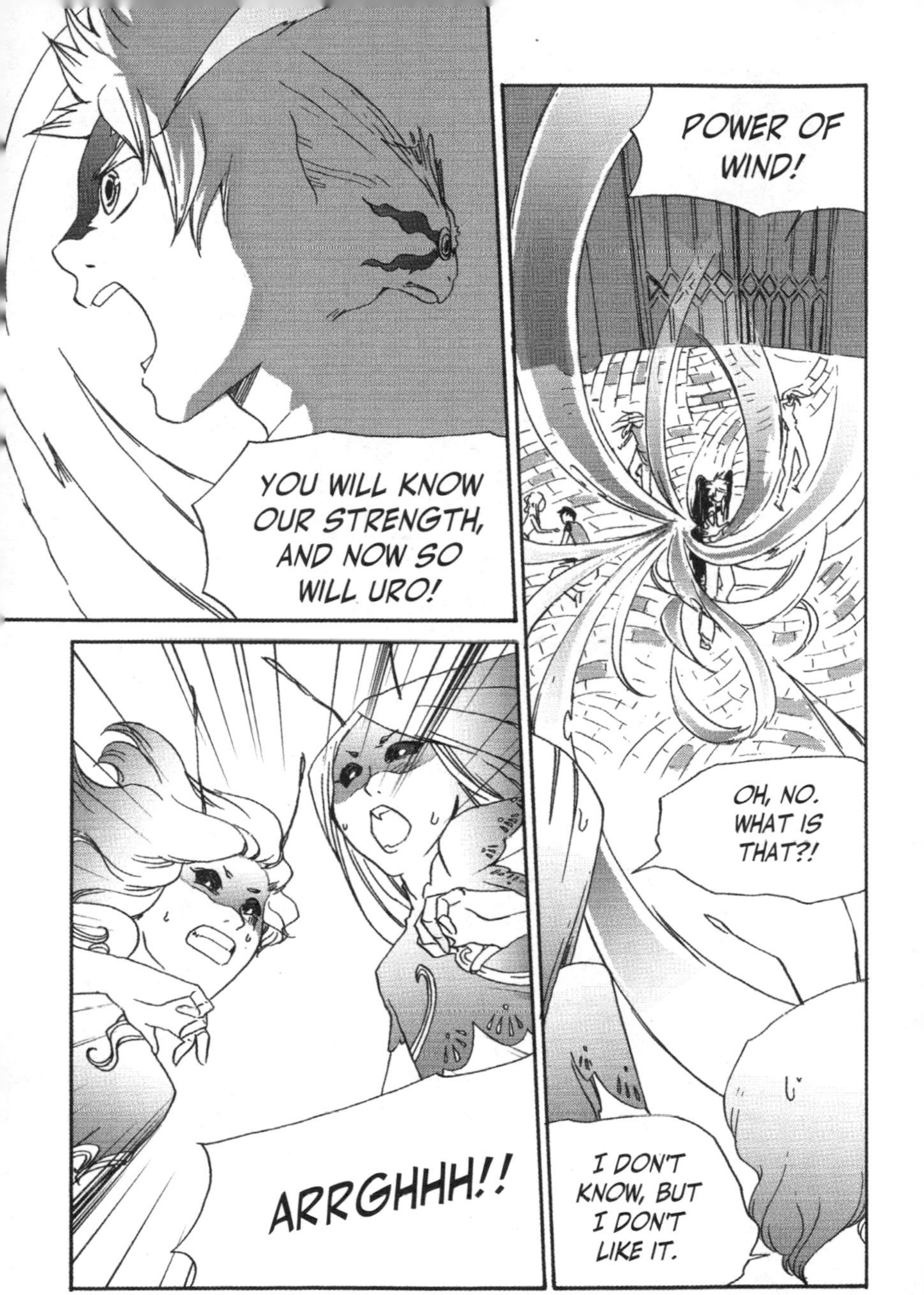
POWER OF WIND!
YOU WILL KNOW OUR STRENGTH, AND NOW SO WILL URO!
OH, NO. WHAT IS THAT?!
I DON'T KNOW, BUT I DON'T LIKE IT.
ARRGHHH!!

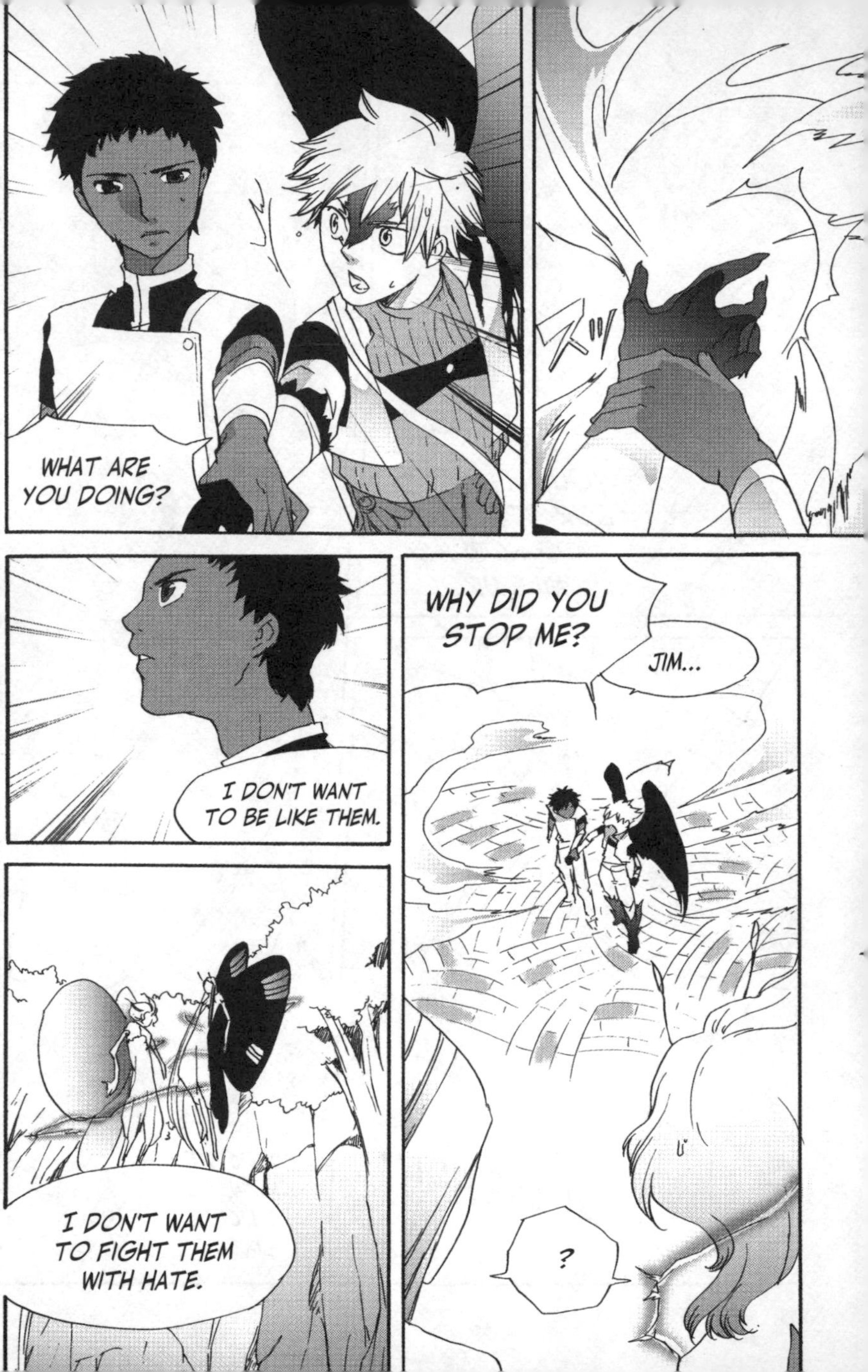
ズッ
WHAT ARE YOU DOING?
WHY DID YOU STOP ME?
JIM...
?
I DON'T WANT TO BE LIKE THEM.
I DON'T WANT TO FIGHT THEM WITH HATE.

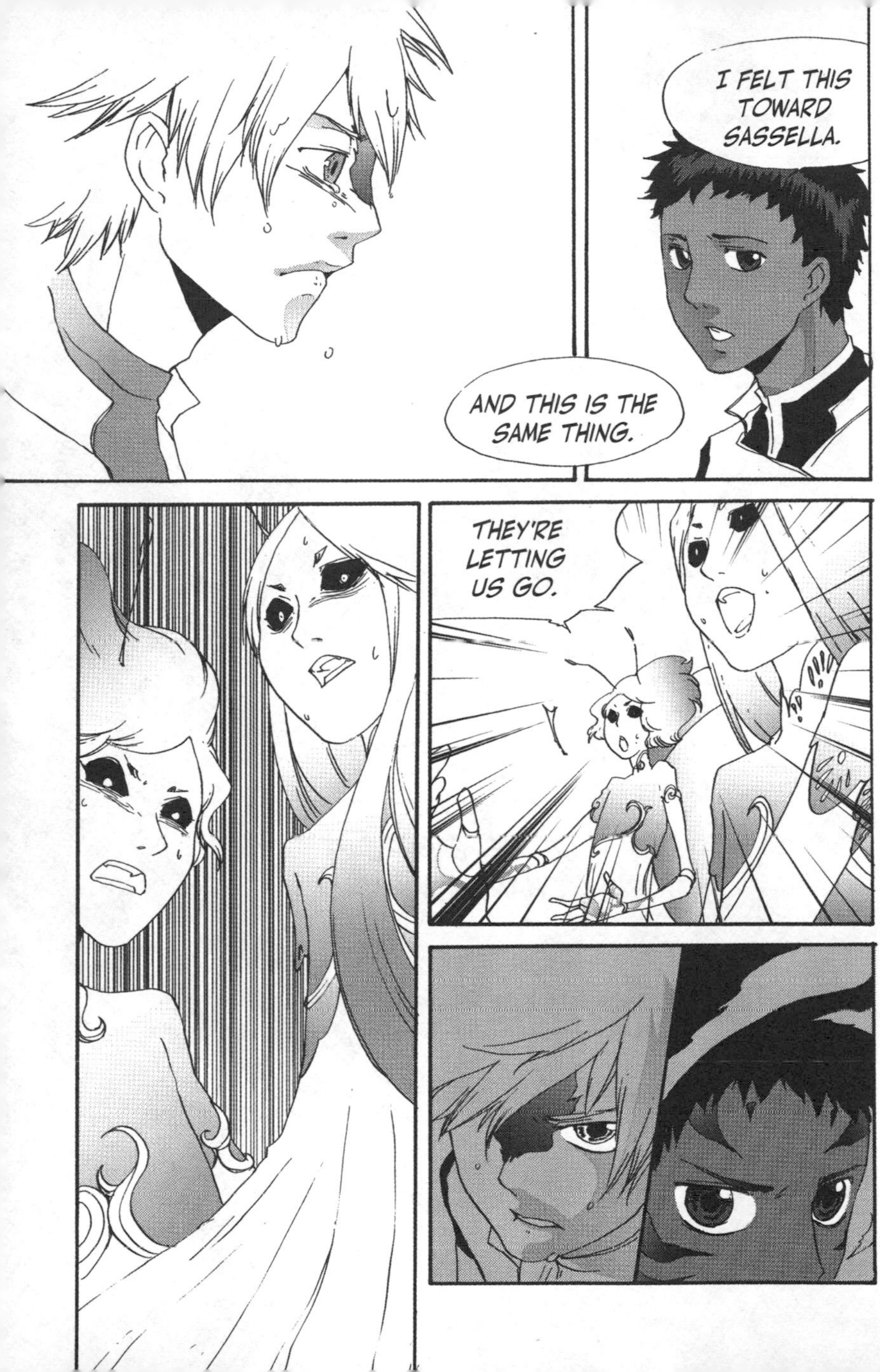
I FELT THIS TOWARD SASSELLA.
AND THIS IS THE SAME THING.
THEY'RE LETTING US GO.

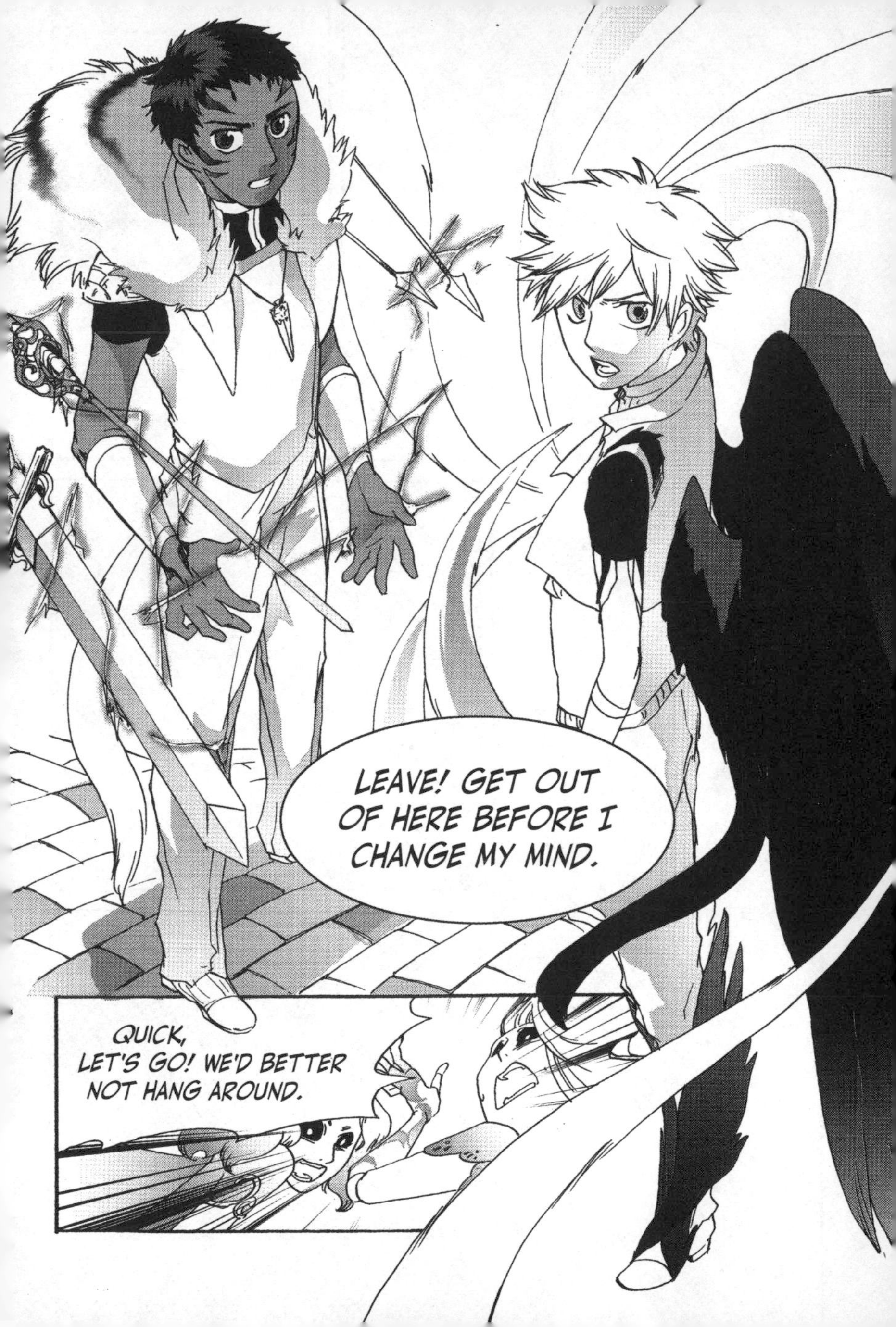
LEAVE! GET OUT OF HERE BEFORE I CHANGE MY MIND.
QUICK, LET'S GO! WE'D BETTER NOT HANG AROUND.

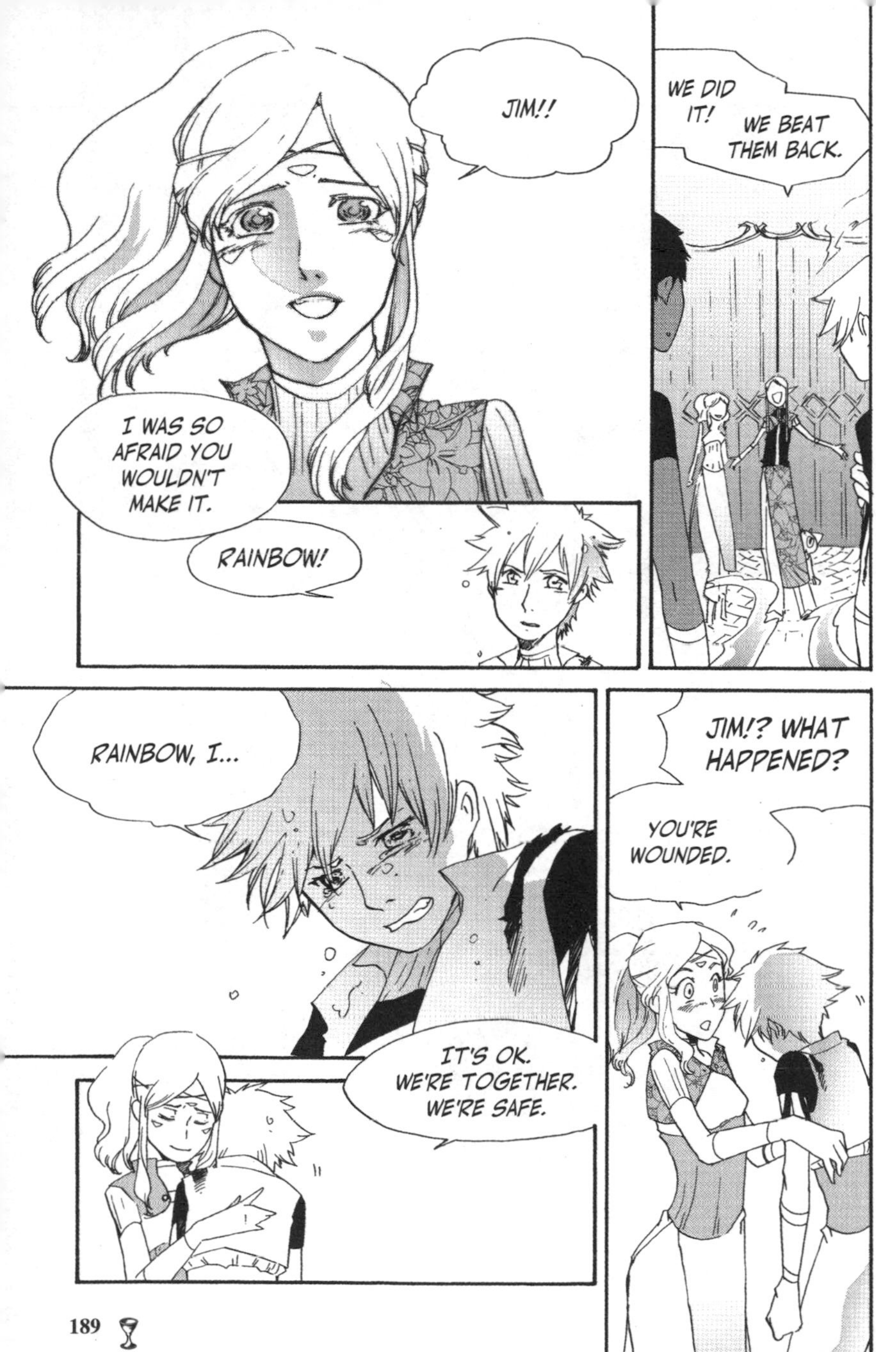
WE DID IT!
WE BEAT THEM BACK.
JIM!!
I WAS SO AFRAID YOU WOULDN'T MAKE IT.
RAINBOW!
JIM!? WHAT HAPPENED?
YOU'RE WOUNDED.
RAINBOW, I...
IT'S OK. WE'RE TOGETHER. WE'RE SAFE.

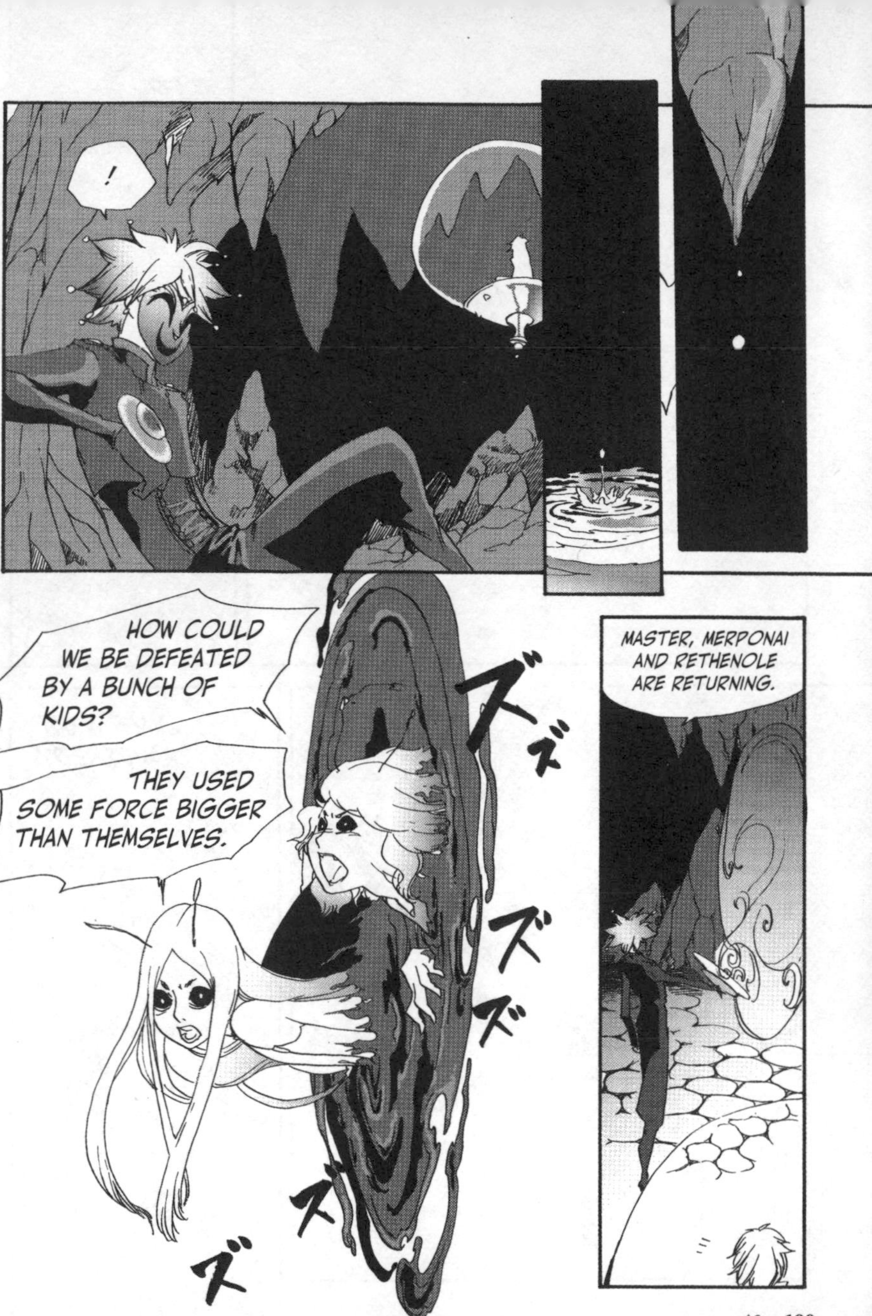
!
MASTER, MERPONAI AND RETHENOLE ARE RETURNING.
HOW COULD WE BE DEFEATED BY A BUNCH OF KIDS?
THEY USED SOME FORCE BIGGER THAN THEMSELVES.
ズズ
ズズ
ズズ

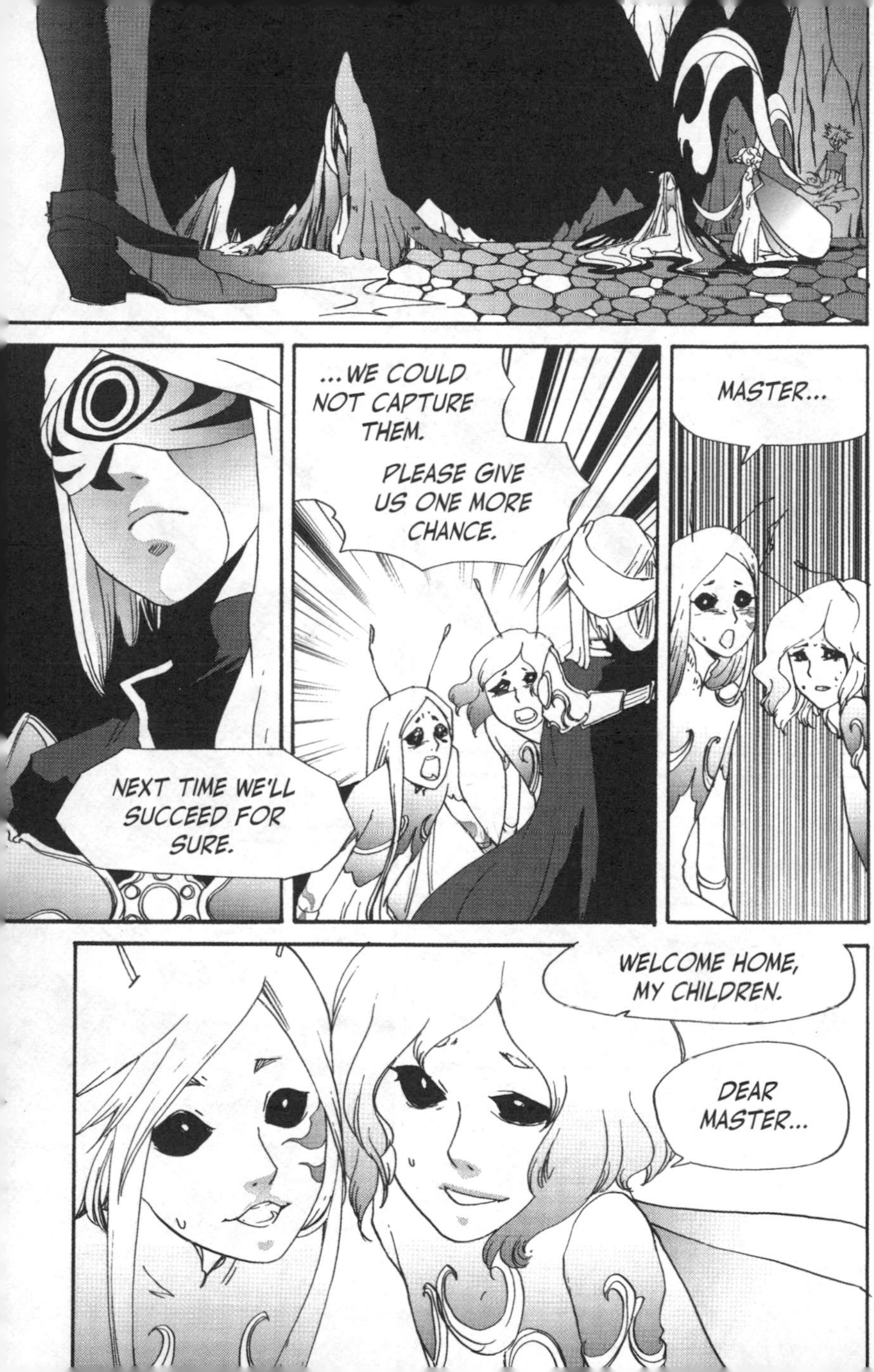
MASTER...
...WE COULD NOT CAPTURE THEM.
PLEASE GIVE US ONE MORE CHANCE.
NEXT TIME WE'LL SUCCEED FOR SURE.
WELCOME HOME, MY CHILDREN.
DEAR MASTER...

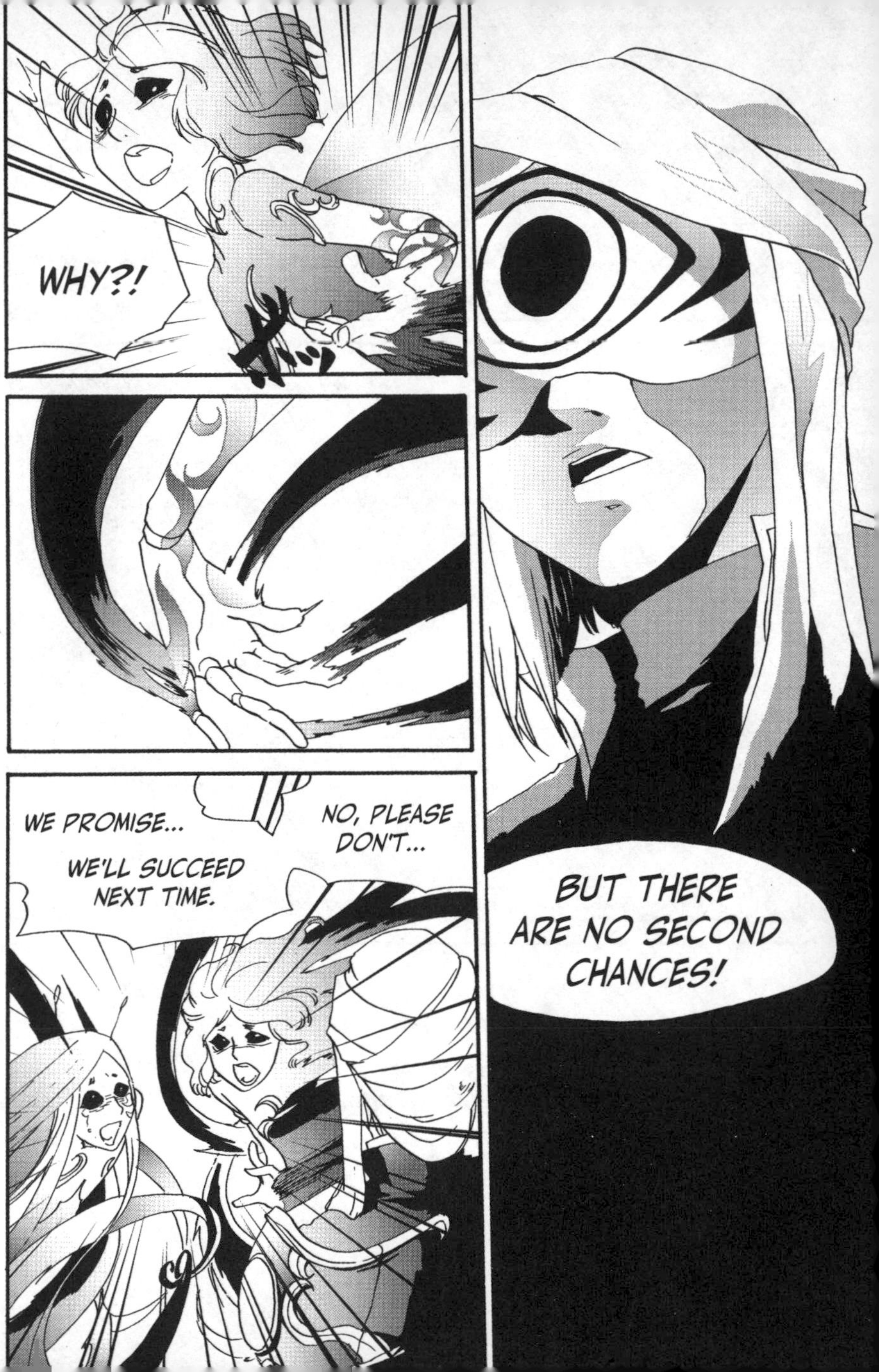
BUT THERE ARE NO SECOND CHANCES!
WHY?!
NO, PLEASE DON'T...
WE PROMISE...
WE'LL SUCCEED NEXT TIME.

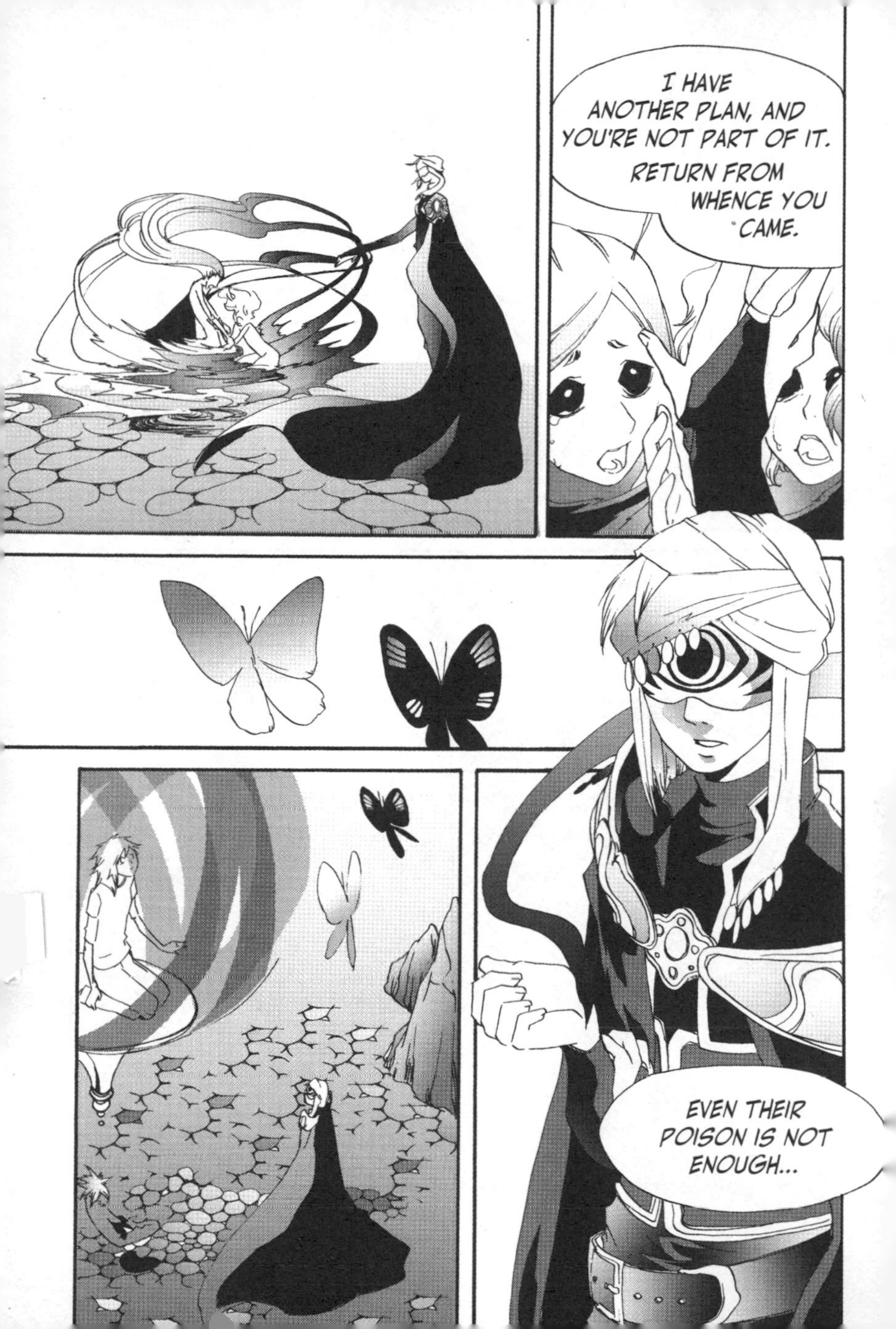
I HAVE ANOTHER PLAN, AND YOU'RE NOT PART OF IT.
RETURN FROM WHENCE YOU CAME.
EVEN THEIR POISON IS NOT ENOUGH...

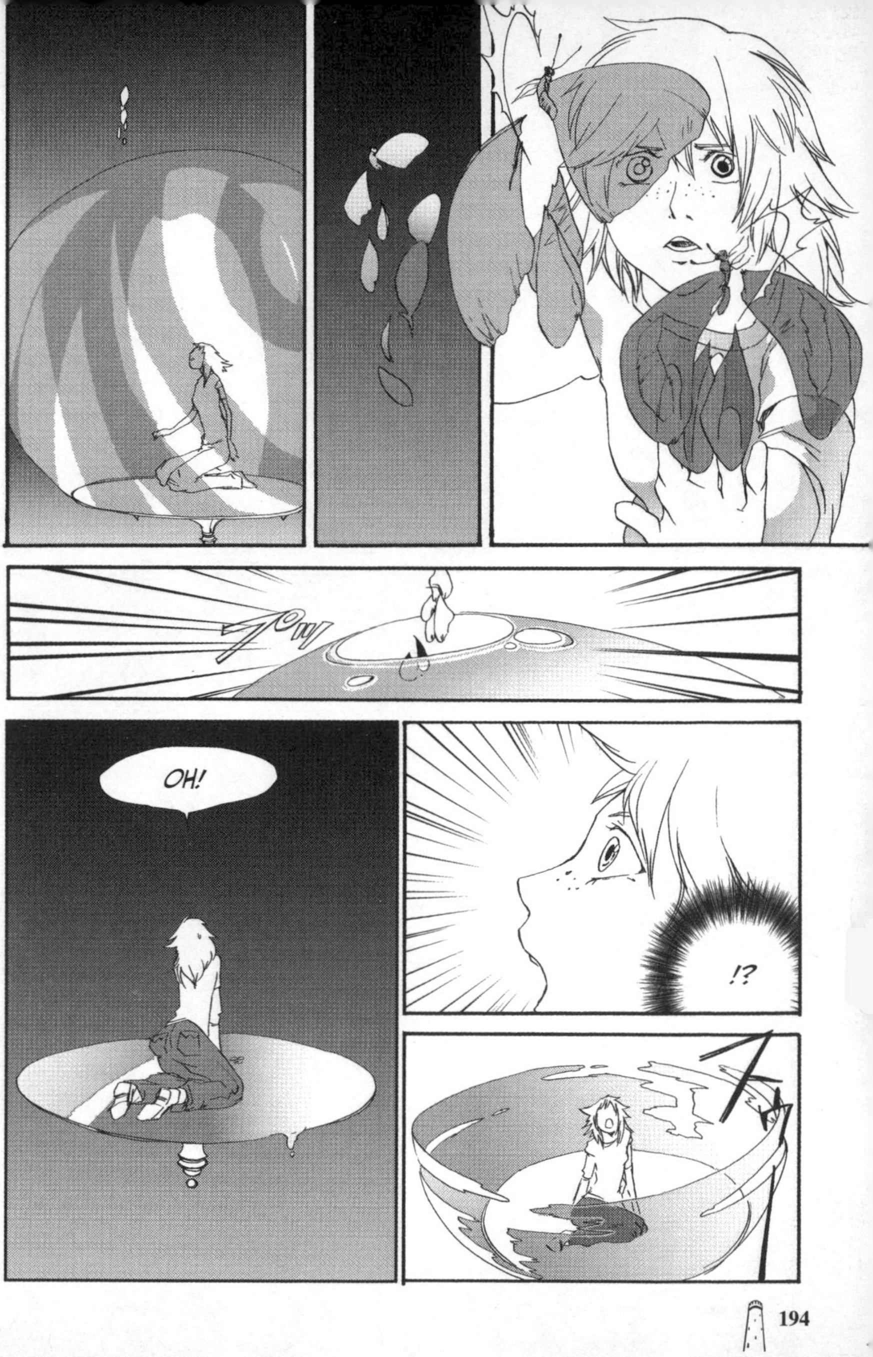
!?
OH!

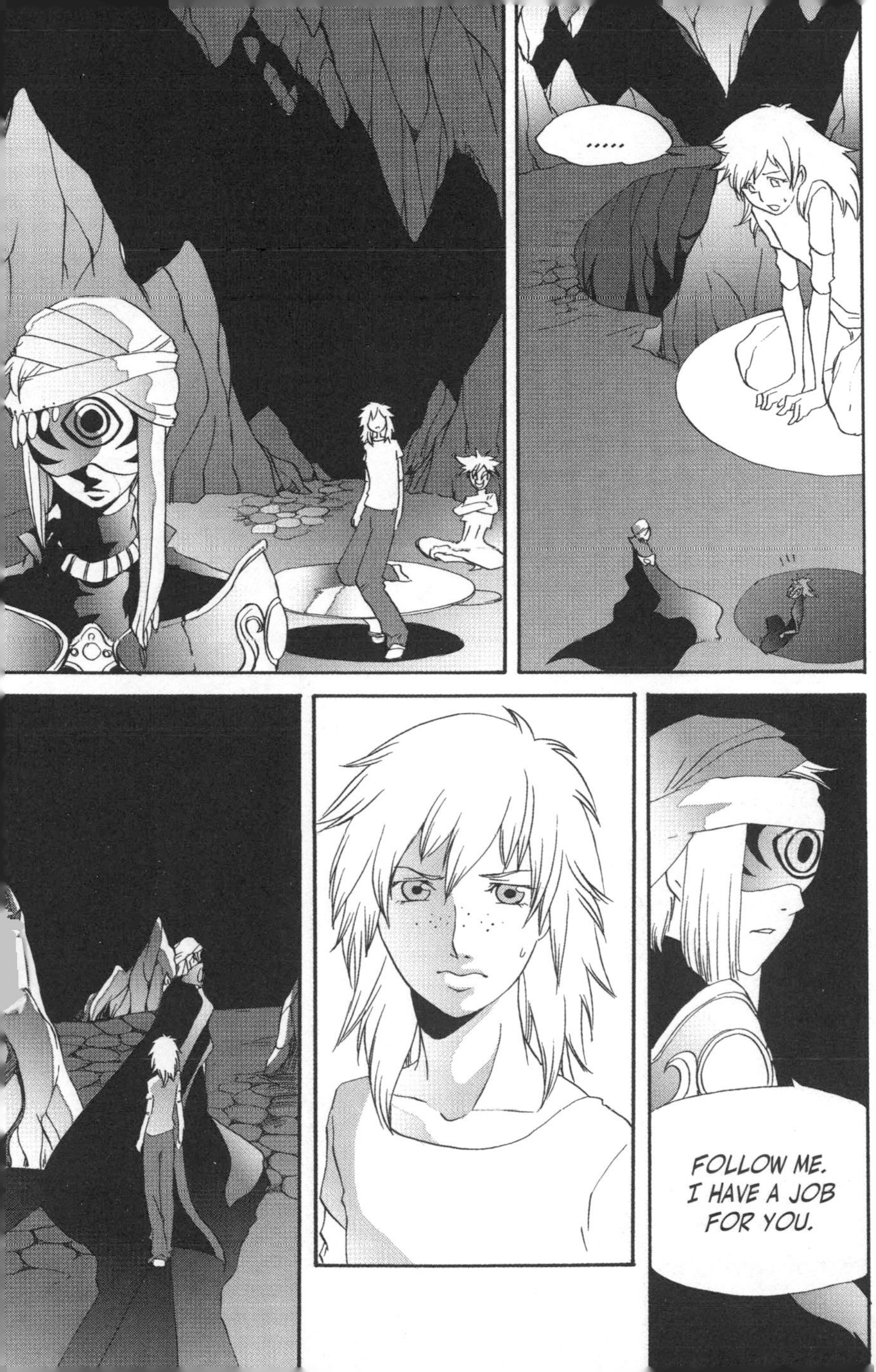
......
FOLLOW ME. I HAVE A JOB FOR YOU.

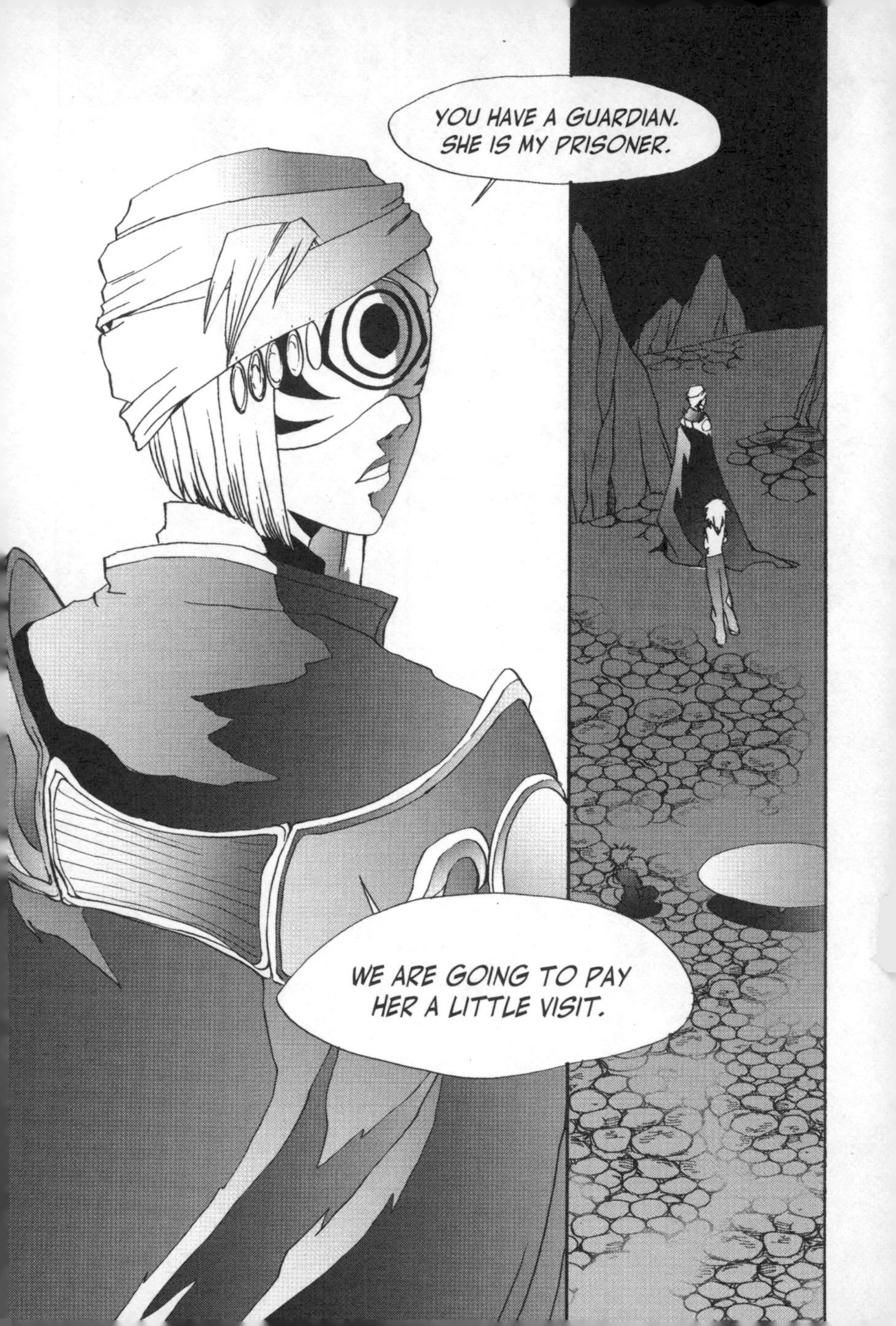
YOU HAVE A GUARDIAN. SHE IS MY PRISONER.
WE ARE GOING TO PAY HER A LITTLE VISIT.

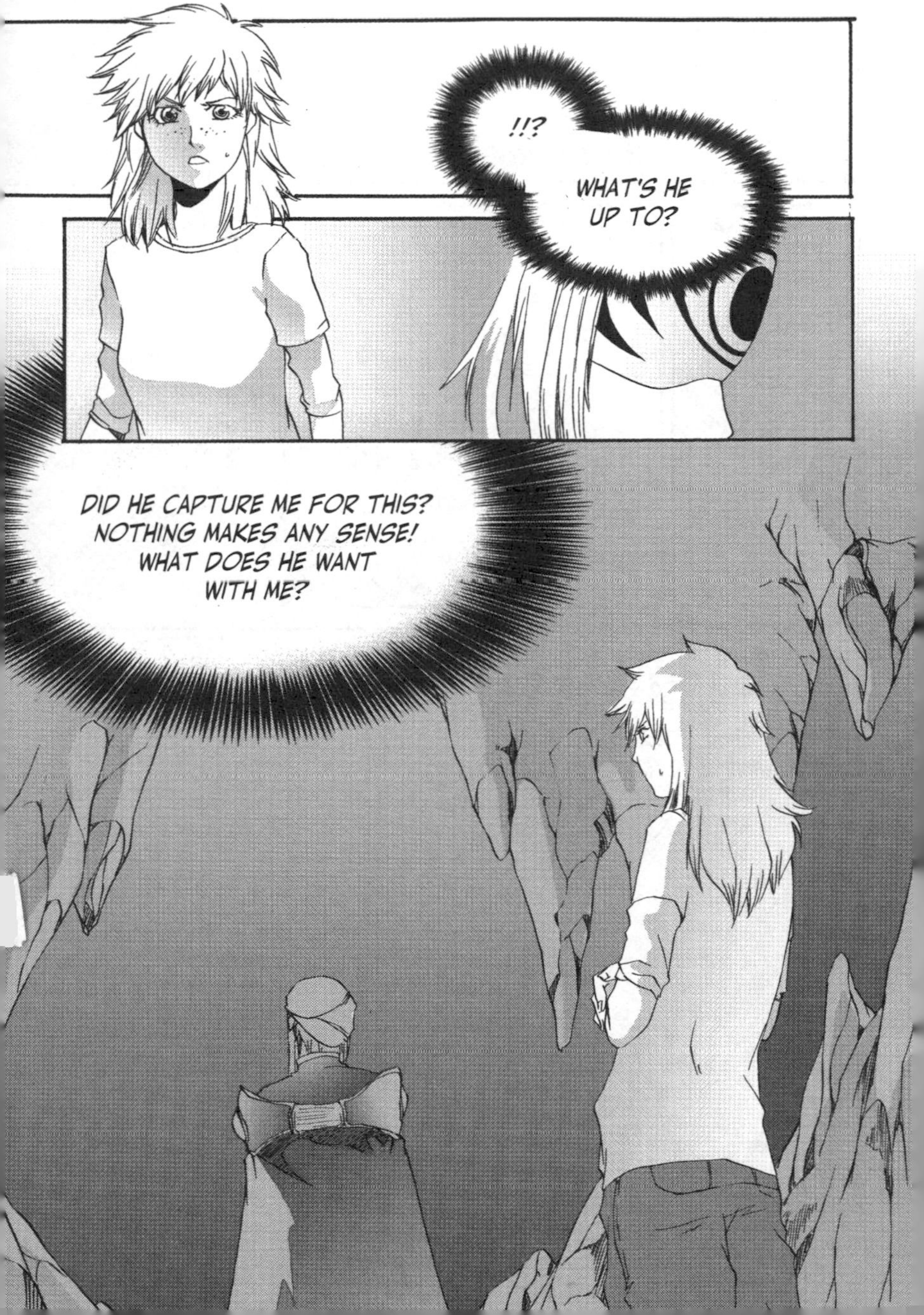
!!?
WHAT'S HE UP TO?
DID HE CAPTURE ME FOR THIS? NOTHING MAKES ANY SENSE! WHAT DOES HE WANT WITH ME?

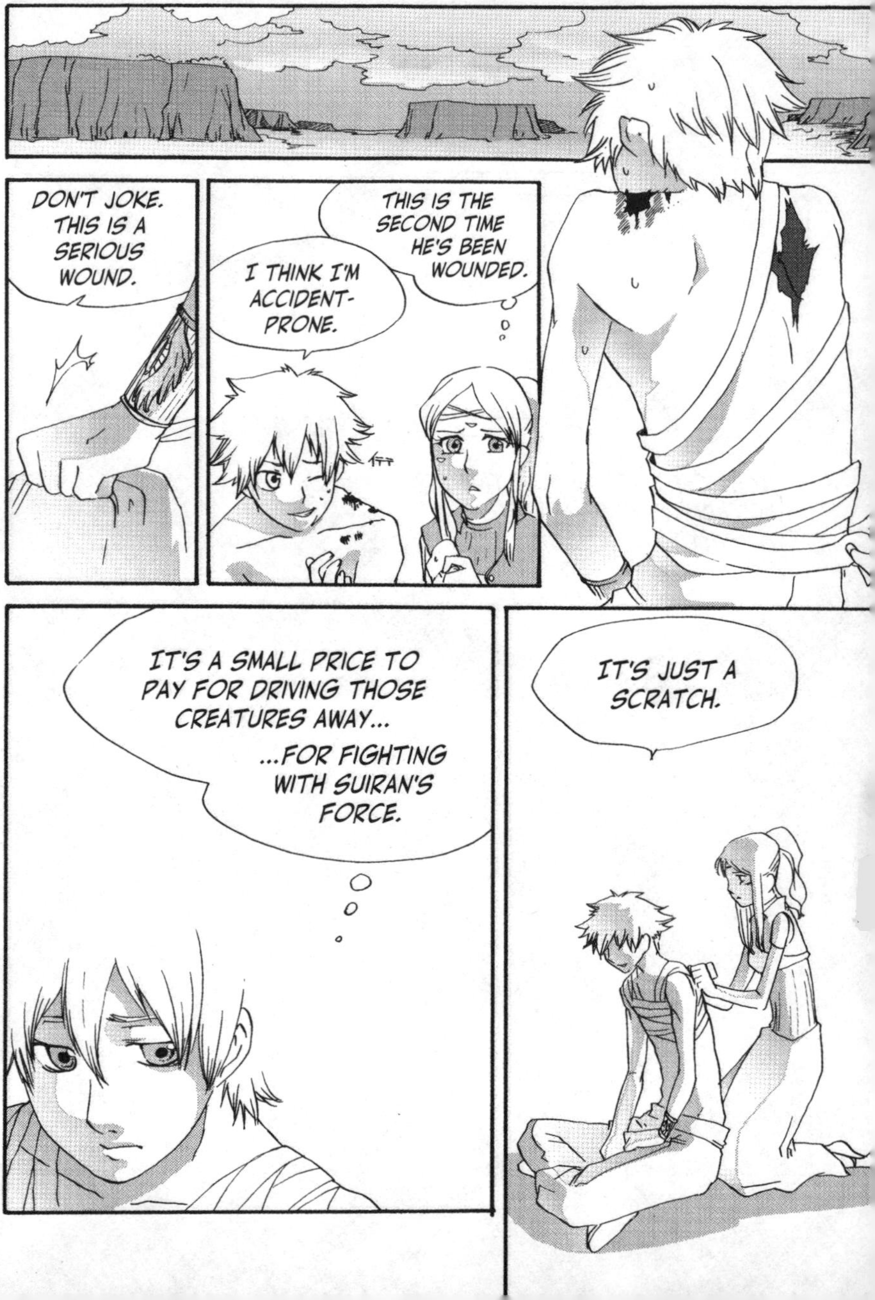
THIS IS THE SECOND TIME HE'S BEEN WOUNDED.
I THINK I'M ACCIDENT-PRONE.
DON'T JOKE. THIS IS A SERIOUS WOUND.
IT'S JUST A SCRATCH.
IT'S A SMALL PRICE TO PAY FOR DRIVING THOSE CREATURES AWAY...
...FOR FIGHTING WITH SUIRAN'S FORCE.

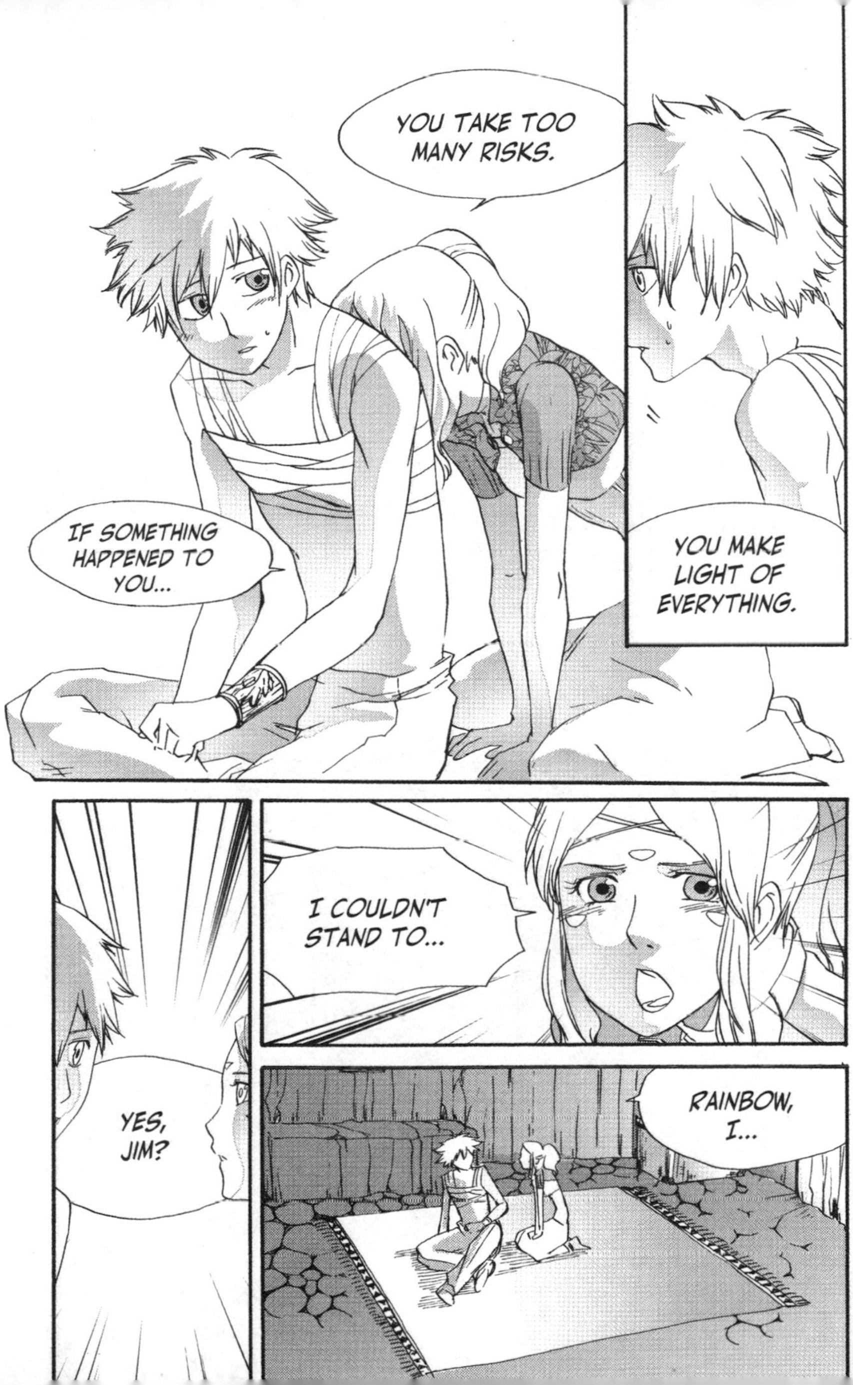
YOU MAKE LIGHT OF EVERYTHING.
YOU TAKE TOO MANY RISKS.
IF SOMETHING HAPPENED TO YOU...
I COULDN'T STAND TO...
RAINBOW, I...
YES, JIM?

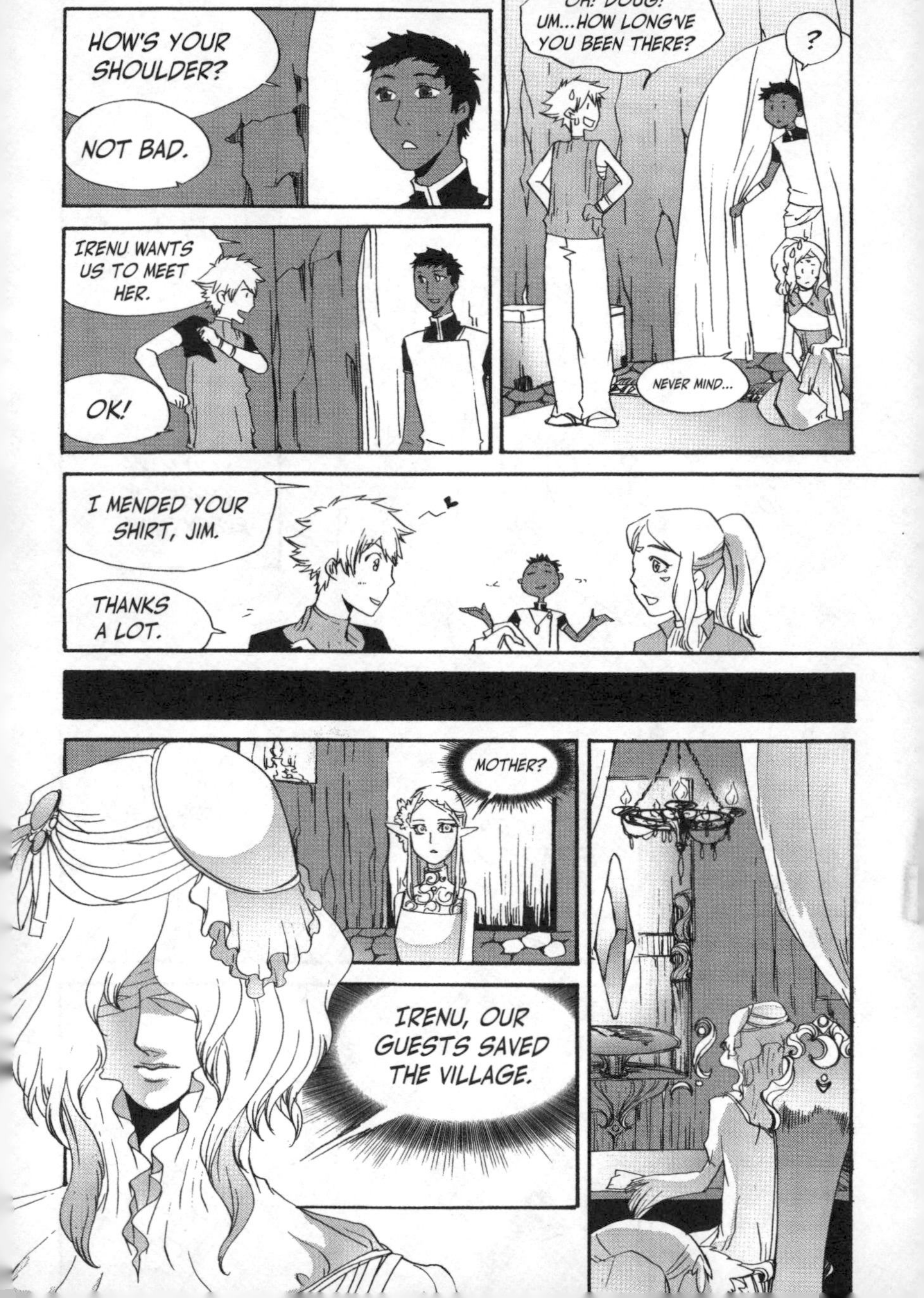
OH! DOUG! UM...HOW LONG'VE YOU BEEN THERE?
?
NEVER MIND...
HOW'S YOUR SHOULDER?
NOT BAD.
IRENU WANTS US TO MEET HER.
OK!
I MENDED YOUR SHIRT, JIM.
THANKS A LOT.
MOTHER?
IRENU, OUR GUESTS SAVED THE VILLAGE.

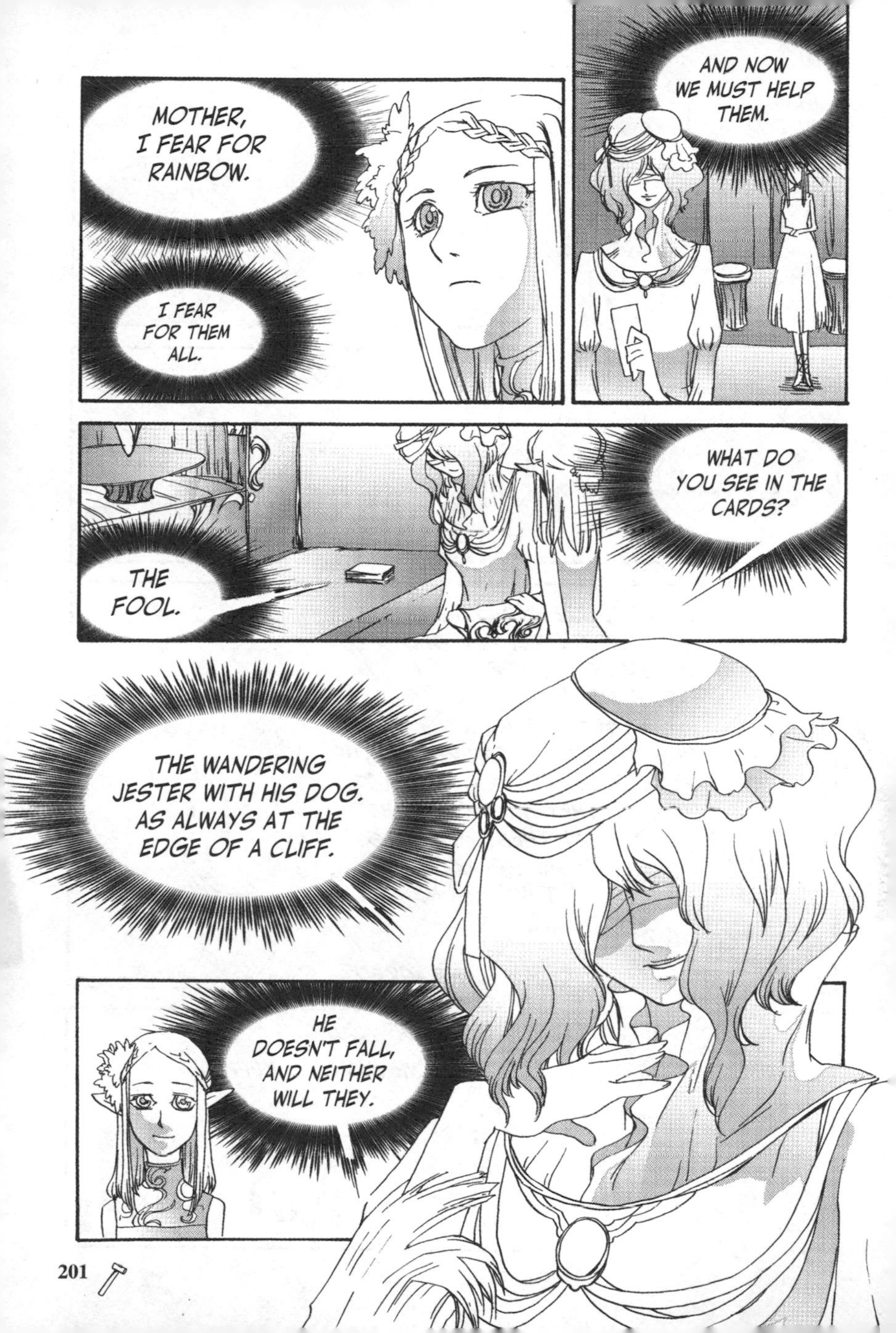
AND NOW WE MUST HELP THEM.
MOTHER, I FEAR FOR RAINBOW.
I FEAR FOR THEM ALL.
WHAT DO YOU SEE IN THE CARDS?
THE FOOL.
THE WANDERING JESTER WITH HIS DOG. AS ALWAYS AT THE EDGE OF A CLIFF.
HE DOESN'T FALL, AND NEITHER WILL THEY.

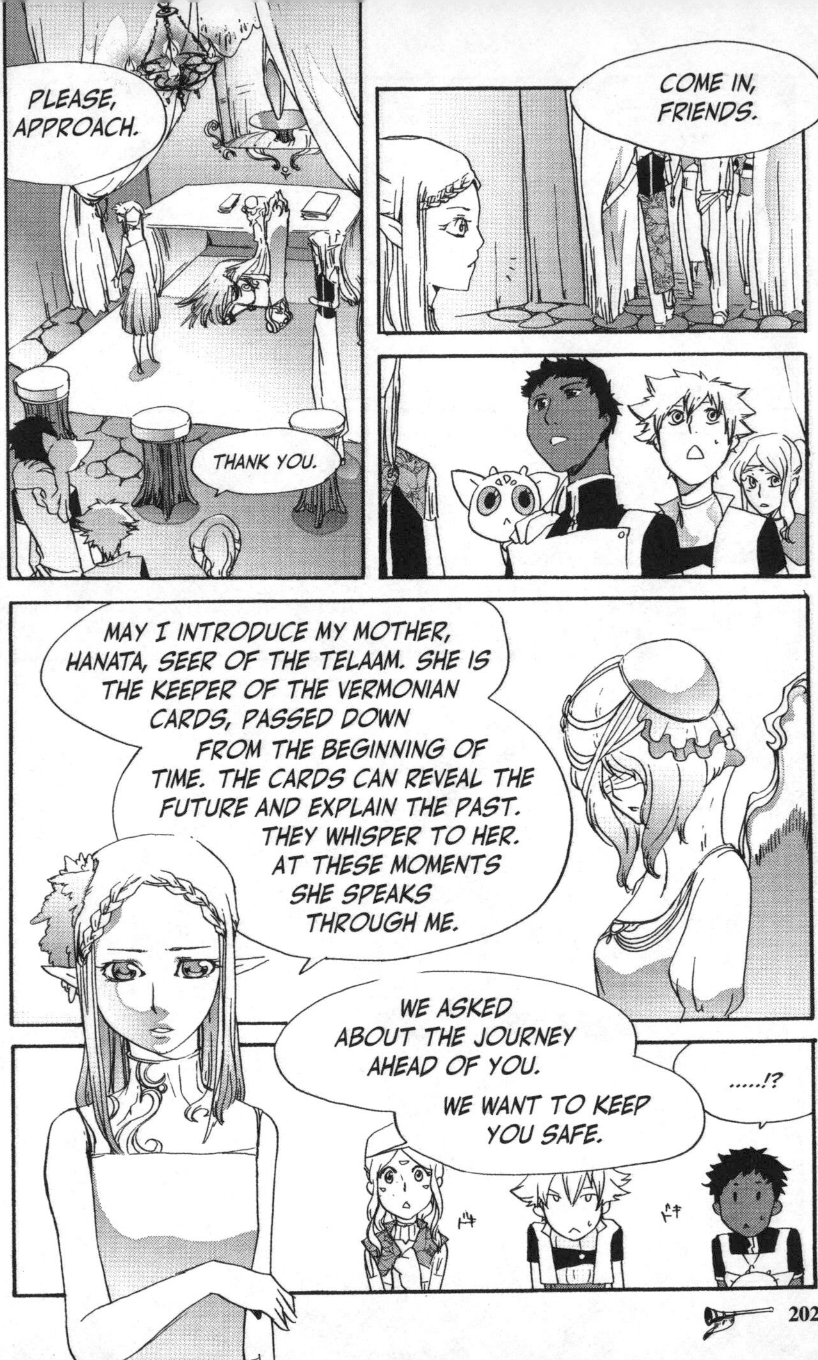
COME IN, FRIENDS.
PLEASE, APPROACH.
THANK YOU.
MAY I INTRODUCE MY MOTHER, HANATA, SEER OF THE TELAAM. SHE IS THE KEEPER OF THE VERMONIAN CARDS, PASSED DOWN FROM THE BEGINNING OF TIME. THE CARDS CAN REVEAL THE FUTURE AND EXPLAIN THE PAST. THEY WHISPER TO HER. AT THESE MOMENTS SHE SPEAKS THROUGH ME.
WE ASKED ABOUT THE JOURNEY AHEAD OF YOU.
WE WANT TO KEEP YOU SAFE.
......!?
ドキ
ドキ

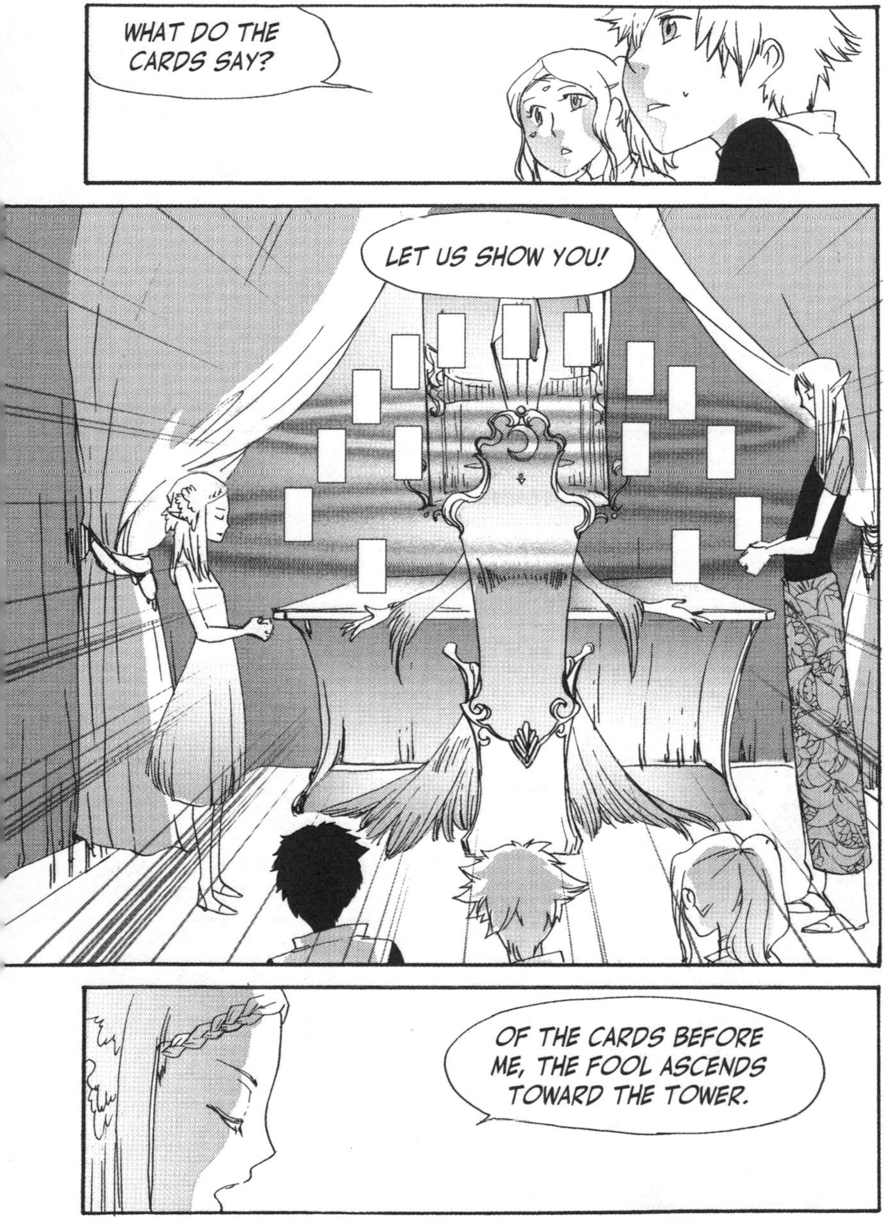
WHAT DO THE CARDS SAY?
LET US SHOW YOU!
OF THE CARDS BEFORE ME, THE FOOL ASCENDS TOWARD THE TOWER.

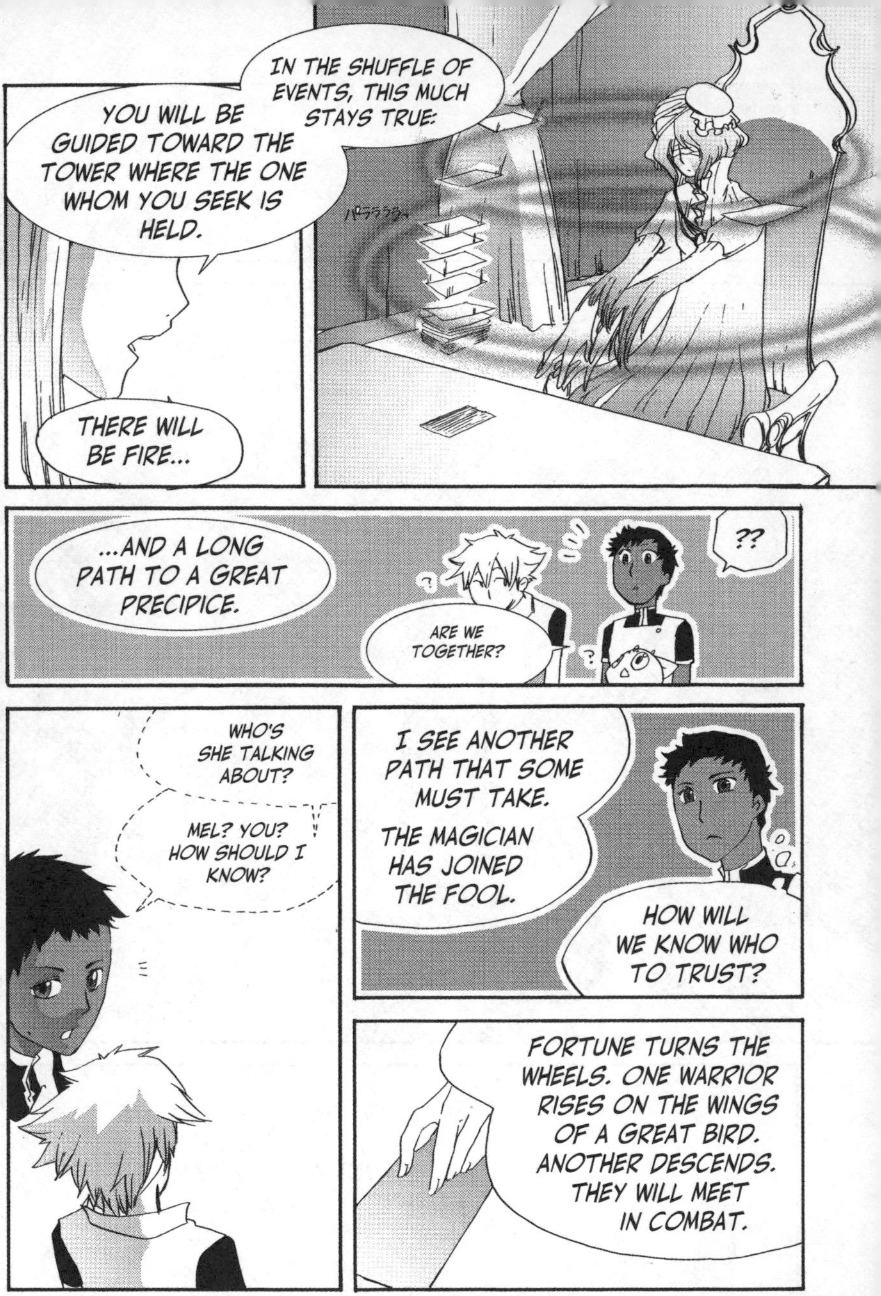
IN THE SHUFFLE OF EVENTS, THIS MUCH STAYS TRUE:
パラララ
YOU WILL BE GUIDED TOWARD THE TOWER WHERE THE ONE WHOM YOU SEEK IS HELD.
THERE WILL BE FIRE...
??
...AND A LONG PATH TO A GREAT PRECIPICE.
ARE WE TOGETHER?
I SEE ANOTHER PATH THAT SOME MUST TAKE.
THE MAGICIAN HAS JOINED THE FOOL.
HOW WILL WE KNOW WHO TO TRUST?
FORTUNE TURNS THE WHEELS. ONE WARRIOR RISES ON THE WINGS OF A GREAT BIRD. ANOTHER DESCENDS. THEY WILL MEET IN COMBAT.
WHO'S SHE TALKING ABOUT?
MEL? YOU? HOW SHOULD I KNOW?

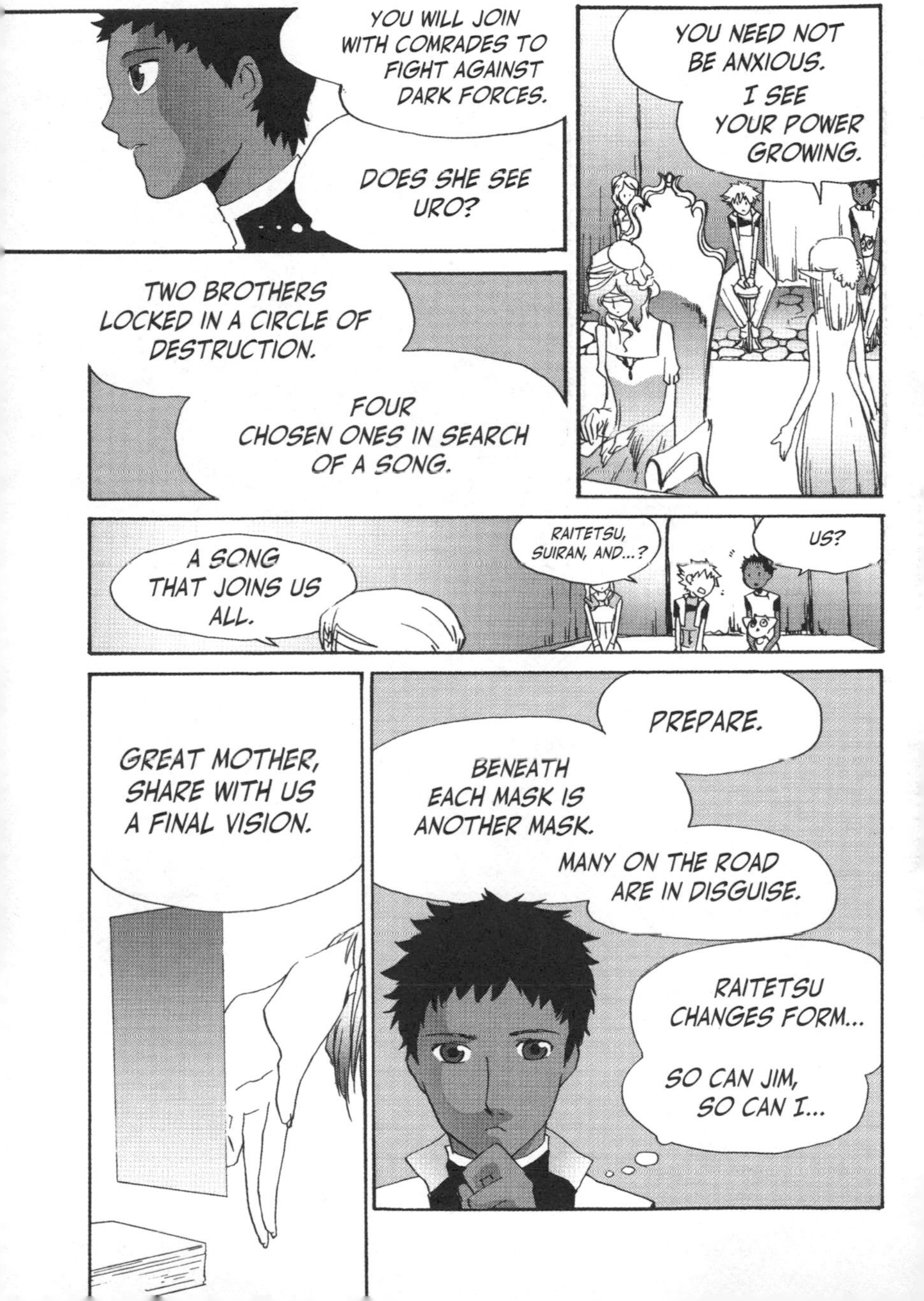
YOU NEED NOT BE ANXIOUS.
I SEE YOUR POWER GROWING.
YOU WILL JOIN WITH COMRADES TO FIGHT AGAINST DARK FORCES.
DOES SHE SEE URO?
TWO BROTHERS LOCKED IN A CIRCLE OF DESTRUCTION.
FOUR CHOSEN ONES IN SEARCH OF A SONG.
US?
RAITETSU, SUIRAN, AND...?
A SONG THAT JOINS US ALL.
PREPARE.
BENEATH EACH MASK IS ANOTHER MASK.
MANY ON THE ROAD ARE IN DISGUISE.
RAITETSU CHANGES FORM...
SO CAN JIM, SO CAN I...
GREAT MOTHER, SHARE WITH US A FINAL VISION.

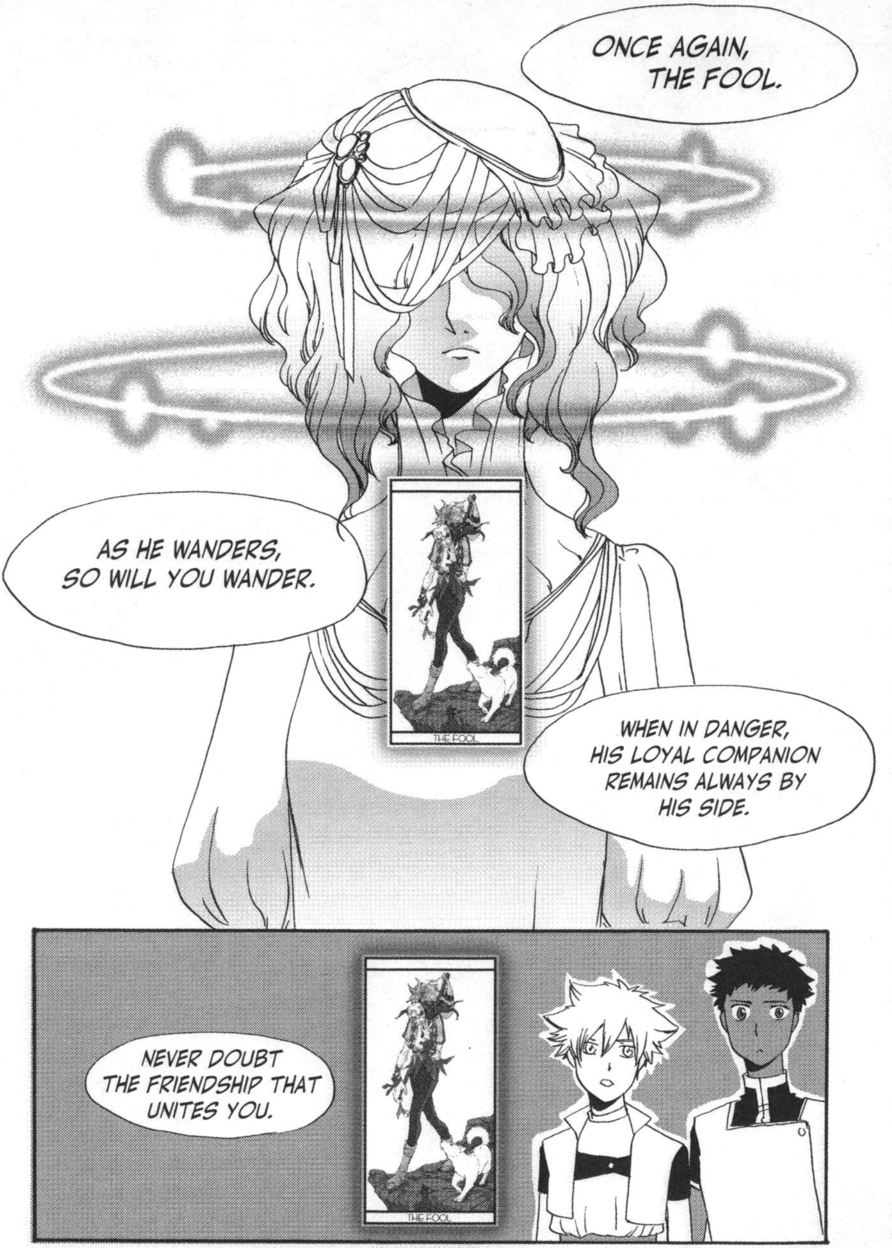
ONCE AGAIN, THE FOOL.
AS HE WANDERS, SO WILL YOU WANDER.
WHEN IN DANGER, HIS LOYAL COMPANION REMAINS ALWAYS BY HIS SIDE.
NEVER DOUBT THE FRIENDSHIP THAT UNITES YOU.

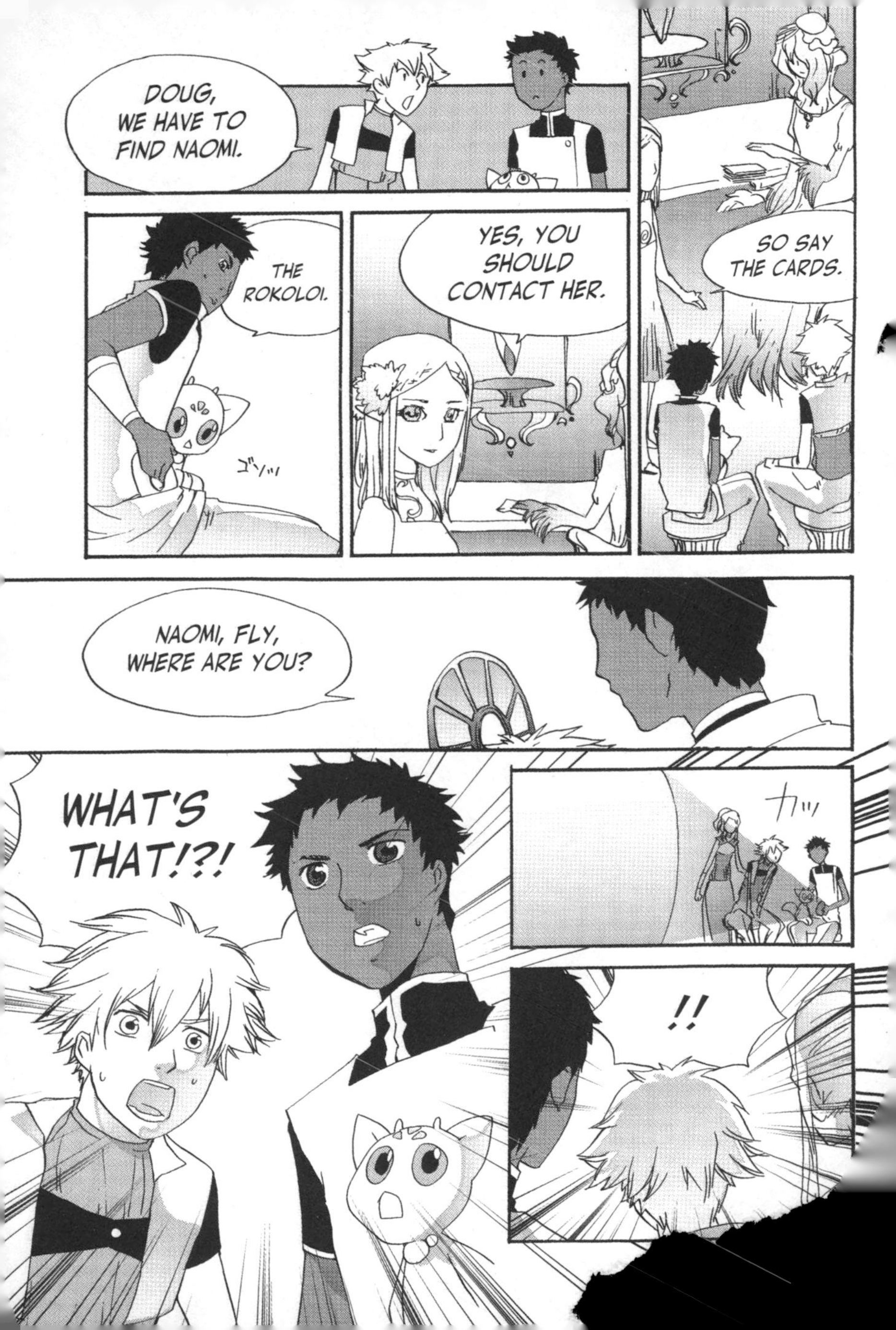
SO SAY THE CARDS.
DOUG, WE HAVE TO FIND NAOMI.
YES, YOU SHOULD CONTACT HER.
THE ROKOLOI.
ゴソッ
NAOMI, FLY, WHERE ARE YOU?
カッ
!!
WHAT'S THAT!?!

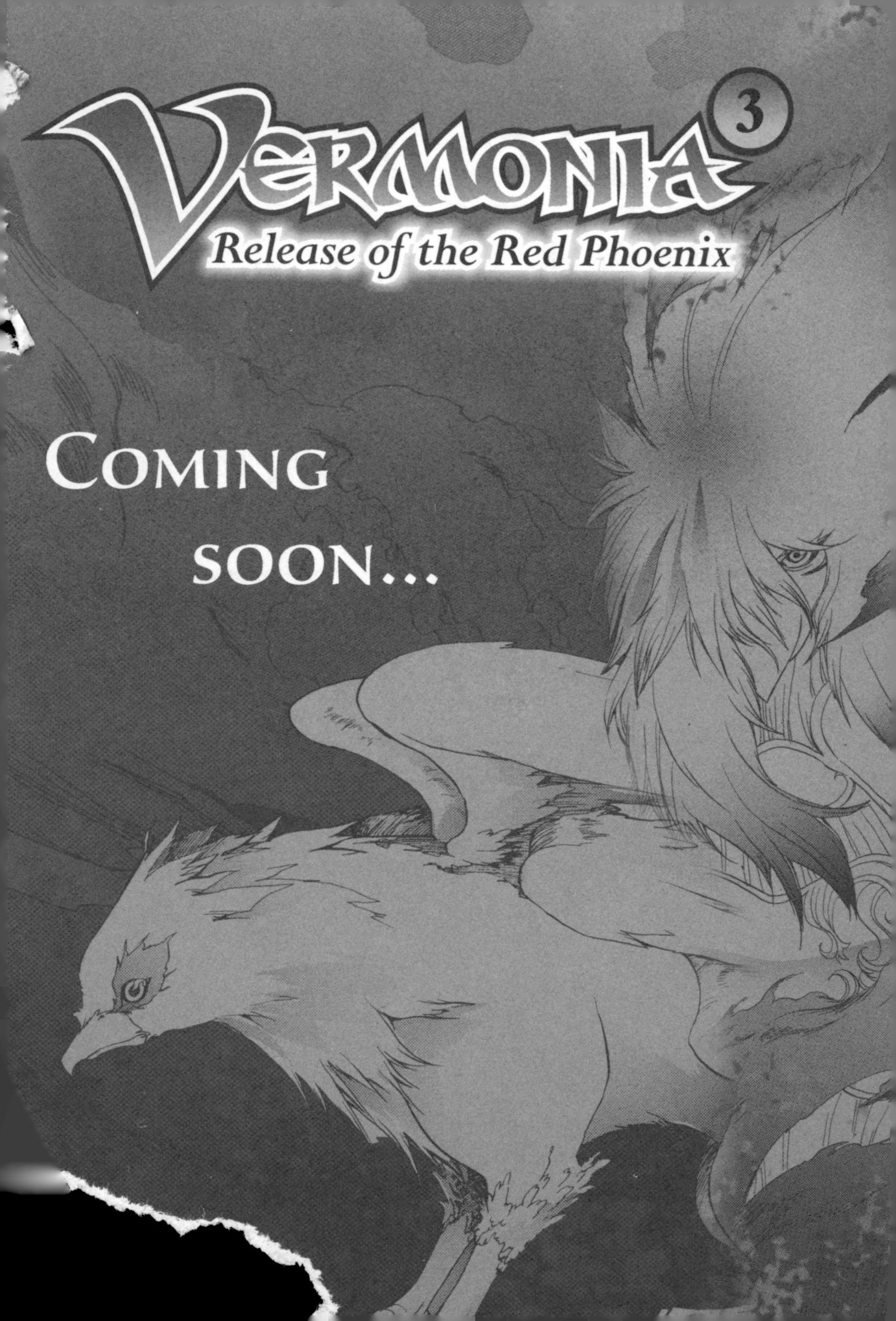
Vermonia 3
Release of the Red Phoenix
Coming
soon...

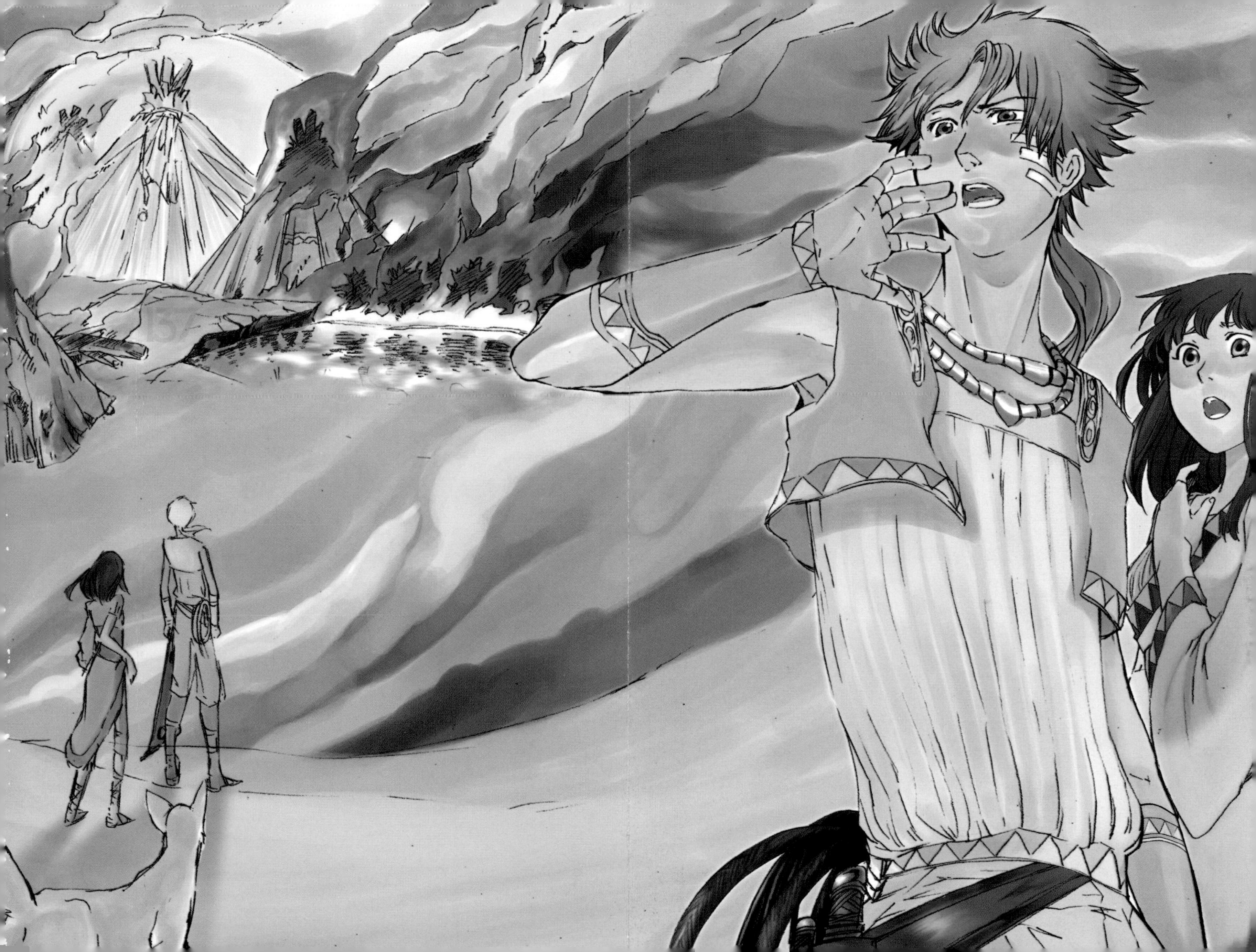

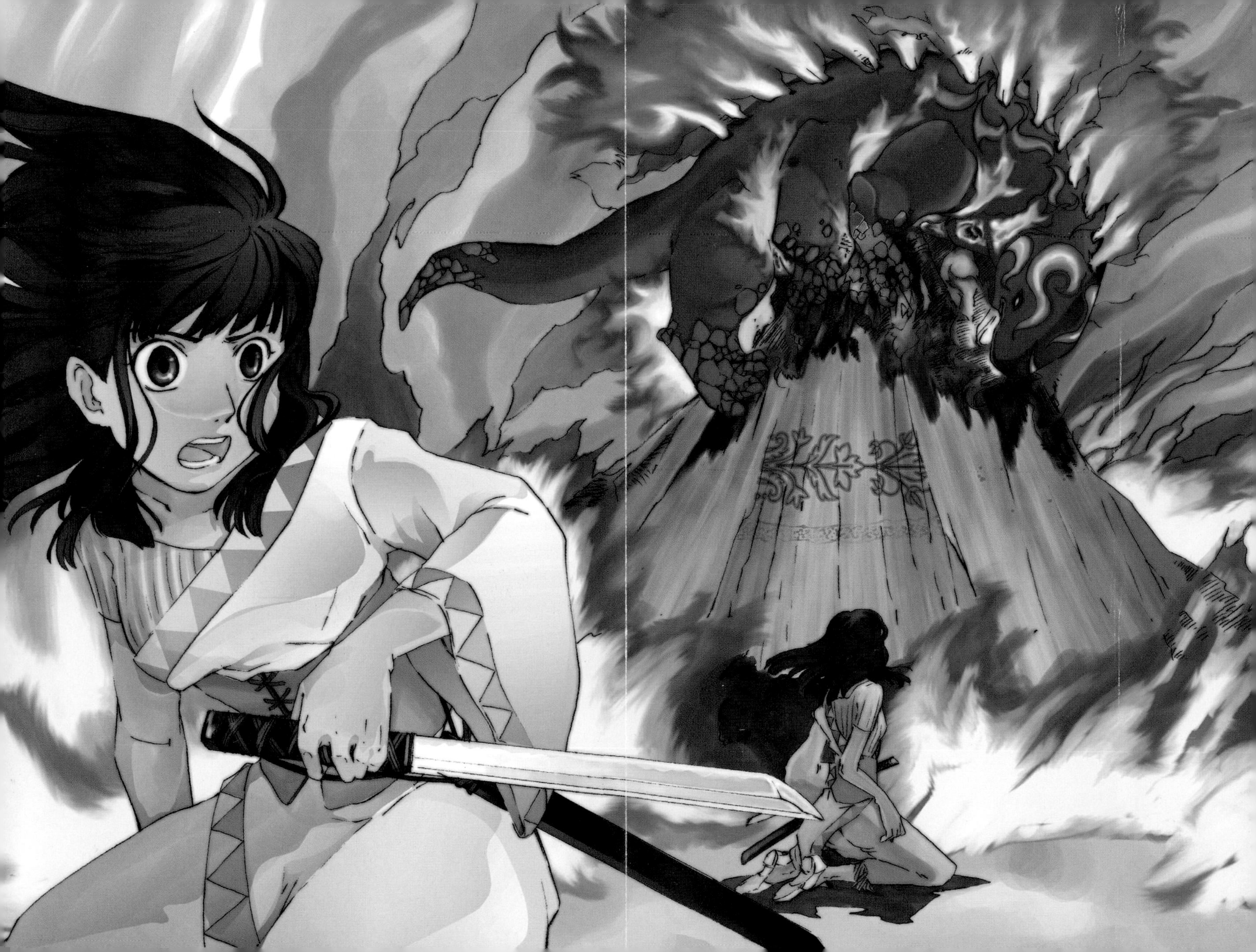

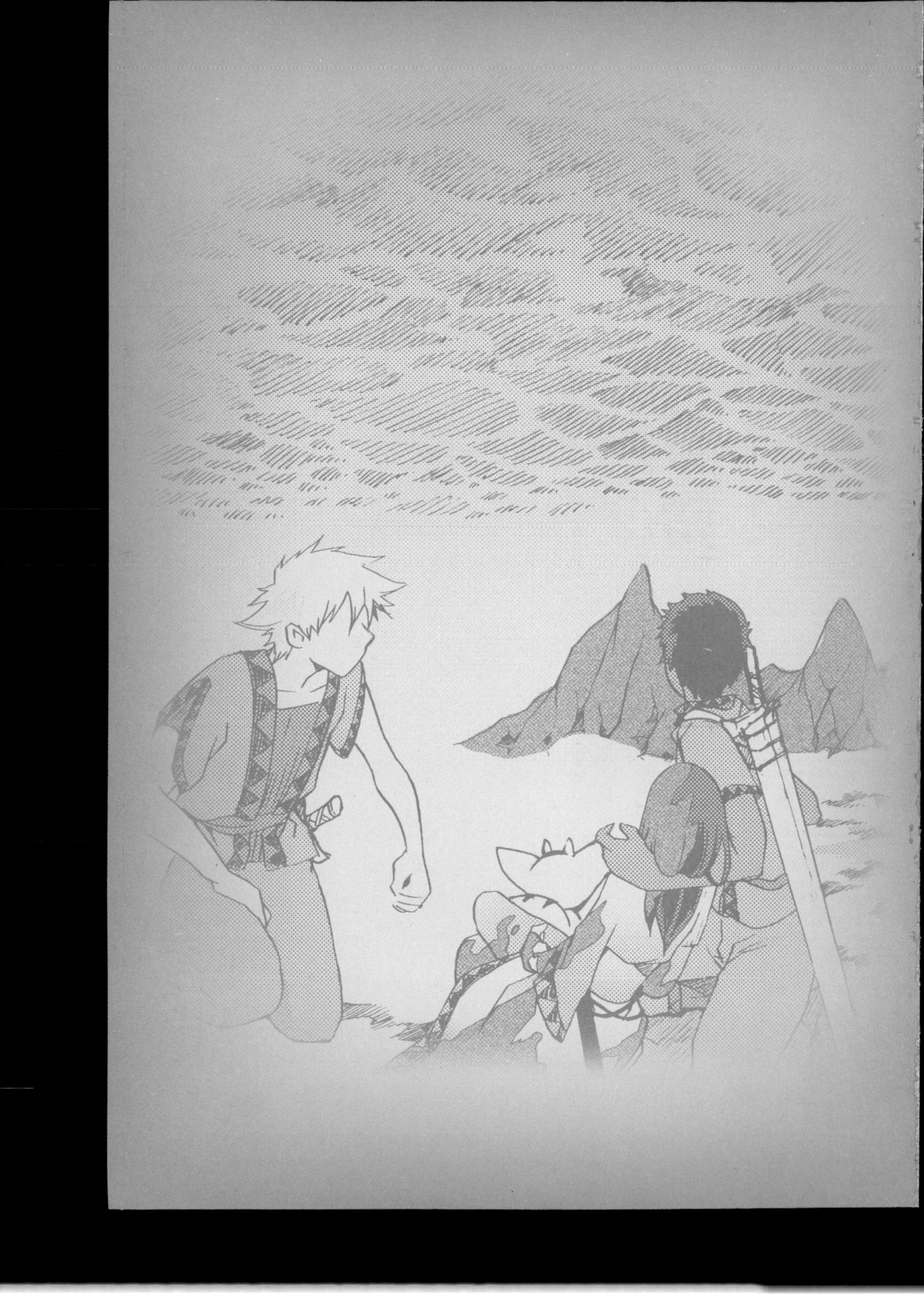

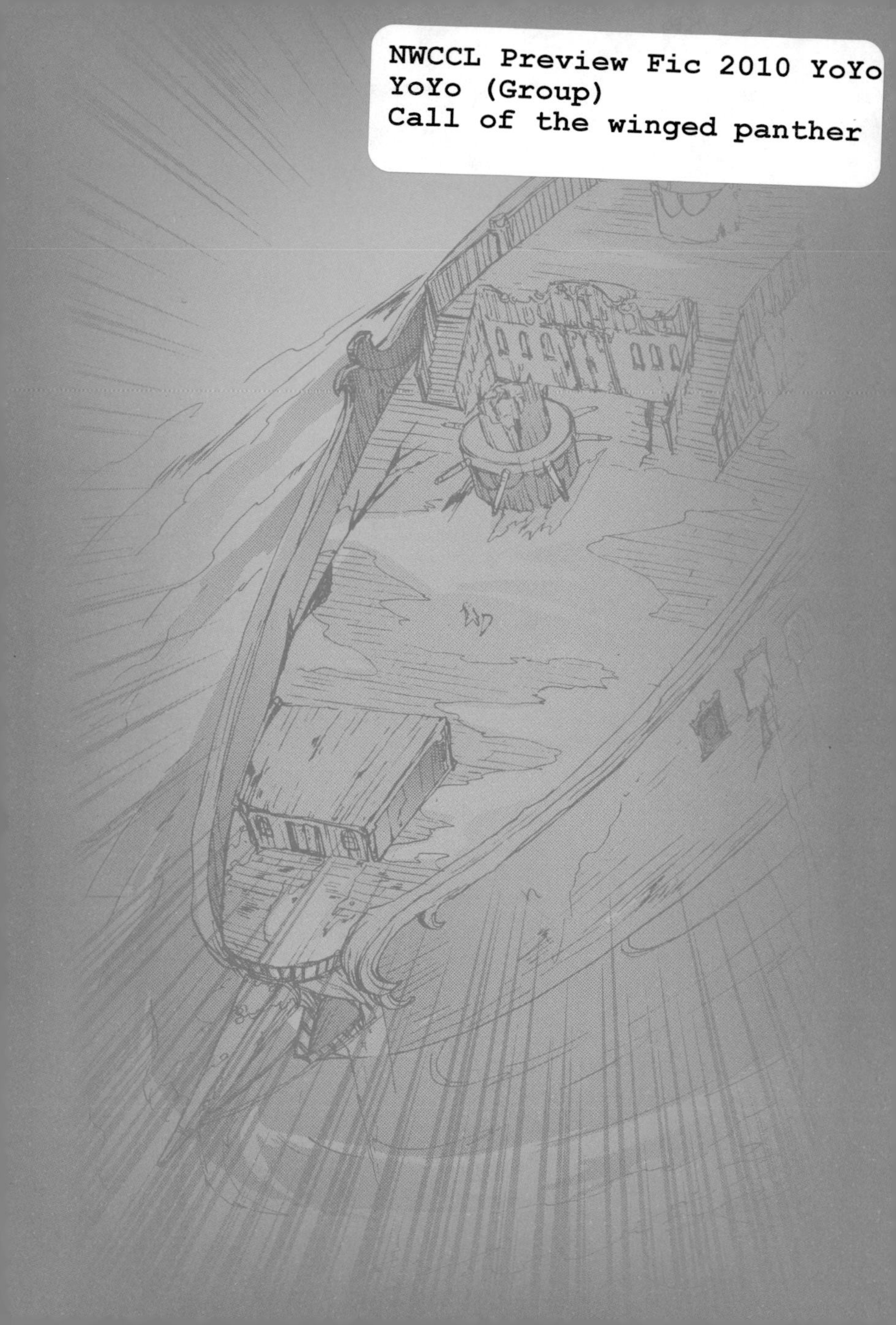